**THERE WAS EXCITEMENT IN THE AIR—
AS WELL AS FEAR . . .**

From all accounts they'd been performing exceptionally, taking great risks and calling down barrages with pinpoint accuracy within a few dozen yards of their forward positions. Still.

The sustained-fire machine-gun platoons checked their tracer for the tenth time. Gonna be a fuckin' party, this bastard.

Peter squinted at his watch, waited for the word from his HQ wirelessman, saw A and C Companies move off into the night. Right.

All went well for an hour, with what was, in effect, a massive advance going undetected. Then 3 Para was discovered on Mount Longdon—someone stepping on a mine, it was immediately hazarded—

And the Argies knew a full-scale attack was underway . . .

THE LAST WARRIORS

WALTER WINWARD

THE LAST WARRIORS

B

BERKLEY BOOKS, NEW YORK

This book was originally published in Great Britain under the title
RAINBOW SOLDIERS.

Map drawn by Patrick Leeson.

This Berkley book contains the complete
text of the original hardcover edition.
It has been completely reset in a typeface
designed for easy reading and was printed
from new film.

THE LAST WARRIORS

A Berkley Book, published by arrangement with
Hamish Hamilton Ltd.

PRINTING HISTORY
Hamish Hamilton edition published 1985
Berkley edition/April 1988

ISBN: 0-425-10749-3

A BERKLEY BOOK® TM 757,375
Berkley Books are published by The Berkley Publishing Group,
200 Madison Avenue, New York, NY 10016.
The name "BERKLEY" and the "B" logo
are trademarks belonging to Berkley Publishing Corporation.

PRINTED IN THE UNITED STATES OF AMERICA

10 9 8 7 6 5 4 3 2 1

This is a work of fiction. Daddy Rankin's battalion did not exist. Its spirit did.

Dedication

Usually these things go to wives, girl friend, friends
or children, but in this instance that is quite impossible.
The dedication can only be:

From one who was amazed at the beginning, and
continues to be amazed, at the incredible fortitude
of everyone who took part

. . . Walking through battalion lines towards last light on June 11, Daddy Rankin looked upon the anxious, grimy, tired young faces around him with affection and pride. Briefly he remembered how they were in full dress kit on the parade square back home, six hundred of them ramrod straight and proud as Punch in their light-blue berets. He supposed the COs of the other battalions were at that moment thinking something similar, remembering their commandos in their green berets, their paras in their red, their Guards. What a sight to see the cream of the British army lined up in the prime colours of the rainbow, though with rainbows, as everyone knew, there was nothing at the other end except disillusion. No, that was wrong, he corrected himself. At the end of any *particular* rainbow there was disappointment at not finding the pot of gold, but there would always be other rainbows, fresh hopes. And one day. . . .

Author's Note

I have attempted to make this story as accurate as possible. However, it remains a story and whenever research and story-line have clashed, I have favoured the latter.

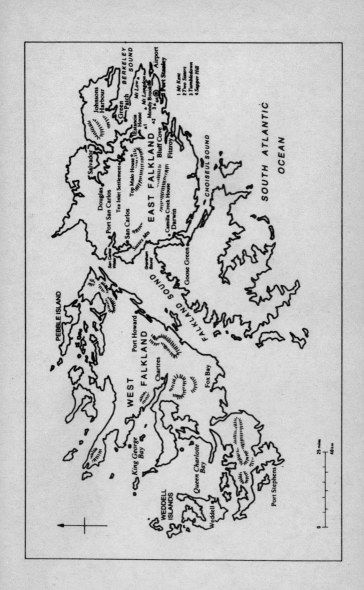

PROLOGUE

EVERY MASSIVE WAVE in the South Atlantic seemed to hit every rivet and bolt in the assault ships *Fearless* and *Intrepid* and, carrying 2 Para, the requisitioned P&O ferry *Norland*; and every shuddering jolt was felt below decks where the assault troops were gathered prior to boarding the LCUs for the amphibious landing on East Falkland. Which would be unopposed, rumour via a clandestine SBS patrol already ashore had it. The bulk of the Argies were elsewhere, waiting for an attack in or around Port Stanley—the 'quick-kill' strategy—sixty miles east of San Carlos Water.

Up top, as the task force made the long run down to Fanning Head, protected by CAP (Combat Air Patrol) Harriers above and wave-hopping helicopters on anti-submarine sorties in front, the weather began to clear hour by hour, causing apprehension on the bridges of the escorting destroyers and frigates. Foul conditions might make life unpleasant below for the marines and the paras and support units, but wind and rain were, for now, their best friends. A landing under the cover of darkness or not, the Argies wouldn't be fooled for ever by the cruiser *Glamorgan*'s diversionary shelling of Berkeley Sound north of Stanley. And none of the senior naval officers, whose job it was to get the amphibious force in a position to make its assault, wanted to be caught out in the open, under clear skies, by the Argentine Air Force, not after what had happened to HMS *Sheffield* on May

4, three weeks earlier. As Hitler had said forty years before about the Allied forces on D-Day, if they could be destroyed before they got ashore or as they came ashore, they wouldn't try it again. A couple of Exocet missiles among the convoy or a low-level bombing raid on the assault ships, and that would be the end of the amphibious force. Without ground troops, the Falklands could not be retaken. The Galtieri junta could win this war within the space of a few hours. The best frontline troops in the British army were aboard the assault ships; there were no others capable of mounting a seaborne offensive.

Few below decks were nervous. Not in obvious ways, at any rate. Some talked more than they usually did, and a handful of normally garrulous individuals fell silent and concentrated on scribbling a final letter home. This was what they were trained for and were paid to do. And, eight thousand miles from the UK and more weeks at sea than they cared to recall, the majority of them wanted to get on with it. Death and mutilation were things that happened to somebody else, and to keep them in that frame of mind their officers and NCOs made sure they were fully occupied: final weapon checks, kit checks. Camouflage cream daubed on.

'Hey, Sarge,' called Private Sammy Finch over the hubbub, 'isn't there a choice of colours like Max Factor? It's bloody ridiculous Jomo having to put this stuff on.'

Henry 'Jomo' Mason was the only black member of 3 Platoon, D Company.

'Shut it, Finch,' said Platoon Sergeant O'Hara.

Men who had finished their preparations joined the snaking queues for what was likely to be their last decent meal for some time. For the first forty-eight hours at least it would be 'ratpacks'—ration packs heated on hexy stoves. The principal ingredient of most ratpacks was what was laughingly called Chicken Supreme, and which was generally considered never to have been, originally, part of anything that sported feathers.

Then the tannoy snapped into life. 'Air Red.'

Below, men cursed. Not men, really. Boys. Adolescents. Kids who, in another time, would have been taking examinations. Some of them, anyway. Others were grown up, had seen this kind of activity before. In Korea, Suez, Aden, Malaya. None of them could move more than a couple of feet in any direction. If the Argie Daggers and Skyhawks had chosen this time for an air raid, they had chosen well.

'Hold your flamin' horses, mate. Don't push. If they hit us, they hit us. There's not a bloody thing you can do about it.'

Then the Air Red was cancelled. False alarm. Radar playing tricks or mistaking Harriers for the enemy.

'Thanks!' shouted someone. 'Bleeding navy,' said another.

'Don't knock the navy,' advised a three-badge Royal Marine. 'They may have to take us off those rocks.'

When the landing docks aboard the assault ships were flooded and the stern ramps dropped, the LCUs reversed out under power into Falkland Sound, the entrance to San Carlos Water. The moon rose, the night brightened. The hills of East Falkland and the designated landing beaches were easily seen. Green Beach—Port San Carlos; Blue Beach—San Carlos Settlement; Red Beach—Ajax Bay. Stealth was unimportant now. Naval guns bombarded Fanning Head. The Argentine defenders fired back—but only with small arms and light machine guns. Nothing heavy. Nothing to knock them out of the water, the LCUs, turn them into floating coffins. And, most important, no planes.

'Nevertheless,' said Sammy Finch, 'I was promised Bermuda and what I get is the Costa Brava.'

'Shut up,' said Captain Peter Ballantine, 2 i/c D Company, in the bows of the same LCU.

Next to Ballantine was Lieutenant Parker-Smith, 3 Platoon's commander, peering over the LCU ramp.

'I knew I was wrong to leave my 12-bore behind. Plenty of game on these islands so I'm told.'

'And lots more at home. Let's get the job done and get there.'

'It was a damned good shoot, that last one.'

'With more to come. Mind you, the one thing this place doesn't seem to have is tall trees and falling leaves. . . .'

PART ONE

'War has its laws; there are things which
may be fairly done, and things which may
not be done.'

—*Cardinal Newman*

ONE

Peter Ballantine

THE EARTH WAS COLD AND HARD. Dead leaves and twigs crackled underfoot like distant rifle fire as the party made its way to the clearing, where several folding tables had been set up. A diffident sun gave scarcely enough light to cast shadows.

The morning shoot had proved disappointing, and after three hours the game trailer contained less than two dozen brace of pheasants, plus a few assorted woodcock, blackcock and a solitary snipe. In the opinion of the Viscount, who had subjected his head gamekeeper to a series of merciless harangues since 10.30, the snipe had given itself up out of sympathy for the guns. It just wasn't bloody good enough, not for eight men. Why, two of the party hadn't sniffed their own powder yet.

Long before noon his lordship had dispatched a Landrover to the manor for flasks of coffee and sandwiches. Returning for a hot lunch was now out of the question; it would take far too long. Being the middle of December, the afternoon shoot would be short enough as it was. The estate's reputation for providing a good day's sport—those who were paying were forking out £400 per gun—would be in shreds unless the bag at least quadrupled. 'The bloody poachers do better.'

'Don't let my father's apparent concern fool you,' murmured Lieutenant the Hon. Rupert Parker-Smith, out of the Viscount's earshot. He strengthened Peter Ballantine's coffee from a handsome silver hip flask containing twelve-year-old malt whisky. 'That bluff old robber baron act is strictly for the paying customers. He has a calculator for a mind, the microchips within it telling him that two or three good days' bags, the pre-Christmas market prices being what they are, will go some way towards curing the damp rot in the west wing. More likely, it'll provide a bracelet or some other bauble for that girl he keeps behind Harrods.'

'Didn't know there was anything behind Harrods, actually,' said their company commander, Major Clive de Winton-Day, known to everyone in the battalion as Winter's Day. He shook his half-empty coffee mug in the direction of Rupert's flask. Rupert poured him a generous measure. 'Besides, that's a bloody unkind thing to say about your father.'

'Not really, sir. The way I look at it, the girl will give the old boy more fun in his dotage than renovating a mouldy old west wing.'

The 'sir' was unnecessary. Socially Rupert was several strata above de Winton-Day and it *was* a shoot, where formality was kept to a minimum. Still, Rupert could not envisage calling Winter's Day, a decade and a half his senior, 'Clive'.

'I doubt you'd be saying that if you were the heir.'

'Fortunately I'm not, for which small mercy I thank God. The estate and all its problems devolve upon my brother. I must say he's welcome to them. Imagine having all these ghastly people a score or more days per season. Horrifying. For a start, how does one collect their loot? Does one go around with a battered hat at sundown and ask them to kindly put in their tenners? Or what? Debrett's Correct Form doesn't say a word about it, would you believe?'

Winter's Day couldn't see that he was being teased. He had earned his sobriquet not only because of the obvious pun on his surname but also as a result of his frosty attitude towards life in general and the company in particular. He was an inflexible disciplinarian when facing men brought before him on a charge (the company clerk, in a memorable phrase, had once described his eyes on such occasions as 'holding less warmth than week-old dog shit'). He had been divorced in 1978 by a semi-wealthy wife whose family now paid the public school fees for their only son. At thirty-seven and a staff college failure, crow's-feet of disappointment parenthesized his eyes.

On battalion exercises he could still manage to keep up, thanks to a daily-more-punishing programme of callisthenics, and occasionally lead from the front a company attack, though more often these days he allowed Peter Ballantine, his 2 i/c, to do what he called 'the energetic bits' while he supervised events from the command vehicle. With no private income and only a few more years in the army, times were going to be hard when he collected his bowler. Although in his case, he sometimes thought, it would be less of a bowler and more of a peaked cap. He knew of several officers who had retired to become security guards or some such. It was a chilling thought.

He cleared his throat noisily.

'Quite,' he said to Rupert. 'Damned decent of the Viscount, incidentally, to allow Peter and me to shoot gratis.'

'Think nothing of it, sir. It's always been the form for as long as I can remember to have two or three chaps in the line who know which end the cartridges go in. These city types may be able to produce four hundred quid at the drop of a hat, but the major object of the exercise is to down the birds for market, much though my father would deny that. Do you know that the estate factor has estimated that each pheasant costs approximately ten pounds to rear. . . . ?'

A broad-shouldered youngster with close-cropped fair hair loped across the clearing and stood a deferential six paces from Peter, loosely to attention. Peter suppressed a smile as he turned away from Rupert's gentle joshing of Winter's Day. Score one for Rupert. At £400 a gun the company commander would scarcely be able to afford twenty minutes. Neither would Peter, for that matter, though he didn't entirely rely upon his pay, as Winter's Day did.

'What is it, Finch?'

Private Sammy Finch's pale-blue eyes held a hurt expression, a sign Peter recognized. It meant Finch was about to make a complaint about someone in authority or about some piece of equipment that did not function as its designers had intended. No mishap involving Finch was ever his fault. If he got lost during night manoeuvres, his compass was on the blink or the map inadequate; if he failed to achieve a decent score on the range with his SLR, the weapon was duff. If he was pulled up for an imperfect shave or because his boots lacked lustre, the platoon sergeant was 'having a go' at him.

One of those Londoners who considered anyone not born in the capital unworthy of serious attention, his time in the army had only served to confirm those metropolitan prejudices. Jocks were thick, Geordies unintelligible, Taffies wet. Scousers, who enjoyed a well-deserved reputation for being hard men, 'wouldn't last ten minutes in the East End'. Yet, belly-aching apart, he wasn't a bad soldier. Peter could think of a dozen in the company who were far worse.

'Twigg and me were wondering if you'd remembered the beer, Captain Ballantine, sir.'

Although strictly against Queen's Regulations, on one of the Viscount's shoots it was customary for Rupert's guests to bring their own beaters to reinforce the estate staff. These were selected on a roster basis from volunteers, of which there was no shortage. The lucky pair pocketed ten to fifteen pounds per man, depending upon how generous the officers felt, and free beer was thrown in; for the Viscount, while anxious to take advantage of as many extra bodies as could be mustered to increase the size of the beating party, was reluctant to provide more than two bottles a head. Rupert's guests invariably brought an entire crate for their men, and it was not unknown for a percentage to be sold at half price to the civvy beaters, there only being a certain number of bottles that even a serviceman could drink in a short lunch break.

'I believe we did, thank you, Finch.'

Peter knew the rules of this particular game. Even though protocol was kept to a minimum on these occasions, come Monday morning he would have to get a hundred reluctant soldiers to do things they would rather not be doing. It would enhance his reputation not a whit if Finch and his inseparable buddy Twigg returned to camp later today with the news that you had only to ask that idiot Captain Ballantine for anything and it would be given, no questions asked. The fifteen or so pounds Finch and Twigg would receive later was guaranteed by tradition. The beer was an extra, designed to keep the men happy and the volunteer roster always full.

Finch didn't bat an eyelid. Not quite twenty, he had been a soldier for close on two years. There was nothing anyone could tell him about handling officers below the rank of colonel.

'In that case, sir, we're running a bit short over there.'

The beaters were eating their sandwiches off a trestle table set up a fair distance from the guns. As far as Peter could see, every man had a bottle in his hand or in front of him.

'Not from where I'm standing.'

'Optical illusion, sir. Parallax.' Finch spelt it out. 'P-A-R-A-L-L-A-X.'

Peter had lectured the company on parallax the previous Wednesday. Before the lecture not one of them had known what parallax was. In the test he had set them on Thursday only twenty per cent had remembered the substance of Wednesday's lesson. Peter had wagered aloud that none of them would even be able to spell parallax by Saturday. Finch had just proved him wrong, and even Peter had to concede game and set.

'Okay, Finch, in the boot of Mr Parker-Smith's car. I think you'll find it's open. The bottle of whisky you'll also see there is not one of your perks.'

'Wouldn't dream of touching it, sir. Nasty stuff.'

Hatless, Finch brought his heels smartly together. Peter nodded.

'Ten minutes, gentlemen,' boomed the Viscount. 'Then we'll show 'em.' He made it sound like an early morning bayonet charge across no-man's land against the Hun.

'Will the weather hold, Rupert?' Peter asked.

Rupert glanced at the sky. 'Should do. Let's hope so anyway. We can well do without anything even approaching the fiasco we had in November.'

Winter's Day had not been present that Saturday, but Peter remembered the occasion vividly. It was the second shoot of the season and the first, that season, to which Peter had received an invitation. Rupert tried to share out the rights he had as second son of a viscount among the rest of the battalion's officers as well as his own company.

One of the 'city' types had brought his own dog, which was perfectly acceptable as he had cleared it with Rupert's father beforehand. The dog, however, though magnificently pedigreed, was very young and had spent six months being trained in Norfolk during a rather dry East Anglian summer. It transpired later that the animal had never seen rain before; at least, it had never been asked to retrieve in a howling gale. When the rains came, they did so with a vengeance, and the few birds the beaters managed to put up were met, on the clear side of the copse, by a young bitch wailing like a banshee at being soaked. The beaters chased the pheasants one way, the dog promptly chased them back—or scared them into eccentric orbits far away from the nearest gun. By the end of the afternoon seven thoroughly drenched and miserable guns were in the mood to commit mayhem on the eighth and his dog.

'And then the wretched animal somehow managed to get into the hen run,' concluded Rupert, describing the scene for Winter's Day who, though he had heard much of the story before, thought that having the son of a viscount in his company gave it a touch of class. Thus he was willing to forgive Rupert most things, including repetition. 'What it wouldn't do with pheasants it was determined to do with the chickens, to earn its biscuits. It "retrieved" half a dozen by the scruff of the neck, killing the lot, before we managed to corner the brute. I'd never actually seen anyone speechless with rage before, but my father exemplified the condition. One could see the words forming, but stap me if he could articulate. I thought my brother was about to become the eleventh viscount overnight.'

On the other side of the clearing Sammy Finch dumped the crate of beer at Chris Twigg's feet, produced an opener from his pocket and deftly uncapped two bottles, one of which he handed to Twiggy. The civvy beaters, who had all finished their allotted two bottles, looked on enviously. Sammy thought he might sell them a beverage or two later on in the day. On the other hand, he might not. At the end of the shoot the officers generally went back to the manor for a drink or three, while the beaters went home to the telly. That meant him and Twiggy hanging around until Winter's Day decided it was time to return to camp, which would hardly be before six. It was an hour's drive back and they'd be stuck in the company commander's car, the same way they'd come up, with Winter's Day driving unless he felt too pissed and turned over the wheel to Captain Ballantine. Lieutenant Parker-Smith (notorious for jumping suddenly on the unsuspecting catching a crafty smoke and thus known throughout the battalion as Zebedee, after the children's television puppet whose legs were springs and whose catchphrase was 'boing, boing') was probably going to stay at home, now that he was here, and not on duty, as far as Sammy remembered, over the weekend.

It might be as well to hang on to the rest of the beer for their own consumption. Sitting behind the company commander and the 2 i/c half cut was better than sitting behind them sober.

'What was that bunny with Ballantine all about?' asked Twiggy.

Twiggy used the word bunny a great deal. It derived from rabbit and meant, in a Londoner's patois, talking. Twiggy was not a Londoner; he'd picked up the expression from Sammy. Twiggy was from Manchester and the only non-Londoner in D Company—in the *battalion*, for Christ's sake— whom Sammy could tolerate, the reason being that he'd felt sorry for Twiggy from the moment he first saw him during basic training. In Sammy's unhumble opinion, Twiggy was an unlikely soldier. He was six inches taller than Sammy and a stone lighter. Where Sammy was a compact five feet nine and eleven and a half stone, with a middleweight boxer's build, Twiggy was constructed like something that held up blackcurrants. He ate like a horse without putting on an ounce. At one time there was talk of giving him his ticket because the MO could see no way that anyone with such a physique would make the grade as a soldier. Twiggy had fought tooth and nail to stay in, going so far as taking solo runs with fifty pounds of equipment on his back and spending his spare time mastering the assault course. Back in Manchester there was only the dole queue and a houseful of brothers and sisters always moaning about something or other. In the army he had mates, most particularly Sammy Finch, even though Sammy thought, and frequently said, that Chris Twigg wouldn't know how to slice bread unless he, Sammy, was guiding the knife.

'Parallax,' said Sammy, answering Twiggy's question.

'Oh, that,' said Twiggy.

'Yeah, oh that. Now drink your ale and think yourself lucky to get it. He wanted to play games, did Captain Ballantine. Didn't want to tell me straight off that the beer was in Zebedee's car.'

'Why not?'

'Christ, don't ask me. You know how they are, officers. One minute they're being Father Christmas, the next Dracula with an invitation to a booze-up in a blood bank. Comes of being brought up among all this.' Sammy made a sweeping gesture with the hand that held the beer bottle, encompassing the clearing, the woods beyond and, for all Twiggy knew, the rest of the county. 'And marrying those skinny women who talk to you as though you had a terminal case of cholera.'

'I didn't know Ballantine was married.'

'Forget it,' said Sammy. 'Skip it. Just forget I spoke, all right?'

Twiggy grinned to himself. In the same way that he had known quite well what parallax was, being one of the twenty per cent who had answered the test correctly on Thursday, he was aware of Captain Ballantine's bachelor status. And, although he would never have admitted it to a living soul in the battalion, he had taken and passed five O Levels at the age of sixteen. It paid dividends to act dumb around Sammy. He wasn't sure Sammy would have liked him so much were he otherwise.

The wind got up during the afternoon, knifing through gun and beater, master and servant alike. Nonetheless, the session was an unqualified success, with each gun getting his fair share of well-driven birds, and Rupert, in particular, hitting everything he aimed at. Afterwards, with characteristic modesty, he gave the credit to his new 12-bore. 'Congratulate J. Purdey and Sons, not me. Wouldn't have hit a bloody thing without it.'

By the time it was getting dark and the party had finished shooting the covers around the manor, the day's bag had risen to over two hundred, the majority of them pheasant. The Viscount confessed to being content. Later, in the gun room, he proposed his customary toast.

'To a successful shoot and the next bag, gentlemen.'

Rupert took his cue. 'May she be more wanton than the last.'

By convention at the manor, the first post-shoot glass of whisky (no other drink was deemed fitting, regardless of a guest's personal preference) was always taken in the gun room, while hands were washed, 12-bores encased, boots swapped for shoes, jackets changed, muddy dogs put in their pens or muddier Landrovers. The second and subsequent drinks were taken in the library in front of a roaring log fire, while the day's hits and misses were discussed. For those who required more solid sustenance, wedges of sandwiches and piping hot soup were already in place on the sideboard, on a help-yourself basis. Shooting days were the only occasions the library resembled a working man's café, and God help the guest who dropped cigar ash on one of the priceless rugs or set down a bowl of soup on the rim of the billiards table.

From time to time the Viscount's grandchildren, Rupert's nephews and niece, all three under the age of seven, put in an unscheduled shrieking appearance, closely followed by their nanny, who swiftly herded them out with apologies to the Viscount. The Viscount was widely known to dislike small children. 'Noisy, anti-social little creatures until they're sixteen, totally dependent upon one's good will.'

'And thereafter,' murmured Rupert in Peter's ear, 'parasites.'

'And thereafter,' intoned the Viscount, 'parasites.'

'I sometimes wonder how any of us managed to grow up without him using his influence at court to get us all sent to the Tower,' said Rupert.

Rupert's elder brother and his wife were in another part of the county, visiting friends. They would not be returning until later, but Rupert's sister Lavinia joined the men briefly around 5.30. At twenty, two years younger than Rupert, almost as tall as her brother and equally slim, they were alike enough in fair good looks to have been taken by strangers not only as siblings but twins. Sammy Finch would have classified her as 'skinny', and so she was in an aristocratic fashion. Nevertheless, she could have outshot Sammy with pistol or rifle any day he cared to choose.

Dressed in a loose-fitting pullover above a tweed skirt, her blonde hair pulled back and fastened at the nape of her neck with a dark-blue ribbon, she circled the library with easy confidence, pausing only to collect a man-sized glass of whisky, chatting pleasantly to each group of 'city' guns before joining Peter, who was standing near the billiards table, watching Rupert doing his well-bred best not to hand out a thrashing at snooker to Winter's Day.

'The blue, Rupert, the blue,' encouraged Lavinia.

'Buzz off and entertain Peter,' said Rupert, knowing full well that if he sank the blue the remaining reds and colours up to the pink were a piece of cake.

'As you wish.' She fluttered her eyelashes coquettishly at Peter. 'How would you like to be entertained?'

'Do you have anything specific in mind?'

'Very definitely. But I think we'd get slung out of the room p.d.q. if I suggested even my mildest notion. On the other hand, if you care to be discreet and leave with me now, say we're going to feed the dogs or something. . . .'

'I'd care for that very much—if I didn't have to get back to camp.'

'Don't concern yourself with that, old boy,' drawled Winter's Day from the table, grunting with satisfaction now that Rupert had deferentially muffed the blue and, in doing so, set up a perfect red.

'There you are,' said Lavinia. 'From the horse's mouth, if the major will forgive me.'

'Consider yourself forgiven.'

'No use, I'm afraid,' countered Peter. 'Whatever my company commander says, I'm expected home for lunch tomorrow and I shan't be there unless I clear my paperwork tonight.'

'You always say that.' Lavinia feigned petulant disappointment. 'I only came down to this mouldy old gin mill because I knew you'd be here. I sometimes think my designs on you are not reciprocated.'

'You'd be quite wrong there. Lack of real opportunity is all that ever gets in my way.'

'Rubbish! Your nose is growing, Pinocchio. What gets in your way is that I'm twenty and you're twenty-eight, which wouldn't matter a damn if you were thirty-three and I were twenty-five. I gave up doing Latin prep a few years ago, you know, so just for telling lies you can get me another drink. To judge from my father's expression among others, I'm several litres behind the rest of you. Oh, hard luck, Major!'

The 'simple red' had missed the yawning pocket, and the white had cannoned off the cushion and sunk the black. Seven away. Rupert wore a pained expression.

Peter took Lavinia's glass across to the drinks table. He had known her for almost a year, though he had met her on less than a dozen occasions in that time and always at shoots or battalion parties, never alone. He found her easy on the eye and he guessed she'd be fun *à deux,* but she'd probably run a mile if he ever seriously tried to take her up on one of her not-quite-joking offers. Perhaps one day he'd surprise her, just to see how she reacted. There were a lot worse fates for a young and ambitious officer than getting involved with the daughter of a viscount, and there was no one special in his life at present. Nor had there been since the long-standing relationship with Cecilia had come to an end in the summer.

He grunted inaudibly, doubting whether he'd ever learn if anything substantial lay beyond Lavinia's façade. The eight-year gap didn't concern him too much, and she was far from the silly ass she sometimes gave the impression of being. Like Rupert, who could also play the upper-class idiot to perfection when he chose, she had considerable strength of character. Not much of a horseman himself and therefore taking minimal interest in matters equestrian, he had it on good authority that she was a front-running candidate for the next Olympic team. She spoke fluent French and excellent German, was an invaluable help, according to Rupert, to her father and eldest brother in managing the estate, and could whip the best of them on the ski slopes. But he'd never pursue her with anything like the ardour she'd expect because he suspected, beneath the veneer of frivolity, that she was a sober-minded young lady who had one eye on marriage, for which he felt nowhere near ready. His reluctance in that direction had caused the rift with Cecilia. He handed Lavinia the refilled glass. She took a sip and spluttered.

'Good God, did you put any water in this?'

'A little.'

'A little is right. You damned near gave me a tonsillectomy.'

Towards six the gathering started to break up, with Winter's Day at last potting the pink and black to give him the frame. Rupert caught Peter's eye and raised both his own to heaven.

After everyone had collected his belongings from the gun room, in the courtyard there was much shaking of hands and revving of Landrovers and Range Rovers. Under the rules of the shoot each gun was allowed to take away a brace of pheasant, which had been placed, during drinks, in each vehicle by the head gamekeeper and his assistant.

Peter and Winter's Day were the last to leave. They shook hands formally with the Viscount and Lavinia at the entrance to the rear hall. Rupert seemed to have disappeared.

'Here they come,' said Sammy, glancing over his shoulder while he and Twiggy relieved themselves in the shadows of some rhododendron bushes. The pair had finished the crate of beer and there had been frequent visits to the bushes.

'And just what do you think you're doing,' demanded a

voice from the darkness, 'relieving yourselves on my rhodo-
dendrons?'

'Jesus Christ!' swore Sammy, taking a step forward in
alarm and, in the process, pissing over his boots.

Rupert appeared out of the gloom, having put his own
brace of birds in Winter's Day's car, for the Mess. 'G'night,
chaps. Make sure the company commander and Captain
Ballantine don't get into any trouble on the way home.'

'That flaming Zebedee!' Sammy was wiping his boots on
the grass when Peter appeared, slightly ahead of Winter's
Day.

''I'll pretend I didn't hear that, Finch, but God help you if
you want to stop at the roadside on the way back to camp.'

TWO

Rupert

WHEN RUPERT GOT BACK to the library the Viscount was walking slowly round the billiards table, collecting the dead balls from the pockets and scudding them across the felt, all the while muttering to himself about the damned gamekeeper constantly saving the best spinneys for the afternoons. It would have to stop.

In Rupert's absence someone had been in to clear up the minor mess the guns had made, and now there was no sign of sandwiches or soup. Empty glasses had also been whisked away and the sideboard and drinks table tidied.

'It's not really McGregor's fault, you know,' said Rupert. He settled himself in an armchair by the fire, opposite Lavinia, who threw him a sharp frown of caution. On the subject of McGregor's shortcomings, the Viscount had a low flashpoint. It was the same every season, and every season saw the Viscount vowing that it would be McGregor's last. Somehow, however, McGregor stayed the course, as he had done since he took over from his father in 1951.

'What's that?'

'I said it's the luck of the draw that the best bags recently have come in the afternoon. McGregor can hardly be expected to know where every bird on the estate is at every moment.'

'Nonsense. That's what I pay him for, blast him, to learn the covers.' The Viscount straightened his back carefully, feeling his years although he was only sixty. '*And* I saw him hanging around outside when everyone was leaving, making it perfectly obvious he was expecting tips. I won't have that. Reflects badly on me. Makes him look like a damned cab driver.'

'Tips *are* part of his perks,' soothed Lavinia.

'Perhaps so. But he shouldn't be so blatant. He'll never be the man his father was.'

If the Viscount noticed the glances that flashed between Rupert and Lavinia at that moment, he pretended not to. They'd said that about *him* too, when his father died, and doubtless one day someone would say it about his elder son Oliver, though in that instance the observer would be on the mark. Oliver didn't shoot, didn't hunt, didn't fish, spent all day and every day at that merchant bank. Whereas Rupert . . . But it was as well not to dwell on that. Rupert had been born second and, as far as the viscountcy was concerned, didn't count. One could not start messing about with historical precedent or the Lord only knew where it would all end. The male line was secure, that was the main thing, although it was something of a tragedy that Rupert had come along ten years after Oliver, when the gynaecologists had just about given up hope that there would ever be more than one child, instead of ten years before. When he wasn't being foppish, Rupert was a genuine chip off the old block—and the block before, his grandfather. Of course they fought and argued; that was only natural. Wouldn't have it any other way. A stubborn young whelp, Rupert. Like his sister. Always had been, both of them. Unlike Oliver, who had always wanted to please, even as a child. Something wrong with that.

Fleetingly, the Viscount wondered if he'd ever shown enough affection to any of his children, but he quickly dismissed that thought as dangerous nonsense. That wasn't the family way, kissing and backslapping like some wretched Continental or American.

'What about these snooker balls, Rupert? It used to be the form in this house that whoever played last spotted them for the next frame.'

'I'll do it,' offered Lavinia.

The Viscount helped himself to a glass of malt and stood with his back to the fire. Rupert hazarded an accurate guess at what the next topic of conversation would be, though it took a moment or two to be given voice.

'Have you seen your mother recently?'

'Yes, earlier in the week. Tuesday.'

'How was she?'

'Don't you know? I thought they phoned you every day.'

'They do, but they don't tell me much. And I don't visit her often these days.' A moment's regret. 'Couldn't take it, seeing her sitting there, staring into some distance I can't share. She didn't recognize me last time. Thought I was one of the doctors or some such. Still, maybe it'll clear up.'

'It'll never clear up, Daddy,' said Lavinia from the table. 'Mummy wasn't just a drunk in need of the occasional drying out; she was a chronic alcoholic. She drank so much that eventually it affected her mind. She won't be coming home. She's in that place for life.'

'Perhaps you're right. Peculiar family, the Harcourts. A couple of cousins went the same way, into the booby hatch. Didn't call it that, of course. Private clinic or some nonsense. Still, it's the loony bin and there's an end to it.' The Viscount was close to tears, part whisky, part bewildered sadness. 'Damned embarrassing when you think about it.'

Rupert stepped in to change the subject. It was now 6.30 and, at this rate, his father would be supine before eight. There were those who could take their drink and those who could not. His father could, even though he passed out and had to be helped upstairs more often than not these days. His mother, for some biochemical reason, should never have touched a drop. That was the way of the world.

'I noticed you were having a good old chinwag with Peter earlier,' he called across to Lavinia.

'Did you? How frightfully observant. And I thought that all you were doing was ingratiating yourself with Winter's Day.'

'Not a bit of it. I had a great deal of time between turns, as you may have gathered. I thought you were getting on rather famously.'

'Lavinia and Peter Ballantine?' The Viscount's eyes were slowly going out of focus. He reminded himself that this must be his last drink before dinner.

'Lavinia and Peter,' confirmed Rupert. 'Didn't you see it?'

'Didn't see a damned thing except the man can shoot.'

'Which was all there was to see.' Lavinia tugged at the ribbon that was holding her hair in place. 'Rupert's simply being objectionable, trying to matchmake where no matchmaking is necessary or needed.'

'Meaning you can handle it yourself, is that it?' Rupert pressed on, aware that he was discomforting his sister but anxious to keep his father off the subject of his mother. 'So those little girlish giggles were part of an act.'

'No girlish giggles and no act. I like Peter very much, but more than that there is not.'

'You couldn't give me the colour of his eyes, for instance,' challenged Rupert.

'I could,' offered the Viscount. 'He's around five feet eleven inches tall.' They stared at him. 'That's his height, of course. His eyes are brownish greenish.'

'Hazel,' said Lavinia. Rupert winked at her. Balls, she mouthed.

'Hazel, then,' said the Viscount. 'He has a widowed mother, a sister and a young brother, the latter still at school, I believe. He obtained, courtesy of the army, a decent degree at Cambridge—quite the wrong sort of blue, I would have thought—and has a little money of his own. He'll probably sail through Staff College and end up a brigadier at the very least. Why are we discussing Peter Ballantine's c.v. incidentally?'

'Because Lavinia has designs on him,' grinned Rupert.

Lavinia aimed a kick at him. 'Rubbish.'

'Nobody tells me anything,' said the Viscount.

Lavinia was saved further embarrassment by the library door opening to admit Oliver, who was the same physical type as his brother and sister though far less robust in appearance. Where it would be obvious to any discerning spectator that Rupert and Lavinia spent much of their time out of doors, Oliver's complexion was that of uncooked bread. With his horn-rimmed glasses, which he was rarely seen without and which he regularly had to push back on to the bridge of his nose, he would have passed for the junior languages master at any minor public school. For all that, it was his brain and financial acumen that kept the estate solvent, using as he did his City connections to evolve complicated tax schemes and obtain loans at advantageous rates of interest during times of crisis. He was thirty-two years old and somewhat shy, particularly in the presence of his father, to whom, he was well aware, he was something of a disappointment. If the truth had been generally known, he too would have much preferred for Rupert to have been born first.

'Hello, all,' he said pleasantly. 'I saw McGregor outside. I gather you had a successful shoot.'

'No thanks to him,' said the Viscount surlily. 'Where's Helen?'

'Helping put the children to bed.' Oliver, feeling absurdly uncomfortable, glanced at his watch. 'Well, I can't stop, have to change. We're dining out tonight. Just popped in to say hello.'

'That goes for me too, I'm afraid,' said Rupert, getting to his feet.

'What, both of you?' The Viscount frowned. 'No one ever seems to be around for family dinners these days. I hope you'll be keeping me company,' he added to Lavinia, who sighed quietly.

'Yes, I'll be here.'

Rupert accompanied his brother step for step up the broad staircase. 'You shouldn't let him get to you, you know.'

'Can't help it,' shrugged Oliver. 'He scares the living daylights out of me if you want me to be frank. You're rarely here. Nor is Lavinia, for that matter. We live here, Helen, myself and the children. The silences at table can be cavernous. We have little in common and we both know it. One glass of whisky too many and he becomes either mildly abusive or chronically maudlin. He's about a glass away from that condition now.'

'He's lonely.'

They paused outside Rupert's bedroom door.

'I accept that,' nodded Oliver. 'Regrettably he's lonely because of the old girl or you, Lavinia to a lesser extent. He is never lonely enough to require my company except as a stopgap.'

'That sounds suspiciously like self-pity.'

'It's more than that, old chap. It *is* self-pity, or it would be if I really gave a damn. Have a good evening.'

Three-quarters of an hour later there was a tap on Rupert's door. He had had his bath and was in the process of finishing dressing.

'Me,' called Lavinia.

'Come in.'

She perched herself on the edge of the bed.

'What colour tie, do you think?' he asked her.

'Let me see.' He held out the rack at arm's length. 'The dark red, I think, with that suit.'

'The dark red it shall be. Something on your mind?'

'There was. It'll keep now, however.'

'Say again. I'm not with you.'

'I thought you were skulking out in Oliver's wake to avoid dinner with Daddy and me. Now I see you have a date.'

'Pray continue, Holmes.'

'Simple, Watson. You'd be in a dinner jacket if it were something formal away from the battalion. You wouldn't be asking advice on a tie if it were a simple get together with a few of your chums. I therefore deduce that it's a woman.'

'I doff my cap to your brilliance.'

'Though I think you might have stayed in this one night,' went on Lavinia, her petulance only half feigned. 'God knows, you're his favourite and he sees little enough of you as it is.'

'In about an hour it won't matter a hoot whether I'm here or not. He'll have had one drink too many and that will be that for the evening.'

'Well, *we* could have talked. I don't see much of you either.'

'We can talk after breakfast tomorrow. I don't have to be back at camp until after lunch.'

'You mean you're coming home this evening?'

'You don't see me packing a razor or toothbrush, do you?'

'And I don't see you wasting your time on vestal virgins, either. Which means she's probably married and you can't stay the night.'

'Now you're being nosy. Besides, there's something incestuously unsavoury about a sister talking to her brother in such a manner.'

'Don't be absurd. I learned a long time ago about adultery.'

'Ah yes, I recall. He was something in advertising, wasn't he? About a year ago.'

'That's below the belt.'

'Sorry,' said Rupert genuinely. 'You're right. I apologize.'

'You're forgiven. But be careful, that's all. If she's married to anyone in the battalion you're walking on eggs. There's probably something in Queen's Regulations about it.'

'Doubtless, but you're fishing in barren waters. For all you know I'm meeting a nice *single* young lady to discuss life's bitter ironies over a bottle of Valpolicella in an Italian restaurant. Her parents are not only rabid socialists but pacifists too. Thus I am disqualified from meeting them on two counts. One, that I am a serving officer; two, that my ancestors were robber barons who wangled a viscountcy several hundred years ago. Hence, I shall be home long before the proverbial larks.'

'Huh,' snorted Lavinia.

From her own bedroom window, out of curiosity, she watched him climb into his Porsche, gun the engine, and roar off down the drive. At the gamekeeper's lodge his headlights swung left. Right would have taken him, after five miles, into the market town which bore the same name as the estate and whose buildings the Parker-Smith family had once largely owned. Left—in, say, forty minutes at the speed he drove—would lead him to the camp; or rather, to the large town three miles outside the camp, where some of the battalion officers and senior NCOs had flats and houses. He could be going anywhere, of course, but she doubted it.

Because it started to rain heavily soon after he set off, Rupert was compelled to reduce speed. It therefore took him fifty-five minutes to reach the small hotel on the outskirts of the town. He was taking something of a risk, he knew, because the hotel was midway between the camp and the centre of town. However, it was a calculated gamble and not much of a one at that. Any officers out for the evening, to his certain knowledge, would aim for one of the bigger watering holes in the town proper, and it was not the sort of establishment to attract the other ranks, there being no jukebox, disco or fruit machines. The ORs, whether in their own transport or by bus or taxi, would head directly for the bright lights on a Saturday night. To all intents and purposes, though they were not strictly speaking in the country, this was a country inn. And, if anyone saw them together, it was a coincidental meeting.

He spotted her car in the car park and Julia Lomax herself in what the landlord called the cocktail bar but which was only the old snug bar tarted up a bit to justify the higher prices at this end of the inn. She was perched on a tall stool to show off, he suspected (and for his benefit he hoped), her astonishingly long legs. She was drinking gin and tonic. Not that he could tell it was gin as opposed to vodka, but he had never seen her touch vodka, which she termed 'a common little drink'. There were half a dozen other people in the bar. He recognized none of them; nor would he have expected to, for Julia, who had a sixth sense in such matters, would have left and waited in her car had she seen even a half-familiar face.

He crossed over to her, exclaiming 'Julia!' in faked surprise.
'Rupert!'

They exchanged chaste kisses on the cheek and a series of
such phrases as 'What a surprise!' and 'What on earth are you
doing out this way?' After they had ordered and been served—
another gin and tonic for Julia and a whisky (Rupert thought
that wiser considering that he had been drinking it since
dusk)—they retreated to a corner, Rupert shaking his head in
answer to the landlord's question of whether they would like
to see the dinner menu.

'What kept you, you bastard?' muttered Julia, squeezing
his hand fiercely. 'I thought you'd stood me up. You said
eight on the dot and now it's a quarter past.'

Not for the first time—and this was at least the tenth they'd
met clandestinely—Rupert marvelled at his good fortune. By
any standards, she was a beauty. An admitted twenty-seven,
five years his senior, her blue-black hair was thick and lus-
trous and her dark eyes full of promises that had been fulfilled, with him, on many occasions. Though not given to
poetry or even minor flights of fancy, Rupert sometimes
thought that, if any woman had been specifically designed for
the sexual act, Julia Lomax was that woman. Fully dressed,
she was sensational; undressed, she was a miracle in the same
category as the feeding of the five thousand.

'Not a chance. The weather held me up. And the old man,
who wanted me to stay for dinner.'

'You persuaded him otherwise.'

'I said I had a more pressing engagement.' Under cover of
the table, Rupert caressed her thigh.

'Don't,' she murmured. 'I'll leave marks on the seat.'

Fifteen minutes and another drink later, they left the inn.
Julia held an umbrella over them as they walked to her car.

'You take it,' she offered, getting in behind the wheel.

'No, I don't mind a bit of rain.'

'I'll towel you dry when we get to the flat.'

'I'll hold you to that. Are you sure you don't want to eat
first?'

'First?'

Rupert felt himself redden slightly. He supposed it would
take him a few more years before he could handle with
aplomb women like Julia Lomax.

'You know what I mean.'

'I think I do. I'll race you there.'

'Done.'

Running with his head down back to his own car, Rupert had to swerve to avoid a stationary taxi, the driver of which had temporarily disgorged his passengers, both desperate to relieve themselves, a few minutes earlier. Outside the Gents, Sammy and Twiggy had both seen Rupert and Julia Lomax leave arm in arm. Now they were standing in the shelter of the inn's doorway.

'I didn't get a good look at her,' said Twiggy. 'Are you sure?'

'Of course I'm bloody sure. That was Captain Lomax's wife. I've seen her with him lots of times around the camp. So've you. Unmistakable she is. Walks like she's dying to get laid.'

'I know Captain *Lomax's* wife,' said Twiggy, 'but I don't think that was her.'

'Then you're friggin' blind. Well I'll go to hell.' Sammy stared after the rapidly vanishing Porsche. 'Who'd've thought old Zebedee was getting his leg across there.'

'Maybe he isn't,' said Twiggy. 'Even if it was her, they could've just been having a drink together.'

'Christ,' said Sammy in disgust, 'your mother must have thrown up when they presented her with you. She went into hospital to have a kid and got landed with a retard. He's giving her one, take my word for it.'

Twiggy shrugged. 'So what if he is? That's their business.'

'Yeah, you're right,' agreed Sammy, after giving his grey matter a whirl to see if this new-found intelligence had anything in it for him. He concluded it hadn't. It would be too dangerous for all kinds of reasons to drop hints to Zebedee that he'd been seen with another officer's wife. Besides, Captain Lomax had to be the most disliked officer in the battalion, and he wasn't in their company. Serve the miserable bastard right.

'Come on,' he said, 'I've got a thirst and that meter's ticking away like a bastard while you're standing here rabbiting.'

THREE

Sammy and Twiggy

DADDY RANKIN, THE BATTALION'S COMMANDING OFFICER, had a theory about all soldiers in whatever regiment below the rank of corporal. After a few gins in the Mess he was prepared to develop it in his rich, fruity baritone for anyone who cared to listen.

'The British soldier, gentlemen, is like Jeremiah's leopard or Ethiopian: he can neither change his spots nor his skin. His priorities are plottable along an upward curve on a graph. Somewhere near the base of the curve are food, shelter, warmth, companionship and dry feet. A slightly higher value is accorded to doing as little as possible for as long as he can get away with it. His ability in this direction, far from arousing the wrath of his peers, is actually greeted with admiration. Higher still come beer and cigarettes, without a ready supply of which Tommy finds it impossible to function. But at the upper end of the curve is his quintessential raison d'être; fornication, which he pursues with a quasi-religious fervour unseen since the time of the Zealots. Getting into the knickers of the town's maidens—and it matters little if the town is in England or Africa—is his major objective in life. Besides this, everything else pales into insignificance. What the maiden looks like facially is frequently of total indifference to him. He is not seeking Cleopatra or the Queen of Sheba or Trojan Helen. The foothills of the mountain are his goal, not the summit.

'He has originated a peculiar vocabulary for these female desiderata. They are, alternatively, bints, wenches, lasses, muff, bits of fluff, nookie—and, since the proliferation of American television programmes, broads and chippies. They are rarely girls or women. A girl is his sister, a woman his mother, and he has a biblical fear—Old Testament, kindly note—of associating the sex act with members of his family. It is curious, therefore, that, in his mind, he has succeeded in desexing that he desires most.

'Saturday, hebdomadal feast of excesses, is the day of the hunt. A Saturday night without a conquest is regarded as a dismal failure at best and vanishing youth at worst. Any responsible and farsighted Minister of the Crown with an eye to the recruiting figures would do well to abjure such mealy-mouthed nostrums as improved conditions and better pay, and replace them with camp brothels on a points system. Thus an efficient soldier would have access to the most nubile lovelies and an inefficient one reduced to that practice eponymised by Onan. Here endeth the lesson.'

Daddy was proud of his vocabulary and exercised it to the full at every available opportunity, leaving many of his officers, after a briefing, in a state of complete bewilderment. There were those who said he was too educated for his own good. There were others who reckoned he was just slightly on the right side of being totally crackers.

Whatever they were called, however—bints, wenches, lasses, muff and the remainder of Daddy's et ceteras—by nine o'clock that Saturday evening Sammy and Twiggy were batting zero. During the thirty minutes they had been in town, they had visited three public houses, drinking a pint in each and leaving quickly when it became apparent that there was no spare muff, bint and so on, on display.

'We've left it too bloody late, that's what we've done,' grumbled Sammy, sheltering from the rain in the doorway of the third pub. 'All the good stuff's been snapped up. Jesus, even the *bad* stuff's been snapped up. Did you get a load of those two in the glasses in there?'

'They weren't that bad,' said Twiggy mildly. 'I wouldn't have said no if they hadn't been with someone.'

Sammy stared at him disbelievingly. '*Weren't bad*? You ought to see someone about those eyes of yours. The fat one looked like a reject from the Muppet Show, and as for the other one, I've seen more meat on a poker.'

'We could try the Black Horse,' suggested Twiggy. 'They've got a disco on a Saturday night.' Despite Daddy's assertions, he was less frantic than Sammy in his pursuit of compliant females. He generally tagged along because that suited him, but it wouldn't have bothered him a great deal if they'd had to settle for a hamburger supper and a late-night film.

'And it's three bloody quid to get in. That's too much of a gamble. Solo muff doesn't spring three quid just to dance around. It either goes with its regular bloke and gets him to pay, or hangs around boozers waiting for a couple of berks like us to put their hands in their pockets.'

'The drinks are cheaper once you're inside,' argued Twiggy. 'And we're not broke. We've each got the fifteen quid Winter's Day and Captain Ballantine gave us.'

'Less two quid apiece for the taxi. Less the money we've just spent on beer. Less the two quid each it'll cost to get a taxi back, three if it's after midnight.'

'You haven't spent all your pay, have you?'

'No, I haven't spent all my pay, Auntie. But I don't fancy spending three notes on spec.'

'So it's another pub, then. That's fine with me. I'm hungry anyway. I could do with a couple of pies as well as a pint.'

'Christ, Twiggy, where the hell do you put it all?'

They ran across the road in the driving rain and ducked into the first pub they came to, removing their raincoats and shaking them before going into the bar, which was barely half full, twenty customers at the most. They recognized one or two faces from the battalion, including their platoon sergeant, Harry 'Scarlett' O'Hara, who was sitting at a table with a young woman they took, correctly, to be his wife. If she wasn't his wife he had some fast talking to do, for she was clearly pregnant. Scarlett nodded affably to them.

Sammy made a big play of pushing his way to the bar, though there was no one in his path.

'Gangway, gangway, mind your backs please. Whoops, sorry, madam.'

No one took any notice of him. This was a barracks town. The civilian customers had seen soldiers before and could recognize them even out of uniform.

Sammy gave his order to an over-made-up barmaid who was examining her nails in between reading the evening newspaper. Although she was the only unaccompanied female in the bar and he had had several successes in the past with pub staff, he dismissed her with scarcely a second's thought. The dark roots were beginning to show through her dyed hair and, in his estimation, she wouldn't see forty again.

'Two pints of best bitter, please, darling.'

She looked at him without moving. 'I'm not your darling.'

'No, you haven't had that good fortune, have you? Still, the night's young and you never know your luck.'

She reached for a couple of glasses and pulled two foaming pints.

And two pies, added Twiggy, wondering if the Christmas tree near the door was real. He concluded it wasn't.

'And two pies,' repeated Sammy. 'No, make that three. What have you got?'

'What you can see.' She indicated the hot food cabinet.

'Are you always this chatty or is it just something about me that makes you talkative?'

'Look, any more of your cheek and you're out. I don't have to serve you, you know. Your money buys you a drink and something to eat. It doesn't buy you conversation.'

'Make it three steak-and-kidney,' said Twiggy. From past experience he knew that Sammy could become argumentative if riled.

They retreated to a corner table. Ignoring the plastic knife and fork, Sammy took his pie in both hands and bit into it.

'Jesus,' he muttered between mouthfuls, 'I wonder what qualifications you need to get a job here. Her personality could strip paint at fifty feet.'

'You ask for it sometimes.'

'What's that supposed to mean?'

'Just that there are some days you ask for it.'

'This is meant to be the season of good will, isn't it?'

Sammy pointed in the direction of the bar. Above it someone had constructed out of silver foil a message that read: A Merry Christmas To All Our Customers. Stuck to the mirror behind the liquor bottles were a few blobs of cottonwool snow and several limp paper-chains. There were also a few early Christmas cards.

'Yessir,' went on Sammy, 'I'm certainly glad we came in here, Twiglet. That was a very handsome suggestion of yours.'

'Mine!' said Twiggy indignantly.

'Well, it certainly wasn't mine. You think I'd be sitting here out of choice? Christ, I've seen more life on a butcher's slab. If this is the runup to Christmas, I'll bet they have a really terrific time on a slack Wednesday in February. I'll bet they burst into a couple of choruses of Land of Hope and Glory if someone buys a half of shandy.'

'Shut up and eat.'

'That's your answer to everything, isn't it? Feed your face. Never mind that it's pissing with rain outside. Never mind that this is the last Saturday for a week. Never mind that I'm feeling as horny as a goat. Stick your face in a pie, that's Twiggy's answer.'

'You won't get anywhere by moaning.'

'They'll put that on your grave, you know that? Twiggy Didn't Moan. He was pushed around and buggered about all his life, but the last thing he said as they nailed him in his box was: You won't get anywhere by moaning. Anyway, I'm allowed to moan. I'm in the army, aren't I? It comes with the contract. You ask Scarlett over there. Christ, this is gnat's piss.' Sammy pushed his beer glass to one side. 'I'm going to get a whisky and make a wish.'

'What are you going to wish for?'

Sammy leered at him. 'Make a guess. A blonde and a brunette to walk through that door by themselves. About nineteen and so high.' Sammy put the palm of his hand up to about five feet three.

'I'll get the drinks,' offered Twiggy, suspecting that Sammy would have more words with the barmaid, who would banish them into the night before he'd finished his second pie. 'I have to go to the bog anyway.'

Three whiskies later it was Sammy's turn to relieve himself. Or so he said. What he really needed was a breath of fresh air. Whisky on top of all that beer with very little solid food in his stomach was beginning to take effect.

While he was away the closest he was going to get to his wish that Saturday night walked into the pub, giggling, shaking umbrellas, click-clacking across the floor in high heels. There were three of them and not one was a blonde. Twiggy didn't think Sammy would mind. He certainly didn't. They were all about nineteen or twenty, all pretty. Twiggy kept an anxious eye on the street door for fear three blokes were going to follow them in, but the door remained closed.

He thought quickly. As a rule he wasn't much good at casual chitchat, preferring to leave that to Sammy. On the other hand, he wasn't a complete idiot either, and this trio were as manna from heaven. But he knew he had to move fast before Sammy reappeared and, perhaps, scared them off by being over-aggressive. At six o'clock in the evening, when there were plenty of other uncaught fish in the sea, the occasional failure of Sammy's technique didn't matter. Now, however, it was 9.30.

Before the girls could order, while they were still fumbling in their purses and discussing what they wanted under the frosty, impatient glare of the peroxide barmaid, Twiggy was beside them, brandishing a fiver.

Two minutes later, how he managed not only to pay for their drinks but persuade them to sit down at the table he and Sammy were occupying, he wasn't quite sure. He'd made the offer; one of them had asked him why he wanted to spend his money on them. He'd mumbled something about he and his mate having had a successful afternoon in the betting shop and wanting to share their good fortune. The same girl asked him if he was from Manchester and if he was in the army. He'd answered yes to both questions; there seemed no point in denying it. After that, and after a little more giggling, she had accepted on behalf of all three girls—vodka and lemonade all round. From there on, it was plain sailing.

They seemed 'nice' girls too, not scrubbers, Twiggy was quick to appreciate. Not that he objected to the odd scrubber, which was all that was usually available, but he had a clear idea of what he meant by 'nice'. Nice girls had jobs in banks or insurance companies; they did not go to work with curlers in their hair. They lived at home with their parents in semi-detached houses and owned dogs. They always dressed smartly, stayed in twice a week to wash their hair, and never fought with their mothers and fathers. For that matter, voices were rarely raised. As for their parents ever getting drunk and breaking things, that was unthinkable.

Twiggy often thought that he would not at all mind having a steady relationship with a nice girl, though being in the army made that difficult. Still, he would have liked to write letters and receive them. As things stood, he rarely wrote home and no one at home *ever* wrote to him. To his certain knowledge, he was the only man in the company who never enquired about mail.

If anyone had accused Twiggy of being naive, he would have accepted it. Nor would he have considered the comment a criticism. If being naive was wanting something better than living as he had done before joining the army, where Saturday nights, *any* night, rarely passed without one of his brothers wanting to make trouble over one thing or another, then being naive was okay with him.

When Sammy returned to the bar, his face damp where he had splashed cold water on it, he blinked and shook his head. 'I do not believe my friggin' eyes,' he muttered incredulously.

So far first names had not been exchanged. Sammy remedied that, introducing himself and Twiggy first.

'Chris,' said Twiggy self-consciously, correcting Sammy. It didn't seem right that the girls should call him by his nickname.

They were Libby, Carol and Sheila. Libby was the one who had asked all the questions at the bar and was evidently, if decisions had to be made, the leader. She had curly brown hair and an impudent expression. She was also slightly plump but not unpleasantly so. 'Well-upholstered' was the description that occurred to Sammy, who found himself, not entirely by chance, sitting next to her.

Next to Twiggy sat Carol, whose perfume Twiggy thought intoxicating. She didn't say much except when asked a direct question, and even then lowered her eyes, blushed a little and answered softly.

First impressions notwithstanding, on closer inspection Sheila proved to be two or three years older than her companions and thus also several years older than Sammy and Twiggy. It showed in her attitude, which was faintly superior. She was pleasant enough and laughed politely at some of the things Sammy said, but she appeared edgy. Twiggy noticed that she was wearing a ring on her engagement finger. Once in a while she glanced anxiously towards the door.

'We were thinking of going to the disco,' said Sammy, after a second round of drinks, all thoughts of wasting the entrance fee now dispelled. Three into two didn't go. There had to be some method of splitting the girls up or the evening would be wasted.

'The Black Horse?' queried Libby. Sammy nodded. 'I shouldn't bother. We've just come from there. It's dull tonight.'

Sammy flashed Twiggy a quick wink. That meant the girls would have re-entry passes and wouldn't cost a penny to take in.

'Maybe you were with the wrong company.' He was dying to get his hands on Libby and there was no better place to start than the dancefloor.

'You can say that again.' Libby ran a hand through her curls and looked at her watch. Sammy panicked. The charm wasn't working. They'd all bugger off in a minute unless he was careful.

'Something to eat, then,' he suggested, saying the first thing that came into his head. A meal wouldn't necessarily lead to anything more exciting tonight, but it might set the scene for next week. 'There's an Indian place a few doors down.' Jeeze, he thought: beer, whisky, pies and a curry. Throw-up time. 'Twiggy'—Twiggy glowered at him—'and I were starting to feel a bit peckish before you arrived.'

'Yes,' said Libby, 'you look as though you could do with some food inside you. Uh-uh,' she added, as the street door was suddenly thrust open to admit three new faces—all male, all civilians, all in their mid-twenties. And all taller than Sammy and considerably heavier than Twiggy.

They lurched over to the table, faces flushed with drink. Sammy reckoned that being a Londoner gave him an edge when it came to anticipating trouble. This wasn't strictly true; he was a naturally wary individual who would have had the same instincts whether born in Cardiff or Glasgow. In any event, these three were trouble. He pushed his chair back a couple of feet to give himself room and side-armed the whisky and vodka glasses out of immediate reach of the newcomers.

'Come on, you, out,' one of them said to Carol, reaching roughly for her arm.

'I'm not going,' said Carol, shying away.

The same man stretched across the table and caught hold of her sleeve. 'I said out and I mean bloody out!' he bellowed.

Twiggy's half-clenched fist uppercut the man's forearm, making him loosen his grip and take an involuntary step backwards. Twiggy stood up. Sammy followed suit.

'She said she didn't want to leave,' said Twiggy.

The man recognized the provincial accent. He sneered.

'Mind your own business, peasant. Nobody asked your opinion.'

'Now that's not nice,' said Sammy.

'Leave her alone anyway,' said Twiggy.

'You heard him,' said Sammy. 'Leave her alone and go outside and play with the traffic.'

By now the pub's other customers were taking an interest, including Scarlett O'Hara.

'Don't get involved,' whispered his wife.

'They're in my platoon,' said Scarlett, as though that explained everything. To him, it did.

Behind the bar the surly barmaid pressed a bell to summon the manager, who was serving in another part of the pub. Two rings—fight imminent. She also called across, without much conviction: 'Here, cut that out.'

'Yes, cut it out, Roy,' said Libby irritably. 'You've had too much. Go home and sleep it off.'

'The bloody hell I will. Tell your girl friend to mind her own business, Doug.'

Now Libby stood up, eyes flashing. 'In the first place I'm not his girl friend. I hardly know him. In the second place, if the police arrive and arrest you for being drunk, what do you think your precious mother will have to say when she has to bail you out? Grow up, for God's sake.'

'Shut up, scrubber,' snarled Roy.

That was too much for Sammy.

'Right, we've tried to be reasonable but you don't want any. So you either walk your chalks now or step outside and take the consequences.'

'Make him behave, Colin,' pleaded Sheila to the third man, the one who, Twiggy thought idly, had probably placed that ring on her engagement finger.

'Come on,' said Colin, after a moment. 'She's not worth the trouble.'

He placed a hand on Roy's shoulder. Roy shrugged it off. In the same movement he made a second lunge for Carol, who backed her chair into the corner, raising an arm to her face.

Twiggy didn't hesitate. Roy's chin, the manner in which he was leaning across the table, made an inviting target. Twiggy hit it, sending Roy sprawling.

Scarlett got to his feet and made for the group. 'Oh Christ,' said his wife to no one in particular.

Colin and Doug helped Roy up. His mouth was bleeding, though it hadn't been much of a punch. Sammy had moved in front of Libby and Twiggy in front of Carol. Somehow Sheila was now fifteen feet away.

Scarlett arrived on the scene at the same moment as the manager. 'It's not this pair's fault.'

'I don't give a bugger whose fault it is. Get the hell out of my pub, all of you, and don't come back.'

'They're not to blame,' persisted Scarlett, without raising

his voice. 'They were having a quiet drink with the girls when these jack-the-lads barged in looking for trouble. Believe me, Arthur, that's how it was.'

Scarlett evidently knew the landlord, who thought it all over for a few seconds. 'Right,' he said finally, 'you three out. The rest of you can stay.'

'I'll remember you,' shouted Roy, a handkerchief to his mouth and addressing Twiggy. 'I'll bloody well remember you. As for you, you bitch. . . .'

The remainder of the sentence was lost as his two companions hustled him into the street.

'Thanks, Sarge,' said Sammy.

'Forget it. But watch yourselves,' advised Scarlett. 'I doubt they'll be back tonight but there'll be other nights.'

Scarlett rejoined his wife with whom he held a whispered conversation before finishing his drink in a single swallow. They left together.

The barmaid came across with a cloth to wipe the table. Twiggy's punch had jarred it, knocking over most of the glasses. From the expression on her face, if looks could have killed friends of Sammy and Twiggy would have been wearing black armbands.

'So what was all that about?' asked Sammy.

Carol was almost in tears. Twiggy put out a tentative hand to comfort her, but withdrew it when she jumped.

No one answered Sammy's question. Instead Sheila said: 'I should go after Colin.'

'Go,' said Libby uninterestedly.

'Will Carol be all right?'

'I'll look after Carol. Go on,' added Libby, less unkindly. 'There's no point in breaking an engagement just because of one stupid man.'

Sheila gathered her handbag and umbrella, and left.

'What we all need is another drink,' suggested Sammy. The altercation had sobered him up considerably.

'Not for me.' Carol shook her head.

Libby waved Sammy towards the bar. 'Get her one anyway. Brandy and ginger.'

Jesus, thought Sammy. Whatever happened to women who used to drink light ale and think they were doing well?

The landlord poured the drinks himself. 'This'll be your last,' he told Sammy. 'I accept it wasn't your fault, but I'd like you to drink up and leave.'

'I repeat,' said Sammy, when he returned to the table, 'what was it all about?'

'We were in the disco,' explained Libby. 'They'd all had too much to drink, but Roy was the worst. He became objectionable with Carol—you don't need the details—and the other two took his side. So we walked out. Sheila didn't want to come at first. She's getting married in the summer and already has half the furniture chosen. That ring might as well be through her nose.'

Sammy understood. 'But she went with you because she knew they'd follow you here.'

'Yes. That was stupid of me, letting you buy us drinks. It would have all blown over otherwise. I'm sorry about that.'

'No problem,' said Sammy airily. And then: 'Is he someone you know well, that Doug?'

'No. Didn't you hear me say so? I hardly know him at all. He's a creep anyway. I only agreed to go out with him because I had nothing better to do.'

'On a Saturday night? No regular bloke?' Sammy brightened momentarily before having a horrible thought. Maybe she did have a regular bloke who was *also* in the army, maybe even in the battalion, but who was now away on leave or on a course.

'That's fishing and none of your business.' Libby glanced at her watch for the second time that evening, again giving Sammy palpitations. 'I think we should be going. Thanks for your help.'

'Yes, thank you,' said Carol self-consciously, looking at Twiggy over her brandy glass.

Twiggy grinned idiotically. One-punch Twigg, king of the ring. It hadn't been a hell of a punch either, but it had made him feel good.

'We could still have that Indian meal,' offered Sammy, 'if you don't want to go back to the Black Horse. It wouldn't take long. You could be home for the midnight movie.'

'Well . . .' Libby looked at Carol. She, Libby, wanted to go. Not that she felt any great attraction for Sammy; he was in the army, after all, and doubtless, like the rest of them, preoccupied with sexual conquests. But she had come out this evening because she was between boy friends, and it was early yet. Why should she ruin her night? What was more, Sammy had stood up to—they had both stood up to—Colin, Doug and creepy Roy when they didn't have to. An Indian

meal wouldn't lead anywhere she didn't want it to go.
'Carol . . . ?'

'I don't mind.'

'Okay, then,' whooped Sammy.

The girls insisted on going Dutch; that, they argued, was
only fair. Neither Sammy nor Twiggy objected. One way or
another they'd both spent a hell of a lot of money for one
Saturday.

Later, they walked the girls as far as the bus stop; it
transpired that they lived virtually next door to one another.
Sammy wanted them to share a cab as it was still raining. He
and Twiggy had to get one back to camp, in any case. Libby
declined firmly. 'The bus will do.'

In the shelter Libby took careful control of Sammy's wandering hands. 'I said I was sorry we got you involved in a
fight. I'm not that sorry.' A few feet away Carol decided she
didn't mind being kissed by Twiggy.

In the taxi, Sammy was full of well-being.

'You just don't know how it's all going to work out, do
you? Without that right-hander, Twiggy, we'd be starting off
again from scratch next week.'

'You're seeing her again, then?'

'Saturday. Earlier if I can manage it. What about you? That
Carol doesn't say much.'

'She says enough.'

He'd asked her where she worked, for want of something
to say. She'd told him the Midland Bank and that, yes, she
would go out with him again if he gave her a ring at the
office. Twiggy thought things were definitely looking up.

FOUR

Elizabeth Ballantine

IT HAD BEGUN TO SNOW an hour before Peter Ballantine arrived home for lunch the day following the Viscount's shoot. From the foot of the drive, despite the outside lights being on, the house was virtually invisible behind a thick curtain of flakes. Peter hoped the snow wouldn't stick. D Company was due a field and firing exercise on Monday, which would be wiped out if this sort of weather continued and give him, as company 2 i/c, a major headache regarding what to do with the men otherwise. A tax-paying outsider might wonder where his contributions were going if elements of the British army were rendered immobile by a snowstorm, but if the troops couldn't see their targets and the support choppers were unable to take off, it was wiser to postpone the manoeuvres. They could do some close-order drill in the undercover shed or, providing no one else was using it, spend an hour or two on the indoor range. After that it would have to be another damned lecture or an afternoon with the PTIs in the gym. Roll on January, he thought, and battalion exercises. Come hell, high water or blizzards, one didn't call those off. If a war ever broke out in Europe, the Russians would hardly be considerate enough to invade only if the weather was fine. He made a mental note to telephone Winter's Day later on in the afternoon; perhaps the snow was local and the vicinity of the camp clear.

He closed the gate behind him and motored slowly up the

drive to the gravelled forecourt, keeping his speed to a minimum in case Barney, his labrador, was out and about, anticipating his master's visit. Not that he could really call Barney his own these days. With his relatively recent promotion to captain and new responsibilities as company second-in-command, it had proved impossible (and unfair to Barney) to keep the dog on the camp, and so he was now left at home, for Sara to look after, or Edward when he wasn't away at school. Barney didn't care for the new regime and regularly tried to climb into Peter's car when it was time for Peter to leave. Once, craftily, knowing he was to be banished, he had tried to hide in the open boot, behind a suitcase and several boxes, and was only ejected after a struggle. Which he almost won since he was the biggest and most powerful labrador Peter had ever seen, built more like a small bear than a dog. He was getting old now—eleven if Peter remembered the passing years correctly—and some of the yellowness of his coat, and especially around the muzzle, was turning grey. He probably hadn't many years left.

As Peter drove up to the forecourt, the familiar sound of his tyres on gravel muted by the new-fallen snow, he reflected how much he loved this house. He had been born and brought up here, as had his sister Sara and younger brother Edward. Compared with the Viscount's mansion it wasn't large, and the nearest neighbours were a mere hundred yards away instead of a dozen or more fields. But it was four centuries old and part of the county's history, having previously been owned, among others, by a hanging judge, a captain who had served with Nelson, and at least one knight who had been executed for offending the first Queen Elizabeth. During World War Two one of the cloak-and-dagger outfits had commandeered it, and within its five and a half acres of garden and woodland young men and women were taught the arts of self-defence and sabotage by hard-bitten, hard-talking NCOs.

John and Elizabeth Ballantine, Peter's father and mother, bought it in 1950, after it had lain empty for five years. The successful barrister and his comparatively new bride had spent time and money making good the dilapidation, restoring the house to its former splendour and beginning the garden afresh. At Elizabeth's instigation and within the framework of existing government regulations, John Ballantine had also cut down those trees that were dead or in a dangerous condition, and planted anew; oaks, copper beeches, conifers, shrubs. John did much of the work himself, which would have been in no way considered remarkable had he not lost both legs above the knee in the Normandy hedgerows, where he had fought as a subaltern with the regiment in which Peter now served.

The elder Ballantines and their three children had lived contentedly in the house until seven years earlier, when Peter's father, on his way home from Kenya after the victorious defence of a client on a capital charge, was killed when the light plane ferrying him and other guests from a celebration party to Nairobi crashed on take-off. He was the only fatality; the others scrambled clear or were pulled clear, but he was trapped by his tin legs while the aircraft burned.

Of all the trees John Ballantine had planted, three oaks were Peter's particular favourites. All were of different ages— twenty-eight, twenty-three and sixteen—having been embedded at the birth of each of the Ballantine children. Next to each tree was a mahogany stake giving the name of the child and date of birth, a useful *aide-mémoire*, Peter often thought, for buying gifts and sending cards.

He could hear Barney's baritone woofs long before he switched off the ignition, and moments later the front door was pulled open for the dog to appear and thunder across the forecourt like an express train. He jumped up excitedly, two huge paws on Peter's chest and pink tongue licking his face. Peter fought him playfully for a few seconds before saying, 'Enough, enough!' Duty done and welcome acknowledged, the dog bounded away.

Edward stood in the doorway, taller and broader than Peter remembered, though that was scarcely possible since the two had seen each other at half-term in October. He held out his hand formally if awkwardly; he revered his older brother and was in two minds whether, like him, to join the regiment one day or pursue a career in civil engineering. Elizabeth Ballantine was against the former and in favour of the latter. In her opinion one son in the army was enough. The options were therefore rarely discussed. In any case, there was plenty of time before Edward need make a final decision, though Peter considered that civil engineering would probably win out in the long run. From all accounts Edward was an exceptional student with his head firmly screwed on. He would look at pay structures, weigh the odds and calculate whether he stood any chance of making colonel. If he concluded he didn't, that the competition was likely to be too fierce at the top in a rapidly shrinking British army where promotion could be snail-paced now that there were no wars to fight, he would remain a civilian. For Peter, there had been no choice to make. For as long as he could remember he had wanted to be a soldier, and still did. The fact that others of his graduating year with similar or inferior degrees were now making twice as much as he was didn't enter into it.

'Do you need anything from the car?' asked Edward.

'It can wait. When did you get home from school?'

'Friday afternoon.'

'Good report?'

'It hasn't arrived yet, but I expect it will be reasonable.'

'I expect it to be the customary brilliance. Did you dress the tree?'

At the far end of the rectangular entrance hall, next to the downstairs cloakroom, an eight-foot-high Christmas tree stood in a half-size dustbin whose true function was disguised behind several layers of Christmas wrapping paper. The dustbin was filled with dry sand to give the tree stability, and draped over the tree's branches were flickering fairy lights in several dozen colours. There would be another, slightly smaller tree in the drawing-room, Peter knew. There always had been.

'Yesterday,' said Edward. 'Almost alone, I might add, since Sara spent most of the afternoon day-dreaming and jumping every time the telephone rang.'

'Any word from Ricardo and Beto yet?'

'Nothing. I suppose they will be coming?'

'If Ricardo said they were, they'll be here. I expect they got held up in Paris. If the weather over there is anything like this, they may be delayed.'

'Not for too long, I hope. Sara will drive herself and everyone else crackers if they don't phone soon.'

The Jordan-Arditti brothers, Ricardo and Alberto, who was generally called Beto, were long-standing Argentine friends of the Ballantines, particularly of Peter, who had been to boarding school in England with Ricardo and who had spent many summers and half-terms in his company, both in England and in Argentina. He had a great deal of affection for as well as a lot in common with Ricardo, not least because the Argentinian was the same age and also a regular army officer. He had written early in December to say that he, Beto and their sister Lucita would be visiting Europe briefly around the middle of the month, stopping over in Paris for a cousin's wedding before flying to England. He sincerely hoped that Peter would not be occupied elsewhere. Peter had cabled back immediately to the effect that he would make sure he wasn't.

The Jordan-Arditti family fortunes had evidently taken a turn for the better, Peter reflected as he washed his hands in the cloakroom to the accompaniment of Edward's incessant chatter concerning some incident that had occurred at school on the last day of term. At one time they had been extremely wealthy; then suddenly, almost overnight, they were poor or at any rate poorish. Peter knew little of Argentine economics that he had not learned from Ricardo, but he was aware of the terrifying rate of inflation that could wipe out, if one was unlucky, whole businesses at the blink of an eyelid. However, it now seemed that the family were in the chips once more. Flying from Buenos Aires to Europe was far from inexpensive and 'a few days in Paris', as he knew from his own experience, could cost enough to make strong men weep.

He wondered briefly what the situation was between Sara and Ricardo. He never enquired; it wasn't his business. Sara was twenty-three and capable of making decisions for herself. He knew his sister was fond of his friend and suspected those feelings were returned, but he didn't know quite how deep it all went. That too wasn't his concern. Certainly she had also spent holidays with the Jordan-Ardittis in Argentina, and possibly something more than mere friendship had developed then. Time would tell.

'You haven't heard a word I've said,' protested Edward, punching Peter lightly on the arm.

'Of course I have. Sticky Cook or someone with an equally absurd name drank half a bottle of whisky before breakfast and threw up in chapel during a doubtless untuneful rendering of "Lord Dismiss Us With Thy Blessing". It happened in my day too, you know. There's always some idiot who believes whisky to be lemonade and can't wait to show how grown up he is. I think mine was called Sos McMasters.'

'Sos?'

'Short for Sausage. He was as round as a weather balloon.'

'And you said Sticky was an absurd name!'

'Well, yes. Anyhow, I was listening.'

'Sorry, I thought you weren't.'

Peter winked at him. 'That's a knack you learn in the

army, keeping half an ear on the briefing while thinking of something else entirely. If you had to sit through an hour of maps and diagrams with my CO you'd know what I mean.'

'Winter's Day or Daddy Rankin?'

'Daddy. Major de Winton-Day doesn't know an awful lot about maps. And you can forget I said that, especially if you come over to the camp some time during the holidays and meet the company commander yourself.'

'Can I do that?'

'We'll see. Maybe for lunch one day. Keep it under your hat, though, or your mother will conclude that I'm trying to get you to enlist in the ranks.'

Peter finished drying his hands.

'Right, I'd better show my face before they come looking for me. Where are they, in the kitchen?'

'Making lunch, yes.'

'Something appetizing, I trust. I'm ravenous.'

'The usual Sunday stodge. Roast beef, roast spuds, Yorkshire pudding and some vegetables, I forget what. But we're having roly-poly for pudding,' Edward added enthusiastically.

'You'll go back in January as fat as a pig. You're already half a stone heavier than when I last saw you.'

In the kitchen Peter kissed his mother and sister, generally got under their feet by looking under saucepan lids to see what the contents were, and, after a minute or so, was chased out to the drawing-room, where Sara joined him a few moments later. Edward disappeared to find Barney before the dog caught pneumonia.

Peter was on his haunches, putting an extra log on the fire. 'Make me one,' he said over his shoulder, hearing Sara at the drinks table.

'Gin and tonic?'

'Please. Not too stiff.'

'Are you driving back today in that muck?' She inclined her head in the direction of the window, where outside, the snow seemed to be coming down thicker than ever.

'Probably not, but I'll be telephoning in later and you never know what sort of flap will be on.'

Sara settled for a sherry and sat by the hearth, her drink at her side, her arms clasped around her knees. Without being beautiful she was nonetheless a striking-looking young woman, with chestnut-coloured hair (a legacy from her mother's side of the family which had not been passed down to Peter or

Edward) framing a pale, oval face that reminded her, she had once remarked caustically, of a genteel Victorian consumptive doomed to meet the grim reaper before her time. 'I should have spent my life on a chaise-longue, leaning bravely against puffed-up pillows and reading slender volumes of verse, preferably in Wimpole Street.' She was small and slim (another quality that had not been inherited by Elizabeth Ballantine's sons, who were, if not outrageously tall, certainly robust). During the week she lived alone in a tiny London flat a short bus ride away from her job at the Foreign Office, where she worked in a medium-grade secretarial capacity. She lived by herself not because she was anti-social—she had many friends, male and female, in London—but because she couldn't stand the thought of sharing with a bunch of twittering females on a regular basis. 'I've seen what happens to others. Someone has always eaten someone else's yoghurt or the last apple, the bathroom is full of everyone's knickers but your own, and once a week there are hysterics because someone's boy friend has thrown her over for a newer model.' If she had boy friends or lovers of her own, she kept very quiet about them. Aside from the fact that she was his sister, Peter was deeply fond of her.

'I thought Mother was looking well,' he said.

'She always glows when the family's together. It doesn't happen often enough, what with Edward at school and you in the army. I don't get down as often as I should, either.'

'Are you saying she's lonely?'

'Well, she misses Daddy, naturally, even after all these years, but no, not lonely as such. She gets stacks of invitations and not just because people feel sorry for her. But that's not the same, is it? The same as having a family around, I mean. Families don't make demands the way outsiders do, however nice they're trying to be. One is always hopping up to get them drinks or having drinks forced upon one. Also, if a member of the family offends you, you tell him or her to shut up. You can't do that with comparative strangers.'

'That's a bit too deep for me.'

'Don't act the military dunderhead. It doesn't become you. You know perfectly well what I'm talking about.'

'Not really. I spend my life with comparative strangers, live with them. They don't bother me.'

'That's because you're too self-contained.'

Peter raised an eyebrow. '*I* am?'

'Of course. Perhaps self-confident is a better expression. You're probably as good at your job as anyone else your age and superior to most. To be so you have to be pretty sure of yourself, which breeds self-containment.'

'The way you say it doesn't make it sound like a compliment.'

'It wasn't meant to be. It wasn't meant to be an insult either. It was simply a statement. Would you get me another sherry? I'm too comfortable to move.'

Peter refilled her glass and topped up his own, heavy on the tonic. 'Go on,' he said.

'With what?'

'With the analysis.'

'It wasn't an analysis and I'd finished anyway.'

'It *was* an analysis and you hadn't finished. You weren't talking about me. Well, not entirely. You were talking about yourself.'

'Was I?'

'You were.'

'Perhaps you're right.' Sara thought about it. 'Yes, perhaps you're right. How very perceptive of you to spot it.'

Peter grinned at her. 'It comes with the rank. We can't tie the troops to cannons and give them fifty lashes these days if they break Queen's Regs. We have to find out why they've committed the offence and make sure it doesn't happen again. Don't you ever read the recruiting blurbs in the colour supplements, the bits that say that five years as a commissioned officer teaches one more about man management than a dozen university courses?'

'It's not the first item I turn to in the Sunday papers.'

Edward, covered in snow, appeared in the drawing-room doorway. 'Barney objected to being brought in. We had a fight which I almost didn't win. I've got to change. Mother says lunch in five minutes and the wine needs opening. I'd do it quickly if I were you, Peter. Sara is the wine buyer this weekend and she's obviously picked up a job lot. I checked the vintage. It's going to need all the help it can get. In my view it doesn't so much need to breathe as about a week on a life-support system.'

'Damned cheek,' said Sara. 'You can go without then, in that case,' she called after Edward's disappearing back.

'Is Edward self-contained or whatever it is?' asked Peter.

'Not yet. He's too much in awe of you to be his own man for a few years.'

'In awe of me?'

'You keep raising your eyebrows every time I state the obvious. Of course Edward's in awe of you. He was only eight or nine or some such when Daddy was killed. Since then you've taken Daddy's place in his eyes. That's only natural. As a matter of fact I was pretty much in awe of you myself until a few years ago.'

'I don't think I can stand much more of this,' said Peter jocularly, getting up from his armchair and taking his glass with him. 'I'll go and do as I'm bid and open the wine.'

He paused by the door.

'As a matter of interest, what happened a few years ago that made me less awesome?'

'I'm not sure I should tell you.'

'Come on now, you can't get away with that.'

'All right, you were twenty-three and I was just eighteen. I'd seen you in uniform and you were an impressive sight. You seemed huge to me, very mature. Then Barney got run over that time you were on leave.'

Peter remembered the occasion well. At dusk, Barney had got out of the gate, down the lane and on to the main road, where he had been hit by a vehicle that hadn't stopped. After calling him and looking for him for several hours, Peter found him at the side of the road late at night, more dead than alive. The vet had wanted to put him down. Peter wouldn't have it. Without much confidence in the outcome, the vet had therefore done his best. Peter sat with the dog, more or less without sleep, for three days and nights, just letting Barney know that someone was near by who cared for him. By the third dawn he drank some milk and brandy from a saucer, and two days afterwards was eating solid food. He made a complete recovery, astonishing the vet. Had the dog not been so huge and powerful, he would surely have died.

'So,' said Peter.

'You sat with him in the red barn. You wouldn't allow me or Mummy or anyone else near him, but I was around anyway, just to see if I could help. I heard you talking to him.'

'I hope you're not going to embarrass me by quoting my exact words.'

'No, I wouldn't do that, but you kept him alive. You

became less awesome then. I realized you weren't a god in a tailored uniform but a human being.'

At lunch Peter sat at the head of the table, his mother on his right, Sara on his left and Edward next to Sara. The table seated twelve and for several years after her husband's death Elizabeth Ballantine had taken precedence during meals. Then gradually, subtly, almost without Peter noticing it, she had bequeathed the position to him, occasionally at first, then more regularly, then permanently. One day it would be Edward's turn, when Peter married and set up home for himself. She hoped he would not be too long about it; she wanted grandchildren. Although in her view (while she had in no manner attempted to influence his decision) Cecilia had been quite wrong for him, being too much of the clinging vine, he couldn't afford to wait for ever for what he considered to be the right woman. She knew her elder son better than he imagined, knew him to be over-critical of people who did not live up to his expectations of them. All very fine and large in the army, where minor imperfections could have major consequences, but nit-picking in the last analysis when choosing a wife. There, loyalty, dependability and character should be the prime qualities looked for.

Elizabeth Ballantine's once-red hair had turned grey within months of her husband being killed although she was little more than fifty then and not yet sixty now. She was the same build and had the same facial bone structure as Sara, and no one could fail to mistake them for mother and daughter. Since the previous winter she had walked with a stick. Arthritis, her doctor told her. Nothing to worry about providing she wasn't in too much pain. Other than that her health was excellent. She would live to be a hundred. 'God forbid,' she retorted.

After lunch the four played bridge for an hour, Sara partnering Peter, Edward his mother, the losers to do the washing-up, by hand since Elizabeth Ballantine would have nothing so totally unnecessary—'and so symptomatic of the commercial hotel mentality of the twentieth century'—as an automatic dish-washer in her house. Edward and his mother wiped the floor with Peter and Sara, as they generally did when paired together.

Later Peter telephoned the camp. It was snowing heavily there too but the forecast was that it would ease and probably clear before morning.

'No sense in taking risks, old boy,' said Winter's Day.

'Might as well take advantage of home comforts overnight. If the Met. men are reading their tea leaves correctly, you'll have an easy run tomorrow.'

Half an hour before dusk, while Elizabeth Ballantine relaxed in front of the drawing-room fire with the *Sunday Times* and one of the few glasses of brandy she permitted herself each week, Peter, Sara and Edward donned outdoor clothes and took Barney for a run in the grounds, bombarding him and each other with snowballs. When they returned their mother had news for them.

'Ricardo telephoned from Paris just after you left. It's snowing there too, but they'll be over as soon as they can get a flight.'

Peter caught the look on Sara's face at the news: a glow of pleasure mixed with apprehension.

FIVE

Sara Ballantine

MARCH, WHEN SHE HAD LAST SEEN RICARDO, seemed an eternity ago. He had written to her, of course, but the tone of his letters was guarded friendliness, and she, taking her cue, had replied in the same vein for fear of appearing pushy or anxious, or becoming an embarrassment. It was as if he'd forgotten—or, worse, regretted—the two days, and nights, they had spent together in Mar del Plata during her last week in Argentina. Perhaps he did. Or more accurately, perhaps he did not but wanted the relationship to go no further. Holiday lovers were hardly unique.

The Happy City, the Argentines called Mar del Plata, two hundred miles from Buenos Aires on the Atlantic coast, and happy is what the city had been for her. What had started as a sightseeing excursion, with separate bedrooms at the Château Frontenac, had ended, the first evening, with an energetic and memorably erotic session of lovemaking after a highly successful tilt at the roulette wheel, number 27, her birthday, coming up twice in succession and four times in an hour, quite against the odds. The following morning they had breakfasted exotically on Havana *alfajores,* soft biscuits topped with caramel and covered with chocolate; and champagne, a combination that would have turned her stomach in London, or had she not been in love. For she was, she admitted to herself, in love with Ricardo, and probably had been for years.

Later they'd walked through the tree-lined squares, and lunched and talked. That evening they'd given the casino a miss, and, after dinner, made love again into the small hours. She wondered what the hotel staff would think on discovering that her own bed had not been slept in. Probably not very much.

She could not remember what they'd said at the airport, but it was not 'thanks very much and goodbye'. Then again, Ricardo wasn't that sort of man. Maybe he hadn't known how to tell her that what had happened was just one of those things that occasionally do after a pleasant evening and, perhaps, a little too much to drink. Not too much to affect performance but more than enough to impair judgment. It was quite an easy matter to say 'I love you' during or just after excellent sex. Men and women said that sort of remark to each other all the time. Sincerely meant too. But not meant to be for ever, which she wanted her relationship with Ricardo to be. For her, it hadn't been just sex, and she had remained celibate since her return from Argentina.

Maybe that was being silly and incurably romantic. After all, they hadn't made any promises to one another—not a promise that could be called a *real* promise, out of bed. But the fact remained that she hadn't wanted to sleep with anyone after Ricardo, and that was all there was to it.

She was worried about seeing him again, she had to admit. How would he react? How would *she* react? She would make some excuse and return to London if he was cool and distant. And there was no indication that he would not be. After all, he hadn't made this trip solely to see her. He, Beto and Lucita were in Paris for a wedding. He was an old friend of Peter's. What could be more natural than his wanting to see his ex-school chum, especially as they were in the same job at the same rank? Or to see his chum's mother, who had once served him lemonade and buns during half-terms and when she, Sara, five years the junior of Peter and Ricardo, had been scolded away from their adolescent adventures, or played an Indian to their cowboys.

If he simply walked in and said, 'Hello, Sara, nice to see you again'—and shook her hand as though nothing had happened between them, she would be in her car and back to her flat before he could blink.

However, she'd wait and see. She was good at that.

SIX

Ricardo Jordan-Arditti

RICARDO WOKE UP with a splitting headache and a mouth that felt as if someone had been burning chicken feathers in it. He opened one eye slowly, cautiously, suspiciously, like an old woman adjusting a wrinkled stocking in a public place. Mother of mercy, was this the end of Rico? He thought it might be. And a damned good thing too. With an entire rugby pack trampling over his skull, death held no terrors.

Gingerly he sat up, bending forward and resting his head on his knees. Parts of the previous day floated back to him. Okay, he was in a room. To be more precise, he was in a hotel bedroom in the George V, 8th *arrondissement,* Paris, though how he, Beto and Lucita had got back here from their cousin's wedding in Chantilly defeated him.

A vee-shaped chink in the heavy drapes let in a slash of daylight, but other than that he had no idea of the time. After a moment he switched on the bedside lamp—an action that brought a muffled snarl of pain and rage from the adjacent bed—and hunted among a pile of loose change for his watch. 8.30. Monday morning, presumably, unless he'd lost a day somewhere.

Naked, he left the bed and padded to the bathroom. After he had cleaned his teeth vigorously, he returned to the bedroom and made for the bar/fridge. There was an empty bottle and a half-full bottle of Dom Perignon on a table, but the latter would be flat and warm by now. To quench his thirst, he debated whether to have a cold beer or a quarter bottle of champagne, before settling for the champagne which he swallowed in two gulps. He then opened the curtains, flooding the room with daylight and bringing another muted bellow of protest from Beto. At least he assumed it was Beto—the timbre of the voice sounded about right and the heap of crumpled clothes at the foot of the bed were definitely his—though it could be anyone. There had been a great deal of drinking and dancing and a certain amount of propositioning at the wedding feast. Better check.

'Go to hell,' mumbled Beto when Ricardo pulled back the covers. Assuming a foetal position, he groped blindly for the sheets and blankets which Ricardo had tossed to the floor, out of reach.

'Wakey, wakey,' grinned Ricardo, feeling a little better with the champagne inside him. 'It's a fine morning, the snow's stopped temporarily, and we've got a plane to catch.'

'Not till this afternoon.'

'It'll take you that long to get up unless you start now.'

Beto refused to budge. Ricardo looked around the room for something with which to coax his younger brother into animation, his eyes alighting on the half-full bottle of Dom Perignon. It was a hell of an expensive way to get someone on his feet, but . . .

Beto let out a howl as the champagne hit his face. He sat up abruptly, fists clenched. Still grinning, Ricardo backed away.

'You bastard!' shouted Beto. 'Have you no pity? I'm dying here.'

'And I'm doing you a favour. Come next month when you start your military service, you'll thank me for getting you into training. They shoot recruits, conscripts or not, who won't get up when they're told. Now, while I'm having a shower, organize some breakfast, lots of toast and several jugs of coffee. And, while you're about it, call Lucita's room and ask her to join us in half an hour if she hasn't breakfasted already.' Ricardo paused by the bathroom door. 'I suppose Lucita *was* with us when we left the wedding?'

'How the hell should I know? I don't even remember me being with us.'

Under the shower—five minutes with the hot spray and then, gritting his teeth, thirty seconds with the cold—Ricardo gradually filled in most of the gaps in his memory of the previous day.

The afternoon and the early part of the evening were easy, from the ceremony to the formal part of the reception and the toasts in his uncle's Chantilly villa. He recalled phoning Peter Ballantine's mother while still relatively sober, but things got a bit murky from the time the dancing really got underway about nine. Ricardo's cousin and his bride had slipped away around then, to the accompaniment of hunting horns and rice throwing, after which everyone got down to some serious drinking. He remembered dancing with a very attractive French divorcee a few years his senior, say thirty-five, who had about as much Spanish as he did French, and conducting a long conversation with her in English, some of it political and relating to the *desaparecidos,* the 'disappeared ones', those men, women and sometimes teenagers who had vanished from their homes since the junta came to power, not to be seen again. The Frenchwoman had become quite heated in her condemnation of the Galtieri regime, the more so when she realized that he, Ricardo, was in the army. She assumed all military personnel were tarred with the same brush. The average Argentine soldier, he had argued, had as much to do with the clandestine security organizations responsible for the *desaparecidos* as the average French soldier had with the SDECE, or the British soldier with MI5. She thought otherwise, and said so, and after a while he began to suspect that she was more than she seemed to be, a journalist perhaps.

Once he made it quite clear that he had no intention of continuing the debate, that a wedding was no place to discuss politics, she changed her attitude, dropped the hostility, became more friendly. Too friendly unless he had misread the signs, the come-to-bed invitation in her eyes. But he avoided her for the remainder of the evening, danced with others, just to be on the safe side. When he wasn't dancing he was drinking—too much, more than he usually did, and for the wrong reasons. Whether she was a journalist or not, the woman had put him on the defensive and he didn't like it.

Of course conditions were not perfect in Argentina; nor were they in any country in the world. But he was a serving officer who had taken an oath of loyalty. Whatever he might think of the junta privately—and like many other officers of his age and rank he was anxious to see a return to democratic government—he could not allow his country's leaders to be criticized openly, especially by the French, who were possibly the most insular and touchy of all Europeans, no matter what anyone said about the British.

Shortly after midnight the party started to break up. There were beds in the villa for everyone, Ricardo recalled being told by his uncle, but he had declined on behalf of his brother and sister. They really had to return to Paris since they were flying to London the following afternoon.

A taxi was summoned and farewells made, but the road from Chantilly to Paris was treacherous after the recent snow, and the journey took two hours. They reached the George V around three a.m., whereupon he had ordered two bottles of Dom Perignon and a bottle of Hennessy XO to be sent up to the room he shared with Beto. Obviously one of the bottles of champagne had been drunk plus half of the second, but he didn't recall seeing the Hennessy in the bedroom. Perhaps Lucita—wiser and older than her eighteen years—had recognized the silence in the taxi for what it was, and had concluded that it would be imprudent, after talking politics, to leave her elder brother brooding with a bottle of cognac.

Politics were not often discussed in the Jordan-Arditti household, not since Ricardo's father had remade—under the junta, in cattle and banking—the fortune he had all but lost during the early Seventies, when some poor investments combined with one of the world's worst inflation rates had driven him to the edge of bankruptcy. Had the family wealth not been lost Ricardo would not have been taken from school in England at the age of seventeen to become a late entrant in the Colegio Militar, the Argentine Military Academy, where the normal admission age was sixteen. (Though shattering at the time, it was a turn of events Ricardo no longer regretted. Now that he had a substantial income from his shares in the family business, he enjoyed being a soldier; it suited his temperament.) Had Alfredo Jordan-Arditti's fortune not been regained, Beto would have followed in his elder brother's footsteps, enrolled as an officer candidate at sixteen, four and a half years ago, instead of completing his studies with a view, one day, after post-graduate work and travel, to lecturing and perhaps writing on South American history, a career of which his father strongly disapproved. With one son in the army, who was to take over the running of the family companies if Beto insisted upon pottering around with the past? Beto didn't care, and frequently said so. In any case, long before firm decisions were made about his future he had to do his compulsory military service in the ranks, something he could perhaps have avoided, using his father's influence, had he been a different sort of young man.

In Ricardo's opinion, Beto was unlikely to make much of a soldier. Academic leanings apart, he had, as did Lucita, a rebellious artistic streak in him, a legacy from their mother who in her youth had sung professionally. He played the piano, painted a little, wrote some verse. He was likely to find military discipline illogical and irksome.

Ricardo wiped the steam from the shaving mirror with a hand towel and studied his reflection. So there it was, for what it was worth. Lucita had been in the taxi and had returned with him and Beto to the George Cinq. Problem solved, though he would take good care not to consume so much alcohol in future regardless of whether or not he was being baited by an undercover journalist, or whether the whole incident was a figment of his imagination. (He recalled one of Beto's witticisms: 'Just because I'm paranoid doesn't mean that no one's after me.') If memory served him, the medical profession said that the first bout of semi-amnesia was not the beginning but the end. Once it started, it was all downhill after that.

He lathered his face with an old-fashioned brush prior to shaving with a cut-throat razor. At five feet ten and one hundred and sixty pounds, a single pound heavier than the weight he had boxed at during his early years in the army, his was the physique of the natural athlete. Though he had given up the ring when he realized that there were other middleweights with far more ability (because it is not in the Argentine character to aspire to be second best), he was an expert horseman, played polo for his division and was an army reserve, and could out-stay all but a dozen men in his battalion on cross-country runs. He had inherited his dark good looks from the cross-breeding of his Italo-Irish ancestors— and somewhere in the lineage was an English great-grandmother—and until the middle of the current year had been considered by the other members of his mess to be something of a lady's man. Then all that had changed, and only the more astute of his brother officers had put down the transformation to Sara Ballantine's visit to Argentina in March. Ricardo wasn't sure that his brother officers were right, which was one of the reasons he and his brother and sister were spending a few days in England before flying home.

Shaved, he brushed his teeth a second time, less vigorously than before. Some toast and coffee and he would begin to feel more like his normal self.

Hearing Lucita's voice outside, he wrapped a towel around his waist before going into the bedroom.

'Now you,' he ordered Beto, who had donned a dressing-gown and was sitting in an armchair, smoking a cigarette that he didn't seem to want, looking as though he'd died a week ago. Less Latin in looks than either his brother or sister—a throwback, Ricardo often thought, to the English great-grandmother—his normally pale complexion was this morning the colour of a dead wood fire. 'Shave, shower and et cetera. At the double.'

Beto struggled to his feet. 'I hope I'm never attached to your battalion.'

'Little chance of that. We don't have much use for historians up the sharp end. The brass will take one look at you and assign you to 1st Corps HQ at Campo de Mayo, probably sign-writing. Did you order breakfast?'

'Yes,' said Beto, disappearing into the bathroom.

'For three?' called Ricardo. But Beto had gone.

'For two,' said Lucita. 'I had mine ages ago, while the so-called men of the family were sleeping it off.'

'Sorry about that. It doesn't happen very often.'

'I know it doesn't. But it shouldn't happen at all.' She made a face. 'God, that sounds very pious, doesn't it. It wasn't meant to be, but you worried me last night. You were incoherent at times, mumbling away about the government and the *desaparecidos*. If an excess of alcohol makes you talk like that and look the way Beto looked when I walked in, I don't know why you drink. There I go again.'

'You're beginning to sound like your mother. And your father.' Ricardo took a cigarette from Beto's packet, and lit it. It brought back the burnt-chicken feather taste to his mouth, and after a solitary puff he stubbed it out. 'And speaking of last night, did I imagine I bought a bottle of Hennessy XO, or did you snaffle it?'

'Guilty. It's in my suitcase. I thought you'd had enough, both of you.'

'So you've said.'

'And have you seen the price of it? I checked with the

room-service menu. At home, whole families could live for a week on the cost of that single bottle.'

'It's one of the world's best cognacs being served in one of the world's finest hotels. What did you expect to be paying for, grappa?'

'Still.'

'Still nothing. And I've had enough criticism for one morning. Make yourself useful. Pass me some clean underwear, socks and a shirt, and then turn your back.'

Lucita limped to the wardrobe, favouring her right leg. Her left was an inch shorter than her right, a consequence of childhood polio which she was lucky to have survived. She refused to wear compensating shoes and would never be able to wear high-heels without, as she put it, 'waddling like an inebriated duck'. But that was the least of it. Until the age of seven, when the polio struck, she had been considered something of a child prodigy as a pianist. She did not have to be forced or bribed, like so many talented children, to practise; she loved the instrument and the magic she could conjure from it with her tiny fingers. A brilliant future was predicted for her.

After her illness she screamed whenever her mother or father took her anywhere near the music room, and wept piteously at the sight of her teacher. Finally she was allowed to discontinue her studies, on medical advice, and it wasn't until she was in her teens that all concerned discovered the rationale behind her post-polio hysteria. It had to be judged doubtful if she had fully understood it herself at the age of seven, but she had apparently reasoned that, with her left leg now shorter than her right and liable to be in an iron brace for several years, she would never be strong enough to operate the pedals. By the time she realized she was wrong it was too late; there was no way she could make up for those six lost years.

However, a minor miracle did take place when she was fourteen. She found that her musical ability was not confined to the keyboard; she had inherited her mother's marvellous soprano voice and had concentrated on developing it and refining it ever since. Perhaps the concert hall would be her salvation, though personally she had far from ruled out the opera stage, in spite of her disability. If looks and dramatic presence had anything to do with it she would make it, for she resembled a young Audrey Hepburn, a determined gamine.

Ricardo accepted the socks, shirt and underwear. Lucita turned her back and gazed out of the window.

'I called the airport,' she said over her shoulder. 'It's clear. Providing the snow keeps away, they expect departures to be as normal. There's a British Airways flight at 12.30 or an Air France at 1.30, space on both.'

'Did you book us in?'

'No, I wanted to talk to you first.'

'Make it Air France. We're in no real hurry. You can do it from the desk downstairs.'

'I'll see to it while you're having breakfast. Should we phone the Ballantines and let them know what time we'll be at Heathrow?'

'No. We'll call them when we land, in case we're delayed. They're a considerable distance away and, knowing them, they'll insist on coming to meet us.'

'How? Peter's in the army, isn't he? Surely he can't just come and go as he pleases.'

'Right. He said in his cable that he'd arrange a few days' leave while we were over, but obviously he wouldn't want it to begin until he knew what day we were arriving. If we call the Ballantines from Heathrow that will give them a chance to contact Peter at battalion and let him know our e.t.a. Allowing for Customs and passport hold-ups, he'll still be there before we are.'

'If we phoned them now you could be sure of it.'

'Weren't you listening to me? If we phone them now they'll insist on meeting us.'

'You mean Sara will.'

'All right, Sara will. It's too far to ask her to drive if we're not on time. We'll hire a car, that's simpler all round.'

'Hmmm,' murmured Lucita.

'What does ''hmmm'' mean?'

'Just practising scales.'

'Fibber.'

'All right, just wondering if you need the driving time to compose yourself before seeing her again. Also'—the thought suddenly occurred to her—'wondering if yesterday's combination of champagne, wine, brandy and whatever else could have been nerves as much as anything.'

'Rubbish.' She was right, however, thought Ricardo. At least on the first count. As for the second, he didn't know that himself. 'Though talking of phone calls,' he added quickly, to get her off the subject, 'we should perhaps ring home, tell them how the wedding went and how much everyone regretted their absence.'

'It's five o'clock in the morning there now. Besides, you've already done it.'

'I have?'

'You have. About 3.30 a.m. French time, if I remember correctly. You were on the phone for about half an hour. At least, you were on it for twenty minutes, Beto for seven, and me for three.' She lowered her voice a couple of octaves and did a creditable impersonation of Ricardo's baritone. ' "Mama, I hope you're feeling better. Everyone was *so* disappointed— hiccup—that you didn't feel well enough to travel—hic—and that Papa felt it incumbent—*incumbent*—to stay at home with you." '

'Don't,' groaned Ricardo, now recalling parts of the conversation.

Lucita refused to stop. ' "Uncle Guille suggests a low-fat diet, plenty of fresh vegetables and lots of rest, and you'll be as right as rain in six months." I must say I was most impressed with your medical knowledge.'

Ricardo walked past Lucita and reached into the wardrobe for his dark-blue suit. 'You're a pig, you know that.'

'Oink, oink,' grunted Lucita.

'And for being a pig you can do the packing for Beto and me.'

'I always do anyway. You and he pack as though you were making a hero sandwich. Two grown men, one an army captain and one a university graduate, and you fill a suitcase as though you were stuffing a goose. God knows what would have happened if I hadn't made the trip.' She paused, slyly. 'On the other hand, this being Paris, God probably does know what would have happened, and we wouldn't want you sullied, would we?'

'Now that's enough,' said Ricardo sharply. Damn it, she was growing up fast. He was away for a few months only, it seemed, on his army duties, and when he came back he expected to see a ten- or twelve-year-old waiting for him, hunting through his kit to see what he'd brought for her. But she was almost a woman, now. No, she *was* a woman. That six months in New York with Signora Benvenutti, the drama coach recommended by her Argentine voice teacher, had matured her beyond recognition. There again, six months in New York would sharpen the softest kitten's claws.

She dropped him a neat curtsey. 'As you wish. Though talking of Paris,' she added seriously, 'we should buy some things for the Ballantines—at the airport duty-free shop I mean. I made a mental list earlier. Havana cigars for Peter, after-shave for Edward, eau de toilette for Mrs Ballantine.'

'You've left out Sara.'

'As if I would do such a thing. Arpège for Sara. That is her favourite scent, isn't it?'

Ricardo glowered at his sister. 'There was a time, you know, when Mama spoke of you becoming a nun. That would have been a profligate waste of talent. You should be on the stage.'

'Oh, I shall be,' said Lucita, 'I shall be. In any case, I'd have made a dreadful nun. Black just isn't my colour.'

She half-limped, half-skipped towards the outside door, reaching it as the room-service waiter knocked and entered, bearing breakfast. She offered the startled young man a sweeping bow and ushered him in. In excellent French she said: 'The gentleman struggling with his trousers, is in fact, a millionaire. Make sure you get a good tip.' In Spanish she added: 'I'll make the airline reservations and be back to pack for you in twenty minutes.'

Beto emerged from the bathroom as Ricardo was pouring coffee and buttering his first slice of toast.

'Okay, so what's the plan of campaign?' he asked, seizing the coffeepot. Ricardo told him the time of their flight. 'Excellent,' beamed Beto. 'That gives us an hour or two. After breakfast I suggest we leave our bags with the hall porter and wander up the Champs-Elysées for some ice cream and perhaps a little champagne in Le Drug-Store.'

Ricardo stared at his brother in astonishment.

'I thought you were at death's door.'

'That was twenty minutes ago. I looked inside, didn't think much of the company, and walked away without leaving a card. Okay, champagne and ice cream?'

'Whatever you say.'

Ricardo shook his head. Everyone, it seemed, was bouncing around this morning with the exception of him. It had to be age.

• • •

Their flight left on time and was uneventful, though from the air, as the plane made its approach, they could see that much of the English countryside was covered with snow. The main roads seemed clear, however.

After clearing Customs and Passport Control, Lucita left her brothers to find a phone while Ricardo and Beto headed for the Hertz desk, where Ricardo, the only one of the three to possess an international driving permit, signed for the hire car and paid with an American Express card drawn on his US dollar account. He had other cards in Argentine currency, but he knew from past experience that European traders, not surprisingly in view of his country's inflation rate, sometimes raised objections to dealing in the peso. They would complete the transaction sooner or later, but frequently there were delays.

Ricardo also did most of the talking on the rare occasions he and his brother and sister travelled together in England, especially at airports, for the single reason that he spoke the language best. At times he had been mistaken for an Englishman who had spent several years abroad. Not that Lucita and Beto couldn't get by; they could and did. Lucita's English was almost perfect, albeit that the North American influence was apparent; Beto's eighteen months in England at Ricardo's (and Peter Ballantine's) old school between the ages of fifteen and sixteen and a half had served him in good stead, and only rarely did he make serious mistakes in construction or have to hunt for a noun. But Ricardo's fluency and accent were useful tools when dealing with such officials as immigration officers, who could be awkward with foreigners. For what purpose are you here, how long will you be staying? And so on. Although Ricardo had rarely, except when first at school, come across the peculiar English attitude towards race, he had heard sneering references to 'bloody dagoes' applied, sotto voce, to others, those who had difficulty with their sentences. With officialdom, to speak English fluently was a *laissez-passer*. It was something he would never entirely understand about the island race, their superior attitude towards foreigners, though in every other respect he liked the English—the British, for that matter—enormously.

In the Hertz compound, Ricardo familiarized himself with the gearshift on the Ford, studied the maps in the glove compartment, and made a mental note to remember that he would be driving on the left. After two false starts trying to escape the tangled-wool maze that was Heathrow, he found the right road. Three hours later, with only a single wrong turn, Beto hopped from the passenger seat and opened the gate at the foot of the Ballantines' drive.

Sara's fears proved to be unfounded, and, although she had no way of knowing that he had experienced any, so too did Ricardo's. The warmth of the embrace they gave each other said it all; nothing had changed since Mar del Plata.

By eight p.m. it was as if the Ballantines and the Jordan-Ardittis had seen each other only the previous week and not, as with most of them, for upwards of two years. Had a stranger chosen that evening to pay a call, he would have assumed he had gate-crashed a gathering of blood kin who delighted in being related.

Dinner was an informal affair taken round the large table in the kitchen, and Peter could not help noticing that Sara had eyes only for Ricardo. In the manner of the proud and (to those who did not know him well) seemingly aloof Argentine, Ricardo was doing his best to include everyone in the conversation, though it was plain that Sara's feelings for him were reciprocated. Which was going to make it awkward, perhaps, when deciding how to entertain the Jordan-Ardittis for the three days they were to be in England. Peter had arranged seventy-two hours' leave, and naturally enough he wanted to spend as much as possible of it with his old school friend, including a lunch in the battalion mess—and taking Edward, as he had promised—where he was sure Ricardo would enjoy the company of fellow professionals. Equally naturally, it was apparent that Ricardo and Sara wished to spend some time together, and alone. Beto and Lucita were no problem; both wanted to take a train to London, see the sights, and buy some gifts to take home.

Eventually—and with a tact that marked Peter as an excellent future staff officer—it was decided that Sara, who had also arranged a few days' leave from the Foreign Office, Ricardo, Beto and Lucita would go to London the following day, Tuesday. Once there they were on their own. On Wednesday, lunch at battalion, and on Thursday evening a formal dinner at home, with perhaps some entertainment from Lucita if she could be persuaded to sing, and if the Ballantines' piano was not totally out of tune.

'Persuaded!' scoffed Ricardo. 'I'd like to see you try and stop her.'

Towards midnight, smoking two of the excellent Havanas bought at Charles de Gaulle, Peter and Ricardo took Barney for his final run in the garden. Although bitterly cold with the prospects of more snow forecast, the night was crystal clear.

'Barney remembered you,' said Peter, knowing that it was an idiotic comment but feeling pleasantly full and mellow on the after-dinner Hennessy XO that Lucita had spirited up from somewhere.

'So he should,' said Ricardo, feigning indignation. 'I've known him as long as you have.'

'So you have, so you have. When was he born? I was trying to figure it out yesterday. The summer of 1970?'

'Easter. He was waiting for you when we got here at the end of term. It was later that year I had to leave England.'

'Ah yes. But everything's all right now, I understand.'

'If you mean what I take you to mean, yes. It comes and goes, you know, wealth, in Argentina.'

'Let's hope it stays this time.' Peter chuckled. 'You may be able to buy yourself a majority. That's the only way you'll beat me to that rank. You'll be calling me sir when we next meet.'

'A wager?'

'A fiver.'

'Done.'

Peter whistled his dog, noticing that Ricardo was shivering. He'd left a temperature in the mid-eighties just a week earlier, of course.

'It's good to see you again,' he said.

'And it's good to see you, Peter. It seems wrong, somehow, that old friends should be separated by hemispheres.'

SEVEN

3 Platoon

WHILE SARA BALLANTINE and the Jordan-Ardittis waited for the 7.50 a.m. train to London, the members of 3 Platoon, D Company, in the freezing cold and under the eagle eyes of Scarlett O'Hara, formed up in three ranks in front of the company office. Due to ground and visibility conditions, the previous day's field and firing exercise had been postponed, to the delight of the company, who could take a dozen lectures from Captain Ballantine if it meant keeping warm. Monday's weather had been strictly for polar bears. With any luck, Sammy had confided to Twiggy, the exercise would not only be postponed but abandoned completely, at least until after Christmas leave, which the whole of D Company, having drawn the long straw for once, was to begin in a week's time. And with Captain Ballantine on a seventy-two-hour pass, not due back until Friday morning, the chances were the company would have a cushy three days, because it was a five-pound note to a spent cartridge that Winter's Day wouldn't want to do anything energetic with his 2 i/c away.

Unfortunately for Sammy's hypothesis, Peter Ballantine was not the kind of officer to take three days' leave without ensuring that the company carried out at least part of its training programme in his absence. After receiving Sara's telephone call on Monday and confirming with Winter's Day that he could take his seventy-two-hours as arranged, he summoned each of D Company's platoon commanders and told them what they would be doing from Tuesday to Thursday. For 3 Platoon, Rupert Parker-Smith's platoon, Tuesday would be occupied, providing the snow held off, with a sixteen-mile route march in full battle order, ending with live firing at fixed targets.

'Does that include me and Double-Eff, or do I leave them to the tender mercies of Sergeant O'Hara?' Rupert had wanted to know.

Double-Eff was 2nd Lieutenant James ffolliott, twenty, just commissioned and still wet behind the ears. Daddy Rankin had given him to D Company to gain experience, and Winter's Day had seconded him to 3 Platoon.

'That most certainly does include you and Double-Eff,' said Peter, 'full battle order and all for both of you. Why, don't you feel up to it?'

'Had a bit of a rough Saturday night after you left, and spent most of Sunday getting over it.'

'Just what you need, then, a good sharp walk to clear the cobwebs. Take them up to the old Marston range. That's sixteen miles as near as I can tell, damn it, and I've checked that it's not being used by anyone else tomorrow.'

'And we truck back, presumably.'

'You do. You can arrange that yourself with MT, who'll also provide the butts party if you twist their arm—unless you've got anyone on light duties you think might be swinging the lead. Clear any would-be malingerers with the MO first, though, or he'll chuck Hippocrates at you.'

'Roger,' said Rupert.

'If you make your e.t.d. 0800, you'll be at Marston before midday. Get the truck to take the long way round so that it doesn't pass the platoon on the way, and don't tell them they'll have transport back. That'll make 'em sweat a bit.'

At 0755 Rupert and Double-Eff appeared from behind the company office. Scarlett called the platoon to attention. In the middle of the rear rank Legless Jones—a heavy, bleary-eyed drinker and so nicknamed to distinguish him from Non-Legless Jones, a teetotal bible-puncher from the Welsh valleys— muttered to his friend and boozing companion, Groggy Butler: 'That bastard Zebedee. I'll bet this was his idea.'

'No chance, man. He wouldn't be so daft.'

'Quiet in the ranks!' bawled Scarlett before marching smartly over to Rupert and Double-Eff. Since the entire platoon was hatless, no salutes were exchanged.

'3 Platoon all present and correct and ready for inspection, sir,' said Scarlett.

'Very good, Sergeant. Mr ffolliott will inspect the third rank, I'll take the first two.'

Which was all going to be a waste of time anyway, Rupert knew. Sergeant O'Hara would have made sure that none of the platoon had tried to lighten his burden, or woe betide him, by filling his small pack with empty boxes or a dozen pairs of socks. But, like much else in the army, certain procedures had to be gone through for the sake of form, and discipline. Without the Damocles sword of inspection hanging over their heads, few of the idle buggers would bother to stick to the rules.

Scarlett ordered the first and third ranks to stand fast, and stood the middle rank at ease. After a moment's hesitation because there were two officers on parade, he elected to accompany Double-Eff. Zebedee would soon shout for him if he was needed, though God help anyone who had cobwebs in his SLR.

Rupert began his inspection with the first man on the right in the front rank, Corporal Mike Tyler, who, though half an inch shorter than Twiggy, next to him, occupied the right marker position through virtue of being 3 Platoon's junior NCO. Rupert gave him a perfunctory once-over. It wasn't done to mistrust corporals.

Behind his back, Tyler was called Two-Shit Tyler, from his habit of trying to top any tall story with a taller one of his own. If someone bragged of having polished off two bottles of whisky at a sitting or having had two girls at the same time, Tyler would invariably claim three bottles or three girls. Thus (the story went), if someone had had one shit, Tyler would have had two.

Twiggy was next, and more or less ignored by Rupert, who knew of Private Twigg's keenness to stay in the army and also of his five O Levels. On Twiggy's left stood the only black in the platoon, Henry Mason, son of an English father and a Kenyan mother and known as Jomo. Jomo's webbing and rifle gleamed; he was an excellent soldier, ramrod-straight and unashamedly proud of his uniform, no matter what his mates at home said about him being an Uncle Tom. Although he had no academic qualifications and had been somewhat of a rootless drifter before joining up, he would make an excellent NCO if he could be persuaded to accept responsibility.

'No cotton wool in your pack, is there, Private Mason?' asked Rupert.

'No, sir.' Jomo's accent was pure Birmingham.

'And if I asked you to open up and let me see your mess tins, what would your reaction be?'

'That you could see them, sir.'

Two down from Jomo was Jim 'Branston' Pickles, a shifty-eyed Glaswegian who considered himself to be, rightly as it happened, a hard man. He was older than many of the others in the platoon, twenty-eight, and had a wife and a couple of children somewhere in Scotland. By nature Rupert was a fair-minded individual who tried to find some good in every-one; he found it hard, however, to like Pickles whom he considered, accurately, to be something of an 'old soldier'. He did as little as he could get away with to justify his pay, though that little was generally enough to keep him out of serious trouble.

Reaching the middle of the rear rank and nervously glanc-ing over his shoulder to see how far Rupert had got since he did not want to finish his inspection first, Double-Eff asked his first question of the morning, addressing himself to Leg-less Jones.

'What's the muzzle velocity of the SLR, Private Jones?'

When edgy, as he was now, Double-Eff's voice became slightly high-pitched, not at all the deep baritone of com-mand he attempted to cultivate when in private. His com-plexion too betrayed his youth. He looked scarcely old enough to shave.

Legless stared at the young officer as though he'd grown two heads. What the hell was the silly sod talking about? That sort of question went out with recruit training. Still, he re-membered the answer.

'Two thousand seven hundred and fifty feet per second, sir,' said Legless, his own voice thick with last night's beer.

'And what's that in metres?'

'Metres, sir?'

'Metres.'

That was too much of an effort for Legless. A metre was about three feet, wasn't it? And three feet into two thousand seven hundred and fifty was . . . No, his brain was jelly.

'Don't know, sir.'

'Well, find out. I'll be asking you again.'

Double-Eff moved slowly up the rear rank. When Legless thought he was safely out of earshot, he grunted to Groggy: 'Where the hell does he think *he* is?'

Double-Eff just about caught the remark but, seeing that Scarlett was pretending not to, elected to ignore it also, aware that he could make a fool of himself by treating it as insubordination. Really, it was very difficult, trying to be a good officer. Pulling rank wouldn't earn respect, but when did one jump on a man and when did one leave him alone? All of these people had vastly more experience than he, and the majority of them were older. Sandhurst, in his opinion, didn't cover man managment in sufficient depth. Oh, there were dozens of lectures, but it seemed to be taken for granted, under the all-embracing heading 'leadership', that anyone who had been to public school and played in the first fifteen would automatically be held in awe by chaps who had been largely to comprehensives and whose first interest, as a game, was soccer. Which wasn't true at all, not these days. It was all very well for someone like Rupert, who had been born issuing orders to gamekeepers and foresters, but it was a different matter for someone like himself, whose father, the poor relation of the ffolliott clan, owned a small village grocer's and who had sweated blood to raise the school fees and give to his son the privileges taken for granted by the richer ffolliott cousins; who had even, for that matter, for trade purposes, dropped the first 'f' from the family surname and capitalized the second, making the name on the shop Folliott, seemingly ashamed that such an ancient cognomen should be seen in its correct form above a window full of tins and bottles of squash.

Notwithstanding having one uncle who had served meritoriously in the army and another who had achieved flag rank in the navy, Double-Eff frequently wondered why his selection board had judged him fit to become an officer, not realizing that most of them, in their time, had been plagued with self-doubt similar to his, nor understanding that his superiors on the board did not expect every candidate to be general staff material.

Conscious that Double-Eff was dawdling and guessing the reason, Rupert quickened his pace, barely glancing at Sammy Finch or, next to him, the religious abstainer Non-Legless Jones, who Sammy felt sure he'd heard muttering some kind of prayer a moment or two earlier. Which was rather unfair, in Sammy's opinion, asking God to intervene on an inspection. Still, Non-Legless was a bit like that, always praying to Jesus in that lilting singsong voice of his about something or other, carrying his bible everywhere. Of course the Welsh were bloody peculiar anyway, crackers, religious or not; had something to do with all those bloody leeks they ate. Although Non-Legless couldn't be that much of a Christian, could he, or he wouldn't be in the army, whose function, when you came right down to it, was to go out and kill people.

On the extreme left of the front rank, and the smallest platoon member, stood Yank Hobart, who reckoned he looked like Steve McQueen, the resemblance beginning and ending with the fact that both the late actor and Hobart were barely five feet seven inches tall in their socks. Nevertheless, Yank combed his fair hair in the manner of McQueen and, whenever possible, sprinkled his conversation with Americanisms picked up from imported TV programmes, to which he was addicted. He never went on parade; he 'hit the bricks'. During the previous year's Ulster posting for the battalion, he considered he'd 'burnt' at least two Micks, though battalion records did not bear out the boast; and an A Company corporal who'd been killed by the IRA on the same tour had 'bought the farm and was out of the ball game'. If the battalion were ever posted back to Northern Ireland or any other trouble spot, Yank was going 'loaded for bear'.

Rupert skipped up the back of the front rank, prodding a pack here, tugging a piece of webbing there. Leaving Double-Eff's side briefly, Scarlett brought the middle rank to attention and stood the front rank at ease. He then rejoined Double-Eff, who had reached the penultimate man in the rear rank, Private Cyril Ball, variously known as Prawn Balls, Fish Balls and No Balls and not objecting in the least because anything was better than being called Cyril. Scarlett saw the subaltern hesitate without, at first, understanding why. Then it hit him. Private Ball had only just, that morning, rejoined the platoon after a fortnight's compassionate leave to take care of, as an only child, his dying mother, a widow. She had finally expired the previous Thursday, being buried on Saturday. Double-Eff hadn't seen him before, did not recognize his face. Oh Christ, thought Scarlett, too late to intervene but correctly anticipating the next question and the response.

'I don't seem to know you,' said Double-Eff innocently.

'Ball, sir,' Cyril Ball had played this game before. He could just as easily have said Private Ball or 4278 Ball, but the alternative was always good for a laugh and after the grim events of the previous week he felt he could use one.

There were the customary muffled guffaws within the ranks, particularly from the man on Ball's left, Private Brian Sweet, whose sobriquet was Three-piece. A twenty-two-year-old from Somerset who was only a fraction of an inch taller than Yank Hobart, Sweet nevertheless had a remarkable and well deserved reputation for pulling women, many of whom towered above him. He was by no means handsome. The rest of the platoon had seen him in the showers and he was no better endowed than average, so it couldn't be that. Nor did he spend a lot of money on his girl friends. However, they laughed a lot in his company; he was a born comedian. Maybe that was his secret.

Scarlett bellowed for silence. Double-Eff went red.

'I beg your pardon?' he spluttered, horrified that his voice had risen several octaves.

Scarlett hastened to the rescue. 'Private Ball, sir. Just back from fourteen days' compassionate. Private Ball lost his mother, sir, last week.'

'I see.' Double-Eff took several deep breaths in an attempt to recover his composure. 'While I naturally regret his bereavement,' he went on, 'perhaps you'd advise Private Ball, Sergeant, that to avoid any further misunderstanding it would be expedient to give his rank before giving his name.'

'Very good, sir.' Scarlett's expression told Cyril Ball that there would be an afternoon of reckoning once the route march was over. Cyril didn't care.

Rupert had occasion to reprimand only one man, Private Binns, Acne Hackney, Davey Binns from Hackney, London. Although the unfortunate skin eruption that had first appeared during his recruit training to disfigure, in part, Davey Binns' face, was now largely a thing of the past, blemishes occasionally reappeared for some reason the MO couldn't fathom—without putting it down to worry or stress, which were diagnoses not easily accepted in Her Majesty's armed forces, the more so since Binns professed not to be worried about anything.

However, from time to time his chin would break out in spots. When that happened he was unable to shave adequately, which was why Rupert had a few words with him.

It was only a reprimand, though, not a formal charge. When questioned, Davey explained that he had not felt the condition serious enough to report sick, and Rupert silently sympathized. A soldier who was unable to shave and was therefore unsightly could not remain in the army. Once or twice, okay; a regular recurrence would mean the man being given his ticket. To Rupert's certain knowledge Private Binns had few friends if any, was something of a lonely, doe-eyed individual with whom no one wanted to pair on two-man assault course exercises. However, he wanted to remain a soldier; to achieve that he had to keep as far away as possible from the MO. Rupert made a mental note to have a quiet word with the medical officer. Perhaps something could be done that had not yet been tried; if not, well, Private Binns would have to become Mr Binns.

The inspection at an end, after conferring with Double-Eff Rupert said to Scarlett: 'Fine, Sergeant. A good turn-out. Let's get going. The sooner we're there, the sooner we'll be back. Mr ffolliott and I will lead. I suggest you bring up the rear to encourage the stragglers.'

'There won't be any of those, sir.'

Although apart from the occasional flurry the snow had held off, the air temperature was zero and the platoon, after standing still for so long, were anxious to get moving, get the circulation flowing. They had done this march before and knew that the first three or four miles were easy, a doddle, virtually flat roads with few undulations. You could crack on the pace there. The next six miles were tougher, downhill for half a mile, uphill for the next half-mile. That was more or less the pattern until mile ten was reached, after which there were three more miles without much climbing or descending, until a one-in-three drop for a mile and a half, with the Marston range visible in the distance, under a thousand yards as the crow flies. Then came the killer, the final mile and a half, which was a brutal uphill slog. Heartbreak Hill it was known as and something like it was familiar to every infantry battalion in the British army.

Miles three to five took them through the outskirts of town, where they were jeered at on occasion by groups of youths.

Okay, let 'em grin, let 'em sneer. Who the hell cared? What the hell did they know about Northern Ireland and ducking and diving into doorways when the bullets started flying and the Mick kids let loose with rocks and petrol bombs? Nothing. One day, maybe, on an exercise such as this, Zebedee or Scarlett or Double-Eff would say, Right, lads, sort the bastards out. Christ, wouldn't they run then. *We didn't mean it, mates. It was just our bit of fun.* Whack! *Honest, we didn't mean any harm.* Whack! And that one with the orange barnet who looked like some crazy kind of Christmas fucking decoration; they'd remember him, shouting 'nigger' at Jomo. By Christ they would. There'd come a time in a disco or in one of the pubs when that jerk would walk in, and that would be it. Goodbye, orange head. Hospital time. They, the platoon, could shout 'nigger' at Jomo, call him Cherry Blossom or Black Ass because he was one of them, part of the team. Anyone else did so, the boot.

Miles six and seven came and went. So did eight. Starting to feel it now. Yessir. Starting to feel it in the thighs and the calves and the fucking lungs. Right, cigarettes definitely to be cut down. Fifteen a day from now on. No, ten a day. Christ, try a bit harder and they could be cut out entirely. Not difficult. Shit, what the hell was so difficult about giving up smoking? Nothing. Piece of piss. Beer too. Three pints a day maximum. Better still, screw beer completely during the week. Yeah, that was the ticket.

Miles nine and ten. Okay, not so friggin' bad, is it? That's way over half and there's an easy chunk coming. Three miles like glass. At the end of that a beautiful big drop. To hell with Heartbreak Hill; that's no problem. One step at a time. That's all there was to it. One step, two step. Some stupid kid's nursery rhyme about that, isn't there? Round and round the garden like a teddy bear, one step, two step . . . And then twenty. After twenty, another twenty. Jesus, a few hundred more and that was halfway. Easy. No sweat.

Come on, Legless, pick your bloody feet up. Where d'you think you are, Yank, in *The Great Escape*? Could use ol' McQueen's motorbike now. Come on, Jomo, you get a free lion skin, a silver spear and eighteen fuckin' goats if you make it. Watch it, Jonesey—friggin' bible's not going to help you now. What's the matter with you, Prawn Balls? Too much pulling your bloody duff on that compassionate?

Okay, here she comes, the big drop to the bottom of

Heartbreak Hill. Fuck it. Forget it. It's only another hill. Look down. Follow the feet of the guy in front. Left right left right. Simple. Think of something else. Those two bits of muff on summer leave. What were they called? No, not those two, they were Gog and fuckin' Magog. The other two. Iris and Pat. Christ, they were something else. I mean, something *else*. In and out like a fiddler's elbow. Wham, bam, thank you, ma'am. Do you love me? Of course I love you. Now shut up. Terrific stuff.

And then there were the pints. Can't get beer like that down here, not down south. Rubbish stuff. Haven't got a friggin' clue south of Watford. A couple of pints later on tonight. No, make that three or four. Give up week-day drinking next week. Shit, next week's Christmas. Can't give up bloody booze at Christmas. Sacrilege. Nor before the New Year. Right after, though. Directly after. Gotta get fit. Gotta keep fit, too, during leave. A little jogging, maybe a game of soccer. Remember what it was like coming back after summer leave? Murder. Put on eight pounds. All beer, all flab, all round the gut. Gotta do some running or something. Just to keep the edge on.

Right, here's the big bastard. Shorten stride. Jesus, what the hell's Double-Eff doing, running up and down the ranks? Encouragement? *Keep going.* I'll give the silly bugger keep going. He's fit, though, the bastard. Gotta give him that. He might be a prize prick but he's fit. Zebedee too. Springing along on the other side. Boing, boing. A few hundred yards now. Can only be a few hundred more yards. Yeah, there's that white friggin' post that leads up to the gates of the range. Piece o' cake. Didn't think we'd do it there a while back. Thought Groggy was going to pass straight fuckin' out and we'd have to send for the meat wagon.

Okay, through the gates, along the path, up to the firing point. Truck's here. Where the hell did the truck come from? Didn't see it pass.

Front rank—ten rounds rapid.

Easy, easy.

Second rank—ten rounds rapid.

No sweat. No problem. See that, Jomo? See that, Yank? Right down the throat. Pity the poor bloody Micks on our next tour.

Third rank—ten rounds rapid.

Good shooting. No, more than good after sixteen lousy miles.

Easy, easy. They don't call 3 Platoon the best goddam platoon in the company for nothing. No, sir.

Okay. Line up. Three ranks. Attention. March to the truck. Heads up. We're soldiers, not a bloody rabble like those snot-nosed punks.

Damned right, Scarlett. Damned right, Double-Eff.

He's a bloody good platoon commander, Zebedee. They don't come any better.

EIGHT

Sara Ballantine

THE TRAIN WAS FORTY MINUTES LATE due to frozen points in several places on the line, and did not arrive at Paddington until 11.30. Sara took the Jordan-Ardittis into the Great Western Hotel and sat them in the bar while she called some restaurants. The nearer it got to Christmas, without a reservation the more impossible it became to get a table. She struck lucky with Au Jardin des Gourmets in Greek Street, where she was known. They reached there at 12.30 and lunched until two. After coffee and brandy—and with what appeared at the time to be consummate skill but which had actually been agreed with Beto the previous evening—Lucita pleaded that she and Beto had a great deal to do and see, and that the pair of them had better get on with it. The 'older folk' could linger over their drinks.

'Here, less of the ''older folk'', if you don't mind,' protested Sara, secretly delighted that Lucita had, without prompting, taken the unspoken hint.

'Will we see you at the station?' asked Beto.

'Yes.' Sara nodded. 'And please be there by 6.15 or we won't get home tonight.'

Lucito smiled wickedly. 'Wouldn't that be awful!'

Ricardo signalled for two more brandies.

'I don't suppose it's too apparent to you,' he said to Sara—somewhat nervously, she thought, now that they were alone—'but those two always manage to make an exit before the bill arrives. It was the same in Paris. Beto looked after the luggage, Lucita ordered the taxi. I was left at the desk.'

'I can call them back if you like.'

'No, don't do that.'

Ricardo stretched across the table for Sara's hand just as the brandy arrived. Damn, she thought.

'Anyway,' she said, 'footing the bill is part of the penalty for being big brother. It's the same when Peter and Edward and I go out. Mind you, Peter generally objects a lot more vocally than you've just done, and twists my arm until I agree to pay my share.'

'Perhaps I should do the same.'

'Mmmm.'

A gale of laughter reached them from the trio at the adjacent table. Sara had overheard some of their conversation during lunch. The tall, bespectacled man in the natty pinstripe was apparently a publisher, the other man nursing a gigantic drink a writer, and the woman the writer's wife. They were evidently celebrating something, and making a fair bit of noise about it. Sara would willingly have consigned them to hell, or at least to another table. How could one have an intimate conversation with that racket going on? One couldn't, that was the answer. Nor had they managed to talk privately for more than a few seconds the previous evening. She felt exactly as she had done after Mar del Plata; she was fairly certain he did too. But she needed the words.

She sipped her brandy. Well, now or never, girl. We can't sit here all afternoon, and on Friday he'll be gone again.

'Have you got any special shopping you want to do?' she asked.

'Not really. We sent home quite a few things from Paris rather than try to bring them into England and then take them out again. Have you?'

'No. And that being the case, my flat's not a million miles from here.'

She waited anxiously for a reaction, wondering if it was Dutch courage obtained from the wine and the brandy that had emboldened her to make the suggestion; wondering if she was rushing her fences. He might have some idiotically chivalrous notion that it wasn't 'good form' to go to bed with the sister of an old and dear friend while he was staying with that friend's mother. It was one thing to sleep with a woman when she was eight thousand miles from home, after a superb day.

It was another to make love to her on her own doorstep, as it were. Yet this was the man she was determined to marry, and she wasn't going to allow him his own sweet time in which to make up his mind that he, too, wanted that.

'Oh God,' she said, 'I'm being a bit obvious, aren't I?'

'Not at all.' Ricardo toyed with his brandy. Hell, maybe his brother officers were right, that Sara Ballantine had got to him in a way that no other woman ever had. There could be no other reason for his palms sweating. 'As a matter of fact, I was going to ask you if I could see the flat you told me about in Mar del Plata.'

This haste is positively indecent, decided Sara, smoothing her coat in front of the mirror by the exit while Ricardo examined his wallet for a pound note with which to tip the cloakroom girl. Considering I'm dolled up in my Sunday best, down to the silk underwear and stockings, it is indelicate, to put it at its mildest, how self-evidently anxious I am to divest myself of the whole seduction kit. It is one thing to be aggressively female or womanly aggressive, depending upon how you like your adverbs fried; it is absolutely shameless to rush your man out of the door before the ink on his credit card voucher is dry.

In the taxi, Sara snuggled close to Ricardo.

'Of course,' she said, 'when I called it a flat I perhaps overstated its proportions. It's little more than a pied-à-terre. Sitting-room-cum-bedroom, bathroom, kitchen. You've no idea how much something bigger costs in central London. I haven't seen it since Friday. I can't recall whether I made the bed or not.' She giggled self-consciously. 'You know, I'm suddenly very nervous. How absurd. Five minutes ago I was acting like Madame de Pompadour. Now I feel like a sixth-former sneaking off to see a blue movie.'

'A very beautiful sixth-former.'

'Thank you, but I'm still nervous and I don't feel much older than a sixth-former. I know I talk like one at times.'

Up a single flight of well-carpeted stairs, Sara's individual front door led immediately into the sitting-room-cum-bedroom. The bed, she was relieved to see, was made.

'See, not much, is it?'

She took Ricardo's overcoat and hung it on the rack, next to her own. Then she switched on the gas fire.

'I'm going to the loo. The drinks are over there. Help yourself. One for me too. I'd better stick to brandy.'

As she washed her hands, Sara stared at herself in the mirror. My God, the lunch-time booze was showing. On a cold day, with her colouring, one drink too many made her face shine like a stop-light. Beautiful? Someone had to be joking.

Carefully, she repaired her make-up.

What next, she asked her reflection? How could she sound so relaxed when she was going through hell inside? Mar del Plata was a different world. What if it wasn't as she remembered? What if it wasn't as *he* remembered? She had some things in the bathroom, a nightdress, a negligee, though most of her good stuff—so much for the forward planning, my girl—was on her bed. Did she undress here, now? Put on anything that was available? Did she take everything off or leave on her bra, pants and stockings? Was that too whorish? She would sink into the ground if, having undressed more or less, she found Ricardo sitting quietly on the sofa reading *Country Life*. Christ, why did she feel so gauche?

Suddenly she saw the funny side of it; or rather, the realistic side. She was just tense, no more. So she wouldn't take any risks and be forward. She would return to the sitting-room, face renovated, precisely as she had left it.

The drinks were on the table next to the sofa. Ricardo had mastered the intricacies of her tape-deck and was now hunting through her cassettes.

'Mozart, I think,' he said over his shoulder. 'It's a Mozart day.'

He pointed to the window. Outside, blobs of new snow were falling.

'Why Mozart and snow?' she asked, sitting on the sofa, crossing her legs and casually sweeping up her brandy glass. 'I'm not an expert, but Mozart isn't cold.'

'Not cold.' Ricardo adjusted the volume. Strains of the Adagio from the A Major Piano Concerto filled the room. 'Pure, untouched. Nonexistent until it's felt.'

'Good grief,' smiled Sara, 'that's a very erudite statement from a military man. I didn't know you were a music *aficionado*.'

'We're not all untutored savages, you know.' He sat beside her. 'But you're right, I'm not. I stole that comment from Lucita.'

Sara swallowed heavily before placing her glass on the table.

'For God's sake kiss me before I go mad.'

Later, she was to reflect that every daydream she had had since March had been fulfilled with a wondrous gentle violence. The waiting and worrying hadn't been in vain and it was true that a woman's most erogenous zone was her mind, for she had played and replayed this scene a hundred times during the past nine months. Where she thought she had been in love before Ricardo, she now knew she'd been fooling herself; where she thought she'd been erotic before, whether because of a man or self-induced, she hadn't. When she'd toyed with her fantasies and cursed them for being inadequate, she now knew why; when she'd wondered whether all the golden times that happened to women in fiction were subconscious *cris de coeur* of male/female longing for the unobtainable, she now knew they were not. This wasn't just a repetition of what had happened in Mar del Plata; this was brand-new, and better.

When they made love a second time, they did so on the rug in front of the fire. It was different now, more tantalizing, slowly rediscovering each other's bodies with unembarrassed pleasure, but equally joyous. Sara could never remember being happier, more alive, more aware. She'd said somewhere in the middle of it all that she loved him, and he had responded that he loved her too. There were no doubts. She knew they both meant it.

It was dark when they finally unwound, colder also, though the temperature, she thought, could have as much to do with what she was feeling inside as the weather outside. She was reluctant to get up, get dressed, leave him, leave the flat, go out into the world again as if nothing had happened to her. But that was being childish. There would be many other days like today, dozens, hundreds.

'I'll run us a bath,' she said.

When she returned, she was wearing her negligee and carrying a robe for Ricardo, a man's robe.

'Peter's,' she said, handing it to him, 'before you jump to sinister conclusions. He keeps a lot of spare stuff here in case he's ever stuck in town overnight.'

While he put on the robe she poured them each another brandy; or, rather, she topped up their earlier drinks, which had hardly been touched.

'Thank you,' he said, accepting the glass. He took a sip

and grimaced. 'You know, I really will have to cut down my alcohol consumption when I get home.'

'Don't talk about that.'

'About cutting down my drinking?'

'About going home. Talk about nice things. Tell me that I'm beautiful again and that you love me.'

He did so, but with less ardour than she would have wished. No, she was being selfish. He too must be troubled to be flying out in a couple of days, as troubled as she was distressed. There was much to discuss before then, such as . . . But no, she wouldn't jump the gun. Let him say whatever he had to when the mood took him.

'How much time do we have?' he asked.

She squinted at the mantelpiece clock, just visible in the firelight.

'Not much. Taxis will be murder at this hour and in this weather. To be on the safe side, about thirty minutes if we're to be at the station by 6.15. If the worst comes to the worst and we can't get a taxi, that'll leave us plenty of time to join the huddled masses in the tube.' Sara tossed her head coquettishly. 'Why, did you have something in mind that can be accomplished in under half an hour?'

He grinned and shook his head. 'No, you've just about exhausted me.'

'Well,' grumbled Sara, feigning pique, 'there goes another illusion. So much for the legendary Latin-American charm. Under the circumstances I've heard more romantic comments.' She realized the implication of her words. 'What I mean is . . .'

'Don't tell me,' said Ricardo. 'It's not only that I don't want to know. It's just not important. Whatever happened before today doesn't matter.'

'If you're sure,' said Sara, doubtfully.

'I am.'

'But something's bothering you, isn't it, and I doubt it's exhaustion. If it is, for exhaustion we have ginseng, if I can remember where I put it. For everything else you have me.'

'In your mother's house?'

'Ah.'

Ricardo sat in front of the fire, his legs crossed under him. He patted the floor, and Sara joined him. 'I agree it's difficult,' she said.

'It's a bit more than that.'

'Is it just Mother, or is it Peter who's really bothering you?'

'I've known him a long time, longer than I've known you, for that matter. He's my friend. I have to confess I don't feel entirely comfortable sitting in his sister's flat and wearing his robe. If we weren't flying out on Friday—no, listen to me— and under different circumstances, I'd tell them all this evening that I love you and want to marry you.'

'Oh Christ,' said Sara happily.

'I've thought a lot about saying that since March. I had a few doubts after your plane took off, as I'm sure you did. Was it the casino and the beach, or was it you? I don't have those doubts any longer. But . . .'

'Does there have to be a "but"?'

'I'm afraid so, when you think about it. For one thing, I'd like to tell my parents about it privately before we make a public announcement. They'd be hurt, feel left out, otherwise, and my mother's not as well as she could be. In the second place, I'd find it hard to tell *your* mother and Peter that we're planning to get married after being away for only a few hours. I can tell you honestly that I'm going to be embarrassed when I see them again tonight.'

'Because they'll guess what we've been doing this afternoon?'

'They would if I told them I wanted to marry you. I suppose that makes me old-fashioned.'

'If it does, I love you for it. What about Beto and Lucita?'

'What about them?'

'Lucita will know where we've been since they left us.'

'How?'

'She will, that's all.'

'She's only a child.'

'She's eighteen and she's lived in New York.' Sara could follow Ricardo's reasoning and, to an extent, sympathize with him; not saying anything to her mother and Peter was as much for her sake as his. But this was the man she loved and was going to marry. She didn't want to wait to make that fact public knowledge.

The sound of overflowing water reached her ears.

'Lord, the bath!'

She raced into the bathroom just in time to prevent a major disaster. After letting some of the water out, she returned to the sitting-room.

'Nearly a ghastly accident. I don't think my downstairs neighbour would appreciate being flooded out.'

She rejoined Ricardo on the floor in front of the fire.

'You're right, of course, we can't say anything this evening. You're also right about wanting to tell your parents first. I'm sure they're fond of me . . .'

'They are.'

'. . . but I can see it might come as something of a shock to be told that their elder son wants to marry a non-Catholic. Will there be any religious objections, do you think?'

'None that can't be dealt with. It's something we can talk about, like everything else. That's soluble. What isn't, not right away, is that I'm a serving officer who's returning home on Friday and who will be more or less occupied until late March.' He took hold of her hand. 'I can think of nothing I want more than getting you out to Argentina as soon as possible, but I'm afraid that too will have to wait.'

Sara understood. Being the sister of an army officer she knew about manoeuvres and duties and how there were times she didn't see Peter for several months. She also accepted that there might be some red-tape involved in order for Ricardo to marry an alien. But March! That was an eternity off.

'It'll take a few weeks to put through the paperwork,' said Ricardo.

'You'll change your mind,' she pouted, only half-joking. 'It's a trick to put me on one side of the South Atlantic and you on the other.'

'I won't and it isn't.'

He would talk to her on the telephone as often as he could. He would tell his parents what their plans were. She would come out to see him next March as she had last March. They would be married in June, probably in Argentina if his mother was still unwell and unable to fly. *Her* mother, he knew from the way she looked, was, apart from some arthritic pain, fully fit. However, the location was something they could also discuss later. He would write a long letter to Elizabeth Ballantine and another to Peter, so that nothing would appear underhand. With the phone calls, they would probably guess anyway long before March.

Sara accepted it all. Argentina was hardly next door; she couldn't expect to pop over for weekends. The waiting she'd cope with; keeping it all to herself was going to be more difficult.

'But I'll do it,' she said. 'At least for two or three phone calls or until Peter or my mother ask me directly. The worst thing will be tonight and tomorrow night and Thursday night, knowing you're only a few doors away from my room.'

'Can you still see the clock?'

'Yes. We now have twenty minutes.'

'That's plenty of time.'

When they met up with Beto and Lucita, both carrying huge shopping-bags, at Paddington, Lucita was far too full of her afternoon to notice any change in Sara.

'We've had marvellous fun,' she bubbled. 'I can't tell you. How was your day?'

'Reasonable,' said Sara, 'reasonable.'

NINE

Edward Ballantine

ALTHOUGH STRICTLY SPEAKING it was not necessary to clear the visit of Edward and Ricardo to the battalion, as a matter of courtesy Peter had telephoned Winter's Day on Tuesday afternoon and informed him that he would be bringing two guests for lunch in the mess on Wednesday and possibly 'the full guided tour' of the establishment afterwards.

'No problem, old boy. We've nothing secret here if one discounts the manner in which the cooks can turn perfectly decent meat into something the cat dragged in. I'll let the adjutant know. I don't think I've met your younger brother, have I?'

'No. He's looking forward to it,' improvised Peter.

'Excellent. Army material, would you say?'

'He has his moments of believing so, but he's only sixteen. He'll make up his mind in the next year or two.'

'Well, use your influence. We need all the first-class blood we can transfuse from civvy street. The other chap's a dago, I think you said.'

'Actually he's a captain in the Argentine army,' replied Peter coolly.

'That's what I said, didn't I?' Winter's Day was genuinely puzzled. 'Show him around by all means. I'm sure the CO won't object. Give us a chance to demonstrate how a real fighting force works. Perhaps he'd like to display his expertise on the small-bore range or the assault course.'

On impulse, after hanging up, Peter called Rupert and explained his luncheon arrangements for the following day.

'If the company commander or Captain Lomax are around and become in any way objectionable, be a good chap and try and give me a hand to steer the conversation in another direction.'

Rupert hesitated. Peter was unaware, naturally, of his involvement with Julia Lomax, and the last thing Rupert wanted to do was to antagonize or bring himself unnecessarily to the attention of her husband, who was not only his superior officer but a thoroughly unpleasant individual to boot. Though entitled to wear one of the most exclusive old school ties, a gentleman he was not except in the narrowest interpretation of the word. If the liaison with Julia was uncovered, Rupert would not have put it past Toby Lomax to 'accidentally' shoot him. Nevertheless, he agreed to Peter's request without demur.

'Will your Argentinian chum be over here for long?' he asked. 'I mean, perhaps I could arrange for him to pepper a few pheasants next week.'

That was characteristic of Rupert thought Peter gratefully. 'No, he's leaving on Friday.'

'Ah well, just a thought.'

'And a decent one. Thank you.'

Peter recalled that 3 Platoon had been up to the old Marston range that morning. He asked Rupert how the march had gone.

'Nobody fell by the wayside if that's what you mean, but it was bloody hard work.'

'I do believe that was the intention,' Peter teased him gently.

'Oh quite, quite. Until lunch tomorrow, then.'

Though invited, Beto declined to accompany Edward and Ricardo. He would, he said mournfully, be seeing more than enough of barracks life starting in January. Sara and Lucita were not asked. Lucita would not have accepted had it been otherwise. 'Dull and boring soldier nonsense.' Peter wasn't so sure Sara would have refused. There was a wistful look about her as she waved the trio goodbye from the drawing-room window, and he'd sensed a definite change in her when she returned from London—more confident and relaxed in one way, more apprehensive in another. He didn't dwell on the reasons. She hadn't been hurt, he was sure of that, and that, for the moment, was enough.

After lunch, which confounded Winter's Day's criticisms of the cooks' culinary skills, Ricardo, Peter and Edward retired to digest their meal over, respectively, two brandies and a glass of Madeira, there being no nonsense about under-age drinking in the mess providing, in the words of Winter's Day, 'a chap proves he can hold it'.

In their tiny group before the huge log fire, as well as the company commander were Rupert and Double-Eff, the latter hovering uncertainly on the periphery. The battalion CO, Daddy Rankin, who had lunched alone in his office while attempting to reduce the mass of bumf in his in-tray prior to Christmas leave, poked his head in around 1.30 for a post-prandial port, was introduced to Peter's guests, and suc-ceeded, in six mind-boggling, polysyllabic minutes, in amazing Ricardo with his analysis of the TAM medium tank's armour, information that was purportedly classified, this particular weapon of war, developed by Thyssen Henschel, being used nowhere else in the world except Argentina. This brought the conversation around to weapons in general and, when Daddy had gone, a minor argument ensued concerning the relative merits of the Mirage III and the Harrier in ground-support roles, with Ricardo, not unnaturally as he was used to work-ing with it, favouring the French-built fighter-bomber because of its superior speed and service ceiling, while the British officers to a man praised the vertical/short take-off and land-ing capabilities of the Harrier. With the debate becoming mildly heated and with Ricardo reluctant, as a guest to prose-cute his case too fiercely, Rupert eased the tension by saying that it was all academic, really, since the damned air forces of *any* nation were never on the spot when required.

'They invest tens of millions of pounds in a single aero-plane and then, when needed most, they can't take off be-cause of the weather or because they might get their shiny new machines dirty or because the moon's in Sagittarius or some such. I do believe I remember meeting a Royal Air Force squadron leader who refused to fly one morning be-cause the laundry hadn't sent back his clean linen. How could he possibly take off in a soiled shirt? I understand flight training nowadays includes a course in manicure, although the scurrilous rumours that air force officers are also being taught how to hold a knife and fork correctly are, I believe, unfounded. Nonetheless, they consider themselves superior even to the cavalry who—if a hoary anecdote will bear repetition—when asked what possible purpose the cavalry have in modern-day battle invariably reply: ''To lend a little class to what would otherwise be a vulgar brawl.'' '

A roar of delighted laughter and a patter of applause greeted the end of Rupert's monologue. In common with all infantry regiments, the present company enjoyed nothing more than cutting the 'glamour mobs' down to size. Rupert acknowledged his audience's appreciation with a lordly bow of his head.

Edward was enraptured by it all: the technical knowledge displayed in comparing two aircraft, the elegance of Rupert's wit, the splendour of the mess with its magnificent oak panelling and full-length portraits of the battalion's past heroes. Perhaps Peter's would be among them one day.

This was a man's world occupied by men of daring and humour. Civil engineering, surely, would be dull stuff by comparison.

Peter read his thoughts.

'It's not all like this, you know, and don't you dare tell your mother that you enjoyed yourself or she'll accuse me of brain-washing and have my hide.'

'The memsahib not too keen on Ballantine Minor joining the rough soldiery?'

This from Winter's Day. Lord, thought Rupert.

'Let's say she has grave reservations,' answered Peter. 'Besides,' he added, 'Edward's very bright. That wouldn't give him much of a future in the army.'

'Oh, I say,' protested Rupert. 'The days are gone when all one needed to command a regiment was a spot of land and a few extra thousands a year. We all have our O Levels now. In fact, I hear tell,' he said pointedly to Peter, 'that there are those among us who have a degree.'

Edward blushed at the reference to his intelligence. Being bright, which he accepted he was, ran a poor last on his list of priorities, as it did for most sixteen-year-olds in English public schools. Near the top were being good at games and being popular, which fortunately applied to him also. His school life would have been hell had he been only clever.

Winter's Day was the first to spot Toby Lomax enter the mess. Unhurriedly he rose to his feet.

'Well, not all of us are on leave. If you can spare a

moment before you go home, Peter, you might have a word with me. On second thoughts, why spoil an otherwise pleasant day. It will keep.'

He shook hands with Edward and Ricardo, reflecting, in the case of the latter, that for an Argentine Captain Jordan-Arditti wasn't such a bad fellow. Double-barrelled name too. He hadn't known they had such things over there.

Toby Lomax strolled across, a glass of beer in his hand. He was known to the other ranks throughout the battalion as a tough, uncompromising officer, and was universally disliked for being so. At thirty, he was three years older than Julia, and for the life of him Rupert could not understand why she had married him. Nor would she tell him when he had asked her. 'None of your business.' They were poles apart. She was slim and bubbly, indubitably very sexy, and he was a hulking brute, built like a barn door and very dour. And hardly interested in sex at all, according to Julia, though she still slept with him, a circumstance that occasionally disturbed Rupert though he was the first to admit that he was in no position to object.

An SAS reject, Lomax stood six feet four inches in his bare feet and kept his dark hair cut somewhat shorter than regulations demanded. No one in the battalion, except possibly Daddy, knew why he had been returned to unit, though there were unconfirmed stories that even that bunch of hardened bandits in Hereford had found his psychological attitude unacceptable. Certainly he would not have been RTU'd for lack of physical fitness or mental stamina, being gifted with an abundance of both. He was a peculiar coalescence of the mystical and the brutal, and he left no one in any doubt that he considered himself wasted in what was no more than an above-average infantry battalion. If ever asked why he did not transfer out to the Parachute Regiment or the Royal Marine Commandos, outfits only slightly less awesome than the SAS, he would tap his nose in a mind-your-own-business gesture. Most of his fellow officers reckoned that he'd probably tried, in secret, and been turned down, or had been told on the grapevine that any application would not be regarded favourably. He was known to have quite a tidy sum of money of his own, and it was something of a mystery why he remained in the army because self-evidently he offended promotion boards. He would never command this regiment or any other, and would be lucky to get his own company.

Rupert had a theory, which he had never revealed to a living soul because it sounded lunatic: Rupert thought that Toby Lomax stayed in uniform because in the army he had the opportunity to kill. He had certainly displayed a taste for blood in Belfast. Provisionals meeting one of his patrols or roadblocks rarely came out of the encounter alive. Any who did were subjected to a thorough beating before being passed over for interrogation. What would have been termed psychopathological behaviour in civilian life was given unofficial sanction in Northern Ireland. The Micks were murdering bastards and deserved all they got—as long as it was kept out of the press.

'Mind if I join you?'

Lomax deposited his huge bulk in the armchair just vacated by Winter's Day before anyone could dissent—not that anyone would have done. It became apparent after a moment that he had heard from somewhere about the presence of an Argentine officer on the base, and Peter had no alternative short of downright rudeness to introducing his brother and Ricardo. Lomax nodded affably but did not offer to shake hands with either.

There then passed an uncomfortable fifteen minutes, after ten of which Rupert excused himself, much to Peter's annoyance. This was scarcely the support he had asked for.

Lomax quizzed Ricardo on the training methods and equipment of what were evidently two crack Argentine units, the *Buzo Tactico* marine commandos and the 5th Marine Battalion, which Peter had never heard of and which Lomax obviously had, probably during his short time with the SAS. His questions were both aggressive and dismissive to the point of giving offence, but Ricardo parried them with easy charm, giving such generalized answers that they could have referred to a brigade of Girl Guides.

Shortly after Rupert's return, a mess sergeant appeared at Lomax's shoulder to inform him that he was required back at B Company immediately.

'They said it was urgent, sir.'

Lomax levered himself from the armchair. 'Nice to have met you,' he said to Ricardo, meaning it had been nothing of the sort.

'I apologize for that,' Peter told his friend. 'He can be very heavy going.'

'It doesn't matter,' said Ricardo. 'We have them in our army too.'

'And you were no help,' Peter accused Rupert. 'I've a damned good mind to send you and 3 Platoon up to the old Marston range again tomorrow. And tell the men why I'm doing it.'

'Oh, I don't know about that,' said Rupert. 'Who do you think asked B Company to make the phone call? Come along, James,' he added to Double-Eff, 'you heard what the company commander said about not all of us being on leave.'

The two junior officers shook hands with Ricardo and Edward.

'Perhaps we can talk horses instead of aeroplanes next time we meet,' said Rupert. 'I'm thinking of going into breeding as a sideline one of these bright days and I'd appreciate all the expert help I can get.'

'I'll look forward to that,' said Ricardo.

'Thanks, Rupert,' Peter called after him.

'Don't mention it.'

During the afternoon Peter showed his guests over the camp. In one form or another Ricardo had seen it all before, though he was impressed by the severity of the assault course and the obvious fitness and determination of the men tackling it, as he was impressed with the general appearance of the battalion. There was a purposeful, efficient air about it. Morale, he noted idly, seemed high.

At the end of the day Peter decided he'd better see his company commander in case the silly old blighter had some problem that would give him, Peter, a headache when he returned to duty on Friday morning. It would only take a few minutes. He left Ricardo and Edward in his quarters, where the Argentine chatted enthusiastically to his young companion about his own days at school. By the time Peter returned, Edward had concluded that he liked Ricardo Jordan-Arditti very much indeed and that he would not at all mind, if that's how Sara wanted it, having him for a brother-in-law.

After dinner at home on Thursday, while Beto played the piano Lucita sang. She had a beautiful voice that even Beto's sometimes inexpert keying could in no way diminish. Later, both families stood around the piano and went through their entire repertoire of Christmas carols. Later still, wrapped gifts were exchanged; those for the Jordan-Ardittis were handed to

Lucita to pack, and those for the Ballantines placed under the big tree in the entrance hall. Under threat of eternal damnation, none was to be opened by anyone until Christmas morning.

Peter left before breakfast on Friday. He had to be back at camp by eight a.m. and he'd said his goodbyes the previous evening.

Once the car was packed, the Jordan-Ardittis drove off at 9.30. While Elizabeth Ballantine retreated into the house because of the cold, Edward and Sara walked down the drive ahead of the car to open and close the gate. It wasn't until the car was out of sight and the sound of its engine fading in the distance that Edward saw Sara was crying.

TEN

Girl friends and wives (i)

BATTALION MANOEUVRES IN SCOTLAND at the end of January were, it was generally accepted, pretty close to catastrophic. The weather was appalling, with blizzards and drifting snow making mobility largely a matter of luck. Observers from Brigade could not see a damned thing and fairly soon made it clear, during one mock battle, that they were going to 'view' the rest of it from the lounge bar of the nearest hotel. The defending company during this assault were, originally, supposed to be firing live rounds from their 'gimpies', general purpose machine guns, on a fixed trajectory, to give the attackers a taste of realism. As the defenders were 'blind', however, it was decided that blanks would be substituted. The signal conveying this change of plan got through to all defensive platoons bar one, who obeyed the earlier live-firing instruction and came close to killing a score of their comrades.

Although his critics frequently accused Daddy Rankin of having a concept of strategy that was stuck in 1945—which would have made him something of a prodigy since he was six at the time—he had never found any offensive doctrine superior to what he termed 3S/CS: surprise, speed, simplicity, and concentration of strength—none of which, he complained to the adjutant, was much bloody good when one could scarcely see a hand in front of one's face. All that would surprise him about this débâcle was finding that he hadn't lost a company or two. 'Gone with the bloody wind.'

Away from Battalion HQ, the field companies, officer and man, wondered how much longer Brigade would let this nonsense go on. They were not learning anything except that the Hexamine stoves didn't always work in a howling gale and that the price of whisky, for those who had been canny enough to fill a spare water-bottle with it, increased in a complicated mathematical equation which involved the number of men who required a tot divided by the amount of liquor available plus a profit margin gauged on the ability to pay minus a quantity left over for the sellers, which could not be bought for a king's ransom. Someone was heard to call this method of doing business The Law of Diminishing Marginal Utility, though no one quite knew what that meant, including the speaker, a second lieutenant from A Company. In D Company, Double-Eff thought it could be expressed as:

$$\frac{N}{L} \times (P\text{-}X)$$

where N equalled the buyers, L the whisky, P the profit margin, and X the unpurchasable quantity. The consensus was that Double-Eff didn't know what the hell he was talking about and that it was a damned good job he hadn't joined the Royal Artillery.

It was universally agreed that NATO exercises in West Germany, where the battalion was due at the end of April, though usually a combination of hard work and tedium in equal measures, would be a picnic compared to this. One or two members of 3 Platoon muttered surreptitiously about mutiny, and Branston Pickles, who had a wife and bairns in Scotland, decided on the third day of manoeuvres that he'd had more than enough and went AWOL. The MPs picked him up next day at home, drunk as a skunk and in the process of setting about his unfortunate wife with an empty bottle. Subsequently he was sentenced to twenty-eight days and reckoned he'd got the best of the bargain.

Day Four of manoeuvres was scheduled to end with a night attack against a hill defended by HQ Company. In the opinion of Sammy Finch, 3 Platoon would do well to leave Jomo behind. What the hell was the point, he argued, of dressing up someone of Jomo's colour in winter gear when the minute he raised his head and flashed his teeth the entire assault was stuffed? He looked like a hundredweight of coal in a flour bag. Scarlett told Sammy to shut up and stop moaning. And any more cracks about Jomo's colour and he'd be on a charge. Jomo didn't mind the cracks. He liked Sammy and he knew Sammy liked him.

In any event, the attack was called off because of the worst storms, according to the radio, Scotland had seen for a couple of decades.

'You should see it in Montana and North Dakota at this time of year,' drawled Yank Hobart, but nobody paid him any attention. They all knew that the furthest west Yank had ever been was Ireland.

On Day Seven Three-piece Sweet made a minor name for himself in battalion history by smuggling two women into D Company's lines. They were Austrian au pairs from Edinburgh, spoke little English, and had planned some skiing in the Highlands before the weather had closed in and trapped them in the tiny village four miles away. Three-piece had spotted the village in the distance during exercises and, with his uncanny instinct as far as the opposite sex was concerned, had taken it upon himself to explore further, especially as the road between the village and D Company had been cleared by snow-ploughs. In the other direction, the way the girls wanted to go, it was still impassable to public transport. He had found them in the village's solitary café looking glum.

However, any ideas that D Company—or at least 3 Platoon—had that they were in for a wild if frozen orgy were swiftly knocked on the head. The girls, while more than willing to alleviate their boredom temporarily in male company, were not prepared to act as groundsheets for the whole platoon. Three-piece reckoned later that it would only have been a matter of time—and a little of the precious whisky that Groggy Butler and Legless Jones had a corner on—but the presence of women in the lines spread like wildfire, and soon there were more bodies than was normal in the vicinity of 3 Platoon's bivouac area, which very quickly attracted the attention of Rupert and Double-Eff. Three-piece suspected that Non-Legless Jones, affronted by the idea of sub-zero sex, had ratted to the platoon commander, but this was never proved and Non-Legless firmly denied it.

The problem of what to do with the girls when Rupert and Double-Eff were reported looming up was solved by putting them in sleeping-bags and placing the platoon's bergen rucksacks around them. Using a combination of pidgin English and sign language ('They findee, they shootee, bang-bang-zip' —which had the rest of the platoon in hysterics), Three-piece conveyed to the Austrians that they would be given a blind-fold and a last cigarette if discovered. Even so, their muffled giggling was only drowned by a hearty singsong, fortissimo, until Rupert and Double-Eff retreated. The girls were then escorted to the road and sent on their way. Three-piece's attitude towards women did not include chivalry when his neck was at stake.

But all bad things had to come to an end though, when manoeuvres were over and the battalion about to return south, the adjutant was overheard to say to the CO: 'I just hope to God these chaps don't have to fight anyone in the near future.' To which Daddy was heard to reply, in a rare departure from eloquence: 'I quite agree. This has to be the biggest fuck-up since the Flood.'

Among the keenest to leave the barracks early their first night back down south was Twiggy, whose relationship with Carol Bannister was coming along nicely. They had been out together half a dozen times since Christmas leave, mid-week as well as weekends, though their physical relationship had progressed no further than some mild petting in the back row of a cinema. If he were honest with himself, Twiggy would admit that he was nervous about pushing her too hard too soon in case she took offence and gave him the brush off. She clearly—if, to Twiggy, incomprehensibly—enjoyed his com-pany, and she had never again mentioned Roy, the bloke whose chin he had punched in the pub, except to say that she wasn't seeing him any longer. Nor was she seeing anyone other than Twiggy. He didn't want to lose her by making excessive demands, certainly not since, miraculously, she had actually written him a letter following their first evening out alone. It was only a few lines—'Dear Chris, Thank you so much for a lovely evening. I really did enjoy myself and I hope you'll call me again. Yours sincerely, Carol'—but to Twiggy it was Holy Writ, the first letter he had ever received in the army. The envelope had been lying on his bunk one afternoon and he had approached it suspiciously, thinking it was a joke or a mistake. But no, it was addressed to him, everything apart from his service number, which she could not be expected to know then. He'd read the lines a hundred times and carried the envelope everywhere he went, transferring it from pocket to pocket. He'd hoped she'd write to him again, with perhaps a little more affection in the closing sentiments than 'yours sincerely', but so far she hadn't and he didn't like to ask. That might have involved confessing that he never received letters otherwise, of which he was somewhat ashamed.

He had yet to meet her parents or any of her friends apart from Libby Rees, which didn't bother him. On the contrary, he was grateful. He knew he would become tongue-tied and embarrassed if he was compelled to pass even a couple of hours with Mr and Mrs Bannister, who doubtless subscribed to the average civilian's opinion of soldiers, especially where their only child was concerned. Anyway, all that could wait. If they continued going out together for any length of time, he was bound to meet the people closest to her sooner or later. Further ahead than that he did not want to think.

He experienced a surge of unfamiliar anxiety when, not seeing her, he alighted from the bus at the town terminus. He had written to her from Scotland telling her when he expected to be back—adding a couple of days for good measure—but he had no idea whether she'd received his letter or if anything had happened to change her mind about their continuing relationship while he was away. Two weeks was a long time. That was the trouble—perhaps the only drawback—with the army; you weren't your own master.

She wasn't there. It didn't take more than a few seconds to establish that. There were the usual crowds at the terminus but no Carol. Had it not been Friday evening he would have called her at the office—which, bloody fool, he should have done earlier in any case, to confirm the arrangement. She wouldn't have been able to hide from him at the bank, pretend she wasn't there, as she could easily do at home. He could hear her talking now, to her mother or father. 'Look, there'll be someone calling me on Friday. He's got a northern accent. Tell him I've gone away for the weekend, please.'

Of course if he had any balls he'd ring her at home anyway, put on one of those plummy voices that Roy had. 'This is Mr Jones from the bank. May I talk to Miss Bannister please. It's rather important.' Then she would come to the telephone and he could ask her straight out why she'd stood him up.

But he wouldn't do it. He couldn't carry it off. Besides, if she didn't want to see him again, she had the right. To her, it had all just been a bit of fun, something to occupy her between Roy and whoever came next.

Feeling thoroughly depressed Twiggy went into The Ragged Staff, the pub next door to the terminus, clinging to a vestige of hope that she would be sitting there. That had happened once before, one night in mid-January when it was snowing heavily and the bus was late and she had grown cold standing outside. She wasn't there, of course, as he'd known she wouldn't be. He bought himself a pint and sat at one of the tables. There were steaming pies in the hot food section, but he didn't feel hungry.

To hell with it. He'd get good and drunk and take a taxi back to camp. He had plenty of money; there'd been nothing to spend it on during manoeuvres.

He wasn't the only Friday-night loser, he concluded midway through the pint; there were eight, ten other guys from the battalion in the pub. Most of them were obviously out to get pissed after Scotland, but a couple looked as if they'd suffered the same disappointment he had.

Bloody little bitch, he thought suddenly. Stringing him along like that until something better turned up. Oh yeah, he could see it all now. She'd had enough of Roy but there was no one else on tap right away to take her to the cinema and buy her drinks. No one except good old bloody Twiggy, of course. Idiot of the year with no danger of competition. Two weeks away—two lousy weeks—and she'd found someone else. Someone from the bank or someone from her friggin' badminton club. Badminton! Jesus Christ on a scooter! He should have known the minute she mentioned she played badminton that he was going to be given the big heave-ho before long. 'Oh, don't you play, Chris? You should. It's invigorating.' Invigorating! Which a sixteen-mile route march up to Marston wasn't, naturally. Or round the assault course in full battle order. And the superior way she'd said it; he remembered that too now. You mean you don't play badminton? No, he didn't damned well play badminton. He wouldn't know a shuttlecock from a ballcock. They were all the same, these middle-class bints. Okay, he was better off without her. Screw her, which is what he should have done instead of pussy-footing around—*respecting* her, for Christ's sake. That's where he'd gone wrong, not trying to get into her knickers. They always said that, didn't they, that no woman likes being put on a pedestal? Flat on her back in the middle of a field, that's what they wanted. All of them, whether they were scrubbers or whether they worked in a bank and played bloody badminton. Give 'em all a jab with the old pork sword, that's what Three-piece would say. Or was it Yank?

He was trying to remember which one when he glanced up to find Carol sliding into the chair opposite, breathing as though she'd been running, her hair dishevelled. She had a letter in her hand. *His* letter. From Scotland.

'It arrived after I'd left for work this morning,' she panted. 'It was waiting for me when I got home . . .'

'But I wrote it on Sunday and posted it on Monday . . .'

'I know, I saw the postmark . . .'

'Bloody post office . . .'

'It was probably the weather . . .'

'It was probably the company clerk playing with his . . . I mean, playing silly buggers . . .'

'I saw the road conditions on television . . . We've had delays with the bank's mail too . . .'

'I think I'll sue . . .'

'I waited ages for a bus . . . I thought you'd gone . . . Then I remembered this pub . . .'

'I thought you'd stood me up.'

'Why on earth would I do that?'

'I don't know. When you weren't here . . . Would you like a drink?'

'Yes please, but somewhere else.'

'Wherever you like. Have you eaten?'

'No, I didn't have time.'

'Then we'll do that too.'

'Good, I'm starving. But can we find a phone before we do anything? I didn't know when you were coming back and I'd arranged to play badminton tonight. I'll have to ring up and say I can't make it.'

Twiggy held the door open for her, grinning idiotically. Maybe Yank and Three-piece didn't know everything after all.

Across town, in a tiny Italian restaurant, Sammy Finch was struggling with the menu. There were English equivalents alongside each of the Italian dishes, but Sammy wanted to have a stab at the Italian pronunciations to impress Libby Rees, sitting opposite him. Like a fool, he'd told her he often ate in Italian restaurants in London, which he didn't. He'd been in a few, of course, though mostly after an evening on the beer when he'd stuck to spaghetti or whatever else looked filling and cheap and which he could eat without throwing up. If the truth were known, he wasn't that keen on Eyetie fodder. She'd let on she was, however, so here they were.

Like Twiggy with Carol, Sammy had seen Libby regularly since the end of Christmas leave. Unlike Twiggy he'd got Libby as far as bed on their seventh meeting, the last one before manoeuvres. She lived at home with her parents and younger brother, and on the night in question she'd invited him back. Her mother and father were at a dinner-dance and would not be returning until the small hours; her brother was staying overnight with friends. Sammy thought it was his birthday. The signals were obvious, weren't they? She'd proved to be pretty passionate in earlier clinches, but he'd judged it was going to take him a lot longer to get her between the sheets. Not so, however. They'd had a few drinks out followed by several glasses of her father's whisky in her sitting-room while listening to records and doing some body-contact dancing. Then upstairs.

And then it was nothing. Not a bleeding thing. She was all over him with her hands and he couldn't raise a gallop. Zero. Limp dick. Brewer's droop.

It had never happened to him before and he was shocked.

She'd told him not to worry, that it didn't matter. It wasn't going to change anything between them. He was in a strange house, in an unfamiliar bed (and *she* seemed to know a hell of a lot about it). It would be different next time.

Big deal. He *had* worried and it *did* matter. In Scotland he'd imagined her talking to her friends, telling them that he was all mouth and no action. It was not that he would never live it down; one day the battalion would be off, another posting, West Germany in April. They wouldn't remember him here then. But he'd remember. And it would scare the hell out of him in case it happened again. He had to make it with Libby, just for the record.

With that in mind, and again unlike Twiggy, he hadn't trusted the mail. He telephoned her during one of the stop-overs on the way down from Jockland, giving her chapter and verse, the date the battalion would be home and his first available night. To other men facing possible rejection or ridicule, such a call would have taken courage. Sammy didn't view it like that. He'd failed with Libby, therefore he must succeed with Libby. And on this occasion forewarned was forearmed. It was the booze last time, too much beer topped off with whisky. There'd be no more self-indulgence. Some wine, maybe, nothing more.

Also, he'd been given a tip when he'd broached the subject with the expert, Three-piece, in a roundabout manner. Lots of starch put lead in the pencil, that's what Sweet had always found. Italian grub, for example. All that pasta and shit. Never failed. Damn near an aphrodisiac.

It could not have been better. Italian fodder did the trick and Libby was a sucker for Italian fodder.

Because it was still early evening, they were two of only half a dozen customers. Over a glass of white wine, recommended by the red-jacketed waiter and not too foul if you could forget about all those Eyeties jumping on the grapes with their great feet, Sammy studied each item on the menu. It would be all A-okay in a couple of hours, whether it was a knee-trembler in the bus-shelter or back at Libby's gaff, if it was free. She wouldn't have come out with him again unless she was keen would she? Of course she wouldn't. Stood to reason. And *there* was a thought. In spite of all that double-bunny about it 'not mattering' and 'don't worry', maybe *she* was worried too. Maybe she blamed herself for not being sexy enough or getting him to swill all that Scotch. Yeah.

Three-piece had also given him another piece of advice: don't flap if you don't get the Italian pronunciation right. Instead, use English and stick the letter 'o' on the end of everything if you weren't sure. Three-piece had met a lot of Italians; they always understood him. If you said 'elephanto' or 'giraffo' they knew what the fuck you were talking about. Sammy could not work out what Three-piece was doing talking to Italians about elephants and giraffes, and Three-piece said they were just examples, for Christ's sake. Sammy said he hoped so, and that his limited knowledge of Italian cooking didn't mean they ate elephant's feet or giraffe heads. Three-piece told him not to be such a cretin.

Well, there were no elephant's feet or giraffe heads, Sammy saw, but, Jesus, there were some weird objects. They didn't go a bundle on Heinz Spaghetti Hoops in this joint.

Calamari all'olio. Squid. Squid? Christ, that was like octopus, wasn't it? Octopus! No chance. He could have eaten some pork, but that wasn't on the menu. Okay, he could ask. Bung an 'o' on the end. Porko. Maybe not, though. That didn't sound right. Piggo? Fat with big ears and a curly tail, waiter? You know, fuckin' piggo. Grunto. Giant bastards that always have their snouts in the trough.

No, stay with the menu.

Right, *gnocchi alla Milanese*. Dumplings and crap. Forget it. He wasn't going to try saying that. Not a prayer. Guh-knocky? Guh-knockio? That sounded like a little wooden puppet and about as Italian as Non-Legless Jones. Go for something easier.

Straciatella alla Romana. Holy shit, soup. Forty-seven syllables to order a bowl of Roman soup.

He became aware that Libby, studying her own menu, had more or less decided what she was going to eat. She would, of course. Probably been in here or somewhere like it a hundred times.

'Any ideas?' he asked casually.

'I was wondering what you were going to suggest.'

You and me both, sweet sister. How about fish and chips? Da fisho and da chippo. Christ, was *this* a mistake. He wondered if he could find some excuse for them to leave. He concluded he couldn't, not if he wanted to sort out his 'little problem' with Libby. Better get on with it.

He signalled the waiter, who, bored by inactivity, was at his side instantly, pad in hand.

Sammy panicked now that the moment of truth had arrived. 'Soupo,' he said. Because he was nervous the word came out several decibels above his normal speaking tone. Startled, Libby gave an involuntary giggle and put a hand to her mouth. Sammy glared at her. 'Is that all right with you?'

'F-fine,' stuttered Libby.

The waiter peered over Sammy's shoulder. He spoke excellent English, but he didn't have much time for the armed services. They frequently disturbed the other customers and often tried to get away without settling their bills. He'd act dumb with this one, just to see how he handled it.

'Soupo?'

Sammy pointed.

'Ah, *zuppa di ciliege al vino*.'

Jesus, thought Sammy, whose finger in his anxiety had hit the first line on the menu it came to. Wine soup with cherries— *served cold*. Cold soup!

But it was too late to back off.

'Yeah, soupo. Zuppa.'

'And to follow, signor?'

Sammy was starting to sweat.

'What about this,' he said, talking partly to the waiter, partly to Libby. 'Scallopp . . . Scalinno . . . Scallipon . . . This bugger,' he finished up, jabbing desperately at the menu.

'Ah, *scaloppine di vitello alla Marsala*. A fine choice. Fresh today.'

'I don't like veal,' said Libby, trying hard to choke back her laughter at Sammy's antics. 'I'd prefer rabbit.'

'Ah, *coniglio*.'

'No—ah, rabbito,' Sammy corrected the waiter before he could stop himself. Libby let out a loud guffaw before diving into her handbag for a handkerchief and pretending to blow her nose.

By this time the two other couples in the restaurant had pricked up their ears and were smiling broadly. Sammy wished the floor would open up and swallow him. This wasn't at all how he'd planned it. They were all having a great joke at his expense, he thought angrily.

'Ah, screw this bullshiterino,' he scowled, throwing his menu on to the table—at which Libby collapsed across it, giggling helplessly, shoulders shaking.

'Oh God,' she managed, 'I've got a pain.'

Sammy was about to storm out in a rage and to hell with Libby when he too saw the funny side of the proceedings. And a way to capitalize on his ignorance. He had the undivided attention of the restaurant. Even the waiter was grinning. Okay, he'd play it their way, play it for laughs.

'Right,' he said, picking up the menu, 'that's two soupos to start with, one scalloperoniono and one rabbito. And take the skin off the rabbito. You know, skinno off the bunny.'

Now the waiter was getting confused. He had to tear off the top page of his pad and start again.

Sammy dug deep in his memory bank for every foreign preposition, definite and indefinite article he had ever heard, which were few.

'With the scalloperoniono I'll have der potatoes mitt eine chunk de spinacho. Comprende?'

The waiter said he did.

Surfacing and wiping her eyes, Libby settled for her *coniglio in vino*, *zucchini affogati* and *insalata verde*, ordering it herself in a passable accent.

'Yeah, a big helping,' said Sammy, not having a clue, apart from the rabbit, what Libby was about to eat.

'And vino, signor?'

'Damn right vino. Mucho vino.' He remembered. 'No, not so mucho vino.'

'Rosso?'

'No, Italian. I can't stand Russian wine.'

'I mean red, signor.'

'Of course Russian wine's red. What other colour would it be?'

The joke had gone far enough for the waiter.

'Rosso *means* red, signor,' he intoned deliberately.

'Oh, right, red. Rosso it is. I thought he was one of their footballers,' Sammy stage-whispered to Libby.

What had begun as a disaster ended up a success. Sammy even enjoyed the food. Once in a while he called for something else—breado, buttero, another carafe of rosso. He was feeling good and a little more wine wouldn't do any harm.

But for him, too, the gag gradually wore thin, and when he finally called for the bill—'Let's have el tabbo, signor'—he'd had enough. There was also the main event to consider. Over dinner Libby had told him that she was glad the battalion had returned when it did, in time for today and not tomorrow. Tomorrow her parents and brother would be at home; tonight they had driven to Gloucester to see relations. On receiving Sammy's phone call Libby had invented incipient 'flu and begged off. The house was theirs for the night.

And a damned good night it was, Sammy was to reflect later. Whether it was the Italian grub or the rosso or because a bloody good laugh had relaxed them both, all was plain sailing on this occasion. There was nothing like it, he thought contentedly, getting the old leg acrossio.

Being eight months pregnant with her first child was far from 'the joyous anticipation promised in women's magazines,' Eileen O'Hara confided to her sister Gwen while Scarlett and Gwen's husband Trevor were in the kitchen of the O'Haras' married quarters, pouring beer for themselves and mixing a gin and tonic for Gwen. Eileen had not touched a drop of alcohol since her pregnancy was confirmed, and very little before that. She didn't really approve of drinking, considering it a waste of money that could be better employed elsewhere.

She only accompanied her husband to pubs to ensure he
didn't overspend his budget.

'Especially with a husband in the army,' she added, loud
enough to be heard in the kitchen, 'when the army can send
him to Scotland for two weeks while I need him here.'

'Not that again,' murmured Trevor.

Scarlett nodded. 'That again.'

At almost six feet tall and twelve stone, Scarlett was the
epitome of the professional soldier from the crown of his
neatly-trimmed hair to the tips of his highly-polished shoes.
Three years older than his wife at twenty-six, he outweighed
her, before she was pregnant, by five stone and could give
her nearly a foot in height. It would therefore have come as a
shock to any member of 3 Platoon or indeed D Company to
learn that Scarlett was close to being the archetypal hen-
pecked husband.

It had not always been like that. For the first eighteen
months of their three-year-marriage, she appeared content to
be a soldier's wife. Then Gwen—two years her senior—had
wed Trevor, and that had started it. Trevor had a good
position with a frozen food combine. His salary plus commission was excellent and he had a company car. Except when
he was on business in another part of the country, he came
home every night. He and Gwen were buying their own
house. 'While we'll be in married quarters for either the rest
of our lives or until it's too late.'

Eileen wanted him to leave the army, quit while he was
still young, make a new career. Scarcely a week passed
without the subject being raised, always with the same time-
worn arguments. 'I miss you when you're away.' 'I don't get
along with the other army wives.' 'I'd like a home that I can
really call my own.' And latterly: 'You'll be a father soon
with a father's responsibilities. Do you think I want my child
growing up on an army base? You've got no consideration at
all.'

Scarlett could not prove it, but he suspected Eileen had got
pregnant on purpose, to force his hand. The child was certainly not planned. As far as he had been aware, she was still
taking the Pill. She denied conceiving to be anything other
than accidental, however. 'Oral contraception isn't one hundred per cent foolproof, you know. Read the newspapers. If
you spent more time doing that instead of burying your head
in training manuals, you might become aware that there is a

world outside the army. Anyway, it's done now.' Then the tears. 'Are you saying you don't want the baby?'

When the nagging first started about his chosen career, Scarlett had dug in his heels. He loved the army, everything about it, even the illogical pettinesses. She couldn't accept that, as she had been unable to accept his going to the assistance of young Twigg and Finch in that pub before Christmas. 'Just because they're in your platoon doesn't mean you have to wet-nurse them twenty-four hours a day.' What was more, he was good at his job. He had nowhere near reached the end of the promotion ladder. He wasn't leaving, and that was that.

But gradually, he realized, she was wearing him down. He couldn't face her whining two or three evenings a week, which recently she'd kept up even when Gwen and Trevor popped over for their customary Friday night visit. Nor was he permitted to put his own case. If he did she would accuse him of not loving her, of not wanting the child, of forgetting her condition. He couldn't win, and she was driving him crazy. Another man in another profession might have said, Right, that's it—and disappeared to begin again in another town. He wasn't another man, however, and his profession did not take kindly to moonlight flits. Besides, perhaps she was right; maybe married quarters was the wrong environment to bring up a child. He just wished he knew what had happened to the blue-eyed, vivacious girl he married.

'Gwen's waiting for her drink, Harry,' his wife trilled from the sitting-room.

'Coming up,' said Scarlett.

Just before midday on Saturday Peter Ballantine, who was remaining in barracks that weekend, received a call in the company office from the guardroom. A Miss Parker-Smith was at the barrier, asking to see him.

Elbow-deep in post-manoeuvres bumf, it took Peter a moment or two to work it out. Lavinia, here?

'Get someone to escort her down to D Company, will you,' he asked the guard commander.

She was shown into the company offices a few minutes later. Peter was about to extend his hand in greeting when she kissed him lightly on the cheek.

'I was in the area driving home from London, so I thought

I'd drop in and persuade Rupert to buy me lunch. Unfortunately the guardroom couldn't find him.'

'He's around,' said Peter. He checked a list tacked on the wall behind him. 'He's not on duty but he's here somewhere.' He indicated the paperwork. 'Most of us are, I'm sorry to say. Did the guardroom try the mess?'

'The first place. And his quarters.'

'Then they should have tried here next.' Peter frowned. 'That's the logical sequence of events.'

'They did. That's how I come to be here.'

'But the guard commander asked for me, not Rupert.'

'Ah,' said Lavinia.

She perched herself on the corner of his desk, carefully arranging the folds of her knee-length skirt.

'Before I get anyone into trouble,' she went on, 'perhaps I'd better confess that I didn't ask for Rupert at all. I knew he wasn't coming home this weekend, which was my excuse. I knew you'd be here, also, because he told me on the telephone yesterday evening. And actually I haven't been to London at all. I drove over from the estate. Forty-five minutes flat from door to door,' she said lightly. 'Rupert can't do much better than that in his Porsche.'

She threw a sidelong glance at Peter, and was irritated to observe that he appeared faintly amused.

'And you can take that superior expression off your face, Ballantine. God knows how many times I've tried to inveigle you into taking me to dinner or lunch in the past year, without success. And, now the shooting season's over, we probably shan't see you at the estate until next October. If the mountain won't go to Mahomet, Mahomet must go to the mountain. So there. Well, say something,' she concluded when Peter remained silent.

'I was just thinking that you must be starving to drive all this way for lunch.'

'Then it's all right?' Lavinia's eyes lit up. 'You're not going to throw me out or think I'm a silly child?'

'Neither. In fact, if you're very good and eat all your pudding, I'll help you with your French homework later.'

'Oh, *you*.' She picked up a sheaf of papers as if to hurl them at him.

'Hey, easy with those. It's taken me all morning to shuffle them into some sort of order. Is your car outside or at the guardroom?'

'Outside. The kindly corporal at the barrier said they had no transport at the main gates. I felt sorry for the poor man, having to march back.'

'That's what kindly corporals are paid for. We'll take your car, then, if that's all right. Mine's half a mile away.'

Beyond the barrier she asked him which direction.

'How hungry are you?'

'Not very. A sandwich and a drink will do me fine.'

There was an inn Peter used occasionally several miles up the road. Peter told her to turn left.

She had brought the estate Range Rover—or rather, one of the estate Range Rovers, Peter reminded himself—which she drove with easy confidence. The perfect picture of an English gentlewoman, he mused, looking at her. A tweed cap, blonde hair tied back with its customary ribbon, battered shooting jacket over an expensive sweater, tweed skirt, low-heeled brogues. And high-cheekboned features that would never make a man avert his eyes. Perhaps he'd been foolish, in the past, not taking her up on her semi-serious advances, too concerned, maybe wrongly, that what she had in mind were wedding bells. Perhaps that would change now, now that she had made the first move.

'Over there,' he said, pointing out the inn.

She eased the Range Rover into a vacant slot in the car park.

The saloon bar and the public bar were packed to bursting. Peter suggested they try the cocktail bar. The first people they saw on entering it were Rupert and Julia Lomax.

Damn it to blazes, cursed Lavinia, wishing she had kept her eyes open in the car park, where Rupert's Porsche must surely be. She had been hoping for a quiet hour or so in Peter Ballantine's company, when she would have done her utmost to ensure that the next move came from him. And soon.

But it was too late now. Rupert had seen them. And judging by the expression on his face he could not have been more startled had the Queen walked through the door. So this, she thought, was the woman he was involved with. Her face seemed vaguely familiar.

Peter, naturally, recognized Toby Lomax's wife at once. Nor did it take much grey matter to deduce that she and Rupert had not met at the inn by chance. He would have liked to have done a smart about-turn, but Rupert was already on his feet, cleverly converting his horror at being found with Julia into astonishment on seeing Lavinia.

'Well,' he said, his voice not quite steady, 'you're a long way from home.'

Sitting at the same table and having drinks together could not be avoided without making an embarrassing situation worse. Lavinia recalled now that she had seen Julia Lomax at battalion functions. A man-eater, she judged. Good God, fancy being dressed in high-heels and stockings on a Saturday morning.

An uneasy quarter of an hour followed, during which Rupert did his best to persuade Peter and Lavinia that he had simply 'popped up the road for a quick one, to get away from the ghastly graveyard atmosphere of a weekend in the mess'.

'And there was Julia.'

Julia herself offered no explanation for her presence unescorted, on the principle of *qui s'excuse s'accuse*. Instead she chatted generally and pleasantly about nothing in particular for the space of a gin and tonic, before glancing at her watch and announcing that she had to leave. 'Otherwise my husband will wonder where I've got to.'

Rupert, of course, did not leave with her.

'You're an ass, Rupert,' was Lavinia's eventual verdict.

'If you mean what I think you mean, old girl, you are emphatically woofing up the wrong conifer,' countered her brother.

'Twaddle. And for God's sake stop talking like something out of Billy Bunter. She's a praying mantis, that one. You'll wake up one morning to find you're her breakfast.'

'And your sister says that,' put in Peter, who had resolved to mention it this once and never again, 'without being familiar with Toby Lomax. Who is not exactly a candidate for the corps de ballet. He'll boot you from here to Easter if he finds out.'

'I repeat,' said Rupert, 'you've got it wrong. But, if we're talking about clandestine meetings, what about you two? Or mustn't I ask?'

'Don't change the subject,' said Lavinia.

'And don't please,' retorted Rupert, pleasantly but firmly, 'try to impose your own standards of morality on me.' He finished his drink. ''Bye.'

'Could he get into trouble?' Lavinia wanted to know.

'If you mean officially, no,' answered Peter. 'We're a pretty broadminded lot these days. Mind you, if it were a colonel's wife instead of a lowly captain's, that would be a different matter. If you mean unofficially, yes. Toby Lomax is a hard man.'

'Will you talk to Rupert?' asked Lavinia. 'Try to make him see sense?'

'Oh, look,' said Peter, 'I don't know that I can do that. I mean, there's only a pip's difference in our ranks and a few years in our ages. I can't come the heavy father.'

'What about ''conduct prejudicial'' or whatever it is?'

'Doesn't apply. You probably stand a better chance than I of getting him to see reason.'

'Then we'll both have a go,' decided Lavinia. 'And we can meet some time next week to compare notes.' She chuckled. 'I don't see how you can turn me down, not with Rupert's well-being at stake.'

'I think I've just been blackmailed.'

'How do you think my great-great-great-whatever-it-was-grandfather obtained the viscountcy in the first place? Is it a deal?'

'Well, with Rupert's well-being at stake, I don't see how I can possibly say no.'

'Good. We'll make it dinner. Lunches seem to be asking for trouble.'

ELEVEN

Ricardo

IN MID-MARCH Ricardo's regiment was stationed twenty miles southeast of Rio Gallegos, capital of Santa Cruz province in Patagonia, near the Chilean-Argentine mainland border. Further south, across the Strait of Magellan, other Argentine units were based on the divided island of Tierra del Fuego. Since January, when the argument over the disputed islands in the Beagle Channel had become critical and the 1972 treaty with Chile was repudiated by Argentina, all Argentine forces in the south, though officially still on manoeuvres, were in actuality on a semi-war footing. 'Show of strength,' the high command called it, which meant, for the officers and men involved, arctic clothing to combat the freezing temperatures and bitter winds, little or no leave, and mail deliveries that were capricious to say the least. The sun didn't rise until 9 a.m., and when it did only weakly illuminated a largely desolate landscape.

For Ricardo—as, in response to a signal delivered by dispatch-rider, he hitched a lift on a half-track back to battalion HQ—the posting meant he had not seen his parents or sister since early February, and Beto not since January, though at least, to the best of his knowledge, Beto's conscription was being served further north, in a gentler climate.

More irritating, however, was not having spoken to Sara for six weeks, and not being able to tell her, even if his letters were getting through—which hers certainly weren't to him—

anything other than he was 'still in the field'. She'd be concerned. They had both expected her to be in Argentina by March, but there was little chance of that now. She would have to wait until this Chilean business blew over or blew up, and that would mean postponing the wedding planned for June, regardless of whether or not his superiors got their skates on and gave the match their blessing, which hadn't happened yet although he had completed the necessary paperwork immediately after Christmas leave. Doubtless his application had been shuffled to the bottom of somebody's in-tray, but that wasn't something Sara would readily understand. Still, military lethargy was a state of affairs she would have to get used to as an army wife, so perhaps it wasn't such a bad thing for her to experience it from the word go.

On the brighter side, when tackled his parents had given the betrothal their enthusiastic approval. As had Elizabeth Ballantine and Peter, by return of post, directly he had written to them. The funny thing was, no one had seemed in the least surprised at his announcement that he intended marrying Sara. Nor was anyone concerned about religious differences. The form of the ceremony and how any children would be brought up could be resolved, was the consensus, without fuss.

Ricardo skipped off the half-track outside battalion HQ and waved his thanks to the driver. The adjutant was about to make a telephone call when Ricardo walked into the office. He replaced the receiver when he saw who his visitor was.

'You're to go straight in.'

The adjutant was the same age and the same rank as Ricardo. They had graduated from the same class at the Colegio Militar, played polo in the same team, and even pursued the same girls once in a while. In short, they were fairly good friends, though the adjutant's expression was anything but friendly now. He looked like a man who had been given command of a firing squad.

'In?' Ricardo did not understand. 'I received a signal by dispatch . . .'

'I know. I originated it.' The adjutant interrupted him impatiently and gestured towards a door. 'The commanding officer wants to see you.'

'Like this? Christ, you might have given me a hint.'

Ricardo was dressed in all-weather combat gear. His company had been on patrol since first light. His boots were filthy and he could have used a shave. This wasn't the way he would have chosen to present himself to Colonel Jorge Filippi.

'That doesn't matter. My orders were to get you up here immediately. The Colonel knows you're out in the field.' The adjutant lowered his voice. 'What the hell have you been up to, Ricardo?'

'Nothing. Look, what is this?'

'Don't ask me. You'd better go in.'

Ricardo flipped his hood off. He had his uniform cap in his pocket. He put it on and straightened it before knocking politely on the CO's door.

Colonel Filippi, also wearing headgear, was seated behind his desk. He was a short, slightly overweight man in his middle forties who chain-smoked American cigarettes, Camels for preference. He acknowledged Ricardo's salute before telling the younger officer to sit down opposite him and make himself comfortable. Ricardo did so, his eyes wandering curiously in the direction of the two men in civilian clothes who were each drinking mugs of steaming coffee. He judged they were not civilians in spite of their attire.

'As of now,' said the CO formally, speaking as if he had carefully rehearsed his lines, 'you are relieved of your duties, Captain Jordan-Arditti. You are to accompany these—ah—gentlemen to Buenos Aires. There's an aircraft standing by at Rio Gallegos.'

'Sir?'

Fleetingly Ricardo had thought that he had been summoned to the CO's presence to be told that his request to marry Sara had been granted. Or that it had not been granted. But it obviously had nothing to do with Sara at all.

'I'm afraid I don't understand, sir. Do you mean right away?'

'Right away, Captain.'

'But I can't simply walk out without telling my company commander where I've gone. Besides, all my kit . . .'

'Your kit will be taken care of, Captain,' said one of the civilians. 'Permit me to introduce myself—Major Vila. This is Major Corino. Colonel Filippi will also inform your company commander of your whereabouts—or, rather, that you are no longer on the strength of this regiment.'

'Am I in some trouble I don't know about?'

'Not unless we don't know about it either.'

'Then am I allowed to know what's going on?'

'Everything will be explained in Buenos Aires.' Major Vila glanced at his wristwatch. 'Now I regret that that must be an end to your questions for the time being.'

Ricardo wasn't sure he liked being ordered about in this peremptory manner. He was, after all, an officer in the Argentine army, not an hotel servant. He elected to make a mild protest.

'Is it your wish that I accompany these officers, sir?' he enquired of the CO.

'No, Captain, it's our wish,' said Major Vila.

Colonel Filippi nodded, the look on his face suggesting that it would be unwise to argue. Well, well, thought Ricardo, majors giving orders to full colonels.

The aircraft was a military version of the Boeing 707. Apart from the crew, the two security majors—Ricardo was certain of their capacity now—and Ricardo were the only passengers. On board, they gave him an electric razor and a complete set of civilian clothes, which fitted almost perfectly even down to the shoes and shirt-collar size. Somebody had evidently gone to a great deal of trouble. At first Ricardo thought that this was out of courtesy, the temperature in Buenos Aires at this time of year being considerably hotter than that of southern Patagonia. Then it dawned on him that it would have been just as easy for the same somebody to provide him with a uniform. Wherever Vila and Corino were taking him, they didn't want him looking like a soldier.

They said little or nothing during the three-hour flight, and Ricardo asked no further questions.

It was dark when the plane landed in Buenos Aires, and Ricardo was thankful they'd let him change out of his all-weather gear. At a guess, the temperature was in the low eighties with humidity about the same.

The passengers were met by an unmarked car being driven by yet another civilian. Major Corino sat next to the driver; Ricardo occupied the back seat alongside Major Vila.

Their destination was a three-storey building in its own grounds in the north-east suburbs. Ricardo vaguely knew the area but had no idea what the building was. Nor were there any clues on the outside to enlighten him, though on the inside, beyond the double doors, were two armed sentries.

Major Corino led the way up a broad staircase to the first floor and along a passage. He rapped on a door at the far end. A deep bass voice bade him enter.

'Captain Jordan-Arditti, sir,' said Corino.

Ricardo did not recognize the officer standing by the huge french windows overlooking the garden, but his rank insignia revealed him to be a general. Automatically Ricardo stiffened to attention. At the same time he was puzzled. There were uniformed sentries in the lobby and the general was in uniform. Where was the sense, then, in dressing him up as a civilian?

It took him a moment to work it out, that it was him that they—whoever *they* were—did not want seen in a uniform. Perhaps Majors Corino and Vila too. Why was another matter.

The general was a medium-sized man, on the lean side, whose age it was hard to determine. Between forty-five and fifty at least, Ricardo conjectured, to be the holder of that rank. He sported a moustache, neither bushy nor pencil-thin, and his hair was mouse-brown. In fact everything about him was average except for his eyes, which were a brilliant, piercing blue and did not smile when his mouth did, which it was doing now as he approached Ricardo, his hand outstretched in greeting.

'Ah, Captain Jordan-Arditti. I'm delighted to meet you. My name is Pastran. Do relax, please. May I offer you a drink?'

General Pastran's handshake was firm and dry, and his welcome obviously sincere. Ricardo obeyed orders and relaxed. Although the way he had been treated by the security majors since leaving Rio Gallegos had more or less confirmed that he was guilty of no offence, it was reassuring to have that corroborated by a senior officer.

'Whisky, thank you, sir.'

'Excellent. I'll join you.'

The general poured his own and Ricardo's drink and motioned Vila and Corino to help themselves. He waved Ricardo to an armchair and took the sofa opposite. Beside him was a maroon folder which he placed on his lap but did not open for the moment. He raised his glass.

'*Salud*. Or what is it they say in England? Cheers? Is that correct? I understand you were in England recently?'

'That is correct, sir, though I wasn't in England recently. It was before Christmas.'

'Well, that's fairly recently, isn't it? In fact, I'd go as far as to say that there are not many men in the army who have been in England as recently as you, not many who speak the language as fluently as you, anyway. That is true, is it not? That you were educated there and speak English fluently?'

'The English might not think so, sir, but yes, I was partly educated in England.'

'Until you were'—Pastran opened the folder and flicked through several pages—'seventeen or thereabouts, when your family lost most of its money and you had to return home. When you enrolled in the Colegio Militar. I'm happy to see your family has regained its former wealth. One thing perplexes me, however.'

'Sir?'

'Most young men of your background do not choose the army as a career. I agree many families found themselves in the same position as your father a decade ago, but ninety per cent of their sons who became regular soldiers subsequently left the services when the family fortune was restored. You stayed on.'

The final sentence was delivered as a statement but evidently required an answer. Ricardo gave the simple truth.

'I enjoy soldiering, sir. Money or not, it's the life I want.'

'And you're ambitious?'

'Yes, sir.'

'You wouldn't be content to remain a captain or possibly a major for the rest of your time and merely use the army as a convenient club to provide a lot of polo and a little excitement?'

'Emphatically not, sir.'

'And you are, of course, loyal—to your service and your country.'

The implied criticism was totally unexpected. Ricardo flushed with anger.

'With due respect, sir,' he said with as much aplomb as he could muster, 'I know of no reason why you should question my loyalty.'

'Really?' The blue eyes flashed impatiently. 'Well, with due respect to *you*, Captain, I find it odd that you have chosen to marry an Englishwoman, a foreign national whose government displays little but hostility towards Argentina. A woman, moreover, who has a brother in the British army.'

So that was it, thought Ricardo, suddenly deflated. They'd flown him up from Rio Gallegos to tell him that marrying Sara would not receive official sanction.

In accordance with the regulations when a serving officer wanted to marry an alien, he had completed the application in full, informing the powers-that-be precisely who Sara Ballantine was and what her family did, right down to Peter's commission. Those were the rules. The armed forces of any nation had to know whether there would ever be a conflict of loyalties. Had Peter wanted to marry, say, Lucita or a European, he would have been asked to fill in a similar form.

But that couldn't be it, he told himself. Turning down his request would have been done through channels. Colonel Filippi would have given him the bad news. 'Sorry, my friend, but they wouldn't wear it.' They wouldn't have sent two security officers to the other end of Argentina to escort him up here. They wouldn't have provided civilian clothes. They wouldn't have granted him a personal interview with an unknown general. They wouldn't have done any of that. Not just to say no.

So who the hell were they? And what did the reference to a hostile British government mean?

Ricardo cleared his throat.

'Am I to understand, sir, that permission to marry Miss Ballantine is denied?'

If it was he would resign his commission and that's all there was to it. Bugger them if they were going to be so trivial.

Pastran ignored the question. Ricardo became aware out of the corner of his eye that Corino and Vila, drinks in hand, had occupied two of the other armchairs in the room.

'Tell me about your few days in England,' said the general. 'For that matter, tell me about the English. I only know the Anglo-Argentine variety. All we ever learn of England in this department is filtered through the Foreign Ministry, which is notoriously unimaginative. Tell me what the indigenous population are like, what they talk about, how they entertain themselves, how they view the rest of the world now they no longer have an empire.'

Without fully comprehending what was required of him, Ricardo did his best. He liked them as a race, though they could be intolerant of foreigners. Many of them were insufferably priggish and infuriatingly narrow-minded; the rest generous to a fault. They had far from adjusted to a world where they no longer 'ruled the waves', and imperialism, in all classes, was never far below the surface. They were a curious amalgam of sheep and wolves, predators and prey.

They could be frighteningly obdurate when their conception of 'fair play' was infringed.

Ricardo mentioned that he had spent an afternoon looking over an infantry battalion. This was of particular interest to General Pastran. How fit were the men? What did their training entail? How was morale? What was the calibre of the officers? And, finally, were political subjects ever discussed—for example, the Malvinas?

Ricardo thought he saw daylight.

'The Malvinas were never mentioned, sir. Of course, you have to realize that I was only in the mess for lunch.'

'But you presumably spent some time with the brother of Miss Ballantine?'

'I did, sir.'

'And you never availed yourself of the opportunity to press the case for Argentine sovereignty over the islands? I find that astonishing.'

'The subject never arose,' said Ricardo. 'Besides,' he added, unable to keep the hauteur from his voice, 'I was a guest in the Ballantine house. Sir.'

Pastran studied him. 'You have, I think, picked up more English mannerisms than you know, Captain Jordan-Arditti. Which may, of course, be no bad thing, providing your Anglophilia does not include subscribing to their claim to the Malvinas.'

'Naturally it does not, sir.'

'Good,' said the general. 'I'm happy to hear you say that.'

He glanced over to Corino and Vila. Ricardo saw them nod imperceptibly.

'Because we have a job for you, Captain,' went on the general, 'one for which I believe you to be uniquely qualified.'

For the next thirty minutes Ricardo listened with growing amazement and excitement to General Pastran as he outlined the top-secret plan to recover the Malvinas for Argentina; not in a year or in six months but in less than three weeks. Diplomacy had failed, that was obvious. Every time the subject of sovereignty was raised either between Foreign Ministries or at the United Nations, the British stalled, as they had done for years, hoping the problem would go away. While it appeared inarguable (according to a recent brief received by Pastran from the Foreign Ministry) that many senior officials of the British Foreign Office wished to be rid of what they called the Falkland Islands 'inconvenience', they blamed not finding a solution on the intransigence of the islanders, their powerful, self-serving lobby in Westminster, and the attitude of some right-wing newspapers which could not accept that the sun had finally set over the Empire. Well, that sort of temporizing could not go on for ever. Enough was enough. Argentina's claim was just. The armed forces would succeed where the diplomats had foundered. South Georgia would be taken during the last week in March, the Malvinas at the beginning of April. The army would spearhead the invasion, backed up by the navy and air force. The landings would become a fait accompli in a matter of hours. Resistance from the Royal Marines garrison was expected to be light. The British government would hum and hah for a week before accepting the situation. Then, from a position of strength, the diplomats could sit round a table and work out the small print for the transfer of sovereignty. The British had given up their other former colonies without so much as a whisper. They would do so again.

Together with Major Corino and Major Vila and perhaps a dozen other specialists, Ricardo would be part of the advance force. Their cover would be that of gas workers, in Stanley to install some additional oil cylinders, since under the 1974 agreement Argentina supplied the Malvinas with all its fuel apart from diesel. They would be equipped with radios, and their task would be to let the invasion force know if any unusual activity or a stiffening of the garrison was taking place. They would fly in quite normally towards the end of March. The exact date had still to be decided.

'So perhaps you now understand why I invited you here,' concluded the general. 'And why your request to marry an Englishwoman was passed to my department. You know the language and you know the people. We don't want any trouble with the inhabitants of the Malvinas. Quite the reverse, in fact. If we can convince them that they will lose nothing under Argentine sovereignty, their Westminster lobby will collapse, thus enabling the British government to negotiate without losing face. Believe me, fewer than two thousand stubborn and somewhat unrealistic people are causing this friction between two nations.

'Also, in an undertaking of this magnitude there are bound to be leaks, rumours. They may even have started already, which is the reason you are in civilian clothes.' Pastran grunted. 'This building occasionally comes under surveillance by outside intelligence organizations. It would hardly do for your photograph to be on file dressed in uniform, and then for you to turn up in Stanley as a gas worker.

'Part of your function there will be to reassure the islanders by being as friendly as you know how. Do not, of course, go out of your way to cultivate them—they're a suspicious lot anyway. But be courteous when it matters.

'I accept that as an infantry officer this kind of clandestine operation is brand-new to you, but you can safely leave the technicalities to Major Vila's and Major Corino's people. You're with them to detect subtle changes of attitude that they would miss. It will only be for a couple of days. Although your commanding officer doesn't know it yet, your regiment is part of the invasion force. You will rejoin it when it arrives. I take it you accept the assignment voluntarily?'

'Of course, sir.'

Ricardo would not have missed it for the world. His part in the proceedings would be entered on his service dossier, and perhaps there would be an accelerated promotion. So much for Peter's prediction that he would reach the rank of major first!

'But doubtless you have some questions you would like to ask me.'

Ricardo had several. The first, did he now return to his regiment until called for?

'No, you'll be billeted with Major Vila here in Buenos Aires. In the two weeks remaining you'll have much to discuss.'

'Will I be allowed to see my parents while I'm here?'

'That wouldn't be wise.'

'The reason I ask, sir, is that my mother has been unwell for some time. I generally write to her once a week, and in the past I've phoned her whenever possible. She'll worry if she doesn't hear from me.'

'How would you explain your presence in Buenos Aires?'

'I'm here to pick up some documents that are too valuable to be trusted to a courier. A flying visit, literally. It would also give me the opportunity to tell her I'll be out of touch for a few weeks.'

'Hm,' murmured the general.

'I don't like it,' put in Major Vila. 'If Captain Jordan-Arditti wants to write a letter, we can arrange for it to be posted in Rio Gallegos.'

'There's also the matter of Miss Ballantine,' Ricardo hurried on. 'We haven't discussed her except peripherally. I still don't know whether my application to marry her has been sanctioned or not.'

'I don't see how that's relevant.'

'It is to me,' said Ricardo, boldly.

'And it's not my decision,' retorted Pastran. 'However, let's say if all goes well it will probably be looked upon favourably in a few months.'

Ricardo had expected that answer, which amounted to a sort of positive maybe. Much would depend upon what happened when the Malvinas came under the Argentine flag. But he hadn't totally asked the question to determine his personal future. There were a few things the general didn't know about Sara Ballantine.

'I haven't heard from her for several weeks,' he said. 'I don't even know if she's been receiving my letters. She is, shall we say, headstrong. It's not impossible that she'll fly out. She already thought she'd be here in March. I don't want her making a wasted journey.'

'I understand,' said the general, 'but I don't see how paying a visit to your mother would stop her. I suggest you write her a letter—which I regret we shall have to censor—telling her that you are still on manoeuvres and will be until, say, mid-April. After the beginning of April it won't matter.' He paused. 'Or you could, of course, inform her that you've had second thoughts about the marriage.'

'*That* she certainly wouldn't believe,' protested Ricardo, 'and it would also put her on the first plane to Buenos Aires. I'll write as you suggest, obviously, but it would also help if I saw my mother. Sara—Miss Ballantine—calls her every so often. At least she talks to my sister. If either or both reassured her that everything was all right, it would solve a few problems.'

The general thought about it briefly.

'Very well, I agree. But I should like Major Vila to accompany you. Please understand that this is not because I think you'll develop a loose tongue or that you will take the opportunity to telephone Miss Ballantine in England. If we had any doubts about you, you wouldn't be sitting here now. But this is not your usual field of operations. I'd feel happier about security if Major Vila goes with you. You can always say he's dropping you off at the airport.'

'Of course, sir.'

Pastran stood up. The two security majors and Ricardo followed suit.

At the door Ricardo asked the general if conscripts would be used as part of the invasion force.

'Ah, yes, you have a young brother doing his military service, do you not. I don't think I can give you that information, but as you know yourself the bulk of our army is conscripted. Their quality for the most part is poor, I agree, but I don't think they'll be called upon to do any fighting. If your brother is among the invasion force I'm sure he'll consider it an honour. He'll also be quite safe.'

Ricardo wasn't at all convinced that Beto would regard the operation as an 'honour'. Nevertheless, he made no comment.

Alone, General Pastran poured himself a second whisky and reexamined the maroon folder. In a pocket at the back were half a dozen airmail letters with British stamps. The return address was Sara Ballantine's, and the contents, which had been carefully examined before the envelopes were resealed, were nothing more than English gossip and sentiments of love. Still, his department had not known what to expect when they were intercepted. Perhaps they could be delivered to Captain Jordan-Arditti in April.

TWELVE

Sara

SHE THREW A STICK FOR BARNEY. He charged after it, barking delightedly, scattering dead leaves and alarming birds. British Summer Time began tomorrow, an hour less for the Sunday lie-in. Only the English would officially start summer before March was over and two weeks before Easter.

She was, she had to admit, a little angry at Ricardo's letter. Well, no, not angry so much. Upset. Her mother had telephoned her at the office the previous day, Friday, and told her that it was waiting for her. Did she want it sent on to the flat or would she be coming home that weekend? She had opted for the country. It had been a dreadful week one way or another. She had reacted with uncharacteristic sharpness to even the politest request, snapping people's heads off. She had seen some of the men rolling their eyes. 'Oh Christ, Sara's got the curse.' Which wasn't the case. She was fed up, that was the case. She had anticipated being in Argentina in March, yet here she was still in England.

And what on earth was Ricardo playing at, sending the letter to her mother's address instead of to the London flat? That was the first time he had done that. He knew she spent all week and some weekends in London. It was as if he wanted there to be some delay between his writing and her reading.

Then some kind of flap had developed late Friday afternoon. Oh, nothing obvious, no one saying anything, but, for someone who had worked in the Foreign Office as long as she had, the signs were there. More telephones ringing than normal. Senior civil servants hurrying hither and thither wearing worried frowns. Junior officers, whose vigour was usually on a par with a piece of week-old Kleenex, positively springing along corridors. Something was very definitely Up. Another African crisis or some such. Or the crazies in Iran threatening to curtail everyone's motoring in the name of Allah. She would find out sooner or later, but, for her, it would have to be later. She'd had enough of Whitehall for one week.

Damn and blast Ricardo. Damn and blast the Argentine postal services. He'd said he hadn't had a letter for weeks, and she'd written seven or eight. He'd also said that he would be 'out in the field' until the end of April. The end of April! At Christmas she'd thought March was a light-year off.

Sara had called his mother immediately, in case Mrs Jordan-Arditti had any further news. Ricardo was so vague in his letter. She had been resting and his father was out. Sara spoke to Lucita, who told her that Ricardo had paid a hurried visit a fortnight earlier, in and out, a matter of an hour on his way back down south. And Lucita knew no more than Ricardo had written.

May he roast! Here he was complaining because his duties kept him away from an international telephone line, and he'd managed to get home for an hour. Surely to God he could have picked up the phone and attempted to ring her.

Not a word about the wedding, either. Well, half a word. 'I don't know whether June will be on. I've heard nothing from the high command yet, and I've now got the CO on to it. It may have to be later.'

So what did later mean? July? August? The millennium?

She was glad, now, that she'd mentioned to no one outside the family that she was to be married in June. She'd wanted to, naturally, but she'd resisted the temptation for superstitious reasons. Bragging about proposed nuptials was asking for trouble. She'd half hinted to the one woman she could marginally call a friend, Poppy Dauncey, that there could be 'mighty tidings' in the offing, but Poppy had scarcely listened, having her own troubles with a married man who couldn't make up his mind whether or not to leave his wife for her. Huh!

Barney dropped the stick at her feet, sat on his haunches, and looked up expectantly.

'Oh, buzz off with your silly stick, you great bear,' she said crossly, immediately regretting her tone when Barney, recognizing admonition without knowing his offence, lowered his head.

She ruffled his ears. 'Sorry, Barney, not your fault.'

She picked up the stick and hurled it. Barney scampered off.

She missed Ricardo dreadfully, that was the root cause of her moods. She missed him more than she'd thought it was possible to miss anyone. Nor was he the most romantic correspondent in the world. 'I can imagine what the house looks like now that the English spring is almost there. Down here in southern Patagonia we're blown off our feet most of the time and soaked to the skin or covered in mud and sleet the rest.'

Covered in mud and sleet! What a tender phrase. Another Latin-American dream shattered. For a wedding present she would buy him the collected works of R. Browning, Esq. Perhaps not, though. Like Peter, he would probably hunt through it looking for pictures of tanks or Sten-guns or whatever they called them nowadays.

'Come on, Barney. Home.'

She retraced her steps.

She would have flown out there if she'd thought it would do any good, but of course it wouldn't. So she'd just sit tight and hope for the best.

Her mother was baking in the kitchen. Scones. She dipped her finger in the mix. Barney recognized food smells and looked at her hopefully. She gave him a biscuit.

'See anyone?' Elizabeth Ballantine asked.

'Ten squirrels, six or seven hundred birds, and a rabbit. At least I think it was a rabbit though it was rather tall. It could have been a flasher in a rabbit suit, though knowing my luck he would have turned out to be impotent and spotty.' Sara exhaled through gritted teeth. 'Damn!'

She put her arms around her mother.

'Sorry. No, I didn't see anyone.'

'Careful, you'll get flour on you.' Elizabeth Ballantine rinsed her hands under the kitchen tap. 'I think I'd like a drink.'

'Before lunch? You never drink before lunch. You hardly ever drink even at lunchtime.'

'How do you know what I get up to during the week? I could be having a wild affair and rolling all over the house from Monday to Friday.'

'Has he got a friend?'

Her mother laughed. 'I'll have a brandy. Pour one for yourself too. There's some of the cooking variety in the larder.'

Sara found the bottle and two glasses.

'Okay, let's have it,' she said over her shoulder.

'Have what?'

'The lecture. How I must be patient. How I must learn that not everything can be geared to my whim. How you were the same twenty-five years ago but you had to cultivate serenity.'

'You think I've asked you to have a drink with me to talk to you like a Dutch uncle? Or aunt.'

'I hope not. I don't think I could stand the accent. Sorry again. Write out one hundred times, I must learn to keep my big mouth shut.'

'What did Ricardo have to say?'

'That he's covered with mud and sleet most of the time, that the rain stayeth not mainly on the plain in jolly old south Patagonia, and that the house must look lovely in the spring. You know, the usual kind of literary goodies that he and Shakespeare scribble. And that June is probably off.'

'Ah.'

'It could be July or it could be August.'

'But it is going to be?'

'Of course. Oh, I see. You judged by my lugubrious expression that Ricardo had given me the Argentine equivalent of the bum's rush, or the *vagabundo precipitar,* as one might say, though I believe an approximate translation of that would be "running vagrant". No, nothing so dramatic as that. Just a little more waiting.'

She handed her mother her brandy and joined her at the kitchen table.

'What say we finish this glass and then have another or six?'

'I have a better idea. I'm going to change into something suitable and we'll have lunch at the pub. My treat. It wouldn't do you any harm to put on a skirt, either. And some proper shoes. Trousers and boots might be fine for walking Barney, but the landlord will think I'm taking in refugees if you appear dressed like that.'

'Do I have to? Change, I mean? I'd love a pub lunch, but I don't think I can face choosing something different to wear.'

'Then I'll choose for you.'

'Oh no. You'll have me putting my hair in pigtails and wearing ankle-socks, which, while exciting the vicar, will do nothing for me. I do believe you sometimes think I'm still ten.'

'Only when you act it.'

'Ouch. Meaning that it's better to suffer nobly than wander about the house looking as if I've lost a pound and found a penny.'

'Meaning that in a few months' time you'll wonder what all the fuss was about.'

'Phrase-maker!'

'Off you pop now. If we get there before twelve we can bag a seat by the fire. For my old bones, you know.'

Sara kissed her mother. 'You're a darling.'

'So are you.'

THIRTEEN

Ricardo

SMALL CHILDREN SHOUTED 'Argie, Argie, you're not wanted here' at him from a safe distance as they passed. Older ones and a few adults added a muttered obscenity or two. They reminded him of football crowds, where the spectators wearing the favours of one team would hurl abuse at those sporting the colours of their opponents without knowing anything about the individuals behind the rosettes. Mindless verbal violence from the *canaille*. Just about tolerable from ill-educated children who knew no better, but not acceptable from adults—even if the perpetrators, on the evolutionary ladder, belonged to the lower orders.

Tomorrow they would sing a different song. Today, appropriately, was All Fools' Day. Come April 2, the islanders would not be so impertinent.

Part of him didn't understand their attitude at all. They were obviously poor, in the main, these people, and he had learned from his briefing that the British government did little for them. Surely they weren't all witless; surely the brighter ones among them were able to discern that living under the Argentine flag would enrich their lives materially? There were plans to develop the airport, he had been told, bring in capital, finance new industry. Did they really want to remain in the Middle Ages?

Presumably yes, at least until someone demonstrated the alternative, which they would have to accept or get out. They were squatters, after all, relying upon big brother across the ocean to support their illegal occupation.

Half the total land area was owned by the Falkland Islands Company, and much of the remainder by a handful of other large landholders. The average islander was tied body and soul to his master, living in houses that belonged to the Falkland Islands Company, receiving his wages from it and shopping in its store. The Shackleton Report, with which Vila and Corino and all other senior officers in General Pastran's department were conversant, had written, in a damning indictment, that while the islanders were mostly honest and physically robust, they were unenterprising and apathetic, accepting that the Falkland Islands Company ruled their lives. Thus the Company was the equivalent of the vocal Unionist minority in Northern Ireland, and via its Westminster lobby had made the matter of British sovereignty indistinguishable from British honour and duty.

Of course (said Vila) Whitehall did not always support minorities, not if it became inconvenient. Look at Rhodesia. Look at South Africa. Perfidious Albion indeed.

Neither did it take a geopolitical genius to work out that international boundaries were drawn up by those who had might on their side. The two Germanies represented a perfect example. One nation with a common language separated by barbed-wire and armed troops because that's how the Soviet Union wanted it.

Argie. Argie.

Across the way a man hawked noisily and spat.

Ricardo was not surprised to find that the taunting irritated him, but was somewhat alarmed to experience an uncharacteristic if human emotion. He began to dislike his tormentors, even the youngest of them.

Then the soldier in him took over. Tomorrow, wait until tomorrow.

They were staying at the Upland Goose Hotel in Stanley, the 'gasworkers', where they were clearly unpopular and had been since they arrived. Several British journalists were also in residence, but on Major Vila's instructions Ricardo and the remainder of the party avoided them as much as possible. Ricardo in particular found this difficult since one of the newspapermen had heard him speak fluent English and had learned, or intuitively divined, that he had been educated in England. The journalist manifestly thought it odd that someone with that background should be doing little more than manual work. Equally dangerous, news had recently filtered through that Argentine forces had landed and occupied South Georgia on March 26. All the journalists tried to bring this up in conversation, which was when Vila told Ricardo to take a stroll and how he found himself in the middle of Stanley on the receiving end of the islanders' abuse.

But gradually it grew dark and the streets emptied. Even so, Ricardo did not return to the Upland Goose. Vila had informed him before his departure that it was highly likely, when it became known in London that the invasion fleet had sailed, and once London, in turn, relayed that intelligence to Government House, that he, Vila, Corino and the other Argentinians would be arrested. That was unimportant; they would be free tomorrow. They had done their job. There had been no stiffening of the garrison in the past forty-eight hours and there could be none now. Buenos Aires had been given that information, together with the numbers, composition and broad disposition of the enemy troops. However, there was no need for Ricardo to spend an uncomfortable night under guard. In fact, it could be dangerous. That he was the only member of the party to speak fluent English would be known to the garrison commander by now, and it might go hard with him if captured. With their peculiar concept of right and wrong, the British troops would be tougher on someone educated in England than anyone else. He should stay away from the hotel. He should also be very careful not to put his life at risk. The Royal Marines were jumpy and likely to shoot at anything that moved. So too would elements of the *Buzo Tactico* who would be landing several hours ahead of the main force.

Where, Ricardo had wanted to know?

Vila would not tell him, for security reasons. He did, however, advise Ricardo to keep well away from the vicinity of Mullett Creek, three miles south of Stanley, and Moody Brook barracks, at the western extremity of Stanley Harbour, from 4 a.m. onwards. If he wanted to see the fun and the magnificent sight of the fleet entering the harbour at day-break, he should make his way to Wireless Ridge above Moody Brook under cover of darkness, and there sit tight.

Ricardo had objected to filling such a passive role in the invasion. For that matter, little use had been made of him since they arrived. His brief from General Pastran had been to establish friendly contacts with the Stanley inhabitants and keep an eye (and an ear) open for signs that the garrison knew an invasion fleet was due long before it sailed. He had failed the first and seen nothing worth reporting of the second.

Vila had nodded sympathetically.

'In undertakings such as this we have to be prepared for every eventuality. You didn't see any changes in the garrison's attitude or composition because there weren't any—for which we should thank God—and it's hardly your fault that the indigenous peasants treat us like lepers. As for taking a more active role, what would you use for a weapon? And how do you think Corino and I are going to feel being under lock and key when the fleet sails in? You'll see it and be able to tell your grandchildren about it. We won't.'

In Buenos Aires Ricardo had daily studied maps and sand models of the Malvinas, particularly the area around Stanley. He knew the ground like the back of his hand. But there were patrols out, motorized and on foot, and it took time to reach Wireless Ridge, on the other side of the harbour from Stanley. To get there he had to skirt Moody Brook barracks. In doing so he got the impression (which was accurate, as it transpired) that the position had been abandoned. He wondered briefly if there was any means of getting this information to the *Buzo Tactico* commandos. He concluded there wasn't, short of setting the barracks on fire, which could be misinterpreted and confuse the assault troops.

By midnight he was in position, overlooking the harbour and Stanley in the distance. Everything seemed quiet enough but he knew that that was an illusion. Once in a while he saw headlights on the road that led from the airport to the capital.

He munched a bar of chocolate. In his anxiety to quit the Upland Goose, that was all he had brought with him by way of food. For more than one reason he hoped the landings were on time and went well. Unless it was all over in a few hours from daybreak, he was likely to become very hungry.

It was a beautiful, starlit night, milder than anyone had a right to expect at this time of the year. In the Malvinas, the beginning of April usually heralded winter.

Although on the climb up to Wireless Ridge he had resolved to remain awake all night, he reasoned that nothing was going to happen for a few hours. Accordingly he set the alarm on his watch for 5 a.m., found a shallow hole on the leeward side of the ridge, and curled up in a ball with the watch under his ear. That done, he closed his eyes and had no trouble dozing off.

When he awoke it was not because of the alarm. Something had disturbed him, some sound. He shrugged off his hood and cocked his head. Maybe it was his imagination but he thought he could hear helicopter blades. Impossible, of course. In a straight line he was five or six miles from Mullett Creek, with the harbour and Sapper Hill between him and it. Still, whatever had broken his sleep had come from due south of where he lay.

Or rather, now stood, because his body temperature as well as the air temperature had dropped since midnight. He held his watch close and squinted at the luminous dial. 4.35.

Nothing else happened for another hour and a half. Then, at ten minutes past six, a series of almighty explosions and blinding flashes took place several hundred feet below his position, in Moody Brook barracks. Phosphorous and fragmentation grenades were followed instantly by long bursts from automatic weapons. There was, of course, no answering fire.

While Ricardo had to admire the skill and stealth of the *Buzo Tactico* commandos—for he had neither seen nor heard their approach—he was puzzled by the sudden pyrotechnics. To the best of his knowledge a court martial awaited anyone who killed a civilian, and the Argentine special forces could not possibly have known that there were no islanders holed up in the barracks. Then again, civilians shouldn't be there and the *Buzo Tactico* were a law unto themselves.

The attack went on for some minutes, until gradually fewer grenades were thrown and the automatic fire dwindled to a trickle as the commandos realized the barracks were empty. But the commotion would have been heard and witnessed miles away, and even as he watched Ricardo saw headlights on the road from the airport, the vehicles heading back towards Stanley now the garrison understood it was being outflanked. A little later, as the Moody Brook force moved off down the ridge, across the harbour came the distant sound of more automatic fire from the vicinity of Government House. The second arm of the *Buzo Tactico* force was attacking.

Ricardo debated revealing his presence to the Moody Brook echelon but decided against it. To attract their attention he would have to stand up and yell. Although he had a small Argentine flag in his pocket, he would hardly expect them to see it in the dark. Nor would their battle plan include a fellow countryman being on the ridge above them, and they were likely to shoot first and ask questions afterwards. He was determined to get in on the action rather than skulk in the hills until it was all over, but on balance it would be wiser to wait until daybreak.

Shortly before then, and with tracer partly illuminating the terrain around Sapper Hill, he dimly perceived east of the airport the massive bulk of the navy's flagship, the *Veinticinco de Mayo,* edging its way up the narrows towards the harbour, accompanied by landing craft and escorted by destroyers. Helicopter gunships flew from the carrier's decks in endless procession, silhouetted against the reddening sky, occasionally spitting fire at possible defensive positions but mainly depositing troops on the airfield, where they were to be picked up by Amtracs put ashore from the landing craft.

A little later Ricardo was scrambling down the ridge in the direction of the road that led to Stanley, taking advantage of what cover there was because there were now fighters in the air, fighters that would be looking hungrily for victims. The air force had been compelled to take a back seat in the invasion and would not be happy at the glory going to the army and the navy.

West of Sapper Hill, about a mile from Government House, he met an armoured personnel carrier coming the other way. Aboard were a dozen infantrymen. Fully aware that the Amtrac's 30mm cannon, let alone the combined firepower of twelve rifles, could vapourize him in an instant, he stood stock still and frantically waved the flag above his head. It was now broad daylight and the colours were unmistakable.

The infantrymen's senior rank was only a sergeant, he was glad to see, but a suspicious sergeant, one reluctant to accept that the unshaven and weaponless individual in front of him was a captain in the Argentine army until Ricardo cursed him and threatened him in such a manner that the NCO gave way. Even then, however, he was unwilling at first to turn the Amtrac round and return to Stanley. The sergeant's assignment was to probe the road as far as Moody Brook. The fighting in Stanley was now at an end, but there were still several members of the garrison unaccounted for. They could have taken to the hills west of the capital.

'They haven't,' said Ricardo bluntly.

After a few minutes' argument, he managed to persuade the NCO to head back for Stanley.

When they reached Government House, it was all over. A score or more Royal Marines were lying face down by the roadside, being photographed. An unnecessary and provocative humiliation, thought Ricardo.

He sought out Vila and Corino, finding the former standing beneath a flagpole from which flew an enormous Argentine flag. Vila was drinking brandy straight from the bottle. When he saw Ricardo his face split into a huge grin. It was the first time Ricardo had seen him express any emotion other than worry.

'We did it,' he whooped, handing Ricardo the brandy bottle. 'And with minimum casualties.'

Ricardo wiped the neck of the bottle and drank deeply.

'Did you see any action?' Vila wanted to know.

Ricardo explained that he'd seen some but he had not been a participant. Vila took a rifle from a nearby soldier and gave it to Ricardo.

'Then fire that. In the air. Another thing you want to be able to tell your grandchildren is that you sniffed powder on the great day.'

Ricardo gestured towards the prone marines.

'What's that for?'

'For? It's for the newspapers at home and throughout the world. To show everyone that the Malvinas now belong to Argentina.'

Ricardo tossed the rifle back to the soldier who owned it.

'You don't want to shoot? It'll be your last chance.'

'I somehow doubt that.'

From an artillery colonel Ricardo established the order of battle. Beto's regiment was among it.

'They're somewhere between here and the airport the last I saw.'

Ricardo set off to find his brother. Until he had seen the humbled Royal Marines he had been quite willing to accept that the British government would recognize a fait accompli and leave the rest to the diplomats. Now he wasn't so sure. When the photographs were printed in English newspapers and shown on television, there would be an almighty roar of defiance. The British public would bay for blood. He would, he was certain, get his chance to 'sniff powder' before long.

PART TWO

One day, you're a hero, the next you're a
bum, so what the hell.

—Babe Ruth

FOURTEEN

3 Platoon

THOSE MEMBERS OF THE BATTALION who were on leave were recalled by telegram and by notices displayed in all mainline railway stations. By the time the last were in barracks, everyone had seen the shocking pictures of the Royal Marines garrison face down in Stanley and heard via the BBC of the jubilation in Buenos Aires. Equally, everyone agreed that the Argentines—or the Argies or bean-eaters or spics as they were now being called in new additions to the armed services' lexicon—had overstepped the mark and that something would have to be done about them. The question was, what? And the second question was: where, precisely, were the Falklands?

Both were answered within a few hours. By nightfall even the dimmest private in the battalion (who was generally reckoned to be a cook in HQ Company) knew more about the longitude and latitude of the islands than he did about his neighbours ten doors away at home. And the 'what' was resolved when Daddy Rankin returned from a top-level meeting to announce to his company commanders that a task force was being made ready and that the battalion would form part of it, sailing as soon as possible. Of course, it was highly unlikely that they would be called upon to fight. A straw poll conducted among other battalion commanding officers considered in a ratio of eighty-five to fifteen that the task force was being assembled to give a cutting edge to diplomatic activity.

A comparison with the Japanese attack on Pearl Harbor became the common currency of conversations, and television 'talking heads', some of whom making well-argued cases for Argentina's claim to the Falklands, were howled down by everyone in uniform and most civilians. What were they trying to do, these intellectuals, spoil a good scrap? The Argies had transgressed, hadn't they? They were marching up and down the Plaza de Mayo shouting that they'd beaten the British, weren't they? Some victory, with odds of about a hundred to one in their favour. Well, like a gang of bullies in a school playground who beat up smaller kids in ones and twos, they'd find out the true score when the kids' big brothers turned up. The return match would be different. The bean-eaters wouldn't know what hit them.

Right.

Galtieri wasn't much of a leader. Did you hear he had a burglary the other day? His library was broken into and most of his books stolen, some of which he had only half finished colouring.

The emphasis within the battalion was now on motion. Get packed and be prepared to move out at a moment's notice. The troops were advised not to take unnecessary items. They weren't going on a luxury cruise though some of them might be travelling by liner. It depended. However they went, space would be at a premium. Take only essentials.

To Rupert this meant his 12-bore, a dozen boxes of cartridges and a shooting-stick. To Daddy Rankin his golf clubs. 'I understand they don't have a golf course in Stanley, but at least I can practise getting out of the rough in the hills.' To Winter's Day an umbrella. 'I checked with the Met. Office re the climate. It can be absolutely appalling down there at this time of year, old boy, absolutely appalling.'

To Three-piece Sweet essential packing meant a dozen foil-wrapped condoms. Making an inspection, Scarlett O'Hara caught him putting them in his kitag.

'Where the hell do you think you're going, Sweet?'

'South Atlantic, Sarn't.'

'You're sure you're not confusing it with the South Pacific—sunlit beaches, coconuts and dusky maidens?'

'No, Sarn't.'

'So why are you packing the johnnies?'

Three-piece was genuinely puzzled. Then he remembered

that Scarlett was married and didn't have to worry about such items any longer.

'Well, for me, Sarge, they're prophylactic as opposed to contraceptive devices, but . . .'

Scarlett cut him short with a snarl.

'I know what the buggers are for, you goon. I'm just curious to know what you plan to do with them when you meet a fierce Argie waving a bayonet in your face. Screw him to death?'

Three-piece beamed innocently.

'Don't they have girls in the Falklands?'

Scarlett gave up.

'Okay, Sweet, okay.'

Through no fault of his own, Scarlett caused the first hiccup in the battalion's preparations.

He was now the father of a three-week-old girl. When it became known that the battalion was to form part of the task force, his wife had kicked up hell. He could not go with them and that was all there was to it. He must see his company commander or the battalion welfare officer and explain that he now had responsibilities. Had he never heard of post-natal depression? Didn't he realize that new mothers needed their husbands beside them to shoulder some of the burden? He must tell Winter's Day that his wife and daughter were more important than a silly game of Cowboys and Indians at the other end of the world.

Scarlett dug in his heels and refused, but behind his back Eileen O'Hara telephoned the camp and pleaded her case with such conviction that Winter's Day called Scarlett into the company office.

'You don't have to go, you know. There are regulations covering this sort of thing. We'll be leaving behind a rear party of which you can certainly be one.'

'Useless mouths, sir.'

'I beg your pardon.'

'Useless mouths,' repeated Scarlett. 'Clerks and skivers and people on light duties and a few mess servants.'

'Possibly. But we can't leave the camp open to every Tom, Dick or Harry who might find it a useful squat. We'd be overrun by gypsies or hippies by the time we got back. The IRA might also consider it an opportune moment to make a nuisance of themselves. Not entirely useless mouths, Sergeant O'Hara.'

Winter's Day examined his finger-nails. He would have been better off leaving the details to Peter Ballantine. Interviews in this vein always made him feel inadequate. It was hard to know whether a man requesting a release from active service had a genuine reason or was simply a coward. O'Hara had always seemed a reliable type in the past, but one never knew.

'And don't think we don't understand, or sympathize. An NCO who has recently become a father—I can well accept that he doesn't want to be eight thousand miles away from his—ah—baby.'

'But I do want to be, sir.'

'I'm sorry?' Really, thought Winter's Day, this was a very confusing conversation. Couldn't the bloody man make up his mind whether to stay or go?

'I want to sail with the battalion,' said Scarlett. 'It's my wife who doesn't want me to go.'

'Ah, I see. The missus being a little difficult, yes?'

'Yes, sir.'

'Demanding hubby dance attendance on her?'

'Yes, sir.'

Winter's Day mulled over the problem. For all concerned it would be a damned sight easier if O'Hara sailed with the battalion. No paperwork, and no awkward confrontation with Daddy, which would reflect badly on his command of the company. Nor anyone else trying the same tactic. 'Look, sir, if Sergeant O'Hara can stay behind because his wife's just had a nipper, I think I have a good case.' It made one shudder to even contemplate it. On the other hand . . .

'Naturally I can't force you to join the rear party, though I would ask you to consider earnestly the consequences of going. And the trouble you might land yourself in with Mrs O'Hara when she realizes her wishes have been thwarted. A formidable woman, Mrs O'Hara. Bent my ear a bit, I can tell you.'

'We're confined to camp until we embus for the ship, aren't we, sir?' asked Scarlett.

'In the main, yes. There are exceptions, of course.'

'And the rear party is confined too, isn't it, sir?'

'Yes.'

Scarlett played his trump card.

'Then my wife doesn't have to know I've gone until we've embarked, does she, sir?'

'I take your point. Yes, I do indeed take your point. Consider yourself most especially confined to camp, Sergeant.'

'Thank you, sir.'

After Scarlett had gone, Winter's Day could not decide whether 3 Platoon's sergeant was an extraordinarily brave man for being willing to face his wife's fury when he returned, or most unheroic for not telling her exactly where she stood straight away. However, it was one personnel problem solved, and the next, which he could hear Peter Ballantine and Rupert Parker-Smith discussing in the general office, was one that could be sorted out at platoon level.

Private Davey Binns, Acne Hackney, was the mainspring of the second hiccup.

Davey's unfortunate skin eruption showed no signs of clearing up. If anything, it had worsened since the battalion got back from manoeuvres, and he was either regularly having treatment from the MO or appearing on parade with a two-day growth of beard. Rupert had shelved making a decision for as long as he could, but finally, two days before the Falklands' crisis broke, he had a quiet word with the MO. The battalion was due in Germany in four weeks. There was no point in taking Binns if he had to be repatriated before the tour was over.

It was just one of those things, said the physician. It could clear up of its own volition in six months or a year, or—curiously thought Rupert—if Binns engaged in an active sex life. ('You're not suggesting the army procures for him, I trust.') Alternatively, it could be something Binns would have to live with for the rest of his days. Sorry and all that, but there it was.

Rupert knew what he had to do without consulting Peter or Winter's Day. Davey Binns would have to be given a one-way ticket to Civvy Street. Rupert passed on the bad news as gently as he knew how.

For a second he thought Binns was going to cry, but the moment passed without tears.

'How long will it take, sir?'

'A week, perhaps a little longer.'

'But I'll have to leave the platoon?'

Davey had seen it happen before, to others who were being invalided out for one reason or another. They became non-persons, the army reasoning that there was little point in continuing to train a soldier who would soon be a civilian.

'Yes. You'll be seconded to HQ Company. What will you do on the outside?'

'Dunno, sir.'

'What did you do before you joined up?'

'Warehouseman, sir. Before that I worked in a hotel as a room-service waiter.' Davey touched his face and managed a rueful grin. 'Then this bugger happened so they sacked me. Can't have blokes with spotty faces delivering the bacon and eggs. Puts the guests off.'

Rupert felt desperately sorry, and said so.

'That's all right, sir. Not your fault. I've been half expecting it for months anyway. No chance of a reprieve, I suppose?'

'None, I'm afraid.'

But the junta's invasion of the Falklands threw Davey Binns a lifeline. As soon as he heard that the battalion was to form part of the task force, he went to find Rupert. And pleaded with him to be allowed to go.

'There won't be any parades down there, sir. I'll bet even the officers won't be shaving half the time. It'll be my last chance. When we get home I know I'll be slung out, but that could be weeks or months away. What'll I say to people in London? They know I'm in the army. They won't believe I've been given my ticket because of a few lousy spots. They'll think I chickened out.'

Rupert had already initiated the paperwork. For all he knew it had left battalion. The army didn't believe in hanging around when it came down to saving a week's pay. But he promised Davey he would do his best, which was what he and Peter were discussing in the general office, the company clerk having been ordered to go and get a cup of tea.

'Give him a break, Peter, for God's sake. This is the rest of his life we're talking about. I know you've got a lot on your mind . . .'

'Such as what?' demanded Peter, sharply.

'Such as making sure the company doesn't leave anything behind,' said Rupert, improvising hastily.

Following the invasion everyone who had met Ricardo in the mess before Christmas and who knew him to be a boyhood friend of Peter had carefully avoided the subject in Peter's presence. Ricardo was a soldier and could be on the Falklands. Peter was going to the Falklands to help recapture them. The implications were uncomfortable, and the whole business further complicated because Peter had made no secret of the fact that his sister and Ricardo were getting married. Or had been getting married. The Lord only knew what their arrangements were now.

'As company 2 i/c you can pick up the telephone and ask battalion HQ whether they've processed the discharge. I can't. You know how bloody-minded the senior clerk NCOs can be with mere subalterns. If you don't, you can forget about shooting weekends this autumn. I'll also let Lavinia know that you've got a string of local girls on the side.'

Since the accidental meeting in the pub in February, Rupert was aware that Lavinia and Peter had been seeing one another regularly, though the precise nature of their relationship he did not know. Nor was he disposed to enquire. He and Peter had a tacit agreement. He wouldn't question Peter about Lavinia providing Peter kept off the subject of Julia Lomax. For the most part the arrangement worked. When it didn't, when Peter adopted what Rupert termed his 'avuncular attitude', Rupert knew that Lavinia had been stirring matters up.

'You can't blackmail superior officers,' said Peter. 'It's against Queen's Regs. Besides, I'm not sure we'd be doing Binns a favour.'

'I'm sure,' persisted Rupert. 'Long sea voyage and all that. Just the ticket for spots. I remember my mother and father taking one once. To Cape Town, I believe it was. They came back right as rain.'

'What was the matter with them before they went?'

'Nothing.'

'Christ,' said Peter. 'You're hopeless.'

'It's the family motto. *Spes protracta aegrum efficit animum.* Hope deferred maketh the heart sick,' Rupert translated.

'You're lame-ducking him.'

'So what. He's my duck.'

Peter sighed wearily.

'Leave it with me. But, if it's gone beyond battalion, you've had it. From brigade upwards they'll be knee-deep in bumf.'

'I'll wait outside.'

Within half an hour Rupert was able to tell an anxious Acne Hackney that he would be travelling with battalion, the discharge papers having travelled no further than a foot-high pile awaiting Daddy Rankin's signature. They would be returned to D Company marked 'no action'.

'Okay, Binns, you're in.'

'You won't regret it, sir.'

'Make sure I don't. Move your kit back from HQ Company and let Sergeant O'Hara or Corporal Tyler know the form.'

Among other items being packed were several bottles of whisky apiece for Groggy Butler and Legless Jones. A rumour (false, as it turned out) had flashed round the camp with the speed of a jungle drum that some ships in the task force would not have canteens serving alcohol due to shortage of space. Panic abounded among the battalion's heavy boozers, the uncrowned kings of whom being Groggy, Legless and a C Company sergeant called Dippy Hendricks.

Together Groggy and Legless borrowed an atlas and a pocket calculator and measured the distance between the UK and the Falklands. As the proverbial crow flew it was something like eight thousand miles, and the average speed of the task force was generally guessed to be somewhere between twelve and fifteen knots. Thus travelling in a straight line the voyage would take anything from three to four weeks. But that didn't include refuelling stops and revictualling stops. It also assumed that the task force would sail directly into Port Stanley like a cross-Channel steamer, without a pause for sea-landing exercises and without taking into consideration that the bean-eaters might not want to move out. To be on the safe side two or three further weeks should be added, giving a grand total from landfall to landfall (or from bar to bar, as Groggy preferred it) of between five and seven weeks. Knowing the army, take the higher figure.

With their arithmetic completed, Groggy and Legless stared at each other in dismay. In a reasonable week—one that did not contain birthdays, high days, holidays or a win on the horses—they would reckon to get through three bottles of whisky each. Seven threes made twenty-one. Twice twenty-one came to forty-two. They would need a ship to themselves or at the very least a cabin trunk to see them through. Not even if they chucked out every piece of equipment that the army could reasonably expect them to take on active service—minor items such as spare clothing and weapons—could they hope to pack twenty-odd bottles of whisky apiece. The maximum was three, and thirty further seconds with the pocket calculator revealed the disturbing truth that three bottles allowed them less than a double snort per day.

Bollocks to that Galtieri and his pantomime army. War might be war but this was ridiculous.

Two very depressed soldiers reopened the atlas and attempted to figure out if they had made a mistake.

Watching their antics from the neighbourhood of his own bunk, upon which his kit was arranged with a tidiness and sense of order that would have sent the RSM into paroxysms of delight, Non-Legless Jones wondered if they would be so concerned about the amount of alcohol in their bags when it came to the fighting. He himself had no doubt that blood would flow before the dispute was resolved. Curiously—at least it would be curious to the others in 3 Platoon if they could have read his mind—the taking of life did not disturb him. Nor did putting his own life at risk. Providence guided his actions and had done every day of his life since he was a child and first saw the light.

He knew that Butler and Sammy Finch and Twiggy and the rest thought him odd. That didn't disturb him either. While he would never have gone so far as to state openly that he had a Christian mission on this earth—unless it was to live up to his beliefs regardless of the difficulties—he accepted that the Lord giveth and the Lord taketh away. The Lord had directed him into the army, he was fully convinced. Otherwise he would never have taken that day trip into Swansea those two years ago, when he could ill-afford the bus fare from his village. Nor would the Lord have sent a thunderstorm, preceded by darkening skies and a flash of sheet lightning, at the exact moment he was standing outside the recruiting office.

He had turned, to seek shelter in the doorway, and had then seen the recruiting poster. The NCO in the picture looked not unlike his conception of the Lord—bold, enthusiastic, a man with a purpose.

He made enquiries inside. The recruiting sergeant was delighted to see him—and see *him* personally, not just anyone who walked off the streets.

He had taken the literature home, studying it avidly on the return bus journey. By the time he pushed open the door of his parents' council house he had made up his mind. He was going to be a soldier. That he was unemployed and that there was no hope of a job, now that the coal mining was almost exhausted in his village, had nothing to do with it.

Neither parent had objected to his decision. A wiser child, irrespective of whether brought up in a household where chapel-going was mandatory, might have deduced that with a father on short-time working and in ill-health anyway, a

mother who subsidized the family budget with a few hours'
cleaning a week, and three mouths younger than Non-Legless
to feed, there was an ulterior motive in his parents' support.
Not Jones. Their approval only went to show that he was
doing God's work.

Surveying his kit prior to packing it, Non-Legless made sure
that his bible and hymnbook were included. There was comfort in both. There could be no comfort in a bottle.

The bible had a marker in it: Revelations, Chapter 9, Verse
2. 'And he opened the bottomless pit, and there arose smoke
out of the pit, as the smoke of a great furnace; and the sun
and the air were darkened by reason of the smoke of the pit.'

A trained psychoanalyst, if invited to hazard an opinion,
might have concluded that Jones (given name Timothy; not
very Welsh but apposite by being the eponymous recipient of
letters written by a man who had also seen the light, St Paul)
was not quite right in the head. Then again, in the army—in
any army—there were always a few like that. Some would
argue more than a few, men with room-temperature IQs.
Equally they would argue that the armies of any nation are
made up of misfits, and that the more dangerous the branch of
service, the greater the loony. Thus the commandos, the
paratroopers, and the specialist outfits should hardly have
enough sense to cross the road unaided. For reasons of self-
preservation, however, those who hold such views in the
groves of academe generally keep them to themselves.

As the time came for the mid-evening news, men left
whatever they were doing and gathered round the camp's
various television sets. The lead story was all about Them—
the army, the task force. It made them feel kind of famous,
like film stars. Pity they couldn't get into town, into the pubs.
It would be drinks all round on the civvies, they were sure of
it. Give 'em hell, boys. Show the blighters who's boss. It's a
long way to Tipperary. Rule Britannia, lads, and Land of
Hope and Glory.

This was the last Night of the Proms for real.

The mood was light-hearted. The bean-eaters were going to
get it in spades, was Yank Hobart's opinion.

'It'll be no contest. We'll burn a few of the bastards and
the rest'll head for the high sierras. Right on.'

For once no one groaned and told Yank to cut out his John
Wayne act. The Argies weren't going to know what fuckin'
hit them. Splat.

Maggie Thatcher was the hero of the hour. Yeah, a hero, not a heroine. If the fact that it was a woman who was leading the charge disturbed the many male chauvinists in the battalion, they didn't let it show. Maggie was okay, not like some of the drips around her who were preaching caution. The hell with caution. Maggie was great.

'A-okay,' roared Yank.

'Can it really be possible in this day and age,' asked one left-wing talking head, 'that the young men of one country are on a collision course with the young men of another country as a political face-saving exercise?'

Abuse was hurled at his unhearing ears. Up yours, you great fairy. Damn right it was possible.

Rule Britt Ekland, Britt Ekland rules the waves . . .

One of the few who would have described the prime minister in different terms from the ubiquitous eulogies was Branston Pickles, now back with the platoon after serving his twenty-eight days. He had done two tours with the battalion in Northern Ireland, the first a bloody sight rougher than the second, the one most of these 'kids' had been on. Branston had been sniped at, mortared, bombed and petrol-bombed more times than he cared to recall. Although one of those who could safely be put in the room-temperature IQ bracket, being under fire had scared him stiff. He was okay with a knife in his hand or a broken bottle in a pub fight where, because of his upbringing in Glasgow's darkest streets, he felt secure in the knowledge that the odds were broadly in his favour. A bullet or shell were different matters. They said you never heard the one with your number on it, which was a big friggin' help. Branston liked his opponents where he could see them.

When the formation of the task force was announced, he'd considered going over the wall again, putting many a mile between him and anything that looked remotely like an armada. But he knew he'd get short shrift when he was caught, as he must inevitably be sooner or later if he didn't want to hide out for the remainder of his life. His wife, the stinking whore, would shop him as soon as look at him. And his father would, as usual, cadge every penny he had. Going AWOL on manoeuvres was one thing; pissing off in the present circumstances was another. They'd toss him in a cell and throw away the key.

No, what he'd do was see it through and keep his head

down. Let the other silly bastards win the medals. Rule Britannia my arse. Britannia had never done anything for him.

Another who was having more than a few thoughts about sailing with the task force was Jomo Mason. He could still hear his mates in Birmingham when the telegram arrived recalling him from leave. 'You gonna fight Whitey's wars for him, Henry?' He supposed he was. He also supposed that he shouldn't want to, yet for the life of him he couldn't see why. This was his country. He had been born here and brought up here. His mates—dumb niggers—couldn't see that. But what did they want? A black England? A black socialist England? Dumb. They were racists in reverse, lounging around street corners, talking sharp, eating soul food, wearing woolly hats and pretending they were in Harlem, New York City. Acting like they were all Richard Priors or Muhammed Ali. And that with Birmingham accents you could cut with a fork.

They were shit. They were black shit, but shit didn't discriminate. They'd failed and they'd continue to fail because they blamed everything on being born black or half black or an eighth black. Cobblers. Being black or white had nothing to do with it. You either made it or you didn't. Your colour didn't matter. There were a lot of white guys on the outside he wouldn't be seen dead talking to. Garbage. The funny thing was, the 'brothers' in the woolly hats and the beads and the ringlets took the piss out of the white punk rockers in much the same way as the punks took the piss out of the blacks. Neither group seemed to know the pride of being smart, of keeping your kit, and yourself, clean. Of holding your head up.

3 Platoon knew. 3 Platoon also knew that one day Jomo Mason would be a corporal. A few years from then he'd be sergeant. Maybe he'd be the battalion's first black RSM. Christ, that would be something for the kids. And when he *had* kids, he'd make sure they didn't grow up with their heads full of rubbish such as black being beautiful. Of course some blacks were beautiful. Some others looked like they'd failed the audition for *The Thing from Outer Space*.

Cyril 'Prawn Balls' Ball slapped a can of lager in front of Jomo.

'What's this?'

'Sheep dip. What does it look like?'

'I mean what's the occasion?'

'The old girl's insurance money came through. I'm buying for the platoon. Eight hundred lovely jimmy o'goblins after funeral expenses, and all for yours truly.'

'Doesn't your dad get any?'

'He would if he knew she was dead, but as he did a runner about fifteen years ago, Jomo, my old mate, I don't suppose he does. By the time he finds out—if he ever does and if he's not dead himself—and starts sniffing around, I'll have spent the friggin' lot.'

'You should invest it,' advised Jomo.

'Not a chance. Once I've had a bit of fun there won't be enough left to invest. Mind you, if it had been eight thousand instead of eight hundred, I'd put most of that in the bank. But eight hundred . . .'

Prawn Balls was a bit drunk. In fact, Prawn Balls was three sheets to the wind.

'Not much, is it, eight hundred quid—for slaving and worrying and being kicked in the teeth for sixty-odd years? I can remember days as a kid when there was nothing to eat in the house apart from a few slices of bread. She tried, my old mum did, but usually there was just too much week left at the end of the money. I'd like to bump into my dad again one of these days.' Prawn Balls' eyes were going slowly out of focus. 'You know what I'd say to him?' Jomo said he didn't. 'I'd ask him first why he ran out on us. Then I'd kick his head in.'

Prawn Balls slurped at his beer. Most of it went down his shirt front. He stared at the mess as though wondering where it came from.

'She died of malnutrition according to the quack. Malnutrition. She'd got out of the habit of eating over all those years. First there was never enough loot and then she couldn't be bothered. There were tins of stuff—hundreds of friggin' tins all over the house when I got home. She could've stood off a six-month siege. Anyway, so when she got ill she hadn't enough strength to fight it. Daft, eh, Jomo? In this day and age you've got people dying of malnutrition.'

Prawn Balls put his head on the table. He'd stopped counting how many lagers he'd had after the twelfth can.

'I'm a fuckin' orphan, you know that?' he mumbled and went to sleep.

Inevitably there were long queues for the camp's few pay

phones. Equally inevitably private conversations, wherein endearments could be expressed, were almost impossible unless the speaker had the thickest of skins. You couldn't tell your girl friend or wife or fiancée that you loved her and would be thinking of her constantly without inviting hoots of derision from all sides. Most of the battalion didn't try, although the number of times the expression 'of course I do' was used ran into dozens.

Sammy Finch and Twiggy were fifth and sixth in one queue. The guy currently on the phone had a stack of tenpence pieces in front of him and, by the sound of it, about a hundred and seventeen brothers, sisters, uncles and aunts to say farewell to.

Neither Sammy nor Twiggy had been on leave when the emergency broke and, separately and respectively, they had seen Libby Rees and Carol Bannister the previous evening. By now Libby and Carol, like the rest of the country, would know what was going on, and Carol for one would be panic-stricken. As of yesterday her monthly period was eight days overdue. Unless her lateness was the result of some biological malfunction that was beyond Twiggy, she was going to be very pregnant by the time he returned from the South Atlantic.

It just wasn't bloody fair. He'd made love to her once, just once, and here she was potentially in the club. To Twiggy's certain knowledge Sammy had been knocking seven bells out of Libby for weeks, with impunity.

To be fair, though, the whole episode had been unplanned. He and Carol had been out one evening, in a pub, and in had walked Roy, her ex-boy friend, the guy Twiggy had clipped on the jaw before Christmas. With him was one of his pals from the same original confrontation, Doug something or the other. They'd made no move in the pub but had stood at the bar, getting slowly tanked. Then, when Twiggy and Carol left, so did Roy and Doug.

In the street there was some pushing and shoving and name-calling before Roy threw the first punch—at the exact moment Yank Hobart, Three-piece and Jomo came round the corner. With that Doug took to his heels. Roy would have followed had Twiggy not backed him into a corner. He didn't want to fight, Twiggy, but there was no getting out of it in front of Yank and the others. Or in front of Carol. Besides, if he didn't teach Roy a lesson, this sort of thing could go on for ever. So he gave Roy one in the mouth and one in the stomach. Fearing the worst, that he was about to face odds of four to one, Roy went down in a heap and stayed there.

Yank yelled for the boot to go in, finish him off. Twiggy would have none of it. The point had been made.

Half an hour later he and Carol were making love on a bench behind the church. It wasn't anything to write home about, not in more than a paragraph, but Carol had let out a couple of squeals of pleasure. Afterwards she told him 'she wasn't taking anything'. She used to, she confessed, but she'd stopped. Twiggy didn't ask for details.

He hoped and prayed that it was all a false alarm. He liked Carol a lot. He would go as far as saying he was in love with her. But he still hadn't met her mother and father, and he dreaded doing so if the circumstances were that Carol was pregnant. ('How do you do. Pleased to meet you. Sorry I knocked up your daughter.') As for marriage, part of him wanted to settle down and part of him said that they were both far too young.

The queue moved up a place.

Sammy's unwitting joke about a new sort of Pill suddenly wasn't very funny. ('Try this one. It's a foot in diameter and has no side effects.' 'How on earth am I going to swallow that?' 'You don't swallow it. You hold it between your knees.')

A buzz swept down the queue. Everyone was to collect their kit and report to their company office. Transport would be arriving before midnight and they were to leave for Portsmouth as soon as loaded.

Sammy saw Two-Shit Tyler walking past—unsteadily, for Tyler had been celebrating, having heard that morning that he had passed his sergeant's exams and would be made up when the battalion returned. It was a pity it couldn't be before they sailed. He would have liked a platoon of his own.

'Do you know if we're moving out tonight, Corp?' called Sammy.

'Hum a few bars and I'll pick it up.'

Berk, thought Sammy. Moose breath. He smiled affably.

'Does that mean yes or no?'

'It means you'd better keep those calls short.'

An RP got the queue organized. Everyone was to be allowed tenpence worth of phone time whether the call was long-distance or local. When the pips sounded, that was it.

No feeding the slot. Groans of 'swindle' went up from those now near the head of the queue.

Sammy wondered what he could say to Libby in a few minutes. Not a lot, he decided, not with half a hundred guys ear-wigging.

As it happened, he did not have to make an immediate decision. Libby's line was engaged. Sammy handed the receiver to Twiggy and changed places with him.

Twiggy held his breath when the connection was made and he heard Carol's voice at the other end.

'It's me, Chris. We're probably leaving tonight. How is—ah—everything?'

'Wait a minute, I'll close the lounge door.' He heard her call, 'It's for me.' Then she came back to the phone. 'Nothing's happened yet.'

'Aw, Christ.'

'But don't worry. I've taken some stuff and it'll be all right.'

'What sort of stuff?'

'The name wouldn't mean anything to you. But I know someone who was in a similar predicament. It worked for her.'

'If it doesn't . . .'

'It will. How are things with you? I've been watching the television.'

'A madhouse. Look, are you sure about this stuff, because if you're not I'll be a long way . . .'

The pips went. Suddenly. One of those things that sometimes happened with pay phones. Twiggy cursed, and was fumbling in his pocket for a second coin when the RP stepped in front of him.

'That's it. No more.'

'But I didn't get my full time.'

'Sorry. That's nothing to do with me.'

Twiggy knew better than to argue. He held the receiver to his ear—the line was dead—before passing it to Sammy.

'Wait for me, Twiglet. I'll only be a minute.'

Sammy was actually two, much of them spent in protest.

Libby's mother answered the phone. She established who Sammy was in a couple of crisp sentences. And no, Libby would not be coming to speak to him. Nor would she be speaking to him or seeing him again. Sammy doubtless understood why.

Sammy did not doubtless understand why, but gradually he found out. Mrs Rees had taken the sheets from Libby's bed that morning, to launder them. The sheets were stained, and Sammy would know perfectly well with *what* they were stained. If he thought he could take advantage of a young girl while her parents were away, he had another think coming.

Sammy couldn't figure it. Normally Libby was careful to bring in a towel from the bathroom. She had done so on the last occasion to the best of his recollection. Of course, the bed usually ended up in a hell of a mess, so it was possible that the towel had not done the trick. But.

'Let me speak to her,' he said. 'I'm off to the Falklands tomorrow. Tonight, as a matter of fact. I might not come back,' he added theatrically.

'I hope you don't,' snapped Mrs Rees. 'I sincerely hope you rot out there. It would be no more than you deserve, you ignorant, *cockney* little man.'

Sammy lost his rag. The old crone was wishing him dead.

'That's a charming thing to say. That really makes you a queen in my book, you know that? And we'll have less of the "taking advantage of a young girl", if you don't mind. What do you think she is, a nun? She knew what it was for, when I was as stiff as a bat.'

Jesus, what the hell was he saying?

'So you got stains on your sheets, so what? I'd guess you don't wash them as often as you should. Anyway, you probably made the marks yourself, you and the old geezer. Sneaking into Libby's bunk for a quick one to keep your *own* sheets clean. No, I'm forgetting. That couldn't be, could it? Libby told me about you, that you've got the sex appeal of a frog. The old man's likely to get it every other Pancake Tuesday if he asks nicely. Lon Chaney's a *Playboy* centrefold compared to you. And another thing . . .'

Much of Sammy's monologue was spoken into a disconnected phone. Mrs Rees had hung up. The remainder of the queue were cheering. Grinning sheepishly, Sammy clasped his hands above his head like a victorious prizefighter.

'That was very bright, Sammy,' said Twiggy, forgetting his own troubles for a moment. 'You certainly hit it off, the pair of you. I wouldn't be surprised if she insisted on a short engagement, so that she can have your grandchildren quicker.'

'Fuck her,' said Sammy. 'Come on, let's go to the Falklands.'

For which 3 Platoon, D Company, the battalion and several other battalions sailed the following afternoon.

As the huge ship pulled away from the quay, Double-Eff found himself sandwiched between Rupert and Corporal Tyler. Two-Shit had scarcely left his platoon commander's side since the battalion came aboard. Now that he was a sergeant in all but name (he kept repeating), he hoped that Rupert would give him greater responsibility. If and when it came to a landing Rupert would be able to rely upon him absolutely. He'd show the Argies what for, just give him a chance.

Finally Rupert had to tell him to seek out Sergeant O'Hara and make sure that all was as it should be with the platoon.

'A case of success going not so much to the head as to the mouth,' said Rupert to Double-Eff. Or rather shouted, for the noise was deafening.

'I'm sorry?'

'Skip it.'

'Incredible, isn't it?' said Double-Eff, a second or two later.

Rupert had to admit that the scenes below the ship were indeed amazing. He had never expected to witness anything like them in his lifetime.

The dockside was thick with people. Thousands of them, possibly tens of thousands. Union flags abounded. So did gigantic handwritten signs. 'Good luck, Bill.' 'Give 'em hell, Gerry.' 'Don't drink the water, Pete.' Hundreds of red, white and blue streamers were being waved, hundreds of multi-coloured balloons released. Some of the younger girls had removed their sweaters; one or two bras somehow got hoisted aboard the ship.

Tugs and pleasure boats sounded their sirens. Songs were tried, from the quayside as well as the decks. Some died the death; some were taken up by acclamation. We are sailing . . . You'll never walk alone . . . Rule Britannia . . . And, naturally, Land of Hope and Glory.

It was all astonishingly moving if one could forget the object of the exercise.

'This day is called the feast of Crispian,' Double-Eff said, surprised to find tears in his eyes but in no way ashamed. His mother and father were down there somewhere, having travelled several hundred miles just to see the ship pull out.

Miraculously in view of the uproar, Rupert overheard the quotation from Henry V's oration to his troops before Agincourt.

'You're right,' he said to Double-Eff. 'Of course the next line goes: He that outlives this day and comes safe home . . .'

'That doesn't sound like you, Rupert,' said Peter Ballantine from behind him.

'No, it doesn't, does it? Except I can't help remembering those television pictures we saw of the crowds in Buenos Aires. Without the banners, I'd find it very hard to tell our lot from their lot.'

FIFTEEN

Mothers and Daughters (i)

NEWS THAT THE TASK FORCE was at sea was greeted in Buenos Aires with a mixture of contempt and alarm, the former emotion being predominant. War fever gripped the streets and was whipped up daily, almost hourly, by junta supporters and non-supporters alike. This was Argentina's finest hour since its football team's World Cup triumph in 1978, and the mob had taken over. If the country could retain the soccer trophy, shortly to be competed for again in Spain, as well as beating the arrogant British, Argentina would be truly on the map as a major power. Anyone who disagreed with that view (and there were some, who learned quickly to keep their opinions to themselves) was a traitor.

Like most of the mobs, the one Lucita-Arditti got caught up in was male-dominated. Men young and old demonstrated their machismo by chanting slogans and dancing up and down in a frenzy, though there were women present too, modern-day *tricoteuses* looking for the guillotine and screaming anti-British abuse for the benefit of the television cameras. Crude effigies of Margaret Thatcher were burned in the Plaza de Mayo, as were facsimiles of the Union flag.

Few of the tens of thousands who crowded the square from dawn to midnight believed that the British would invade the Malvinas. The amateur strategists pointed out the logistic difficulties of supplying a task force across such a vast distance. If they did invade, they would be repulsed. The British could not possibly muster more than two or three thousand troops; the Malvinas garrison was already that strong and would outnumber the 'worst case' British threat in a ratio of three or four to one within days. No, the task force was just a tub-thumping exercise on the part of Downing Street. There would be no blood spilt, US Secretary of State Haig would see to that. After all, wasn't Argentina one of the United States' best friends in South America? A compromise solution would be found, one giving Argentina justice. Those with long memories recalled Britain's last imperialistic adventure of any magnitude, the Suez débâcle of 1956, when the Americans rapped the British across the knuckles. It would be the same this time. Uncle Sam would tell John Bull to lay off, and the British fleet would turn for home, tail between its legs.

Lucita thought otherwise, but knew better than to say so. Not that anyone would have heard her had she chosen to voice her misgivings, and not only because of the noise. These people were crazy, in a world of their own, victims of mass hysteria.

In some respects she didn't blame them, though curiously she didn't feel part of them. For far too long now they'd had little to shout about. They had been promised elections that never materialized. They had seen the purchasing power of their savings and salaries diminish weekly. Some had had friends among the *desaparecidos*. Rival factions had almost succeeded in tearing the heart out of Argentina. But now there was unity, an indivisible purpose, an identifiable enemy.

Enemy?

In common with most Argentines—and certainly every member of the Jordan-Arditti family—Lucita firmly believed that the Malvinas belonged to her country as of right. But enemy? Sara Ballantine? Peter? Edward? Mrs Ballantine? That was absurd. And frightening. Did Sara now view her as an enemy? If it came to fighting—God forbid—would Peter see Ricardo as an enemy? And Beto, who was on the Malvinas but who scarcely knew, she was sure, one end of a rifle from the other?

Quite suddenly Lucita found herself crying. She couldn't understand it but neither could she stop. It was ridiculous. She just wasn't that sort of girl, to cry for no reason.

People around her asked what was the matter. She couldn't answer. All she could do was shake her head. How could she tell them when she didn't know herself?

Willing and kindly hands guided her and occasionally pushed her to the outskirts of the mob. Make way. There's a young girl here in tears. Look out there. Mind your backs. She's a cripple.

She wanted to scream. Damn them, she wasn't a cripple. She limped but she wasn't a cripple. But they meant well, she knew. They were only trying to help. She shouldn't have come. They were right, those who were saying she should be at home.

A hand gripped her elbow, propelling her gently out of harm's way. 'Would you like me to get you a taxi?'

She glanced up at her protector, a young man only a couple of years older than herself. His expression was anxious. She probably looked a fright with her reddened eyes, though the tears had stopped.

'No, it's all right.'

'It's no trouble. Look, let's cut across there. We'll find one easily by the Plaza Inter-Continental.'

'What about your friends?'

'Friends?'

'Whoever you were with—back there.'

'I was by myself. And it's time I was leaving anyway.' He smiled. 'Besides, I expect that'll be going on for some time, if I want to go back.'

Without making it obvious he slowed his pace to match hers, though he was considerably taller than she was and doubtless, normally, walked much faster. She judged him to be a student of some sort. At least, he wasn't dressed as if he worked for a living though his shirt, trousers and shoes were of good quality.

'I found it a bit scary myself,' he said, making conversation.

'Found what scary?'

'The crowds back there. It wouldn't take much to become a riot. In fact, I heard there was a riot outside the British Embassy earlier, but the police broke that up. Strange, isn't it? The police are part of the state and the state is at war, or as good as, with Britain. Yet the police as an arm of the state make sure that no Briton gets hurt or British property damaged. It doesn't really make much sense.'

'None of it makes any sense.'

Lucita had a handkerchief out and was doing her best to make her face presentable. She wasn't quite sure why this young man was still with her. They were away from the worst of the crowds now and she could see a taxi from here.

'You don't agree with the invasion?' he asked.

'Whose?'

'Ours.'

'I'm not sure. My two brothers are in the army and one of them, at least, would. The other probably wouldn't.'

'Are they regular soldiers?'

'The older one is.'

'And he'd agree?'

'I think he would. At least, he'd probably justify it as an illegal act in a just cause.'

'I've heard that expression before somewhere.'

'It's not original.'

'What did you mean by "whose" invasion?' asked the young man. 'There's only been one.'

'There'll be another when the British arrive.'

He looked at her curiously.

'You don't think there'll be a settlement?'

'No.'

'That puts you in a minority. Everyone else I've spoken to or listened to seems to think there will be.'

'I don't.'

'Do you know something the rest of us don't?'

'No. My elder brother's a captain, not a general.'

'Then how . . . ?'

She completed the question for him.

'How can someone of my age and a mere girl be so sure?'

He had the grace to admit that was what he had meant.

'Because I know the British. I don't know them as well as my elder brother does, but I know enough to recognize that they are not sending a task force merely as a show of strength.'

She remembered her father's words earlier in the day. 'It's worrying, Lucita. I don't want to say this to your mother in her present state of health, but more often than not business-men are more capable of reading between the lines than politicians. I have many contacts in London and the signals I'm receiving are not encouraging.'

'You've been to England?' asked the young man.

'Yes. The same brother was going to marry an English girl. Perhaps still is.'

'Why don't you call her up and ask her.'

He had intended the comment as a joke. Lucita took it seriously.

'I've thought of that,' she said. 'I'm sure Sara . . . the girl

. . . has thought of calling me also. I don't suppose either of us will before all such calls are forbidden by both sides.'

'Why not?'

'What could I say? What could she say to me? Her brother's in the British army. As a matter of fact, he and my brother went to school together. They're close friends. Yet they're going to kill one another.'

'You can't possibly know that.'

'Oh, I don't mean they'll meet face to face and have to do something idiotic for their respective countries. But, if it comes to war, my brother will be on one side and her brother will be on the other. One of them may make a decision that leads to the death or injury of the other.'

'You have a very gloomy outlook on life, don't you?'

'No, I have a very gloomy outlook on death. All those people in the square, leaping up and down, screaming, shouting slogans. No one's being hurt at the moment, but what will they do when the first bomb drops or the first ship is sunk or soldier killed?'

'Scream louder, I suppose. For revenge.'

'That's right.' It could escalate suddenly, her father had told her. At present there was a chance, a faint chance, of peace. But the first death would alter all that. There would be no going back. 'And they'll be doing just the same in London. Ten British will be killed so they'll demand ten—or twenty or thirty—Argentine lives. Then those idiots in the Casa Rosada will want a hundred British lives by way of compensation. And so it will go on. After the first deaths no one will remember that the argument was originally about who owns the Malvinas. It will just be a question of winning.'

The young man glanced about him nervously. It was unwise to call the chief occupant of the Casa Rosada, the President, an idiot. The sooner he put this young lady in a taxi, the happier he'd feel.

'So what you're saying is that we shouldn't have invaded at all.'

'What I'm saying is that a few thousand hectares of land aren't worth dying for.'

The young man hailed a taxi.

'Perhaps you're wrong. Perhaps it will all work out and there'll be no war. I've never been to England but my maternal great-grandmother was English. I presumably have some distant cousins over there. I hope I don't have to shoot at them or anyone close to them, or they at me.'

'I don't understand,' said Lucita.

'Of course you don't. I didn't explain. You see, I'm in the same position as your younger brother. I'm a conscript. They're building up the garrison on the Malvinas. I leave in a week.'

Lucita gave her address to the taxi driver.

'Perhaps you'll meet one of my brothers out there.'

She gave the young man the names and ranks of Beto and Ricardo, together with their regiments.

'Maybe I'll meet the younger one but, with the greatest respect, I'll steer clear of the captain.'

'Why?'

'To the regular army we conscripts are the lowest form of animal life. They don't like us and we don't like them. They treat us like dirt.'

'Not Ricardo,' said Lucita firmly.

'Of course not.'

Lucita asked for the young man's name, in order that she could tell Beto and Ricardo in a letter that they had met. The young man hesitated before propriety got the better of him. He told her he was called Ernesto Martinez.

'But I'd rather you didn't write to either of them about me. I want to do my service and get out, back to university. This country needs more architects. It doesn't need any more soldiers.'

He shook hands with her formally, and she thanked him for escorting her away from the mob. It wasn't until the taxi was out of sight that he realized she hadn't told him her baptismal name. Not that that mattered. He was hardly likely to see her again. She was pretty enough, more than pretty, but the address he had heard her give to the taxi driver was one where only the very rich lived. She was way out of his league, though he could understand, now, why she had been crying. At least he thought he could. Anyone who felt as melancholic as she did had a right to a few tears.

He'd bet his life she was wrong about a general war, however. Come to that, betting his life was exactly what he was doing.

When Lucita got home she threw some cold water over her face, applied a little eye make-up, and went directly up to her mother's bedroom, knocking softly before entering.

The curtains were drawn and Maria Jordan-Arditti lay apparently asleep. At least she was breathing evenly and didn't stir when the door opened.

Lucita tip-toed over to the bed and peered down at her mother, whose eyes were closed. Gently, Lucita rearranged the sheets around her mother's shoulders and quietly left the room. The hired nurse should have been in the guest-room across the passage, but wasn't. Lucita sought out her father, finding him behind his desk in his study, a dossier open in front of him, a weak glass of whisky and water by his right hand.

'Where's the nurse?' asked Lucita.

'I allowed her to go out while your mother's asleep. She'll be back later. Will you be staying in for the rest of the day?'

'Probably.'

'Because I have a meeting I can't avoid this evening, and the doctor will be calling in around eight. I know he'll tell the nurse whatever's necessary, but I'd like one of us to be here also.'

'Has something happened?' asked Lucita, alarmed.

The doctor didn't generally visit more than once or twice a week unless summoned. Apart from the pills, the physician's prescription was rest and more rest. With luck, Maria Jordan-Arditti would then recover, though she had to avoid undue excitement or stress since her heart was nowhere near as strong as it should be for a woman still only in her early fifties.

'Nothing,' answered Alfredo Jordan-Arditti, 'but she refused lunch, even soup. She doesn't do that often and she must eat or she won't get well. I'm hoping that the doctor can suggest something to improve her appetite.'

'She should be in a hospital or a nursing home. They'd be able to look after her properly there.'

'She won't go.' Lucita's father ran his fingers wearily through his greying hair. He'd aged visibly since Christmas, Lucita reflected. Before then he could have passed for Ricardo's elder brother. The thought of her parents getting older and one day dying frightened her. Until recently, she'd never viewed either of them as anything but immortal. 'She believes that if she goes in she'll never come out. It's absurd, but the doctor wants to keep her relaxed at all costs.' He shook his head and smiled grimly. 'Relaxed! With all this going on.' He gestured vaguely in the direction of the window and the outside world. 'And she was coming along fine, looking forward to the wedding. I think the knowledge that there won't be one now, or not in the immediate future, has worsened her condition. It's depression as much as anything.'

Lucita drew a chair up close to the desk. Without asking she took a sip of her father's whisky and water, swallowed, and pulled a face.

'How on earth can anyone drink that stuff for pleasure?'

Her father smiled indulgently. Although he rarely admitted it even to himself, of the three children Lucita was his favourite. And not just because she was a girl or because of her physical handicap. In some ways she was more like him than either of the boys.

'Where have you been?' he asked.

Lucita told him, leaving out her tears, of which she was now thoroughly ashamed, and meeting Ernesto Martinez.

'They're going crazy down there. I swear to God I've never seen anything like it. They all seem to think that wishing something to be true will make it true, that the Americans will perform miracles and force the British fleet to turn round in mid-Atlantic.'

'Which it won't.'

'Which it won't.'

Lucita echoed her father's words without, at first realizing what he had said. She looked at him.

'Have you heard something?'

'Nothing definite, and nothing that I should be telling you.'

'But you will.'

'But I will. I was talking to New York earlier. After that I spoke to some of my colleagues here. There's a rumour that the British Foreign Office will shortly advise all British passport holders in Argentina to leave the country.'

'What does that mean?'

'It means that the British don't believe that this can be resolved peaceably. I haven't heard yet what advice our government is giving our people in England, though I imagine it will be something similar unless they're married to British nationals. Even then, they'll probably be advised to keep a low profile if they intend staying.'

'Then you think there'll be a war?'

'Perhaps.'

Lucita understood her father's reluctance to commit himself.

'I'm not likely to say anything to Mama, you know.'

'I know. If there is a war, there's no way we can keep it from her anyway. Which is one reason I'm not insisting that she go into hospital. So yes, I think it will come down to a shooting war.'

Alfredo Jordan-Arditti sipped his whisky. Lucita was right. Why on earth did anyone drink this stuff for pleasure?

'In business communities, particularly my sort of businesses which overlap national boundaries, one learns to read between the lines. Sometimes, to keep ahead of the competition, one's intelligence services in a general way have to be more efficient than any government's. Whenever there's a war or a threat of war, paper currency reflects the uncertainty. Gold becomes buoyant. There are other indicators also, but you may take my word for it that banks and bankers keep their ears very close to the ground. The bankers in England and New York don't want this war any more than the bankers in Buenos Aires. But they tend to believe it's coming—unless someone makes an abrupt volte-face. I don't see Whitehall doing that. The present British government is going through a phase of unpopularity, and it's cost tens of millions of pounds to put the task force to sea. The British tax-payer will want to see something for his money, and the government feels it can win a cheap victory. That is what my American informants tell me. I know what the Casa Rosada thinks. It has taken a huge step, even a justifiable step, and gained universal acclaim. It can't retreat or it's finished. So we have an irresistible force and an immovable object.

'We may be lucky. A few skirmishes by both sides may satisfy honour all round and allow diplomacy to take a hand. I hope so. But one major incident would change all that.'

From another part of the house came the sound of a bell. One ring—which meant no panic.

'I'll see to her,' said Lucita, standing.

'Yes, I think she'd like that.'

Lucita started for the door before returning to the desk and putting her arms around her father and kissing his cheek.

'Don't worry,' she murmured. 'Ricardo will be all right and he'll take care of Beto.'

Maria Jordan-Arditti was sitting up in bed, fumbling with the mechanism that automatically pulled the drapes and controlled the angle of the shutters.

'Damn this thing,' she said, glancing up at Lucita. 'I can never get it to work.'

Lucita's mother was built from the same apparently deli-
cate blueprint as her daughter, but prior to her illness, and
again like Lucita, she was about as fragile as a storm shelter.
Her strength, however, was internal, in her will power and
determination. Judged a considerable beauty as a young woman,
neither age nor ailment had much impaired her looks, though
her once-blonde hair, a legacy from her Anglo-Saxon ancestors—
and one which, to a certain extent, Beto had inherited but not
her other two children—was now fading. Not so her temperament, which remained that of the opera singer she had been
before her marriage.

'It's because you're too impatient,' chided Lucita, taking
the controls and arranging the drapes and shutters to her
mother's satisfaction. 'Now, let's look at you. Good God,
you're a messy sleeper. Here, let me fix the pillows.'

'Don't fuss.'

'Don't argue.'

Lucita stood back to review her handiwork and, surreptitiously, examined her mother. The sleep had evidently done
her some good, but Lucita had seen this sort of thing before.
Within an hour or two, her mother would be tired again.

'Would you like a glass of water?'

'I'd actually like a gin and tonic'—Lucita shook her head
emphatically—'but I'll settle for a glass of water.'

Lucita poured one from the fridge that was a feature of all
the main bedrooms. She handed it to her mother and sat on
the edge of the bed, near the foot.

'Better?'

'Disgusting. Now, tell me about your day. Did you practise
your scales?'

'No.'

'Why not? Not because you thought it would disturb me, I
hope? Which, in any event, would not suffice as an excuse.
The music-room was designed to be sound-proof.'

'Because I didn't feel like it.'

'And what do you think would have happened to Suther-
land, Callas or de los Angeles, if they'd decided at your age
not to practise?'

'I don't know. Is it a quiz?'

'Don't be impertinent. When I was little older than you I'd
completed several professional singing engagements.'

'You have an incredible memory.'

'I have an incredible right hand, which will shortly descend upon your head. You know, I really would like a gin and tonic. I'm allowed two a day providing they're weak.'

Lucita mixed her one, with several cubes of ice and a fresh lime. Her mother tasted it.

'I know I said weak, but they are meant to be able to stand up without aid in the glass. So, what did you do, having forsaken the music-room?'

'Went out.'

Her mother raised an eyebrow.

'That sounded like a full-stop when I was expecting a semi-colon. "Out" is rather vague. I presume you didn't lunch on the Hotel Claridge's pressed duck or visit a museum.'

'I went to the Plaza de Mayo.'

'And?'

'And nothing.'

'You mean it was totally deserted, as usual, apart from one poor street vendor selling peanuts. There were no crowds, no students, no demonstrations. Everyone was dutifully at his desk or in his lecture-room. Or in *her* music-room.'

'Mama,' said Lucita patiently, 'you don't really want to know what they were doing.'

Maria Jordan-Arditti's eyes flashed angrily until she remembered who she was talking to. Even then, she could not quite keep the rancour from her voice.

'With two sons on the Malvinas I don't want to know what the people were doing who sent them there? Or who are encouraging them to remain there? Is that what you're telling me?'

'No,' murmured Lucita. 'It's just that . . .'

'Come here. Move closer.'

Lucita did so, easing her way up the bed. Her mother grasped both of Lucita's hands with her own.

'It's just that you don't want to upset me.'

Lucita nodded miserably. 'It won't do any good.'

'I know, I know,' soothed her mother. 'I know.'

'There's nothing we can do, that's the terrible thing.'

'I know.'

'We just have to sit here and hope.'

'Yes.'

'How can they all be so *stupid?*'

Lucita loosened her mother's grip and half-turned her head. She felt close to tears again, which was pathetic. She really would have to pull herself together.

'Would you like something to eat? Papa said you didn't have lunch. Some soup, perhaps.'

'Yes, I think I'd like that.'

'I'll just be a few minutes.'

Her mother watched her leave the room, remembering her daughter as a child. Remembering her other children too. For all their sakes, she had to relax, rest, obey doctor's orders. Lucita didn't know it but there might have to be an operation, major surgery; a messy, complicated business that she and her husband had discussed endlessly. The chances of success were fifty-fifty at best. Worse, she wasn't at present strong enough to survive surgery, in her doctor's opinion. And without it she was daily growing weaker.

She had no fear of dying, she had discovered rather to her surprise. But she refused to risk the operating table at the odds offered before her sons were safely home. Until then she would rely on the prescribed drugs. While they would not make her well, they would keep her alive.

When she was sure Lucita was not about to return to ask if there was anything else she wanted, she reached into her bedside drawer and took a blue pill from a small box. She swallowed it with the last of her drink.

It had also crossed Sara Ballantine's mind to phone Buenos Aires, but in the end she didn't for reasons more or less identical to those Lucita had given Ernesto Martinez. Besides, she was confused. The middle-class Englishwoman was outraged by Argentina's perfidy, and by Ricardo's undoubted part in it. As the wife-to-be (or should that be phrased, she occasionally thought, wife-that-was-to-have-been?) of Ricardo Jordan-Arditti she was concerned for his safety. She was equally concerned for the safety of her brother. There seemed no way out of the dilemma. She could not compartmentalize her emotions and allow so much caring for Ricardo, so much for Peter; so much anger at the junta's unwarranted actions, so much despair and rage at the manner in which the entire business had been fudged by head-in-the-sands politicians and incompetent, time-serving civil servants in the Foreign Office, men she saw daily. If it came to war—and this was what scared her—she feared she would not be able to stand aloof and impartial, blame events. Blood and country would get, as a due, her loyalty before love. And that would mean the end of her relationship with Ricardo. If anything happened to

Peter—if anything happened to men in Peter's command or with whom he was remotely associated—she would be unable to look at Ricardo again.

To occupy herself, as well as viewing every television debate on the rights and wrongs of the potential conflict, she read everything possible on the history of the Falklands, any Foreign Office memoranda she could lay her hands on as well as general literature. She came to the same conclusion as hundreds of others before her: she didn't know who had the better claim.

She did, however, learn to dislike the Falkland Islanders and their Westminster lobby. At the bottom of it all the two thousand or so souls who occupied the islands and those who pleaded their cause were responsible for what could well be a catastrophe of cataclysmic proportions. They appeared to be an intransigent bunch, refusing to budge an inch. Her reading left her in no doubt that the Foreign Office would have been delighted to get rid of the whole shoddy mess—were it not for the islanders and those with vested interests there, whose attitude seemed to be: 'Look after us but leave us alone.' Well, that sort of bloody-mindedness was not permissible in the last decades of the twentieth century. In this case, 'no man is an island,' was the *mot juste*. Good God, they flew to the mainland—courtesy of the Argentine airline LADE—for hospital treatment because it was more convenient and less expensive than flying to England, yet they couldn't see the practical advantages of allowing Argentina to raise its flag over Stanley. And because of that men might die.

Naturally Galtieri and the other members of the junta were a bunch of thugs looking for ways to hold on to power and earn themselves a chapter in the history books. Of course the whole muddle was the result of irresolution on the part of Downing Street and Whitehall. But the bloody kelpers and their backers were the real irritants.

If an analogy between Gibraltar and the Falklands ever crossed Sara's mind, she elected to ignore it. Indeed, had she been challenged, she would have been horrified at any suggestion that the Rock be given to the Spanish against the wishes of the Gibraltarians. It was simply that, like most thinking people in the United Kingdom, she was bewildered by it all. Unlike most people she had a foot in both camps.

On the day the Foreign Office finally announced that it was advising British nationals to leave Argentina, Sara lunched with Poppy Dauncey. And lunched too well, much of it liquid.

It had been a bad morning, one that had brought home to her just how close, personally, she was to the problem.

Shortly after eleven, her section head had summoned her to his private office. He was a nice enough man, Charles Percy; he was also a wily and experienced public servant, one who had not so much walked the corridors of power as skulked along them, seeking decisionless corners, red-taping his way to an index-linked pension and prize petunias in some dreary little Home Counties suburb. His wife (Sara had no doubt) would be a card-carrying member of the Women's Institute and play an average game of tennis twice a week. She would have the regulation two point eight children and worry about diets. Percy himself would play golf to a handicap of twenty-four and be almost invisible in the local pub. He was the original faceless mandarin, and his middle name was obfuscation.

With Percy was an immaculately dressed creature in his late thirties. Not a hair out of place, not a wrinkle in his suit, not a spot on his shoes. He made Sara feel quite shabby, a chrysalis in the presence of an imago. His smile, which he revealed only twice throughout the course of the whole interview, was that of a piranha accidentally finding itself in the deep end of a municipal swimming pool.

Although Percy did not introduce him by name or rank, it took only moments for Sara to deduce that the creature worked for one of the intelligence agencies. After the introductory niceties, he got straight down to business.

'We understand you are engaged to an Argentine army officer, Miss Ballantine.'

Sara didn't bother to question how that was known or how it had reached the ears of the hugger-mugger warriors. She'd kept it pretty much to herself, but she hadn't made a big secret of it either. However, she was not in the mood for games.

'Who's we?'

'Interested parties. Would you mind confirming it?'

Sara saw no reason not to.

'Yes. I mean I am. Was. I'm not sure now.'

'And he stayed with you before Christmas.'

'He stayed at my mother's house. So did his sister and brother. And my two brothers. It was not what one would term a *menage à deux.*'

'One wasn't about to.' The creature tried the first of his smiles. 'You sound hostile, Miss Ballantine.'

'I'm not responsible for the way you interpret my mode of speech.'

'It will be easier if you just answer the questions, Sara,' said Percy.

'It would be helpful if I knew why they were being asked.'

'We're attempting to build up a picture of Argentine forces on the Falklands,' said the creature candidly. 'We have many sources for doing this, of course, but we can't afford to overlook anything. It would therefore help if you would tell me your fiancé's name and rank, his regiment, and when you last spoke to him or heard from him.'

Sara felt wretched. She knew perfectly well that the creature had every right to ask and that she had a duty to answer. Nevertheless, in doing so she considered she was somehow betraying Ricardo, marking him out for special attention.

The creature made notes.

'And the letter saying he was still on manoeuvres was the last you received?'

'Yes.'

'Would it be possible for me to see it?'

'No. Much of it was personal. I'd rather that didn't go on record.'

'Very well. However, he did say he would be out of touch until the end of April?'

'Yes.'

'And what do you deduce from that?'

'Present tense?'

'Yes.'

'At the time, nothing. I was annoyed, of course, because it all seemed so vague. Now . . .' Sara hesitated.

'Please continue.'

'Now I've come to the same conclusion that you doubtless have.'

'Which is?'

'That he knew about the invasion and was part of it.'

'The letter was written when?'

'Mid-March. I forget the exact date.'

'Strange,' mused the creature. He was thinking aloud. 'A fortnight or so before the actual occupation. Our information is that no one outside the Argentine top brass knew anything about the junta's plans until the last moment. Yet you say your fiancé is not special forces.'

'I'm afraid I don't understand that expression.'

'Of course.'

The creature came to a conclusion. Captain Jordan-Arditti's regiment was probably on the Falklands and Jordan-Arditti himself originally part of the advance force, the so-called gas workers. It wasn't much, but it was helping to build up the dossier.

He delivered the second, and last, of his smiles.

'Thank you, Miss Ballantine, you've been most helpful.'

Sara paused by the door. The creature had studied her progress across the office. Attractive woman, he thought. Now why on earth would she want to marry an Argentine, give up her job and roots and move to a foreign country?

Sara shuffled papers from side to side and did very little that was constructive between the end of the interview and 12.55 when Poppy Dauncey approached her about lunching together. Belatedly Poppy had woken up to the fact that Sara was more or less engaged to an Argentine army officer. As Sara's only friend in the department, the opportunity for a womanly heart-to-heart was irresistible.

Sara's first inclination was to decline. Poppy was still heavily involved with her married lover, and the tribulations of the affair were generally the limit of her conversation—and usually a monologue. But talking to the creature had left Sara dejected, and Poppy, a stunning blonde a year Sara's senior, could be fun when she chose. Her family owned several acres of Chelsea, and her salary served little greater purpose than keeping her in shoes. She wasn't the brightest person in the world, but knew it. ('Men don't go out with me for my brains. My horse has more O Levels than I. If all else fails, I leave my chequebook where I know they'll see it.') Peter had met her once and described her as living proof of socialism's argument against private education and inherited wealth.

They elected to lunch at Bentley's in Swallow Street, away from the hustle and bustle of Whitehall. While waiting for a stool at the counter—only the *hoi polloi* with their American Express cards ate at the tables, in Poppy's opinion—they had several gin and tonics. And then several more because the place was crowded and there were delays. Poppy stuck to singles. After the third drink, Sara switched to doubles.

'My God, darling, you're shifting it.'

'With justification I think you'll agree,' said Sara. 'Those damned kelpers.'

Poppy didn't know what a 'kelper' was. She wasn't even sure that 'kelper' was the word she had heard.

'Quite,' she said. 'What did Faceless Percy want you for? You were in there rather an age.'

Sara wondered if the subject matter of the discussion had been meant to go no further than the four walls of Percy's office. She concluded not. The creature hadn't classified the interview as confidential. She told Poppy what had transpired.

'Good grief, how frightful for you. I saw him, of course, your creature, but I didn't have him down as a spook or whatever the current argot is. I rather thought him to be a male model who'd wandered in by accident. Sartorially exquisite, though I feel one would have to wait one's turn for the hair-drier. Do they shop in Savile Row and at Turnbull and Asser nowadays? Whatever happened to belted raincoats and snap-brimmed fedoras?'

A waiter came over and said their stools were ready. They ordered at the counter: a dozen oysters each and a bottle of Entre-Deux-Mers between them. The man on the stool to Sara's immediate left overheard what they were about to eat. He was around thirty, Caribbean-bronzed, and a good fifteen pounds overweight. He reminded Sara of a suntanned pig.

'They're not an aphrodisiac, you know,' he smirked. 'I had a dozen last weekend and two of them didn't work.'

Oh Lord, thought Sara.

'Bitte sprechen Sie langsamer,' she said. *'Oder bitte schreiben Sie es auf.'*

The man understood he was being snubbed.

'Lovely girl,' he remarked to his male companion in a stage whisper. 'Pity about the personality.'

Poppy read the danger signals and laid a cautionary hand on Sara's arm.

'I didn't know you spoke German.'

'What you heard is what I've got. My command of the language is limited to asking people to speak more slowly or write it down.'

It was perhaps unfortunate that the man and his companion were talking about the growing Falklands crisis. It was not unusual; practically everyone in the restaurant was debating some aspect of it. But the duo next to Sara were regularly referring to Argies and spics and bean-eaters and Argiebashing in a singularly unpleasant way. In particular they were discussing Rear Admiral Woodward's recent widely publicized statement that the coming battle was going to be a 'walkover'.

'Rubbish,' said Sara.

By this time she had eaten only half her oysters but consumed two glasses of wine. On top of the gin and her inner conflict, the combination was lethal.

'I beg your pardon?' The 'suntanned pig' swivelled to face her.

'You don't know what you're talking about,' said Sara. 'You seem to be under the impression that the Argentines are a pack of spear-wielding natives who'll race for home as soon as the gunboats appear. They won't.'

'Is that right?'

'That is right.'

'And that's also enough,' said Poppy decisively. She pushed the remainder of her oysters and wine to one side. 'Time we left.'

'But . . .'

'No buts.' Poppy handed Sara several five-pound notes. 'Here's my half. You pay the bill. I'll see you outside.'

After Sara had gone, Poppy asked the suntanned pig if he was doing anything that evening. The pig beamed. The blonde was, if anything, better looking than the redhead.

'No.'

'I'm not surprised,' said Poppy.

In the taxi Poppy said, 'Home for you, my girl. I'll let Faceless Percy know you weren't feeling well, which is close enough to the truth. A couple of Alka-Seltzer and bed is my advice.'

'Thanks, Poppy. I could have made a fool of myself in there.'

'He and his sort aren't worth the trouble. It's not easy, I know, but bear with it.'

'It's all I can do.'

Sara dropped Poppy off in Whitehall and continued home in the cab. In her flat she undressed and put on a robe. After the Alka-Seltzer she lay on the bed. Christ, was it only at Christmas that Ricardo had been here? She felt like crying but fought it before she fell asleep.

Around seven the telephone rang. And again at seven-thirty

and eight. Sara ignored the persistent bell. She didn't want to talk to anyone.

After the third attempt to call her daughter, Elizabeth Ballantine gave up. She must be out for the evening.

Later, when it was dark, she took Barney for a walk in the grounds. Or rather, Barney walked, Elizabeth Ballantine stood and looked at the stars. She wondered if the Plough, almost directly overhead at this time of year, was visible from wherever Peter was. She decided it couldn't be. The last she had heard he was on Ascension Island, and Ascension was south of the equator. If she remembered correctly, the Plough couldn't be seen south of the line.

Although she had passed many evenings alone in the house, somehow it seemed more deserted tonight. Probably that had something to do with Peter being thousands of miles away and not just a few hundred, not likely to pop in unannounced as he occasionally did. Edward—bless him—had perceived her unhappiness and offered to fake illness for a few weeks. She had insisted he return to school. His education was more important than a middle-aged woman's fears.

She would perhaps call Sara again later, or tomorrow, suggest that they meet in London, perhaps even stay in the flat for a few days. Barney could go to kennels, which he didn't mind because they fussed over him there. Yes, that's what she'd do, visit her daughter. Sara had to be going through agonies.

For the first time in years Barney was allowed upstairs, on a rug, in Elizabeth Ballantine's bedroom. He was puzzled but delighted. Also for the first time in years, Elizabeth Ballantine said a short prayer before going to sleep.

SIXTEEN

Archie Buchanan

'SICK TRANSIT GLORIOUS MONDAY,' Rupert remarked, nodding in the direction of Double-Eff's rapidly disappearing back.

The second lieutenant had had a miserable voyage, retching regularly whether the sea was as calm as a millpond, which was rare, or whether the ship was being tossed about the South Atlantic like a cork, a more usual state of affairs. Neither pills nor potions seemed to work, and Double-Eff wondered if he was going to be any bloody use at all to the operation when they reached the Falklands.

For some peculiar reason he found the motion of exercising helped, and he reckoned that in some respects he was the fittest man aboard. Where everyone else in the battalion ran between five and ten miles a day around the promenade decks and was drilled for an hour or two by PTIs or platoon NCOs, Double-Eff ran a dozen miles daily and exercised alone when the regular sessions were over. Which made him fit but tired. And which would mean bugger all when they were jammed in a landing craft. He would doubtless hit the beach like a gazelle—and then puke.

There was something spectacularly unsoldierly, unmasculine even, about seasickness. If you suffered from it you knew all about the misery it induced. If you didn't you looked like some poofter clown in front of men who strutted the messdecks with plates of bacon and eggs and huge chunks of gooey fried bread. Especially if those men were Royal Marines or paratroopers, who had less time for ordinary infantry regiments of the line than they did for each other. Some of them could eat everything in sight and then go back for seconds, which made them feel even more superior than usual to pongo second lieutenants who threw up after so much as a slice of unbuttered Hovis. Especially this second lieutenant, who'd had the dubious distinction, when they were berthed in Freetown, Sierra Leone, of being sick while leaning over the rail to observe the bootnecks and the paras and some of the battalion bombarding the bumboats with empty tins or anything else that came to hand. His 'long yellow yawn' had scored a direct hit on the unfortunate owner of one of the boats, whereupon the troops were unsure whether to cheer or jeer. In the end they jeered.

Most of the battalion had found its sea legs within a few days of leaving the UK. Double-Eff hadn't and doubted he ever would. Dry land was a dream. The Argies could mortar him, machine gun him, bomb or strafe him with fighters once he was on terra firma. He wouldn't give a bugger. And, if the brigadier was looking for a volunteer to be first man ashore, he need look no further than 2nd Lieutenant James ffolliott.

It was the day after the bulk of the amphibious task force set sail from Ascension, May 9. Five of the RFA-manned LSLs (Landing Ship Logistics) had, being slower, sailed on April 30, which left no one in any doubt, once they were gone, that there would be no diplomatic solution. But much else had happened between the time the task force arrived at Ascension and the time it departed to bring everyone to the same conclusion, though rumours (and rumours of rumours) occasionally made it difficult to separate truth from fiction. Several facts were indisputable, however.

On April 25 South Georgia had been retaken by elements of the Royal Marines in conjunction with the Special Boat Squadron and the SAS. Many aboard the ships at Ascension then wondered if Buenos Aires would see the light and pull out of the Falklands before the main force arrived. But that was not to be and, on the day after the Total Exclusion Zone (TEZ) came into being on April 30, Stanley airfield was bombed by the first Vulcan raid and the Sea Harriers from the carrier group went into action.

May 2 was at first regarded as a good day by the British troops when news filtered through that the Argentine cruiser *General Belgrano* had been sunk by a submarine. ('One nil, one nil,' the ship chanted.) The extensive loss of life was not immediately known, but as it was gradually learned that between three and four hundred sailors had been killed when the ex-American warship went down, the cheers became muted among officers and other ranks alike. In these early days the British quarrel was seen largely to be with the intransigent junta in Buenos Aires, not with men like themselves and those who sailed the ships they were on. Only the genuine hard cases viewed every Argentine soldier as a potential target, though that too would change with time. Besides, what a British sub could do to an Argie cruiser, an Argie sub—or the Argie air force, flying from its convenient mainland bases—could do to a British ship.

Which proved to be the case two days later, when HMS *Sheffield,* hit by an Exocet missile, was mortally damaged and abandoned. She subsequently sank, and twenty-one men lost their lives. Many others were appallingly burnt or otherwise injured.

The shock of losing the *Sheffield* to a solitary air-launched missile, against which she was purpose-built to defend herself, reverberated throughout the fleet, as much among the Ascension Island units as among their comrades attempting to enforce the TEZ 3,000 miles south. It made everyone feel less confident about the eventual outcome, more aware of his own mortality. Apart from 'whistling in the dark' kind of comments, there was also less disparaging talk now of 'beaneaters' and 'walkovers'. The Argentine air force, at least, had proved it had teeth. And it was to the air force that the surface ships would be most vulnerable.

Someone drew an analogy between the present conflict and the Second World War. Viewed in retrospect, WW II read like fiction. At the start the bad guys had it all their own way, scoring victory after effortless victory. Nothing, apparently, stood in the way of their conquering England, which eventually would have made it either impossible to launch the second front from the British Isles or have reduced England to rubble from American long-range bombers in order to dislodge the Nazis.

Then the good guys won the Battle of Britain. A little later the 5th Cavalry appeared in the shape of the Americans, and the good guys were also victorious in North Africa and at Stalingrad. After that, with the minor hiccup of the Battle of the Bulge ('We need the drama, Mr Screenwriter'), the goodies went on to final triumph among the ruins of Berlin.

Loud applause. End of movie. Up grams. Roll credits.

The analogist, Archie Buchanan, wondered if he would be able to write it like that. He concluded he wouldn't. The minders—MoD press officers—would have kittens at the copy. This was a war of right versus wrong, good versus evil, justice versus oppression—with the virtues all on one side and the malevolence on the other—with no doubt about the outcome. The minders would permit no dispatch from the task force to allude otherwise. In fact the minders, along with many senior officers, looked upon the hacks as something of a fifth column in their midst, men who wanted nothing more than to show up the military as uncaring dunderheads. Secrecy, after all, was anathema to all newspapermen, which was Archie Buchanan's occupation.

Now aged forty, with thinning red hair and freckled features, Buchanan had covered wars for various newspapers for as long as he could remember, in Vietnam as a younger man but mostly in the Middle East and Africa. He had seen the Iranians fight the Iraqis, the Angolans the South Africans, the Rhodesians other Rhodesians, and the Israelis just about everybody. He had witnessed the Lebanon tearing itself apart without fully understanding who wanted what from whom.

He had reported long wars and short wars, guerrilla wars and international wars; those that were 'dirty' and those that were reputedly clean—the latter adjective a contradiction in terms, in his opinion, like Welsh culture. He had seen superb troops in action and troops who scarcely knew one end of a rifle from the other. But apart from Northern Ireland—which he didn't really count since, like the poor, it was always with us—he had never gone to war alongside British troops before. He had missed Suez and the latter days of EOKA in Cyprus, and he had been elsewhere during Aden.

Frankly he wasn't sure what to make of the younger ones. They were keen enough, of course (which meant nothing), and very fit (which could mean a lot). Virtually every one of them had done a tour in Northern Ireland, and had therefore been under fire. But what they would be facing in a week or two was very different from street fighting and anti-terrorist patrols. The IRA had no ships, no aircraft, no heavy artillery. Exercises on Dartmoor and the Brecon Beacons and Salisbury Plain were no substitute for the real thing.

On Ascension, when their physical training hours were over, their small-arms drill and equipment checks at an end, the lectures on what to expect on the Falklands concluded for the day, he had watched them sunbathe like any other group of youngsters, and heard them talk. He was convinced that few of them had any idea what they were coming up against. They saw everything with the insouciance of ignorance. When, after the *Sheffield*, an announcement came over the tannoy that medics would be asking for blood-donor volunteers, they treated it as a joke. (Medic: 'Come on, cough up. You might want it back in a fortnight.' Soldier: 'Then fuck it, I'll keep it where it is and save you the trouble.') News that two thousand body-bags were being flown in was greeted with derision. ('Shit, that's less than one apiece. I'm not sharing mine with Smithy.') Or Jonesy or Browny. The older officers and NCOs were well-seasoned, but as for the others . . .

When he'd first spoken to Rupert the second day out from the UK, he had been astonished to learn that the twenty-two-year-old aristocrat had brought along his shotgun, cartridges, and a shooting-stick. This was something out of World War Two, perhaps even World War One. Had the eccentric behaviour been confined to just one lieutenant, Buchanan would have put it down to personal idiosyncracy. But the commanding officer of the same battalion had brought his golf clubs and a company commander an umbrella. Where on earth did the silly buggers think they were going? Keeping up morale by treating the whole thing as a game was one thing; but shotguns, golf clubs and umbrellas? He hadn't been allowed to report it, either. One of the minders had blue-pencilled the paragraph. 'Can't have the folks back home believing we're all going on a South American cruise at the tax-payer's expense.'

Out of genuine curiosity Buchanan had asked Rupert a simple question. He had not believed that everyone could be so gung-ho. 'Are you really going down there to "bash" the "Argies"?' And Rupert answered: 'I think we'll have to, old boy. They're almost impossible to house train, you know.'

Amazing. And as for that pun on *sic transit gloria mundi* . . . Well, all Buchanan could think was: They don't talk like that in the Israeli army.

When he bothered to think about himself in depth, which wasn't often now that he knew he would never write the definitive English novel or indeed any novel at all, Archie Buchanan considered himself tough. Not physically strong—at five ten and one hundred fifty pounds the youngest soldier aboard could have turned him into hamburger—but conditioned to take nothing at its face value, to view the world through dun-coloured spectacles. In his lexicon military men were self-serving opportunists, business tycoons heartless guttersnipes, and politicians liars. Yet for all that he was impressed with what he had seen so far. In spite of his cynicism he had grudgingly admitted while observing the crossdecking of stores in Sierra Leone and the landing-craft drills on Ascension that the senior combat officers and NCOs knew their business. The staff problems for the brigadier and his immediate advisers had to be immense, for this was, to a large extent, a political war, where Britain must always be seen to be behaving with honour. The War Cabinet in London would be putting intolerable pressure on the planners, limiting their parameters of action just in case a diplomatic solution could be found at the eleventh hour. In Buchanan's experience the soldiers would be wanting to do the right thing, the military thing, which was to get the campaign over as swiftly as possible with the minimum loss of life. That was difficult enough when facing an enemy of the calibre that could knock out a warship, but the politicians would be saying, Sorry, we can't have that. Try it another way. We have international public opinion to consider.

Also in Buchanan's experience, six weeks ago he would never have believed it possible that Britain could mount an operation such as this within a few days of taking the decision to recover the Falklands. In another era—Suez, for example—such an undertaking would have been termed post-colonial adventurism, and he would have agreed instinctively with that assessment. Now, he wasn't so sure. Although he was no supporter of Margaret Thatcher—or indeed of the political persuasion of the newspaper which paid his salary—there was a certain atavistic magnificence in what was taking place.

He shook his head at such thoughts. Either he was growing soft—in which case he should retire to the country and write verse—or the Oriental gentlemen behind the bar which served (and thus classified as equals) officers and hacks alike was giving larger measures than were being paid for.

Double-Eff returned looking sheepish and slightly green about the gills.

'Sorry about that,' he apologized.

Buchanan studied him, and Lieutenant the Hon. Rupert Parker-Smith. They were not Israelis, that was for sure, but for the first time since sailing he was not unduly disappointed at being assigned for the duration of the campaign to Daddy Rankin's battalion. He had rather hoped to be attached to 40, 42 or 45 Commando, or 2 or 3 Para. They would be where the action was, as the major shock troops of 3 Commando Brigade. But it was likely that Rankin's battalion would go ashore with one of the glamour regiments, and Buchanan decided that the green berets and the red berets would not gather all the headlines.

'See you,' he said, downing his glass.

'I think you upset him, James,' said Rupert, 'with your sudden exit.'

'Not really, surely.'

'No, not really, but I have to confess that you've been up-setting me somewhat. I'd forgotten about it while we were at Ascension, but being underway again has brought it back to mind.'

Rupert and Double-Eff shared with two other officers from the battalion what would have been, in peacetime, a normal two-berth cabin. Now, to say the least, it was crowded.

'Go on,' said Double-Eff.

'When you rolled over last night I felt distinctly uncomfortable. I have to remind you that I am your platoon commander, not your girl friend or popsy or whatever one has in the wilds of Norfolk.'

'I don't live in Norfolk.'

'Very wise.' Rupert did a creditable impression of Noël Coward. 'Very flat, Norfolk. Nevertheless, if you touch me there again, and in that manner, I shall scream.'

'It's my bladder,' said Double-Eff feebly.

'It felt like a shipment of boloney. If you must become so excited by the motion of the vessel, I suggest you avail yourself of one of the dozen or so ladies aboard . . .'

'That's a court martial offence.'

'. . . Or the services of one of the stewards. Failing all else, do what our bootneck friends do—but in private.'

A bootneck captain from 40 Commando, a man they had got to know well since the UK and whose weather-beaten features boded ill for any Argie he might happen to meet, overheard the remark.

'Royal Marines don't go in for the nifty-fifty. We leave that to you pongos.'

It was from this commando officer that Rupert and Double-Eff and others in the battalion had picked up the weird and occasionally wonderful slang the bootnecks used. All regiments had their own way of saying things, but the Royal Marines, with their long association with the Royal Navy, had developed a means of communication that was almost unintelligible to the outsider.

Pusser's onks were best parade boots; the oggin was the sea, any sea, anywhere. Tiddy oggies were Cornish pasties, and screech was Marsala wine, generally of the variety served in Malta. A 'run ashore' was a trip into town, usually with some evil, drunken purpose in mind, whether one was leaving a ship or simply walking out of barracks. Being 'in the rattle' was being in trouble. Nutty was any form of sweets but generally chocolate. Marines didn't march, they yomped. A pongo was any serviceman, including Paras, who wasn't a Royal Marine. Gus was Plymouth, a man's pit his bed. When a bootneck was heaving something as in a tug o' war, the command was 'two-six', from the days of the jolly boats when the coxwain would order numbers two to six oars to pull. Though it was all meant to be fun, Royal Marines disliked Paras with a loathing that was otherwise saved for mothers-in-law. The feeling was mutual. In a Royal Marine's opinion, a Para didn't need a 'chute to jump with. You could shove him out of an aircraft at ten thousand feet and if he landed on his head he'd be okay. Within seconds he'd be looking around for someone to show him how to piss, and where. And a nifty-fifty was self abuse.

'It wasn't me at all,' complained Double-Eff, after thinking about it. 'It was your damned Purdey. You shouldn't sleep with the bloody thing.'

'You mean I should leave it propped up against a bulkhead and have one of these uncouth Royal Marines pinch it in the mid of night.'

'Now, now, children,' chided the 40 Commando captain, 'spoons and pushers to the rear. Save all that lovely aggression for the Argies.'

'What a rude fellow,' said Rupert, deadpan. 'I do hope the battalion will not have to share a landing craft with the masses.'

'You'll know soon,' said the Royal Marine. 'A buzz is going around that there's to be a senior officers' ''O'' Group tomorrow.'

SEVENTEEN

3 Platoon

ON MAY 10 helicopters ferried all unit commanding officers, their 2 i/cs and intelligence officers, and the COs of the special forces' contingents from the troopships to the assault ship *Fearless*. There, in the wardroom, they were told the order of battle. The place would be San Carlos; the date would be somewhere after May 19. 2 and 3 Para, 40 and 45 Commando would spearhead the attack, with Daddy Rankin's battalion supporting 45 to begin with and probably remaining with that unit for the duration of the campaign. Theirs would be Red Beach One, Ajax Bay, on the west side of San Carlos Water. 42 Commando would remain in reserve. The task was to secure a beachhead and probe only as far as was sensible until the arrival of reinforcements in the shape of 5 Infantry Brigade, shortly due to leave the UK aboard the QE2.

It was to be hoped that whatever day was eventually chosen, the landings would take place at 0600 Zulu (GMT), 0200 local time, and all units were to have secured their first objectives by daybreak since the Argentine air force would represent a major threat once alerted. Crossdecking of the battalions to the assault ships would take place a few hours before H-Hour.

On returning to the troopship Daddy gathered his company commanders and company 2 i/cs together and briefed them on what had transpired aboard *Fearless*. Although he mentioned it to no one, he was slightly overawed to be flanking 45

Commando on Red Beach One. The commandos and the paratroopers were crack units. Still, it was up to him to convince his officers that the battalion could hack it with the best.

Later, company commanders went back to their companies and lectured the soldiers, using slides, on what they could expect to meet on the Falklands. 105 mm howitzers certainly, and possibly the 155, which outranged anything the amphibious force had brought with it. The 75 mm, 90 mm and 105 mm RCLs (recoilless rifles), the 105 being a high-explosive anti-tank weapon whose shell could penetrate 400 mm of armour. Bantam and Cobra ATGWs (anti-tank guided weapons). The principal infantry small-arms were the Belgian FN, the same calibre and virtually the same weapon as the British SLR, and the FMK 3 9 mm submachine gun, similar to the Israeli Uzi. In the air, Mirage-IIIs and Daggers, A-4 Skyhawks and the Pucara, the latter a turboprop aircraft basically used by the Argentines for counterinsurgency. The ground troops would have to be particularly wary of the Pucara. Anyone caught out in the open could expect to make his wife a widow.

'Study the slides,' said Winter's Day, 'until you can recognize any of these aircraft in your sleep. You—especially you Blowpipe teams—won't have a hell of a lot of time to decide whether or not to fire. The first man who brings down a Harrier because he mistook it for something else will have his pay docked until he's a thousand and twelve. After that he'll face a court martial and be shot. And the first man to mistake a Skyhawk for one of ours and who stands up and waves to the pilot will be spread in very small chunks over very large parts of East Falkland.'

This remark did not get the reception Winter's Day expected. The company shuffled uneasily; they had never heard Winter's Day make a joke before, and they did not appreciate the unprecedented. Most of them—though they would have scoffed at being called superstitious if challenged—carried mascots: locks of a girl friend's hair, intimate items of her clothing, pieces of her jewellery, small bears or other animals won at fairgrounds or bought as souvenirs. They would not have dreamt of going into the coming battles without these talismans. Neither did they want Winter's Day to become anything other than the miserable bugger he was. That was too reminiscent of the condemned man eating a hearty breakfast.

The calibre of the ground troops, they were told by Peter Ballantine, taking over from Winter's Day, was believed in general to be poor. Many of them were conscripts with only a few months' training; many of them were very young. They could be expected to run or surrender if the battalion went in hard. Those who would not run were the *Buzo Tactico* commandos and the 5th Marines.

'How will we know them?' someone wanted to know.

'Because they'll kill you, you berk,' Scarlett O'Hara shouted to rapturous applause.

None of the company was in much doubt that opinions concerning the quality of the ground troops and the type and number of the Argentine hardware had been obtained by units of the SAS and the SBS. Nevertheless, Rupert enquired just how solid the information was.

'I wrote and asked them,' said Peter.

'Then if the reply's coming via BFPO,' yelled someone, topping the joke to general acclamation, 'we know bleedin' well you haven't had it.'

Mail was a sore point with most of the troops in the task force. Sometimes post arrived in huge batches, as it had on Ascension; other times the 'drops' to the troopships were irregular. Often the mail brought unpleasant news, as it had to Twiggy on Ascension. Carol Bannister's 'stuff' had not worked the miracle. She was emphatically pregnant though she had said nothing to her parents as yet, and she wouldn't consider an abortion. It was her fervent hope (she wrote) that Twiggy would be home soon and that they could get married. She loved him. She wouldn't mind being an army wife. Twiggy had told only Sammy Finch that Carol was in the club. Sammy had called him a fucking idiot. He'd known all along that Twiggy wasn't allowed out by himself. Still, he might get lucky, Twiggy. He might get the chop on the first day, then all his worries would be over. Twiggy didn't think that was funny.

Peter's address was followed by a lecture from the CSM, Scrunch Watkins. Scrunch was rightly reckoned to be a hard individual, his face resembling a cross between W. H. Auden's and the far side of the moon, though he was only thirty-six. As a younger man he had served in the Royal Marines, mainly with 40 Commando. He had left when his hitch was up, discovered that Civvy Street didn't agree with him, and applied to re-enlist. To his dismay they wouldn't have him.

He was over-qualified for the ranks, but into the ranks he would have had to have gone before any question of his former status as a senior NCO could be considered. In their wisdom the Marines judged that having an ex-sergeant in the same intake as eighteen- and nineteen-year-olds just wasn't on. He'd lead them into bad ways, shortcuts, almost unwittingly, and the evil little buggers would learn all about how to cut corners in their own good time, thank you very much. So Scrunch joined the battalion as an ordinary soldier and was a sergeant within three years. He had been CSM D Company for two years.

Scrunch had done his homework and tapped his ex-oppos in 40 Commando for information about the Falklands terrain, intelligence that was not included in the normal handouts and lectures no matter how comprehensive they purported to be. Since the Royal Marines were the forces originally humiliated in and around Stanley when the Argies invaded, it stood to reason, in Scrunch's view, that they would know more about the land mass than any other unit. He also considered it his function to impress upon these youngsters how easy it was to get killed if you weren't careful. Never mind what the newspapers back home were saying about heroes and all that crap, a posthumous Military Medal wasn't going to buy anyone's grieving mother so much as a loaf of bread. Heroes had to be survivors. The Royal Marine Commandos (and the Paras, Scrunch reluctantly conceded) hadn't made their reputation by being idiots. They were tough, sure, but they were also canny.

Because the company commander was present, Scrunch abandoned his normal manner of imparting information, though he found it difficult not to say that the bunch of fucking deadbeats in front of him would get their fucking heads blown off by the fucking Argies unless they listened to every fucking word he was going to fucking well tell them. And he'd be asking fucking questions later.

Although all the officers present, from the company commander down, used obscenities as verbs, nouns, adverbs and adjectives just as frequently as any NCO or grunt, it was considered impolite to address the troops in the company commander's presence as though he were not there. A bit like the butler saying 'shit' to the domestics in front of the houseguests. Only once or twice did Scrunch forget himself.

There was very little cover on East Falkland, he said. No

trees or bushes they could get their stupid thick heads behind when the Argie air force came out for target practice or the Argie artillery wanted to play Space Invaders with their nuts. Trenches were also going to be dodgy. In many places the ground was too hard to dig in properly with any hope of survival; in others too soft; their trenches would be full of water within an hour, and they were going to need their feet, their PCLs—Personnel Carriers Leather.

'But if it comes to getting your heads shredded or your feet wet, get wet feet.'

The alternative was a sangar, a stone wall built from any rocks they could lay their hands on.

The weather was going to be wicked. They could see outside the window—actually they couldn't, since all the windows were blacked out—that they weren't going to Brighton in June. Frostbite and trench foot were going to be enemies as vicious as any Argie. A soldier was no use if he couldn't march. He was worse than no use. He needed someone to look after him, someone else to take his place and kit, and someone, perhaps, to cart him back to the rear for treatment.

'In other words, you're not only going to be a pain in the arse to someone who's relying on you to give him cover, you're going to lose a finger or a toe or a foot or . . .' He paused. 'OR . . .' he shouted.

'Or our cocks!' yelled the company.

'Right! Or your cocks! Though judging by what I've seen in the showers on this gash boat, you're not going to be missing much. Even Corporal Tyler's girl friend'd do just as well with a chipolata.'

The company screamed with delight at this. This was more like it, after all that shit from Winter's Day and Captain Ballantine about Pucaras and 155s and conscripts. Two-Shit Tyler was renowned for bragging that he possessed personal equipment that would stop traffic on the M1. He had the wisdom to grin, anyway. Not that he could do much else with Scrunch until his stripes came through and he could address the CSM more or less as an equal.

It was going to be hard to keep their feet dry, Scrunch warned them. They'd be seeing rain, hail, snow, sleet—all kinds of shit. And the Argies probably wouldn't be kind enough to give them time to build a fire, dry their socks, warm their tootsies.

'You'll just have to do the best you can. Frostbite's a different matter. Anyone seen *Scott of the Antarctic?*' A few had. 'Then you'll remember—Oates, I think it was. He went all kind of greenish-white, and disappeared saying the others might not see him for some time. On this outing no one disappears for "some time". You're relying on your oppo and your oppo's relying on you. Otherwise you're fucked. You may get a chance to use your sleeping-bags, you may not. You may be just about to curl up in your pits when the Argies decide to do something evil. You're fucked again. Even if you can use your bags, if your feet are cold when you get in, they'll stay cold.' Scrunch feigned a glower at Rupert. 'That applies to people with blue blood also.'

'Mine's the normal red variety, CSM,' called Rupert, and paused before adding: 'Mind you, it is B Rhesus-negative.'

'I thought rhesus was a monkey, sir,' said Scrunch innocently.

Scrunch squashed the minor uproar at this remark with a wave of his hand. He liked Rupert, and he was fairly confident Rupert liked him. However, enough was enough.

'So your feet are cold. So what do you do? You stick them in your oppo's crotch or under his armpit to warm them up, that's what you do.' He waved his hand again. 'Yeah, I know, not a pretty thought. But that's how you stay alive. If you're tall and skinny like Twiggy down there, you can stick them up your own crotch.'

'And the same to you,' chorused a handful of voices from the back, to the tune of Colonel Bogey.

Scrunch grinned.

'Next, water—don't drink it without sterilizing it first. It's got all sorts of horrible bugs in it.'

'Like HQ Company.'

'Like HQ Company,' agreed Scrunch. 'But don't drink it anyway, even if you've got livers like Legless and Groggy. Boil it on the hexy stoves.'

The company groaned. They had a feeling they knew what was coming next. They'd lived well up to now from the ship's galleys. Once they landed it would be ratpacks until— and if—field kitchens could be set up.

'Don't knock 'em,' bawled Scrunch. 'Christ, you've got chicken, you've got curry, you've got stew. You've got hardtack, you've got stock cubes. You've got nutty and dehydrated fruit. You've got enough for a dozen brews a day.

You've got peas and rice and beans and all that stuff. And what ain't you got?'

'WE AIN'T GOT DAMES.'

'And what have you got?'

'WE'VE GOT THE SHITS.'

'Right. Except you haven't. Because if you'd been paying attention to your earlier briefings and learned from your earlier experiences, you've also got anti-laxative. Use it.' Scrunch paused. 'And on the third day . . .'

'We'll all rise to heaven on a great big pile of SHIT.'

'Right.'

'The hexy stoves didn't work too brilliantly in Scotland, Sarn't Major,' someone shouted.

'No bugger worked in Scotland,' Scrunch shouted back. 'You all thought you were on a winter wonderland holiday. But I agree, there was a problem. However, that's now been sorted out. Okay, that's it for now. Any questions, see your platoon commanders or NCOs.'

Peter leaned forward and whispered something to Scrunch, who held up his hand.

'Hold it, hold it. I've just been reminded that there'll be a lecture on first aid and wounds in the cinema at 2000 hours. Be there.'

With that sobering thought ringing in their ears, the company was dismissed.

On May 12 an unconfirmed report spread like wildfire throughout the amphibious force that HMS *Glasgow* had been hit off East Falkland. It transpired that she had been unbelievably lucky, a bomb from a Skyhawk passing clean through her hull without exploding. However, the damage was such that she was forced to withdraw.

Also on May 12 the first 'Air Attack Yellow' was broadcast over the tannoy, the second degree of readiness between White (possible danger but no flap) and Red (attack imminent). Everyone was sent scuttling to their battle stations and lifeboat assembly points, but the Yellow proved to be a false alarm. At least, the intruder was a Tupolev Tu-95 Russian 'Bear', the USSR's frontline maritime reconnaissance aircraft, and not the Argentine air force. The 'Bear' took a long and curious look at the amphibious force before sheering off. The Russian's presence made everyone feel uneasy. Was it just anxious, for future reference, to see precisely what naval elements were with the amphibious group—because whatever ships were there could not be performing their customary NATO role—or was it flashing information to the Argentines? No one knew then and no one found out afterwards.

On May 15, in filthy weather that rolled and buffeted even the biggest ships and made the lives of men like Double-Eff a total misery, Archie Buchanan and the other journalists with the landing force were formally placed under military discipline by a reading of the Declaration of Active Service. Strictly speaking, they could now be told what to do and when to do it by lance-corporals, although in the event of capture they were informed that they held the rank of Captain.

Gradually the flotilla increased in size. Through occasional gaps in the mist and rain, there were ships to be seen in all directions. Up front, destroyers and frigates screened the more vulnerable parts of the fleet—'darting around like Pompey whores on a Saturday night,' according to Scrunch Watkins. Helicopters roared overhead on endless antisubmarine patrols, while Harriers flew Combat Air Patrols in case the Argentine air force ventured further afield than it already had, or in case the *Veinticinco de Mayo*, rumoured to have fled to her home port, either hadn't or was about to reappear. Every piece of equipment was lashed down. Every anti-aircraft system aboard every vessel was manned round the clock by men (and in many cases boys in their teens) in anti-flash gear.

The main amphibious force had already linked up with the LSLs which left Ascension on April 30. Between May 16 and May 18, when the whole group rendezvoused with the *Hermes*, every man aboard the troopships completed his checklist. There would be no going back for items forgotten. The current buzz was that the battalions were to be transferred to the assault ships via their LCUs on May 19—rubbish-skipping as it was known generically, for in appearance the LCUs looked very like oversized versions of the skips found outside building sites.

Among 3 Platoon there was much argument about whether the paratroopers' glass fibre helmets were superior in quality to the regular steel variety worn by the battalion and the Royal Marines. Those who said they were pointed out that the Paras didn't do anything by halves; those who said they were not said that neither did the bootnecks. Overhearing the discussion, Rupert settled the debate in a couple of pithy sentences. 'I had a fibreglass boat once. First piece of jagged rock we encountered ripped the bottom clean out.'

This made even the doubters in the platoon feel a lot better, though they would have been less sanguine had they heard Rupert remark to Scarlett O'Hara, sotto voce, a few minutes later: 'Mind you, I'm a rotten sailor.'

Still, Zebedee was all right, was the general opinion. He might be a royal pain in the backside in barracks, for ever jumping out on people with his 'Boing, boing'—but they trusted him to get them wherever they were going without killing too many of them, which was about as much as any junior officer could expect from the grunts in his command.

For that matter, they had begun to trust Double-Eff also. Okay so he threw up if the mess waiter so much as slapped down his soup too hard, but he'd stuck it out and not retired to his bunk like some maiden aunt. He'd lolloped around the promenade decks and done physical jerks when the rest of the platoon—the company and the battalion, for that matter—were fucked. One or two of the platoon had even begun to call him 'Boss'—a sign of respect hitherto granted only to Rupert. Double-Eff had never been more pleased, and he had written telling his parents that, after five months, he was beginning to fit in. He had not told them he had made a will, or rather rewritten the one he updated from time to time, being a somewhat conservative young man who believed in order and discipline. In his testament he had left everything he owned— which was very little—to his mother and father, together with the insurance money if he didn't survive. That was as it should be and as it always had been (not one of the various girls he knew being special enough to warrant even the smallest memento). But he had also added a codicil to the effect that he loved them very much and was grateful for everything they had ever done for him; that he believed Britain's cause to be just and had no fears. He had thought long and hard about the codicil. The bit about Britain's cause struck him as highly melodramatic, too much First World War. It would be bad enough for his parents, his mother in particular, if he were to die; to have a formal declaration of love might be more than either of them could handle. But he concluded that they deserved to know how he felt.

Most of the rest of the platoon had made wills also. Some hadn't because they were superstitious, some because they had no one to leave anything to. Among those who drafted a testimony though told no one of its contents was Prawn Balls. From somewhere in the dim recesses of his memory he recalled a conversation with Jomo the night before the battalion embarked. He didn't entirely remember the substance of the discussion, but he knew Jomo was a decent bloke and would use wisely what was left of Mrs Ball's insurance money.

Packing the kit they would take ashore was interrupted frequently by air-raid and lifeboat drills, which many of the troops loathed and considered useless since in the event of a genuine emergency it would be chaos trying to reach the lifeboat muster stations. Besides, what the hell could they do if a Super Etendard launched an Exocet at them? Fuck all. Good night Vienna. The Royal Navy would do better to let them get on with their packing in peace and quiet, because it was hard enough without interruptions trying to figure out what would be essential for the first forty-eight hours and what should be left in their big bergens to be brought ashore by the battalion QM.

Groggy and Legless Jones had no problems with excess baggage, not of the kind they would have wished anyway. In spite of promises to each other—and notwithstanding a bottle of Johnny Walker Black Label won from a 3 Para corporal in a marathon poker session—their whisky supply had been consumed before Ascension, the rumour (untrue) being that one could buy more from the Americans on the South Atlantic island. Since then they had been surviving on their ration of two beers a day plus whatever they could beg, borrow, buy or steal from teetotallers like Non-Legless. The deprivation had had one curiously unexpected side effect. Together with the daily runs around the promenade decks and the other exercises, they both felt much better than for as long as they could remember. Groggy had been heard to remark in the presence of a shocked 3 Platoon: 'If I'd known I was going to feel this good I'd've given up drinking years ago.'

Three-piece was tossing up whether to jam his supply of condoms into his small kit (and take a chance on some bastard Argie shooting holes in them) or leave them in his large bergen for the QM, when Scarlett sought him out.

'Bit of a flap,' explained Scarlett. 'Some bugger's mislaid the cartons of johnnies we're going to use to cover rifle muzzles when we rubbish-skip to the assault ships. We're running a bit short. All platoon NCOs have been asked to do a grab-bag on randy little sods like you.' Scarlett waited for a response, received none. 'Thought you might like to help out, Sweet,' he added patiently.

'There's no charge for thinking, Sarge,' said Three-piece nonchalantly.

'Come on,' urged Scarlett. 'There's bugger all down there you'll be able to get your greedy little paws on.'

'I'll look a right berk if there is, won't I?' said Three-piece, though he was inclined to agree with Scarlett.

To begin with he'd expected the Falklands to be something like the newsreels he'd seen of France after D-Day, when thousands of luscious Frog bints threw themselves at the liberators. After listening to Daddy Rankin and Winter's Day, he was starting to believe it wouldn't be like that at all. Still, he wasn't handing over the johnnies as easily as that.

'They cost money, Sarn't.'

'Don't give me that. You get them free from the sick bay. Do you think I came down with the last shower of rain?'

'Yes. I mean no. But the sick bay stuff's heavy duty stuff. You could retread a Mercedes with a boxful. You've got to be drunk or desperate to use them. Mine are civvy gear. Some have got feathers on the end, some have got bobbles.'

God spare us, thought Scarlett.

'You're a dirty little man, you know that?'

'Maybe, Sarn't,' said Three-piece impudently, 'but the fact is that I've got the johnnies and you haven't.'

Scarlett could see the angle. Three-piece was holding out for payment, but he'd be damned if he'd give the little bugger cash. However, there was a genuine shortage of condoms. Doubtless the missing cartons would turn up in time, but that might not be before the battalion crossdecked to the assault ships. Zebedee had asked him to scrounge around and see what he could do, it now being a case of each platoon looking after its own. He'd told Mr Parker-Smith that he knew just the bloke to solve the problem and, by Christ, solve the problem was what he was going to do.

'There's talk of the platoon getting an extra gimpy,' he said.

Three-piece's eyes lit up, but he held his tongue. He'd been a regular soldier long enough to know that you didn't show enthusiasm when some guy with three stripes on his arm became friendly. Volunteer the information that you knew how to play the piano and you'd find yourself shifting the fucking thing from one floor of the sergeants' mess to

another—on a wet Sunday morning in November when everyone else was lying in his pit. Tell a senior NCO that you were
keen on photography and he'd have you sweeping the camp
cinema.

'A gimpy, Sweet,' repeated Scarlett.

On this jaunt everyone would be carrying spare barrels and
ammunition belts for the gimpies, the 7.62 mm general purpose machine guns. Some unfortunate bastards would get the
tripods—nasty, heavy things that weighed thirty pounds and
which meant the man carrying one had to stick close to the
machine gunner in case the tripod was needed in a hurry. All
of the hard work and none of the glamour.

The platoon's usual machine gunners were Two-Shit Tyler
and Jomo Mason, who had both proved in the past that they
were more accurate with the weapon than anyone else in 3
Platoon. Empty, each gimpy weighed twenty-four pounds
compared with the SLR's nine and a half pounds, which
didn't matter that much because machine gunners weren't
customarily asked to carry extra grenades and mortar bombs
and crap like that. On exercise and on the range everyone
liked to fire the gimpy because of the damage it did and the
reassuring rattle it gave out, but few were keen on being
groomed for permanent machine gunner status because that
usually meant serving an 'apprenticeship' as the number two—in
other words, carrying the spare ammo belts and the tripod. If
any forced marches across East Falkland became the order of
the day, the average weight each man would have to carry
would be in excess of one hundred pounds. The poor sod with
the tripod would be struggling with something between one
hundred and twenty and one hundred and thirty pounds. That
kind of load would see off most people; it would bury someone the size of Three-piece. His build was what had militated
against his ever becoming a machine gunner in the first place,
because he'd never have survived the apprenticeship.

Scarlett could see that Sweet was interested, figuring that
these were peculiar times and that maybe—just *maybe*—there
was a possibility of getting hold of a gimpy without serving
the obligatory period as number two.

'What do you say, Sweet?' asked Scarlett.

'I haven't heard the question yet, Sergeant.'

'The question's the same as before. How about handing
over the johnnies?'

This is flaming ridiculous, thought Scarlett. Here we are in the middle of the South Atlantic in a Force 7, part of the biggest battle fleet to set sail from British shores since World War Two, about to transfer to assault ships and get involved in a punch-up with the Argies, and I'm arguing with this little bleeder about condoms with feathers on the end.

'You mentioned something about the platoon getting an extra gimpy.'

'If we get one, it'll be yours.'

Scarlett could say that with his hand over his heart. Sweet wasn't a bad shot with a machine gun; he wasn't the best in the platoon but he wasn't the worst either. An extra gimpy could just as easily be allocated to him as it could be to someone like Sammy Finch, who would undoubtedly want his oppo Twiggy to be number two. The weight of the tripod on Twiggy's skinny frame would drive him into the ground like a tent peg under a six-pound hammer. Anyway, the question wouldn't arise. There *had* been some talk at an earlier conference between company officers and senior NCOs of trying to grab three or four extra gimpies for D Company. It had come to nothing. Whatever spares were going the paras and the marines had snaffled.

'Okay,' said Three-piece, handing over a dozen foil-wrapped condoms. 'Hang on a sec,' he added, as Scarlett accepted them. Three-piece hunted through the packets until he found what he was looking for. 'I'll keep this one.'

'Why that one?'

'It's a tickler, got a red feather on the end.'

'And you're going to put that over your rifle muzzle, feather an' all.'

'Why not?'

'Because you'll look like a flaming medieval knight going to a tournament, that's why not.'

The mental image did not displease Three-piece.

'Well, I am, aren't I, sort of?'

Scarlett shook his head. 'I've never noticed this about you before, Sweet, but I'm beginning to have grave doubts about your sanity.'

'Then maybe I should put in a chit to see the quack,' said Three-piece cunningly. 'If I'm crazy I should be hospitalized and stay here while all the other clever buggers dive ashore in the LCUs.'

'Forget it. It's because you're crazy that you're going.

You're with the battalion for the duration, until we go home or until some Argie blows a hole in you.'

'Just a thought, Sarge.'

Scarlett grinned wryly as he fingered the packets. He'd better make good and sure he distributed them all and had none about his person when he got home. Eileen would throw a fit. Already he was in big trouble because of the 'underhanded and thoroughly shameful manner' in which he had deserted his wife and child. Every letter brought another ten pages of savage complaints, coming at him like tracer shells. If *he* was scared of anything it wasn't an Argie rifle; it was Eileen O'Hara with an axe to grind.

Fear was a subject that was rarely, if ever discussed. It was there all right, in every member of every company of every battalion, and it manifested itself in different ways, according to the temperament of the individual, during the hours that remained before crossdecking to the assault ships. Some men talked endlessly, about anything, finding it impossible to keep themselves to themselves. Others cleaned and repeatedly cleaned their personal weapons, polished their bayonets until they gleamed, and resisted the temptation to serrate the cutting edge in obedience to the rules laid down by the Geneva Convention. Still others went on the scrounge for items of foul-weather kit they had either lost or which had been 'liberated' by someone while the owner's back was turned. At least one group continuously sang Nazi marching songs. They knew all the lines too, though it had to be considered doubtful whether the composer of the Horst Wessel had ever expected his lyrics to be sung by British soldiers fifty-odd years after they were written. Many men played hands of cards for absurd stakes. ('Your million and up a million.' 'Right, I'll see your million, raise a million, and throw in my mother and my sister Sadie.') Yank Hobart ran one of these poker schools, wearing a green eyeshade he'd dug up from somewhere and believing he was the Cincinnati Kid or at least Sergeant Bilko. But most men wrote letters, knowing that there would be little room and possibly little time to do so once they crossdecked.

Since Ascension, Twiggy had had several stabs at replying to Carol's pregnancy bombshell. None of them had sounded right until he concluded that he did, after all, want to marry her anyway, and not just because of the sprog. After that words flowed easily.

He told Sammy of his decision. Sammy hooted with derision.

'Christ, Twiglet, you're not capable of looking after yourself, never mind a wife and nipper. How're you going to live on a private's pay?'

'We'll manage.'

'They said that when they were counting the lifeboats on the *Titanic*.'

Sammy, too, was in regular correspondence with Libby, though he wrote to her at the office ever since he had compared her mother unfavourably to Lon Chaney. In some respects he was surprised that she answered his letters without criticizing him too heavily for insulting her old lady, but he guessed that a lot of girls in the UK liked the idea of having a bloke with the task force. She'd even sent him a clipping of her pubic hair, which he kept in a waterproof wallet. To him the hair was what toy bears were to others, though he might have been surprised to learn just how many of his oppos had a similar talisman. Maybe he'd try to make it up with her mother when he got home, though logic suggested that that was impossible. In any case, he doubted he'd have the nerve or the inclination to face her. What the hell would they talk about anyway if she accepted his apology? ('Hello, Sammy, nice to meet you. Have a sandwich. Now, would you like to watch BBC or ITV or go upstairs and screw the backside off my daughter, you horny little sod!') Stuff it. Not to worry. Unlike Twiggy, he wasn't interested in marriage.

He had a thought.

'You'll be living in married quarters or a flat or something when you get hitched, won't you?' he asked Twiggy.

'That's what usually happens,' answered Twiggy grumpily, not too sure that he cared for Sammy Finch this red-hot minute.

'In that case I approve,' said Sammy. 'I think it'll all work out fine. You'll be needing a best man, and I hope you'll look no further than yours truly.'

'You've got a deal,' said Twiggy, beaming. 'Though we'll keep it all to ourselves for the time being, shall we?'

'Of course, Twiglet, of course.'

Right, thought Sammy, that's the accommodation problem on a Saturday night sorted out, especially as Carol and Libby were mates. And who knew, before Carol Bannister (or Carol Twigg, rather) got as big as a house, they might all end up four in a bed. Yessir, the future held interesting possibilities.

As the evening of May 18 wore on, an episode which was known ever afterwards as The Great Erection Race was enacted in one of the troopship's lounges. It began as a good-natured argument. Someone, a marine, suggested that the bootnecks were superior to all other mobs in every way. Balls, responded a para. Only a handful of marines had the jumping wings that every paratrooper wore, and paras could force march—'tab' in their vernacular—just as far as any bootneck. A lance-corporal from Daddy's battalion—with considerable nerve—submitted that the marines and the paras lived on their past reputations alone.

But how to prove it before they all proved it by dumping the Argies in the sea in a few days? Fighting each other was out; the penalties were severe. Besides, they were all good mates now and needed to conserve their energy for the bean-eaters. They couldn't test endurance with it being dark outside and with the weather, in any case, a bit like the week after Noah got the Met. forecast. And arm-wrestling would establish nothing more than a strong guy from one outfit being able to whip a strong guy from another outfit. That wasn't general enough. What they needed was a test between, say, half a dozen blokes from each battalion. Ideally that should be a drinking contest, but alcohol was at a premium. A demonstration of sexual prowess was obviously out.

But was it? Suggestions flew backwards and forwards until someone had a bright idea—or, rather, one that was considered bright under the circumstances but which otherwise would have qualified the originator and the eventual participants for the rubber room in the funny factory.

Since approaching any of the women aboard was out of the question, the alternative was utilizing photographs from the various soft-porn magazines most men had with them, and other pin-ups that one or two troops had carried for years. The rules were simple. Each unit would select up to half a dozen men, or as many loonies as could be persuaded. They would strip naked and stand in front of their peers. The photographs would be shown to each group of contestants in turn, the object being to induce sexual excitement. No pictures of actual couplings would be permitted, or anything other than an individual girl in a pose. Each team would choose its own photos with a maximum of twelve. The men must stand with their hands behind their backs; the touching of personal parts was forbidden. The man who achieved the highest angle of erection would be declared the winner, and his unit the undisputed best. Any contestant who failed to make a right-angle with the deck from the pendant position after the first round of photo-displays would be eliminated automatically.

Although the contest was greeted with thunderous approval, there were few volunteers to participate. Hearing of the event and having pocketed eight million two hundred thousand pounds in markers, Yank Hobart raced around D Company to scrape up a team and, still in his Cincinnati Kid role, perhaps make a few ackers on the side. The obvious place to begin was with Three-piece Sweet, who had an enviable collection of girlie magazines and who, as a womanizer of repute, was a natural candidate for the battalion 'eleven'. Three-piece wouldn't play but he offered to act as team coach and adviser as well as lending magazines, and photos from other sources, providing he could choose the running order of display. Yank agreed. He also found out quickly that the forthcoming event was regarded very much as a spectator sport. Everyone wanted his oppo to compete; no one wanted to take the plunge and possibly make himself look ridiculous.

Yank tried Corporal Tyler, remembering Scrunch's crack about Two-Shit at the briefing. Two-Shit didn't want to know either. He and Jomo were stripping their gimpies for something like the fifteenth time since sun-up.

'Bloody silly kid's game,' scorned Two-Shit. 'Walk your chalks, Hobart.'

'How about you?' Yank asked Jomo.

'No.'

'You'd be perfect,' persisted Yank. 'You know what everybody says about you guys.'

'No, I don't,' said Jomo. 'What does everyone say about British citizens who come from Birmingham?'

'Aw, come on,' moaned Yank. 'Don't act dumb. Let's get this show on the road. You know what I mean.'

Because he'd heard similar comments for most of his young life, frequently with racial undertones which he knew Yank did not intend, Jomo had the answer off pat.

'What you honkies don't understand is that to move something this weight'—he jabbed at his groin—'through an angle of roughly one hundred and sixty degrees takes more effort and therefore happens less often than moving something that weight'—he jabbed a finger at Yank's groin—'through the

same angle. Basic mechanics, man. You're so little you'd
need a machete to hack your way through a field of toadstools.'

'Huh?' said Yank.

'Bugger off,' said Two-Shit.

In the twenty minutes allowed to round up participants,
Yank found one man from 4 Platoon, D Company, willing to
have a try, and another from A Company. Acne Hackey,
smelling suspiciously of gin, volunteered, but Yank turned
him down. His cock was probably the same texture as his
face, and that not even six weeks' sea air had improved. The
honour of the battalion was at stake.

'Thanks but no thanks,' said Yank.

Non-Legless Jones considered the whole idea disgusting.
He'd read a girlie magazine once and found the experience so
disturbing that he'd resolved there and then never to read
another. He had, of course, and continued to, but he always
felt frighteningly guilty afterwards.

'Nobody asked you, dummy,' said Yank. 'You keep your
leek in your pants.'

Yank was crestfallen. Two wasn't much of a team. He
thought of competing himself just to make up the numbers but
concluded he didn't want to make a bloody fool of himself.

He found Three-piece sorting through a stack of magazines
and single photographs, waiting for him. With Sweet was
Branston Pickles. Branston also smelt of gin. Yank would not
find out until much later that Acne Hackney had carried an
entire bottle of Gordons with him from the UK, determined
not to open it until the landings became inevitable, which he
now judged was the case. He'd sold half-share in the bottle to
Branston earlier.

'Hearyezfockinlookinfaesomeonefaeacompo,' said the Glaswegian.

Branston was hard enough to understand when he was
stone cold sober. Half cut, his accent was virtually impossible
to fathom. However, Yank deduced that Branston was trying
to confirm that Yank was looking for people to enter a
competition. Still, it would be as well to make sure.

'What did you say, Branston?' asked Yank.

'NaefockinBranstontaeyemate,' said the Scot. 'TisfockinJim.'

'But you want to get on the team, is that it? You're
volunteering?'

'He is,' said Three-piece, picking up his magazines and
photographs.

'Are you sure this is wise?' asked Yank. 'I mean, he's half drunk.'

'Naefockindrunk,' grunted the Scot. 'Anyways, anyJock-fockindrunkbetterthananySassenachfockinsober. Soputthatin-yourfockinpipeandfockinsmokeit.'

'Come on, let's go,' said Three-piece, leading the way. 'How many others did you get?'

'Two. A guy from 4 Platoon and a guy from A Company. I sent them up to the lounge.'

Three-piece stopped in his tracks.

'Two! And Branston makes three. That's not much of a bleeding team, is it?'

As it turned out the commandos and the paratroopers hadn't done much better, mustering only four apiece. Eleven contestants, most of them intoxicated in spite of the apparent shortage of alcohol, were outnumbered in a ratio of twenty to one by spectators, all bellowing for their grinning favourites.

The paras and the bootnecks had coaches also, and piles of magazines the equal of Three-piece's. Amid the uproar Three-piece and the other coaches went over the rules for their own benefit and then for the benefit of the competitors, who were in the process of sheepishly disrobing. The coaches would also act as each other's referees. Anything that even looked like hard-core porn would mean the immediate disqualification of that team.

Three-piece and Yank had a quick squint at the covers and some of the displays that the paras and the marines proposed using. No problem there, confided Three-piece. The usual stuff. A few Bo Dereks, some *Penthouse, Playboy, Mayfair* and so on centrefolds. Some Page 3 girls—one or two not bad but no cigar, according to Yank. A famous pop artist moonlighting before she became a household name had Three-piece worried when he saw her, but he thought he could top that. The rest were of the black-stockings-and-tufted-muff brigade, okay for beginners but about as erotic as Peter Rabbit for old timers.

Money was changing hands rapidly. Yank wanted in on the action but was a little worried when he examined the opposition, all men now being fully stripped and facing the audience, some of them clasping their hands above their heads. One para in particular Yank judged to be a serious threat. Balls like cantaloupes. Compared with him—and a couple of others—Yank's entries looked about ready for the infirmary.

The teams divided into three groups, the paras, the marines and the battalion. A marine corporal set himself up as starter. On the command 'Go' the coaches would show their teams the display photographs. They could hold each page open as long as they liked, but they could not return to that page once they had switched to another until the end of the round. No suggestive phrases were to be allowed from the coaches, only words of encouragement such as 'come on' and 'concentrate'.

'Get some money down,' said Three-piece to Yank. 'Put me in for a tenner.'

'Who on?'

'Our lot, you berk.'

'Our lot?'

'What are you, a parrot? Specifically Branston. You'll get good odds.'

Yank studied Branston. He was hung well enough in a kind of knobbly Scottish way that reminded Yank of a prize parsnip his father had once grown on the allotment, but that was about all. There again, none of the other contestants was showing much sign of life.

'Sure?'

'Trust me.'

'Go,' yelled the starter.

Pandemonium reigned supreme for several minutes. The Royal Marine coach needed a lesson in tactics. He rushed from one man to another in his quartet, showing them only briefly each girlie-pic. The para coach had used his head, sorting out his pile of magazines and photos in ascending order of eroticism. Three-piece took his time, turning each page and displaying each photo quietly and patiently.

Getting through nine pictures to the accompanying bedlam took approximately four minutes. At the end of that it was patently obvious that three-quarters of the marines and the same number of paras were going to be eliminated at the end of round one, even if their coaches had produced snapshots of half Hollywood being gang-banged by the other half with sound effects. The big para was showing interest sufficient to raise him close to the horizontal, and a marine who resembled the Incredible Hulk seemed as if he would make it to round two. Of the battalion's entrants, the representatives from 4 Platoon and A Company were about to join three bootnecks and three paras on the sidelines.

'No hands!' screamed Yank, who had twenty pounds down

at four to one against Branston, and Three-piece's tenner at the same odds. 'Referee, that bastard's taking his hands from behind his back!'

'No hands!' yelled the starter.

'We should have handicapped the circumcised,' lamented Yank. 'They're not doing better but they look as though they are.'

The paras and the bootnecks got through their twelve pictures in a further forty-five seconds. Three-piece showed only eleven, keeping the twelfth under wraps and concentrating mainly on Branston, who was grinning drunkenly but who would make it to round two.

'Straight on!' shouted the starter above the din when eight out of the original eleven retired, amid jeers, to their respective corners. 'Round two!'

The para coach and the marine coach took it slower on this occasion, learning from Three-piece and glancing anxiously across at Branston, who was doing best of the remaining trio. They murmured words of encouragement, some of them illegal under the rules, causing Yank to jump up and down with rage.

'Foul! Foul!'

On picture eight of round two the Incredible Hulk folded. Just like that. It was apparent he'd reached the apex of the semi-circle being described and, rather than humiliate himself, he said 'Fuck it' and withdrew. The big para had managed twenty degrees from the horizontal and his coach had been bright enough to realize that it was a Charlie's Angels clone at picture nine in the red berets' repertoire that turned his oppo on. Tits like pumpkins. He stuck with that, saving ten, eleven and twelve as back-ups in case it came to a race in the home stretch. Branston was shading the para by a degree at picture ten in Three-piece's portfolio, but Branston was also sweating a bit and it was going to be a damned close run thing if it came to a third round. In Three-piece's judgment Branston wouldn't make it that far. But neither, in his estimation, would the big para. It was time to play his ace, demoralize the jumping-jack.

He flashed through picture eleven, to the accompaniment of Branston protesting: 'Yedidnaegi'mefockintimetaeseethatfocker.'

'Next one, Branston,' Three-piece encouraged. 'This one.'

'No hands, no hands,' yelled Yank.

The situation remained iffy, with maybe a degree or so in Branston's favour, when Three-piece produced a ten-by-eight photo of Jane Fonda he'd had since he was sixteen. It would be difficult to say how old Ms Fonda was when the photo was taken, but she was no chicken. Neither was the picture soft-porn in any accepted sense of the term. It was simply La Fonda sitting cross-legged in a short dress, fishnet tights, and thigh-high black leather-look boots. But it was also the expression on her face—sexy and arrogant. There was something in those eyes that the Bo Dereks and the *Penthouse* centrefolds would never have. Class told.

'Oohfockinhell,' groaned Branston, already in fantasy land, and gained an immediate fifteen-degree advantage.

The big para folded under the pressure. His mates conceded. Grinning hugely, Yank went around to collect the winning bets. Branston disappeared. Fonda had won by a couple of lengths.

Later, during the share-out—and Yank felt it only right that Branston should have a fiver's worth at four to one from his own gains—Three-piece said, his magazines spread out at various pages: 'How could we fail? Branston's seen everything in this collection a million times. I mean, look at that lot. No style. After a diet of meatballs, who wouldn't give an arm for a thick steak? Mind you, it's always as well to begin with a prawn cocktail or some soup, just to get the juices going.'

'But Branston's got a thing about Jane Fonda, right?' asked Yank. 'I mean, you knew that and that's why you saved her for last?'

'No way.' Three-piece shook his head. 'But I do know Branston. And I know you. Now take a look. What would you prefer on a rainy night in Macclesfield, one of those bimbos or Jane Fonda?'

Yank had to admit that Three-piece had a point. She was a Women's Libber, Jane Fonda, and had funny politics as far as he could remember, but, in looks, she was streets ahead of the usual dough-faces who flashed their prats at the guy with the box Brownie. Still, he was unhappy.

'You mean it was just a hunch? I had twenty flaming notes riding on a *hunch?*'

'It wasn't a hunch,' said Three-piece severely, offended. 'Jesus Christ, Yank, no wonder your success rate with women can be measured in single figures.'

Branston came back from wherever he'd been, fully dressed, to pick up his share.

'YedidnaefockinthinkIcouldnaedofockalldidye?'

Whatever he was drinking it was powerful stuff. Three-piece and Yank glanced at one another, bewildered.

'You said a mouthful,' said Yank.

'Right,' said Three-piece.

Later still that evening, Peter was studying with Winter's Day a large-scale map of the land surrounding Ajax Bay when Toby Lomax appeared in the cabin doorway.

'Seen Rupert Parker-Smith about?' asked the heavy-set B Company officer.

'No, sorry,' answered Peter, barely raising his head.

'Right, thanks.'

An alarm-bell jangled in Peter's brain as Lomax disappeared.

'Excuse me a sec,' said Peter to Winter's Day, and chased after Lomax. Catching up, he asked, 'Is there anything special you want to see Rupert about? I'll probably bump into him before I turn in.'

Lomax was carrying an envelope. The address appeared to be written in a woman's hand. Peter didn't care for the implications.

'It'll keep.'

'I mean, if I can save your legs,' offered Peter.

'Oh, very well. Daddy collared me earlier. Parker-Smith's apparently not the only officer with a shotgun aboard, but it will not, repeat not, be rubbish-skipped when we crossdeck. Can I take it you'll tell him and strike that from my list of things to do?'

'Oh, sure, sure,' said Peter weakly. 'I'll pass it on. Many thanks.'

'Are you all right?' asked Lomax. 'You look a little pale.'

'No, I'm fine. Be glad to see dry land, though.'

'Won't we all.'

Peter discovered Rupert hunched over a table in one corner of the bar, a gold pen in his hand.

'Just scribbling a final few lines to Lavinia,' he smiled. 'Should I give her your love?'

'I've already written to her. About your Purdey—you're not to crossdeck it. It stays here.'

'I wasn't thinking of doing so anyway. This is not going to be the jolly old shooting expedition I first thought. I've already made arrangements to keep it under lock and key aboard.'

'Good. That order came from Daddy incidentally, not the company commander. It was delivered to me by Toby Lomax, who was looking for you.'

Rupert contemplated the nib of his pen.

'I see. And you thought when you saw him he had mayhem in mind. I shouldn't worry about that, old boy. The lady in question is hardly likely to write anything silly to her husband by way of confession now that D-Day's close, and it was agreed before we sailed that she wouldn't write to me while I was away.'

'But you'll be seeing her when we get home?'

'*When* we get home,' said Rupert, 'I doubt I shall be more than a vague memory to the lady. However, if it's otherwise I'm afraid I have to repeat that it's my business only, and I don't much care what you promised my sister. She said some very nice things about you, by the way, in her last epistle to me. I hope she's giving you the same message.'

She was. Between February and the Argentine invasion, she and Peter had had half a dozen dinners together and a shared weekend in the Cotswolds, booking into the hotel as man and wife. The sex had been excellent, as had the walks and the talks and the laughter. Peter no longer thought of Lavinia as Rupert's twenty-year-old sister. Whether anything would come of it only time would tell, and the time to think about it was not now.

On May 19, in a South Atlantic that had, providentially and temporarily, ceased to be angry, the assault ships *Fearless* and *Intrepid* launched their LCUs several hundred miles outside the Total Exclusion Zone and, they hoped, out of range or at least out of observable contact of the Argentine Air Force.

One by one the 'rubbish-skips' came alongside the lower galley doors of the troopship carrying the marines, half the paras and Daddy's battalion, whereupon men, in groups of a hundred and heavily laden with arms and equipment, made the hazardous leap to the assault craft. When an LCU was full, it trundled back the three-quarters of a mile to its parent ship, disgorged its passengers, then returned for another load. Overhead Sea Harriers flew CAPs.

By late afternoon the crossdecking was complete, though

not without tragedy. A helicopter carrying SAS personnel to the *Intrepid* hit a bird—an albatross, it was thought—and crashed into the sea. Those aboard were killed, drowned under the weight of their equipment, before they could be reached.

Space aboard the *Fearless* and *Intrepid* being at a premium, 2 Para remained on the *Norland*. For the landings they would be rubbish-skipped ashore from there. After close on six weeks at sea and eight thousand miles, the amphibious force was ready. All it now needed was the green light from London—the code word PALPAS—and weather sufficiently dirty to disguise its intentions.

EIGHTEEN

Girl-friends and Wives (ii)

In the UK they knew the landings were imminent when the Ministry of Defence imposed a news blackout. In most people's view this was as good as telling Buenos Aires to stiffen the Falklands defences and get the Mirages airborne, for no one believed the officially encouraged rumour that there would be no full-scale assault, only a series of hit-and-run attacks. The MoD's handling of public relations and the distribution of information would be criticized again and again in the coming weeks, particularly by the task force, whose lives might become forfeit because of an ill-judged statement from London. Major attacks were occasionally speculated upon, which was tantamount to giving the enemy a situations map and order of battle.

On the morning of May 20 Carol Bannister's mother heard her daughter being sick in the bathroom. She knew instinctively that Carol was pregnant. After Mr Bannister had left the house for work, and before Carol could do so, she tackled her daughter.

'Yes,' said Carol—there was no point in denying it—and burst into tears.

When she calmed down, Mrs Bannister asked her who the father was. Carol told her, and that Chris Twigg was with the task force. Strange, thought Mrs Bannister, how little one knew one's own children, and how secretive they could be when the mood took them.

'You poor dear,' she murmured.

'You're not angry?'

'No, *I'm* not angry, though I can't answer for your father. When's the baby due?'

'The middle of December. Do we have to tell Daddy?'

'He'll have to know sooner or later. But perhaps we can leave it until later and hope that—Chris?'—Carol nodded—'will be home long before then. Will you get married?'

'Do I have a choice?'

'Of course you have a choice. It won't be much of a life, marrying a soldier. Apart from the money, or lack of it, it will mean living in married quarters, going with him if he gets a foreign posting—or staying at home in England and letting your child grow up only half knowing its father.'

'I'm not getting rid of it.'

'No one's suggesting that. But do think seriously about marriage.'

'You mean I shouldn't? I should let the baby be born illegitimate and bring it up by myself?'

'I don't know. There's a great deal of folklore involved in a child needing a father. This is all brand-new to me, don't forget. In my day it would have been quick-march to the altar as soon as the pregnancy was confirmed and a later claim of premature birth to keep the neighbours from gossiping. Nowadays it doesn't seem to matter so much.'

In spite of herself, Carol was surprised at her mother's attitude.

'I didn't know you were so liberated.'

'Liberation's not new. I wasn't born with a kitchen sink round my neck. Or a cooker. Or a husband and a daughter.'

'It's that Open University,' said Carol, feeling giggly and frivolous. It must be relief, she decided. She had someone to share her burden now.

'Perhaps. However, have you discussed marriage?'

'Hardly. A little, in letters.'

'Do you love him?'

'I don't know. I think so. Yes—I think so. It's difficult to tell, isn't it? When this—something like this—happens, the first reaction is panic. That's followed by a need for respectability, something solid. But I think I love him.'

'Don't marry him if you don't.'

Carol glanced at the kitchen clock. 'God, I'll be late.'

'No work for you today, young lady. I'll ring in and tell

them you're sick. You can take today and tomorrow off, go back on Monday.'

'But . . .'

'No buts. Let's spend the day together. It's been ages since we did that. I want to know a great deal more about . . . Chris. We should also discuss whether to tell your father. I don't know, perhaps it would be better if he knew. Then at least it would be out in the open.'

'I'm going to dread that.'

'He'll be hurt, I agree, perhaps even angry. But it can only get worse the longer we put it off. Does anyone else know?'

'Just Dr McCauley, who advised me to confide in you, by the way. And Libby. She won't tell anyone.'

'I'll make some tea.'

Her daughter a mother, thought Mrs Bannister. And the father little more than a boy, by all accounts—and a boy, moreover, who might be risking his life any day now. Who might not come back. God forgive her for having such thoughts, but the possibility must have also crossed Carol's mind. The loss of the *Sheffield* and the *Belgrano* had demonstrated that this was a war in which people got killed. Open University notwithstanding, the world was insane. Did Mrs Thatcher and President Galtieri know what they were doing? Did they care? All the fine words about sovereignty and 'ensuring that naked aggression did not succeed' counted for nothing to every son's mother who would not see her child again.

The same morning Libby Rees's newspaper horoscope read: Taurus. A confusing year ahead. News from abroad may bring a surprise. The perfect time to give way to sudden impulses. Romance in the air.

Huh, she thought, on the bus taking her to work. Huh and double huh. 'In the air' romance might be, but in the air was where it was likely to stay if her mother and father had anything to do with it. The atmosphere at home had been anything but cordial since her mother's discovery of the stained sheets and Sammy's titanic row with her over the telephone. Not that Libby had ever heard the details, but her mother had come into the sitting-room after slamming down the receiver with her face the colour of an over-ripe plum. And then it had started. *If you want to remain in this house you'll obey house rules. You'll also be indoors by ten o'clock each evening.* (For God's sake I'm almost twenty years of age.) *I don't give a damn if you're thirty years of age. If you don't do as we say, out you go.*

For several days Libby had considered calling her parents' bluff, packing her bags, finding a flat, either alone or as an extra girl. But a detailed examination of her finances had shown her how impossible that was. She had it easy at home, she was forced to admit, the amount she paid her mother for her keep being about a quarter of what she would have to pay in rent and food and so on if she were on her own. Damn Carol for getting pregnant. They could have shared and halved the expenses.

And there's to be no further communication between you and that . . . that . . . (Soldier, Mum?) *Don't be impertinent.*

Well, there *was* further communication, and that was that, though God help her if Sammy slipped up one day and sent one of his 'amorous' letters to her home address instead of the office. Amorous, though, hardly being the word. Lecherous would be closer, and even that was putting it mildly. He was hardly oblique in his comments regarding what he would do to her when he got home, but she had found she looked forward to what she privately termed Sammy's 'dirty talk'. He could easily get a job writing those phoney letters in girlie magazines, which she sometimes found lying around the office. By the same token she wouldn't be so bad at writing them herself. Nor would she pose for photos inadequately— which was something Sammy had also suggested in one of his less serious moments. Pose, that is, and send a print to him by mail. 'Gets bloody lonely down here without something to remind me of what I'm missing.'

Less serious? Not Sammy. And she would be delighted to appear in black stockings and corset for someone with a Polaroid, where the negatives did not have to be processed by randy lab technicians. Nor would she really mind the end product being shown around the ship by Sammy. If she could find a girl friend with a camera, she might just do it. Girl friend? She sometimes wondered if she were not a bit dikey.

God, her mother would have a *fit*!

She chuckled aloud at the thought, hastily turning the chuckle into a cough and covering her face with a handkerchief when several of the other bus passengers glanced across at her curiously.

But what was so wrong in being dikey? It might be fun. It would certainly be different.

It couldn't last, of course, she and Sammy. For that matter, if it were not for her parents' curfew she doubted she would have remained faithful this long, something Sammy continued to ask in his letters and to which she could always reply in the affirmative. Men were funny like that. She had absolutely no doubts that if Sammy had been posted where the battalion was originally due to go, Germany, and not the Falklands, he would have been lifting many a fräulein's skirt every weekend. Yet he'd complain bitterly if *she* went to bed with someone else.

She could, perhaps—as a ploy—introduce an extra girl friend or woman friend to her mother and father. Someone whose respectability was beyond dispute. That might give her some latitude. Someone from the office, maybe. Or there was that nice Julia Lomax, the officer's wife who had put an advertisement in the local rag suggesting regular meetings for all wives and girl friends of men with the task force. A sort of therapy. Julia—she liked to be called Mrs Lomax though Libby always thought of her as Julia—had been most charming. They had got along immediately, Libby felt, when Julia had circulated during the coffee and biscuits after the first meeting. And she was some beauty; even another woman had to admit that. A little distant, perhaps, a little uncertain. Libby wondered what her husband was like.

What Libby had taken for uncertainty was actually unadulterated horror at having to mix with and be pleasant to the frumps and the dowdies who largely represented, in Julia Lomax's view, the battalion's distaff side. What on earth did one say to such people?

Julia was finding out in the middle of the morning on May 20, when she was in the chair at one of the welfare clinics that had been held periodically since the task force sailed. Although there were channels through which could be funnelled run-of-the-mill complaints and requests for assistance because of hardship, Heather Rankin, Daddy's wife, had decided at the outset that it would be an excellent idea for the battalion's officers' wives to become involved in the day-to-day problems of the other ranks' wives and girl friends.

'My dear,' she had said to Julia during a sherry morning early in April, 'some of these poor creatures find it difficult even to fill in a form properly. That's the trouble with army life. When their husbands are at home everything is done for them. They make virtually no decisions for themselves. Now they may have to. The Lord only knows how long the battalion will be gone, and while they're away all sorts of difficulties will arise, you mark my words. From those tiresome unexpected pregnancies—among the unmarried ones, you understand—to the wives who'll take lovers. And *that*, believe me, causes all sorts of disciplinary problems in the long run. You remember the battalion's last Ulster tour? But of course you do. I think we had five young girls, at various intervals, turning up tearfully at the main gates, asking what they should do now they were expecting. Then there was the drink problem. I have it on very good authority that the manager of the local off-licence telephoned the camp to ask if a party was being planned. If so, could he cater for it? Apparently he was receiving unprecedented requests for sweet sherry. I ask you, *sweet sherry.'*

Four years older than Daddy and the daughter of a career diplomat, Heather Rankin had spent much of her girlhood in what were then the Colonies. Although she could hunt, shoot and fish as well as any boy her age by the time she was fifteen, she had been sheltered from many of the harsh realities of life and had, as a result, never fully developed emotionally. Thus 'the other ranks' wives took lovers, whereas what they actually did, in their own parlance, was have a bit on the side if they could get away with it without the old man finding out. It would have been unkind (and untrue) to call her a snob. Her observation regarding the semi-literacy of some of the 'poor creatures' was genuinely held, and in a few cases accurate. Nevertheless, she would have been alarmed (alarmed, not astonished) to learn that a handful of NCOs' wives had university degrees. She belonged to an era when it was considered enough for those not of her class to be able to read a little, write a bit, and do a few sums. Anything more was dangerous, revolutionary nonsense. Daddy loved her dearly but sometimes despaired of her. In his view, often voiced, she was an anachronistic old fascist, an abandoned nenuphar secretly pining for a long-lost Indian summer.

'So what do we do?' Julia had asked that same April morning.

'Do, my dear?' boomed Heather Rankin, her voice sandpaper and silk. 'We organize them, get them all together at regular intervals. To begin with, we put an advertisement in the local paper. To be more precise, you do.'

'*I* do!' exclaimed Julia, appalled.

'You do. I'm allocating tasks, and you're the perfect person to set the ball rolling. Don't despair, you'll have plenty of back-up once we're underway. Ah, now there's someone over there I simply must talk to. Good luck, my dear.'

Anachronistic old fascist Heather Rankin might be, but she wasn't foolish enough not to realize that Julia sometimes strayed from the marriage bed. At least, she *looked* as if she would. There'd been a beauty not dissimilar to her in the Punjab just before Partition, and the tales that had circulated about *that* one, my dear, even among the boys, fairly made one's hair stand on end. Putting Julia in charge of the advertising would give her something constructive to do.

The clinics were held at varying hours, to suit everyone's timetable. Women with young children often could not get away in the evening. Neither could women with evening jobs. Those with daytime jobs preferred their get-togethers after seven. It was unlucky for Julia that she was chairman the morning the imminent landings were being speculated upon.

The twenty or so women in front of her in one of the battalion's recreation rooms wanted information. She could give them none. Nor was the pleasant young man who represented the local Department of Health and Social Security much help. He was there to assist Julia in fielding any awkward questions regarding wives' rights under existing law. Regrettably there were few of those, and by the time the gathering broke up towards midday, when toddlers were howling out of boredom and hunger, Julia felt as if she had been put through the wringer. And achieved nothing.

The DHSS representative, John Maxwell, asked her if she'd care for a large gin and tonic somewhere: 'Not in the camp, outside.'

Julia read the signals. All right, nothing could happen that she did not wish to happen and, after the last hour's coven, she could use some male company. She also needed the suggested gin.

'I'd love to,' she said. 'Can you give me a few moments to tidy up?'

'Sure.'

But at the door to the recreation room Eileen O'Hara collared her.

'If you can spare me a few minutes, Mrs Lomax.'

Julia groaned inwardly. Eileen O'Hara was her *bête noire*.
Nevertheless she put on her best smile.

'I'm in rather a hurry, Mrs O'Hara, and I thought we
covered everything in there. Besides, don't you have to get
back to your daughter?' (It was a daughter, wasn't it, Julia
asked herself? Yes, a girl. Nine or ten weeks old. Colleen?
No, Kathleen. Kathleen O'Hara. Good God, *Kathleen* O'Hara.
Did the Irish always have to be—well, so *Irish*?)

'She's being looked after. I said I might be late. This won't
take long.'

Julia threw a glance over her shoulder at John Maxwell.
Sorry, she mouthed. Maxwell shrugged and picked up his
briefcase.

'Let's go into the anteroom,' suggested Julia, and when
they were both seated on the uncomfortable wooden folding
chairs added: 'And before you go any further I can't do
anything at all about getting your husband back from the task
force.'

That had been Eileen O'Hara's first request at the first
meeting six weeks earlier.

'*You don't seem seem to understand, Mrs Lomax. He ran
out on me without so much as a by your leave. We need him
here.*'

'*And you don't seem to understand, Mrs O'Hara, that the
men haven't gone on a continental holiday, to be recalled by
a Thomas Cook cable.*'

'No, it's not that. I know I can't get him back now until
it's all over, but he hardly seems to answer my letters. I
mean, he replies as if he hadn't read my letter at all.'

'You mean you nag him,' said Julia. To blazes with her.

'Nag him? I don't nag him. If you mean do I let him know
that what he did—without telling me—was disgraceful and
underhand, yes I do. But that's not nagging.'

'It might be construed as such by someone who doubtless
has other things on his mind.'

'Well, it isn't,' Eileen O'Hara repeated stubbornly.

Julia waited; there had to be more.

'The fact is,' said Eileen, 'I want him to leave the army,
get a job outside.'

'We've been over all this in the past,' said Julia patiently,
'and it's not my business. I can't interfere.'

'But he should at least write and tell me he's thinking about
it! And he doesn't.'

'Because he doesn't agree with you.' This is absurd, thought Julia.

'Then he should write and tell me *that*. He doesn't. He tells me what the weather's like and what they're doing on board, stories about the men in his platoon. I'm not interested.'

Julia held her tongue, feeling very sorry for Sergeant O'Hara. What a life the poor man must have. No wonder he'd preferred the task force to staying with the rear party.

'So someone should tell him to answer my letters properly,' persisted Eileen. 'Make him. Someone should write to an officer on board.'

'That someone being me?'

'Well, Major de Winton-Day's divorced so I can't talk to his wife, and Captain Ballantine isn't married.'

'My husband isn't in Sergeant O'Hara's company. I don't think Major de Winton-Day or Captain Ballantine would take kindly to Captain Lomax giving one of their NCOs advice.'

'Then you should ask Captain Lomax to have a word with Major de Winton-Day. Or you could write yourself to the Major or Captain Ballantine . . .'

'I scarcely know them well enough.'

'. . . Or another officer in D Company.'

Julia looked up sharply from her fingernails. Was this little virago hinting that she knew of her relationship with Rupert? No, there was nothing to suggest that.

'I'll see what I can do,' said Julia wearily, intending to do nothing of the kind but knowing that making the offer was the only way to be rid of Eileen O'Hara. 'I'll think of something.'

'I hope you do. Because if that doesn't work I'll have to ask for an interview with Mrs Rankin.'

'Good God, no! I mean, Mrs Rankin is very busy, what with one thing and another.'

Heather Rankin would have a fit if she were cornered by Eileen O'Hara and had to listen to her moans. In the battalion's matriarchy, Heather Rankin was the CO and Julia Lomax her adjutant. It was up to the adjutant to prevent the CO being pestered by cranks.

Later, at home, Eileen would say to her sister Gwen, who was staying with her for a few days while Gwen's husband Trevor was away on a sales trip and who had been looking after young Kathleen all morning, that 'she thought she would get some action now, now she had told that snooty Mrs Lomax how matters stood'. Gwen murmured encouragement but otherwise said nothing. She, too, occasionally felt pity for Harry O'Hara. Even as a youngster, Eileen had been a bully in spite of her diminutive size.

John Maxwell was waiting for Julia outside the recreation room. Julia had never been so pleased to see anyone for ages.

'I thought you'd have given up the ghost.'

'No, I promised you a gin and a gin I'll buy you.'

'A large one was the promise.'

'As large as you like. Did that one give you trouble?' He indicated Eileen O'Hara's disappearing back.

'A little. She seems to think the entire world revolves around her axis.'

'I meet them every day. After a while it becomes hard to tell the genuine cases from the charlatans, the needy from the habitual complainers. So one ends up by treating everyone as a fraud. Do you have anywhere in particular you'd like to go?'

'Well, there's an inn a couple of miles up the road . . .' Julia remembered February and the unfortunate meeting with Peter Ballantine and Lavinia Parker-Smith. 'But it can get crowded. I'll let you choose.'

'Do you have a car or should we go in mine?'

'We'll take both. You lead, I'll follow.'

'I'm delighted to hear it.'

Barely an hour's drive away from where Julia and John Maxwell sipped the first of several gin and tonics, Lavinia left her father and the gamekeeper McGregor talking, or rather arguing, about whether it would be necessary, and if so in what quantity, to buy in some six-to-seven-week-old pheasant poults to supplement those already hatched on the estate. Although the pheasant-shooting season was five months away, in McGregor's view buying-in would be necessary. Balking at the expense, in the Viscount's opinion it would not. Lavinia's brother Oliver, taking a legitimate day off since the estate was a client of the merchant bank of which he was a director, accompanied his sister, on foot, back to the house. The Viscount would return in the Range Rover later. Or McGregor would drive, depending upon who was the most sober after they retreated to McGregor's cottage to continue the discussion over a dram or two.

'My money's on McGregor,' wagered Oliver. 'He pours in a ratio of three to two in favour of the old man. That's how he always wins arguments. You wouldn't think they hated the sight of each other, would you, the amount of time they spend together?'

'They don't hate each other, silly,' laughed Lavinia. 'Quite the reverse. We're all of us—you, me and Rupert—less important to Daddy's day-to-day existence than McGregor. They're like the colonel of the regiment and the RSM, who began life, respectively, as a wet-behind-the-ears subaltern and a canny lance-corporal, and who learned how to hide their true feelings behind a facade of propriety.'

'You'd think it was *his* money,' grumbled Oliver, 'the way he moans about the price of a few poults.'

'Isn't it?'

'Of course it's not. It's the estate's and yours and mine and Rupert's, a few trusts, partly the bank's . . . I doubt he could dig up more than five hundred quid of his own if I asked him this afternoon.'

'I was teasing you,' said Lavinia. 'I can read a balance sheet.'

'Sorry,' apologized Oliver. 'I'm not very good at recognizing a tease. But Christ, he lives like a mediaeval baron, and I have this terrible vision that one day we'll have to open the grounds to tourists. Put in lions and tigers like the others. Or vintage motor cars.'

'The "others" you're talking about are dukes, or at the very least earls,' smiled Lavinia. 'A viscountcy is rather nearer the bottom of the pile. Besides, instead of tigers and lions we can show them Daddy. He should be worth a bob or two as an exhibit.'

'Idiot,' grinned Oliver.

Lavinia changed step smartly to match her brother's stride.

'You're getting very military,' commented Oliver. 'Peter Ballantine must be having quite an effect.'

Lavinia flushed. 'I also have a brother in the army.'

'But he didn't put the spring in your heels. Serious?'

'Mind your own business.'

'Nothing to do with me. Just making conversation. Anyway, he's a nice bloke, Peter, for what it's worth from a dull old banker.'

He *was* a nice bloke, thought Lavinia. In fact, he was an extraordinarily, exceptionally nice bloke, and she missed him fearfully.

'I hear his sister's very pleasant also,' added Oliver.

'I didn't know you'd met her.'

'I haven't to the best of my knowledge. Rupert must have said something. Or you.'

'I hardly know her myself. I've seen her a few times at battalion functions, but that was ages ago, before I really knew Peter.'

'You should look her up,' said Oliver. 'Give her a ring. Didn't I hear you say she's engaged to an Argentine?'

'I may have mentioned it.'

'Then she must be having rather an uncomfortable time. She might appreciate a call, seeing that you have Peter in common.'

Lavinia stopped in her tracks, causing Oliver to halt also. She kissed her brother fiercely on the cheek.

'What was that for?' asked Oliver.

'You're amazing,' said Lavinia. 'Do you know, in all the weeks since I last saw Peter I never once thought of calling Sara. Perhaps I'll do it. Whatever do you mean about bankers being dull? That's a positively inspired notion.'

'I'm glad you think so.'

'Though perhaps I'll wait a day or two. Just in case.'

'Superstitious?'

'Let's say I believe like you, like Daddy, that the landings can't be far off. Poor Sara Ballantine has two people to worry about. I'd hate to be chatting merrily to her about Peter if something had happened to her Argentine. We've been bombing and shelling Stanley fairly heavily, haven't we?'

NINETEEN

Ricardo

ONE MAN who could confirm with absolute authority that Stanley—the airfield, at least—had been bombed and shelled heavily since the beginning of May was Colonel Jorge Filippi, Ricardo's commanding officer, whose regiment formed part of the perimeter defences around the airfield, where some intelligence gatherers suspected that one prong of the impending British assault would be directed.

Filippi had lost several kilos in weight since the first RAF Vulcan attack on May 1, code-named Operation Black Buck though the colonel would not know that until many months later. It had seemed inconceivable at the time that the British could launch a heavy bomber from their only available base, Ascension, on a round-trip of something approaching 10,000 miles, and carry out a precision attack on a target the size of the airfield. But they had, and at 4.46 a.m. local time the first of the twenty-one bombs had fallen, the pattern of the whole cluster temporarily rendering the field unserviceable. The Stanley anti-aircraft batteries had replied with everything they had, to no effect. It was a case of too little, too late. The blitzkrieg had been sudden and devastating, not so much in the damage done but to morale. If the British were that determined, what would happen next? The kelpers had walked around all day on May 1 wearing broad smiles. You've had it all your own way up to now, they appeared to be saying, but that's over.

Of course, it was realized later that the Vulcan could not possibly have made it there and back with a full pay-load without a number of mid-air refuellings. But that, as far as morale was concerned, only made matters worse. An air force that could accomplish such a mission, with the innumerable difficulties involved, with the Vulcan needing to miss only one rendezvous with an airborne tanker for the crew to end their lives in a watery grave, could accomplish anything. And, as if to prove that the sortie was not a one-off affair, later the same morning Sea Harriers carried out attacks against the anti-aircraft positions on Mary Hill and Canopus Hill, north and south of the airfield, while another squadron bombed the Goose Green airstrip, killing the pilot and ground crew of a Pucara in the process.

Also on May 1, three British warships, later identified as the *Glamorgan, Arrow* and *Alacrity,* moved in as close as was deemed prudent to Stanley to shell the airfield with their 4.5 inch guns. Sea Harriers flew cover and were regularly engaged, often at low level, by the Argentine Air Force flying from mainland bases, but at the end of the day, against the loss of not a single Harrier, four Argentine aircraft had been destroyed (one, a Mirage, shot down by mistake by the ground defences, to the great delight of the kelpers). All three warships received minor damage.

In Filippi's opinion, if these were the opening shots in what could become a full-scale war, they had gone badly for Argentina. The major prizes as far as Brigadier Lami Dozo's air arm was concerned, the task force carriers *Hermes* and *Invincible,* were evidently going to keep well out of harm's way. While they remained afloat, the Sea Harriers could not only engage the Argentine Air Force, they could also give cover to the amphibious troops when they arrived. Without the carriers, there could be no landings.

Moreover, the younger conscripts were terrified (and as a consequence largely ineffective) by the noise and bedlam, which none of them had ever experienced before. Nor, for the most part, had they seen comrades wounded and in several instances killed. Although, already being a chain-smoker, he would have thought it impossible to smoke any more, Filippi found he was getting through an extra packet a day, there being no shortage of supplies for senior officers. C-130 Hercules transports continued to get through from the mainland, in spite of a second, though in this case unsuccessful, Black

Buck operation, bringing in luxuries as well as ammunition, and ferrying out casualties.

Then on May 2 the *Belgrano* was torpedoed and sunk.

Until that catastrophe, on strict instructions from Buenos Aires, the penalties for transgression being a court martial, the Argentine occupying force had, with few exceptions, done its utmost to get along with the Falkland Islanders, albeit under difficult circumstances, the kelpers, naturally enough, resenting the conquerors. There were rules, certainly. Short-wave radios capable of picking up the BBC World Service were supposed to be handed in, though in many cases they were not. Pedestrians, when eventually allowed to go about their business without carrying a white flag or piece of cloth, were warned to be careful, since all driving would now be on the right-hand side of the road instead of the left. The Union Jack would not be displayed anywhere, and anyone caught defacing an Argentine flag was liable to a fine or imprisonment. Uncomfortable conditions, to be sure—and felt more in Stanley than in the outlying settlements—but not totally unbearable now that the occupation was a fait accompli, though a temporary one in the view of most kelpers. The new regulations, pesos as currency, stamps overprinted *Islas Malvinas,* the overweening arrogance of many officers: all these things could be tolerated until the task force arrived.

Then the *Belgrano,* and attitudes hardened. Mild looting, an inevitable consequence of any invasion by any armed force at whatever period in history (because soldiers see no reason why they should suffer hardship while civilians, pleading non-combatant status, continue to eat and drink more or less as before), became more widespread. Only in the most extreme cases did Argentine officers take action against the offenders, and they virtually turned a blind eye to the sheep rustling and butchery that went on outside the capital. Though there was never any brutality in the purest sense of the word, islanders found that they were jostled and prodded with rifle butts whenever they encountered squads of Argentine soldiers. Even the conscripts, who to a man did not want to be there at all and with whom, to a certain extent, the islanders could feel sympathy because of their youth, began to get more aggressive. They no longer asked for food, they took it; they no longer searched for discarded wood to make fires, they tore down fences. Their officers allowed them to get on with it. Whenever those islanders who could speak Spanish asked the conscripts why they were stealing food instead of living off their rations, the youngsters would shrug fatalistically and occasionally answer, with nervous glances over their shoulders, that in the Argentine army they were considered useless dregs by all officers and regular NCOs. The less they got (so the reasoning went), the harder they would fight when the time came. The supplies flown into Stanley by the C-130s rarely reached the distant outposts in sufficient quantities. A man was expected to forage for himself if he wanted to stay alive.

Partly because he was well-travelled and had seen other cultures, partly because he possessed his fair share of natural humanity, but mostly because he had a younger brother who was a conscript and therefore knew at first hand the deprivations suffered by some nonregular units, in the beginning, and in his own company, Ricardo had done what he could to ensure that every man received his due in terms of food, warm clothing, cigarettes. But gradually the Hercules transports delivered fewer creature comforts in favour of more ammunition and weapons, in particular 155 mm artillery pieces which at least gave the defenders a chance to return fire against the murderous bombardments delivered by task force warships standing offshore and shelling the airport. The 155s were essential; not only did they now compel the British frigates and the cruiser *Glamorgan* to retreat to a safer distance, they would enable the defenders, when the landings came, to outgun the amphibious force. However, with the Sea Harriers marauding at low level whenever there was a break in the weather, C-130 logistics flights were risky, and cargo space taken up by ammunition and artillery could not be used for anything else. Every man had to make do with the clothes he stood up in and whatever food and fuel he could 'liberate'.

But long before the shortage of calories and foul-weather kit became critical, Ricardo, too, discovered that his attitude towards the islanders changed with the sinking of the *Belgrano*. Where in the third week of April he had placed on a charge an NCO he had seen striking a civilian, though the blow was scarcely more than an irritable cuff, now he didn't much care if every non-cooperative inhabitant of Stanley was beaten black and blue. Although he would have been the first to admit that few items of war news received from Buenos Aires could be taken as gospel truth, even the BBC World Service, to which the Argentines tuned daily, revealed that the ancient cruiser had been outside the so-called Total Exclusion Zone when it was torpedoed. Whether it was steaming home, as Buenos Aires declared, or towards the task force, as the British government argued, was neither here nor there. The British had made a rule and then broken it. As a result they had escalated the war. No one had died, no islanders or British service personnel anyway, during the invasion. But the first casualty figures from the *Belgrano* suggested that close on four hundred mariners had been killed, and the Falklanders were openly jubilant (which proved that some of them still had radios tuneable to the World Service, at any rate), if not at the loss of life, certainly at what they saw as a Royal Navy victory. To hell with them, then. A hearts-and-minds campaign would never have worked anyway. Majors Vila and Corino, General Pastran and Colonel Filippi were right. There was no reasoning with these people, as there had been no reasoning with successive British governments. This was a fight to the finish, and one that Ricardo personally did not expect to survive. In the meantime, he could no longer afford to be concerned about the odd outbreak of vandalism, the occasional rough stuff. Let the men take what they wanted where they found it.

The sinking of the *Sheffield* by a Super Etendard-delivered Exocet on May 4 gave Ricardo a grim sense of satisfaction, the more so when he saw the gloomy expressions among the islanders in Stanley. Take that, you bastards! The loss of the *Sheffield* also gave the garrison a more tangible reason for celebration. Recognizing that it was vulnerable, the task force commander withdrew the carrier group east, abandoning, for the present, daylight shelling of Stanley airfield, and giving the Sea Harriers less time over target when in their bombing role.

But throughout the middle of May the night-time bombardments continued, softening up the defences, sapping an already shaky morale, robbing the Argentines of sleep, and making a life already grim because of the incessant rain and flurries of snow more miserable. Frostbite and trench foot were commonplace, tearful hysteria not unknown, the occasional self-inflicted wound suspected. The regular officers and NCOs grew intolerant of malingerers. All right, no one wanted to be here, but here they were and here they would stay until they were dug out. Right?

On May 14 on Pebble Island, a twenty-mile-long irregular-shaped islet north of West Falkland, eleven aircraft on the airstrip were destroyed, in appalling weather, by British special forces. The knowledge that some elements of the task force were ashore and causing mayhem did little to stiffen the resolve of the garrison. It also gave senior officers a further headache, particularly those concerned with intelligence. The Stanley airfield had been shelled and bombed repeatedly; so too had the anti-aircraft emplacements north and south. The Goose Green airfield had been attacked on several occasions by Harriers. Now Pebble Island was out of action so far as local air defence was concerned. But where, precisely, would the British attempt a landing?

Some argued that it would be a direct assault on Stanley airfield and the peninsula on which it stood; others that Stanley and the high ground were too well defended, that the cost in lives of going for a 'quick kill' would be unacceptable to London. These officers favoured an amphibious landing along the length of Berkeley Sound, a wide bay ten miles north of Stanley Harbour; or Cow Bay, even further north. But if they were right, came the counter-argument, what was the purpose, other than a ruse, of continuing to attack Goose Green? And wouldn't somewhere on West Falkland be more logical, where there were fewer Argentine troops, where the attackers could quickly set up their Rapier missile batteries and possibly construct something of an airstrip for the jump-jet Harriers, thus allowing the carriers to stay well out of range of Lami Dozo's fighter-bombers? That done, the British could dig in and fight a war of attrition until the arrival of 5 Infantry Brigade (no secret that it had sailed), with no further forward movement before then.

Few considered San Carlos Water for the beach-head and a breakout by the assault troops before 5 Brigade appeared. Those who did didn't argue their case forcibly. Port San Carlos was a hundred kilometres from Stanley and, with the prevailing weather conditions likely to worsen in the long run rather than the opposite, rugged terrain every inch of the way. Intelligence sources had made a guesstimate that the task force possessed far too few helicopters to ferry the ground troops forward in huge leaps in more than a piecemeal fashion, and unless they could be dropped at a selected map reference in at least battalion strength, and all at once, they would be wiped out. A forced march from San Carlos to Stanley, man-packing all the equipment that would be needed and always in danger of being attacked on the flanks by infantry, or from the air, was reckoned to be out of the question. No senior Argentine officer underestimated the resilience of the British soldier, but a hundred kilometres across defended country with no roads, and sometimes no tracks, was asking the impossible. It couldn't be done.

However, in one respect the weather favoured the attackers. As darkness fell on the afternoon of May 20, visibility on East and West Falkland and far out to sea was reduced to a few hundred yards by driving rain falling from low-lying fat-bellied clouds. Macbeth weather, thought Ricardo, making his way from his own company lines north of Stanley airfield to York Point, north-west, where he knew Beto's regiment was dug in. Not an earthly chance that Lami Dozo's aeroplanes would take off in this muck.

It was on impulse that he'd decided to visit Beto, whom he had not seen for a week. Impulse, and the almost certain knowledge that all hell would be breaking loose before long. At the midday "O" Group, Colonel Filippi had warned his regimental officers to keep the men on their toes from now on.

'Intelligence says to expect the invasion within the next forty-eight hours, probably within the next twenty-four. The Met. people reckon that this stuff'—he thumbed skywards—'will clear for a day or two after that, which the British will know too. They've already been at sea a long time. They'll want to get ashore and get on with the job. Regrettably, intelligence can't tell us where they'll land. There was a Harrier attack on a fuel dump at Fox Bay earlier, but that doesn't necessarily mean anything. If I were a gambling man, which I'm not, I'd wager that we'll see some action here around the airfield, or perhaps a bit north of here. Anyway, keep them at it, the men, especially the younger ones. Remind them that it's their own lives they'll be fighting for now, not a piece of territory known as the Malvinas.'

Filippi had then managed a tiny smile and a joke.

'The British are going to be remarkably cross that we've dragged them eight thousand miles when they could be watching the World Cup on television. They won't be giving any quarter.'

With those words ringing in his ears, Ricardo had decided to seek out Beto, stuffing his pockets full of cigarettes, some thick slices of mutton in a waterproof wrapping, and half a bottle of brandy before setting off.

The password for the day was 'Ongania', after the general who had led the military takeover in 1966 and on the assumption that no British serviceman, even if he somehow learned it, would be able to pronounce it well enough to deceive an Argentine. Ricardo had to repeat it five times in the half-mile between his company lines and York Point. He did so loudly on each occasion. The men were jittery, ready to shoot at shadows now they knew that British special forces were on the Malvinas.

Ricardo found Beto and several others roughly Beto's age doing picket duty forward of a 35 mm gun belonging to the 601st Anti-Aircraft Battalion. Their positions overlooked York Bay, and they were huddled beneath their ponchos in the lee of a sand dune, wet and miserable and depressed. Also unprepared. Christ, thought Ricardo, if the SAS were in the area they could be amongst these silly bastards before they knew what hit them. Which wouldn't only mean four useless deaths, one his brother's, but also the loss of a valuable weapon.

'Come on,' he snapped, not needing to fake his anger, 'look alive. Get on your damned feet.'

The youngsters made a pathetic stab at standing to attention. They shivered, part fear, part cold, holding their rifles like the amateurs they were, limply, loosely. Beto recognized Ricardo even beneath the hood, but he had been a soldier long enough not to take advantage by greeting his brother by his given name. By way of contrast, Ricardo hardly recognized Beto. In the week since their last meeting he appeared not to have shaved, and his cheeks were hollower, his eyes large, like a photograph of someone released from Belsen.

Ricardo was shocked at the change, and worried; worried enough, anyway, to decide not to bawl out the other pickets. Instead he reached into his pocket and handed them a couple of packets of cigarettes ('Thank you, sir'—amazed) before taking Beto to one side, out of earshot. Fleetingly he remembered Beto in the George V, in December, lounging around in a dressing-gown, smoking, complaining of a hangover, drinking Dom Perignon. Could that really be only five months ago?

'Are you all right?' Ricardo had to raise his voice to make it heard above the elements.

'Yes, thank you, sir.'

'For God's sake, Beto!'

'Sorry . . . Ricardo. Yes, I'm all right.'

'You don't look it. Don't you ever shave in this battalion? And when did you last eat?'

'Earlier.'

'What did you eat? And don't get me wrong, I'm not playing the protective brother. But if you don't eat you can't fight.'

'Some rice, beans, a chunk of meat.'

'Hot?'

'Cold.'

'You look terrible.' Ricardo glanced about him, peering out across York Bay. They could have the whole damned fleet out there and he wouldn't know it. 'How is it up here?'

'It's all right. Well, no, it's not all right. It's bloody frightening, if you must know. We lost a man the other day. Sea Harrier attack. I'm beginning to recognize them now. He was younger than me actually. He was walking across the open ground over there, when whoooosh. Then he was in bits. A bit here, a bit there. I helped collect and bury some of him and didn't feel a thing. Not until later. What are you doing here?'

'I brought you some cigarettes, some mutton, half a bottle of brandy.'

Beto backed away. 'I don't want any favours.'

'Don't be a bloody fool,' snarled Ricardo. 'How the hell do you think I got the stuff? Because someone likes the look of me? I got it because I'm a captain and you're not. You get it because you're my brother and no one else is. Share it with your friends if you must, but take it.'

Ricardo handed over the mutton, the cigarettes, the brandy. Beto took it all and pocketed it without a word.

'It'll be soon,' said Ricardo. 'Tonight, tomorrow night. But I guess you've heard.'

'They don't tell us anything.'

'Then I'm telling you. My CO reckons part of the assault will be launched around here. I don't know. We're all guessing. But be ready. And keep your damned head down.'

Ricardo wanted to add that Beto should throw up his hands and wave a white flag at the first available opportunity, if the British landed anywhere near him, but found he couldn't say the words. Like everyone else, his brother would have to take his chances. In any case, he wouldn't have accepted the advice.

'Are we going to win?' asked Beto.

Ricardo did not understand the question at first. Beto was an historian, a poet, a painter, a musician, an artistic academic. Such individuals never discussed anything in terms of winning and losing; everything was relative. What in God's name was he, Beto, doing here? What were any of the conscripts doing here? They were not only useless, in a military sense they were worse than useless. A commander had to be sure his back was covered, his flanks secure. Otherwise the best-laid strategy was ineffective. These part-timers couldn't do it, and wouldn't do it when confronted by the highly professional British army. Given an equal balance of weapons, determination was everything. The manual said that for a successful assault the ratio of attackers to defenders should be three to one at least and preferably five to one. The British had nothing like that. If anything, on paper they were outnumbered. On paper? That was the trouble. The defenders were largely cardboard cut-outs, bodies to fill gaps.

'Of course we're going to win,' he answered confidently. 'They'll try to land and establish a beach-head and we'll knock them back into the sea. That will be the end of it. They have only one throw of the dice in an operation like this. Beat them back the first time and Buenos Aires and London will decide it's better to get their heads together. By Monday morning it will be stalemate. Look, I have to be getting back.'

Ricardo hesitated before holding out his hand. Beto shook it tentatively.

'Good luck,' said Ricardo.

'Thanks,' said Beto. 'And to you.'

Ricardo was a hundred metres away when he thought he heard Beto shout something else. But he couldn't make out the words.

TWENTY

3 Platoon

THE CODE WORD was flashed from the UK, the signal to go: Operation Corporate, the liberation of the Falklands, was on.

PALPAS.

Throughout May 20 the assault ships plunged through heavy seas in tight formation, flanked by an aggressive escort of destroyers and frigates, the overall picture from each warship's bridge seeming to each naval skipper like something from a World War Two newsreel. From the north-east, outside the exclusion zone, the first course steered was south-west, a feint towards Stanley had the enemy been in a position to see. He could not. The weather was filthy. Above the convoy Harriers flew CAPs while closer to sea level helicopters darted about on anti-submarine patrols like angry wasps.

Daddy had given the battalion its final briefing, the emphasis on the first syllable of that word. Good luck and go in hard.

'And kill the officers. They'll be the chaps waving their arms about.'

This useful piece of intelligence had come from the SAS who, on a clandestine sortie, had surprised a squad of Argentines. The SAS had shot the man 'waving his arms about' and the others had taken to their heels.

'Our officers or theirs?' someone wanted to know, to resounding if nervous cheers.

Later in the day the convoy turned due west for its rendezvous point sixty nautical miles north of Fanning Head, the peninsula at the entrance to Falkland Sound.

Aboard the assault ships conditions were mildly chaotic, with scarcely any room to move. Weapons were cleaned for the thousandth time, notes scribbled, sleep snatched.

Dinner was taken in relays from mid-evening. Most men found they were hungry, belying the fable that fear of the unknown removed appetite.

Perversely the weather changed for the better on the run down to Fanning Head. The rain stopped, the seas calmed, the night became cold and clear.

Men made final checks of their own equipment and that of their oppos. Rucksacks, helmets, rifles, machine guns, mortars, ratpacks for forty-eight hours. And daubed camouflage cream on their cheeks and foreheads.

'Hey, Sarge,' Sammy called to Scarlett, 'isn't there a choice of colours like Max Factor? It's bloody ridiculous Jomo having to put this stuff on.'

'Shut it,' said Jomo tersely.

Sammy broke wind by way of reply. Okay, it took different people different ways. Now, as for him, he wasn't scared at all. Though maybe he should take a leaf out of ol' Non-Legless Jones' book, over there mumbling to himself. At least his lips were moving and his eyes were closed. Not that that meant anything with Non-Legless. He could be eating nutty. Funny buggers, the Welsh. They didn't so much eat as chew cud. Came from being brought up on leek soup and leek pie and leek and chips. Leeks! Bloody hell. Like eating soft boiled string.

Sammy nudged Twiggy in the ribs, and jerked his head at the Welshman.

'Jesu joy of man's desiring,' he sang to the tune of *Deutschland über Alles*.

Non-Legless opened his eyes.

'That's not funny,' he lilted, 'mocking a man's religious beliefs.'

'It is from where I'm standing, Jonesey, old son. You look like a hamster.'

'No, it isn't funny,' said Twiggy, wondering if there was a queue for the heads. He'd relieved himself ten minutes ago but now he wanted to do so again. Bugger it. He'd be up to his waist in water before it mattered.

'You as well, Twiglet?' said Sammy, feigning surprise.

'Jeeze, you've all got the shakes. Are you sure you remembered to put the gas out? And the cat? Cancel the milk?'

'Please shut up,' said Rupert politely. 'You really are getting on everyone's nerves.'

'Well, as you put it so nicely, sir . . .'

'Shut it, Finch,' barked Rupert, in a tone that brooked no argument. Sammy shut it.

Rupert then changed the subject, picking up the earlier theme of camouflage cream.

'You won't be needing any either, James,' he told Double-Eff. 'You've gone a most attractive shade of green. Reminds me of an MG I used to have. Matched the sea perfectly. The sea off St. Trop. naturally.'

'Naturally,' groaned Double-Eff who felt, after his experiences of the last few weeks, that he'd be sick taking a bath.

Yank found himself standing next to Acne Hackney and opposite Dippy Hendricks, the C Company sergeant who rivalled Groggy and Legless Jones when it came to shifting whisky. Dippy was doing something with his mouth. When he took his hand away Yank was surprised to see a gap where four front teeth in the upper set should have been. He hadn't known Dippy wore a plate.

Dippy carefully put the dentures in a handkerchief, folded it and stowed it away. Seeing he was observed, he grinned toothlessly at Yank.

'If all else fails,' he whistled, 'I'll gum the fuckers to death.'

Yank grinned back. Being small, with all his gear on he looked like a child in his father's cast-offs. But this was all right, he thought, the battalion being on a war footing. Even senior NCOs acted like human beings, which they most surely were not.

'We're going to be famous tomorrow morning,' he said to Acne Hackney. 'Front page news all over the world.'

'Or dead,' muttered Davey Binns lugubriously. Maybe it hadn't been such a bright idea, persuading Zebedee to bring him along.

'Naw. You heard what Daddy said. The Argies are elsewhere. The SBS recce said so. The landing won't be opposed. It'll be fame, just you wait. And a medal at the end of it.'

CSM Scrunch Watkins overheard Yank.

'Fame costs, Hobart,' he called, 'and right here's where you start paying.'

'Can you dance with your legs in the air, Sarn't Major?' Sammy wanted to know.

'I'll dance your bleeding legs in the air.'

Peter asked Scrunch to tell all platoon NCOs to organize a roll-call.

'Can't have some of the little buggers hiding in the heads and claiming later they missed the boat.'

First time round, Scarlett found Groggy and Legless Jones missing from 3 Platoon. They appeared after five minutes, shouldering their way along the crowded passage. They had heard a rumour that a corporal in B Company had produced a bottle of Mount Gay rum and was selling tots, but that's all it had turned out to be, a rumour. They would have to go ashore stone cold sober.

'I haven't dragged you away from anything, have I?' asked Scarlett sarcastically. 'I mean, I'd hate a little thing like an invasion to interfere with your social life.'

'Sorry, Sarn't,' said Groggy and Legless in unison.

'Had to pump the bilges . . .' said Groggy.

'All this hanging around . . .' said Legless.

'Oh yeah? They serving scotch in the heads nowadays, are they?'

When Scrunch had confirmed that all platoons were present and correct he reported to Peter, who in turn told Winter's Day. The company commander was in conversation with Archie Buchanan, who would be going ashore in D Company's LCU.

'Fine, thanks,' said Winter's Day.

Buchanan had his portable tape recorder out. In between muttering into it he held it above his head to record background noise. He also appeared, in Peter's absence, to have been interviewing Winter's Day.

'Do you think that's a wise idea?' Peter asked the company commander.

'What?'

'Making comments now that you might not want on the front page of a newspaper come Monday morning.'

'Public has a right to know,' said Archie, who had spent a lifetime overcoming that sort of objection.

'Cobblers,' said Peter, who quite liked Archie but who had

been detailed by Daddy to look after the journalist until they were safely ashore, and who resented it.

'Can't do any harm, surely,' said Winter's Day uncertainly, trying to recall exactly what he'd said to Buchanan.

Peter shrugged. 'Please yourself.'

Although later no one ever remembered being given a command to move, suddenly the company, a naval officer leading, was making for the bowels of the ship and the landing dock.

Lugging their gimpies, Two-Shit and Jomo were behind one another when the tannoy crackled into life with something about enemy air activity. In the dim red light that was the only illumination permitted on the ship now that they were close, Two-Shit paled beneath the camouflage cream.

'Jesus, we're going to be fried.'

All around, men cursed at the prospect of being trapped below the water-line while the Argentine Air Force carried out an attack. But a few moments later the air-raid warning was cancelled as a false alarm.

'Ahthinkahjustfockinshitmeself,' swore Branston Pickles.

Scarlett understood the sentiment if not all the words.

'You've probably got a lot of company.'

Come on there, move it along. Don't you know there's a war on?

The procedure was to board the LCUs in the landing dock, which was then flooded. Both assault ships, *Fearless* and *Intrepid*, carried four LCUs apiece, each capable of taking one hundred men, roughly a company, and four smaller LCVPs, which were lowered from the ships' davits. Not only men and personal equipment were aboard, of course. Some LCUs contained the armoured vehicles of the Blues and Royals.

Someone gave an unseen signal. Water rocked the LCUs, throwing men off balance. The stern ramp dropped and the landing craft reversed out under power into Falkland Sound, at the entrance to San Carlos Water. Then there was open sea and the hills of East Falkland close enough to spit at, easily perceivable as the moon rose and the sky brightened.

'Jesus,' said a voice, 'we'll catch it if there's anyone up front.'

'Keep quiet!' roared Scrunch, causing apprehensive chuckles since the landing craft and Scrunch were making more noise than anyone else.

Sixty miles east, the *Glamorgan* was shelling Berkeley Sound as a diversion and making a quartet of young Argentines guarding an anti-aircraft gun huddle deeper in their ponchos. To the immediate left of D Company's LCU, naval guns were bombarding Fanning Head in a secondary diversion. Disturbingly for the company, fire was being returned. And that when everyone had been told that the Argies were nowhere to be found anywhere near the landing beaches.

'So much for the frigging SBS,' called Prawn Balls.

'I wouldn't let them hear you say that if I were you,' advised Double-Eff.

But the SBS was right. There might be enemy positions on Fanning Head; there were none either side of the bay that was San Carlos Water.

In relays the landing craft made for their respective beaches. 3 Para and 42 Commando to Green Beach, Port San Carlos; 2 Para and 40 Commando to Blue Beach, San Carlos settlement; 45 Commando and Daddy's battalion to Red Beach, Ajax Bay, where their first task would be to occupy the abandoned refrigeration plant and dig in, secure their positions, before daybreak, when the Argentine Air Force, absent up to now, could be expected in strength.

There was a clattering of metal as the landing craft ramps went down, and then the troops were waist-deep in icy water, Archie Buchanan muttering into his tape recorder, Three-piece Sweet looking ridiculous, the feathered condom he refused to part with covering his rifle muzzle. And not a shot fired at any of the invaders although there was still a hell of a racket going on over at Fanning Head. Intelligence had got it right. The landing was unopposed.

Then they were ashore and commands were being issued at rapid-fire speed. Break left. Over there. 2 Platoon right. Gimpy defensive fire posts, there and there. D company, fall in on me.

In spite of everything Daddy Rankin, on the basis that rank has its privileges, had brought ashore a very old four-iron and an equally ancient golf ball. He put the ball down and swiped it, at the third attempt, into the sea. Then he threw the club after it. 'Just to say I did it,' he told the adjutant. 'Mind you, I've played better courses.'

Rupert left Double-Eff and Scarlett to organize 3 Platoon and gazed at East Falkland reflectively. Was this what all the fuss was about?

'Is this it?' he asked of no one in particular. 'What a tame war. I want my money back.'

Later, as dawn approached on what was to be a terrible day, one in complete contrast to the uneventful landing, Three-piece came across a Falkland Islander, a woman, who should not have been on that side of San Carlos Water at all. She had a flask of hot tea in one hand and a bottle of spirits in the other, and was going from man to man, offering sips of both. She kept on repeating, 'Thank you, thank you. We knew someone would come to free us.' And Three-piece, usually so gallant with the ladies, more or less summed it up for all the assault troops when he said: 'What's freeing you got to do with it? We're here because it's our job. You could be Japanese as far as we're concerned.'

The woman went off in a huff.

PART THREE

The essence of war is violence, and moderation in war is imbecility.

—*Macaulay*

TWENTY-ONE

Archie Buchanan

THE ARGENTINE AIR FORCE in the shape of six Daggers, the Israeli-built version of the Mirage V, arrived a few minutes after 10.30 a.m. on the morning of May 21, looking for the ships. And making a tactical mistake it would learn to regret in targeting the warships and not the transports, now running a shuttle service via the LCUs and the LCVPs and off-loading supplies and rear-echelon personnel onto the landing beaches.

Broadsword and *Argonaut* patrolled the north of Falkland Sound, the extreme right, as one faced the Argentine mainland, of the 'gun line'. *Yarmouth, Brilliant* and *Ardent* held the left of the line, with *Ardent* southernmost of all, in Grantham Sound, which was overlooked by Sussex Mountains, 2 Para's first objective en route to Goose Green once the beaches were secure. HMS *Antrim* was positioned off Fanning Head, guarding the entrance to San Carlos Water against possible submarine incursions, though it had to be considered doubtful whether any sub not already in the Sound—and the navy reckoned there were none—would get past the gun line.

The alarm went up: Air Raid Warning Red—given in full during these early hours but soon to be shortened to simply Air Red.

The Daggers came in over West Falkland, well away from the CAP Harriers, and went for *Broadsword, Argonaut* and *Antrim*, letting fly with 450-kilo bombs and 30 mm cannon.

The warships responded with everything in the armoury: 4.5 inch guns, Oerlikon anti-aircraft cannon, Seacat missiles, and, in one case, an ancient Seaslug, designed by its makers, British Aerospace, as a long-range surface-to-air missile and not as a low-level anti-aircraft weapon. A Seacat scored a direct hit on one of the Daggers, causing it to crash into the sea. The remainder then ran south down the Sound, attacking *Ardent* on the way. After that they raced for the mainland, home, before the Harriers could intercept, though one let loose a Sidewinder that detonated short.

The entire action was over in a few minutes and much of it out of sight of the troops digging in on the slopes above the landing beaches. But the altitude at which the Daggers flew returning to Rio Gallegos airfield, no more than fifty feet above the hills in some cases, made all but the slowest of the assault troops bury themselves deeper in their trenches and cover their heads, so terrifying was the noise and suddenness of the sortie. In days to come they would learn to recognize whether or not they were the targets and treat the enemy aircraft with almost suicidal insouciance. But this was the first day and the majority of them had never been under air attack before, the transports having been kept well out of range of the Argentine planes until the landings were given the green light from London. Nor were the Rapier missile batteries yet in place for the most part, and the operators of the hand-held Blowpipe SAMs had hit the trenches with the rest at Air Red. These missile teams would soon realize that it was one thing to man a Blowpipe on exercise, when the incoming target aircraft was not about to emit a fatal burst of cannon fire and where the only 'deaths' were those judged by the war-games umpires; it was quite another to stand up and face a low-flying enemy plane, approaching at a mile every few seconds, release the missile and guide it visually onto the target, all the while wondering whether the cannon fire coming the other way would get to you before your missile got the plane. Part of the operating procedure for the Blowpipe stated matter-of-factly: 'Once he has acquired the target visually, the operator has merely to aim along the sight, fire, and control the flight of the missile by means of the thumb control.' That word 'merely' was to be the object of much gallows humour among the Blowpipe operators between May 21 and the second week in June. The weapon could, of course, be fired at an aircraft tail-on, when it had overflown the operator. But adopting that method any plane in this war, or any other war, would be halfway home before the operator got a fix. As a consequence of its performance in the Falklands, many senior officers suggested that Blowpipe be 'junked' for the future, in favour of a fire-and-forget SAM, where at least the operator stood a chance of surviving an encounter with an enemy plane.

The most serious damage occasioned in this opening attack was to the *Antrim*, which was hit by a bomb that narrowly missed a Seaslug missile, and which failed to explode. *Antrim* then moved closer inshore in order that a disposal team could work on the UXB. *Broadsword* avoided the bombs but was hit by cannon fire, suffering casualties. The remaining ships were unscathed.

Once it was certain that the Daggers had gone for good and that neither radar nor the CAP Harriers could detect, for now, a second wave, the serious business of consolidating positions and off-loading stores continued. For the ground troops there was a more immediate potential threat than sudden death from the air: the danger of a counter-attack against the beach-head by Argentine army units, who, if intelligence had it right, held a considerable numerical advantage. The time-honoured strategy against a seaborne assault was to hammer the invaders with everything the defenders had, instantly, before the invaders had their supply lines going. There seemed to be no sign that the Argies were about to play it by the manual, but the unit COs could afford to take no chances, and the Harriers and support helicopters could not be everywhere, scouting. Coordinating by wireless so that there would be no accidents, each battalion would probe within the parameters of its assigned beach and the hills above in company strength. The objective was not to give advance warning of enemy infantry en masse—the Harriers and the choppers would soon spot anything like that—but to secure the high ground and search it thoroughly for dugouts or hides that might conceal forward artillery spotters. The Argies were known to have 155 mm howitzers, which were capable of slinging shells halfway across East Falkland with great accuracy.

Over at Blue Beach, San Carlos settlement, 2 Para and 40 Commando would find themselves hampered throughout the day (and for some days to come) by small children and a few older ones plus parents who, oblivious to the dangers and treating the whole business as a rather intriguing adventure, insisted on helping with the digging-in, acted as scouts and amateur cartographers, provided tea and coffee, and begged for headgear, berets, and other souvenirs. On Red Beach, Ajax Bay, 45 Commando and the battalion had no such worries, now that Three-piece had succeeded in chasing away the only islander on that side of San Carlos Water.

Daddy called an 'O' Group of company commanders and 2 i/cs, at first intending to give C Company the task of armed reconnaissance until Archie Buchanan asked if he could go along rather than hang around Battalion HQ. He had no story to file as yet. The hacks still on the warships would have covered or be about to cover the Air Red; he needed something different for his own first report.

Daddy recalled that Peter Ballantine, not necessarily with good grace, had taken care of the journalist coming ashore, and thus assigned the first recce to D Company on the principle of better the devil you knew. Like most of the senior officers, Daddy viewed the presence of the media as, at best, a necessary evil. Ballantine would make sure that Buchanan didn't get in the way or, worse, get his stupid head shot off.

On hearing of the arrangement, Archie glanced across at Peter and shrugged his shoulders. For a while thereafter, until Peter threatened to chuck him and his tape recorder into Falkland Sound, he referred to Peter as 'Nanny'.

Back at D Company's lines, Winter's Day briefed his platoon officers and senior NCOs with the aid of a map. Since the battalion was on the right flank, facing west, of 45 Commando, and D Company on the right flank of the battalion, there should be little danger of 45's recce coming anywhere near D Company. However, Company HQ would keep in touch with 45 by wireless, to be on the safe side. The 'spread' of the recce would be to the top of the hills facing them, and north, that is, right, as far as Chancho Point at the tip of Wreck Point North—if it was possible to get there and back before dark and if Daddy decided that another company should leap-frog D and take up permanent positions on the heights. 'We can expect their air force over again periodically so it won't be a morning hike.' The whole of Wreck Point North overlooked San Carlos Water, and that's where an artillery spotter would be if at all. Winter's Day considered it unlikely, that the greatest danger might come from chopper-borne troops attempting to occupy the high ground.

'The ships would have heard all about it by now if they had

an observer up there. Besides, if the Argentines had expected a landing at San Carlos, we'd have had more opposition earlier.'

Peter wasn't so sure, and said so. The Argies could well have placed artillery spotters at various vulnerable points, on spec. The reason that nothing had happened up to now to the ships in the bay could be because the Argies did not have a 155 within range.

Winter's Day accepted that that was a possibility.

Double-Eff wanted to know if artillery observers in general would not be redundant, now that the enemy air force knew precisely where the task force was. Winter's Day pointed out that the enemy air force did *not* know precisely where the task force was. Every ship had moved since the Dagger attack and the 155 batteries would need overshoot and undershoot corrections called rather than just lob shells in the general direction of San Carlos Water. Double-Eff nodded, chastened. Being on terra firma and lacking sleep had made him light-headed. He resolved to keep his mouth shut until he'd grabbed a few hours' kip.

'Anti-personnel mines,' went on Winter's Day. 'The IO reckons the odds are against, and I agree with him. They'd have mined the beaches if they'd thought we were coming this way. They didn't. It's therefore most unlikely they've mined the tracks in the hills. However, we're new to this part of the world and those buggers have been here for weeks. God knows what they've been up to, so be prepared for anything until we're sure. If in doubt . . .'

'We send the CSM on ahead with a long stick and a prayer book,' said Rupert, grinning at Scrunch, who made an obscene gesture with fist and forearm and who seemed to be thoroughly enjoying himself.

'No, I think we'll send you,' said Winter's Day, not at all unpleasantly. '3 Platoon can spearhead the advance, say a hundred yards ahead of the line.'

'Thanks a lot,' said Rupert.

'My pleasure. Someone has to do it. We'd look a mite foolish if the whole company crested the ridge to be met by a squadron of fighters coming the other way.'

'So, instead of the entire company looking foolish, 3 Platoon becomes the first to win a cluster of posthumous gongs.'

'Something like that.'

'Message from Sunray, sir,' said Winter's Day's HQ signaller; Sunray was the wireless code for the CO. 'He wants to know when we'll be ready to move.'

'Reply: in five minutes. Anything I've forgotten?' Winter's Day asked Peter.

'Not that I can think of. Have all the men had something to eat and a brew?' Peter asked generally.

There was a chorus of affirmatives. The first of the ratpacks had been broken into and the hexy stoves fired almost before Daddy had thrown his four-iron into the sea.

'Any questions?' asked Winter's Day.

'Blowpipes, sir,' said a 4 Platoon sergeant, the platoon commander of 4 who was applying for a commission from the ranks and who had thus been permitted to keep command of 4 since it would assist him with his board if he performed well; since, also, Double-Eff, who might otherwise have inherited the platoon after a few months under Rupert's wing, had not been considered experienced enough (or, for that matter, familiar enough with the men of 4 Platoon, who would resent change) to take over when the crisis blew up. 'Do we take them? I know it's not much of a climb but those bastards weigh a ton. Unless we're staying up there . . .'

Actually they weighed just under fifty pounds, but Winter's Day took the point. His immediate orders were to reconnoitre, not dig in at the top. If those orders changed, he'd think again.

He scanned the hills overlooking 45's position via binoculars and saw a Chinook helicopter depositing, inter alia, a Rapier battery. That would be operational before long and there were other helicopters in the air.

He referred to his map.

'Its actually about nine hundred feet at its highest point, but that bit's 45's pigeon. We have about seven hundred tops.' He considered the problem of weight. 'We'll leave them behind. For the moment it's not our job to take on aircraft, but keep your eyes peeled and be ready to hit the dirt when they come again. They won't be interested in us except as secondary targets and we should have a few minutes' warning of an Air Red, but you never can tell. We'll leave the ships and the Rapiers to take care of enemy planes. Move out as soon as you're ready,' Winter's Day added to Rupert.

'Did you volunteer us for this, Boss?' asked Sammy impudently, finding himself within a few yards of Rupert as 3 Platoon set off at the head of one hundred beaters in what was, for now, the biggest shoot in this part of the world. The trouble was, on this occasion the pheasants could shoot back, and Sammy wanted reassurance that Zebedee did not intend winning himself an early MC by offering the platoon as guinea pigs for all the dirty jobs up front.

'Save your breath, Finch,' Scarlett called across.

'Fuck me,' muttered Sammy, 'we're starting, are we.'

Because the purpose of the reconnaissance was just that, a recce, D Company were not manpacking rucksacks. Thus their advance to the top of Wreck Point North was reasonably swift, in spite of the boggy terrain that reminded many of the company of Dartmoor or Scotland. Nor did the weather impede progress; it was a virtually clear day with few clouds.

3 Platoon led in the form of a flattened 'W', the left and right upper arms of the 'W' being the machine gunners, Two-Shit and Jomo respectively. In the middle of the 'W', where it became an arrowhead, were Rupert and his wireless operator, Double-Eff and Scarlett. The rest of the platoon occupied the diagonals of the 'W'. With a greater lateral distance between each man than would have been considered prudent had the platoon been attacking and not reconnoitring, say fifteen yards, three hundred separated Two-Shit on the left from Jomo on the right.

Some way behind 3 Platoon came the rest of the company in the same rough form of lazy 'W', with Winter's Day, Peter, Archie Buchanan and the remainder of HQ Platoon occupying positions similar to Rupert and Co. at the arrowhead of the larger 'W', though here the men were closer together. Thus the distance between the outermost man on each flank was some six hundred yards.

At the top of the ridge the left flank would wheel while the right flank marked time. Then the whole of D Company would proceed in the same formation towards Chancho Point.

At least that was the theory and would doubtless have been executed perfectly had it not been for Acne Hackney and Yank Hobart, within a few yards of each other and slightly to the left and behind Jomo, taking the first prisoner not captured by special forces in the campaign, and introducing the word 'ostrich' into the battalion's lexicon.

At the top of the crest, with thankfully no sign of the Argie Air Force anywhere though there were CAP Harriers and helicopters aplenty in sight, Jomo halted and took up a defensive fire position behind the gimpy while waiting for the rest of the platoon to swing round in a straight line using him as marker. Then he heard a shout from behind. The ground had literally opened up in front of Acne Hackney and Yank, and from the hole emerged a youth whose age they later discovered to be sixteen. His face was filthy, his combat gear soaked and stained, his eyes wide with terror. And his hands straight up in the air, one of them clutching a rifle.

'Am your ostrich!' he shrieked.

Had the frightened figure represented the vanguard of a *Buzo Tactico* battalion, neither Acne Hackney nor Yank would have got in a shot, so startled were they by the sudden appearance of this underage apparition. Nor would Jomo have let fly, but for different reasons: Yank and Davey Binns were in his direct line of fire.

'Am your ostrich!' cried the youth.

'The fuck you're my ostrich!' Yank yelled back, wondering what the silly bastard was on about.

Then Rupert came galloping over, closely followed by Double-Eff.

'Hold ranks and get down, you dozy bastards!' bellowed Scarlett when it seemed that everyone wanted to take a look.

'Am your ostrich!' said the youth for the third time, on this occasion addressing Rupert, whom he recognized as authority.

'You might at least take his rifle,' Rupert suggested harshly to Acne Hackney. Acne Hackney relieved him of it. It was in poor condition, full of shit, he noted idly. The safety was on. Was this who they were expected to fight? He didn't look old enough to get a hard-on.

'What the fuck does he mean, Boss,' asked Yank, bewildered, 'that he's an ostrich?'

'I must have walked right over him,' said Jomo disbelievingly, to no one in particular, peering down into the hole the young Argentine had climbed from. In actuality it was no hole at all, just a shallow trench, very wet, a foot and a half deep and covered with gorse. There was no sign of any tools; the kid must have dug it out with his bare hands.

By now the rest of the company had seen that something was going on. Winter's Day, Peter and Archie Buchanan came towards Rupert and his prisoner at the double. Scrunch remained with HQ Platoon and via radio informed the other platoons that they were to stay precisely where they were until further orders. 'And tell them to keep on the qui vive,' he told the HQ wireless op.

'I think he means he's your hostage,' Rupert said to Yank. 'He's probably got the word hostage confused with prisoner.'

And so it proved to be. But thereafter all Argentine prisoners taken by the battalion were known as ostriches.

In the meantime, however, Winter's Day had arrived and was anxious to know if this youngster was the only one up here or if there were others. If alone, why was he there? If others, where were they? Winter's Day had no Spanish. Peter had a little from his time spent with Ricardo and in Argentina, and Archie a little more. But neither of them could work out the verbal conjugations and they were reduced to thrusting half-remembered nouns at the terrified adolescent, who remained standing with his arms stretched to the sky until Peter gestured him to lower them.

'*Solo?*' asked Peter. '*Solitario?*'

'*Si, estoy solo.*' The youngster tried a smile which didn't quite make it.

'*Mina?*' offered Archie, thinking about how he could write this up. *Bedraggled and bewildered, the Argentine army rose from a hole in the ground, a teenager and scared.*

'*Aqui?*'

'*Si, aqui.*'

'*No hay minas aqui.*'

There then followed a stream of Spanish accompanied by hand movements pointing south, from which direction they gathered the youngster had come. But they understood not one word in ten.

'What do you think?' asked Winter's Day.

'I think he's trying to tell us that he's up here by himself and that there's no one else around, neither fish nor fowl,' said Peter.

'Deserter?'

'I doubt he's unique.'

'Bloody funny place to desert to,' muttered Winter's Day, 'but if we could take that supposition as gospel I'd forget this whole recce.' He glanced anxiously at the sky and then at D Company, spread out in defensive positions over a few acres. Without trenches or sangars, stone-built breastworks constructed from whatever material was available, this was no place to be caught in the open when the bean-eating fliers came back. It was a question of either getting on with the job, completing the reconnaissance, or getting dug in.

'The IO speaks good Spanish,' Rupert remembered. 'Better

now than in the UK, I shouldn't wonder. He was mugging up with cassettes all the way out.'

'Wireless?'

'That'd take for ever. Get him up here,' suggested Peter.

The Intelligence Officer was with them in ten minutes, hitching a ride in a Wessex ferrying supplies to Red Beach. The helicopter didn't hang around. It was only just becoming known that two Royal Marines Gazelles had been lost to enemy machine gun fire off Fanning Head in the early hours. The crews, once the helicopters ditched, were gunned down in the water, with three fatalities.

The IO's Spanish wasn't perfect ('I'm going to ask Linguaphone for my money back') and of the Castilian variety, but it was good enough. The boy was indeed alone and a deserter from his battalion at Goose Green. He had known there was fighting to come and had wanted to get away, being frightened. His officers were brutes who treated conscripts like dirt. He had left the battalion last night, wandered off, climbed these hills, hoping to find an islander who would take him in and keep him safe until the English arrived. He had brought his rifle, an FAL 7.62, as a gesture of good will. Then he had heard the naval bombardment and seen the ships, and so had dug a shallow trench with his hands and rifle butt. The English, his officers had warned him, would torture him first and then kill him, slowly, if they captured him, especially as he was of Indian extraction. The English didn't like Indians.

'Christ,' said Peter.

He hadn't eaten for twenty-four hours, the boy confessed, and little for several days before that. Were they going to torture him?

Hearing the translation, Double-Eff gave the youth a slab of chocolate. They watched him tear off the wrapper and eat greedily, his eyes never leaving them, as though he hadn't broken his fast for a week, let alone twenty-four hours. He started when Acne Hackney absently uncoupled the twenty-round magazine of his SLR and examined the cartridges before slamming the magazine back into place. For that matter, everyone jumped.

'For God's sake, Binns,' snapped Rupert.

'He sounds genuine enough to me,' said the IO. 'Look, I'd better get him down to Red Beach for a thorough interrogation. If he's from Goose Green, 2 Para can use whatever he's got.'

'Then can I take it there's no point in reconnoitring any further?' asked Winter's Day.

'Christ, I don't know, Clive,' answered the IO. 'You'd better ask Daddy. Is that the lad's rifle? I'll take it with me.'

'Do you want an escort?'

'Are you kidding?'

Against a background of aircraft noise and machine guns establishing arcs of fire, Winter's Day talked to Daddy via the HQ wireless. Daddy agreed that there was little sense in proceeding with the recce in company strength on present evidence. But, as D Company was already up there, it might as well stay there, occupy the high ground, just in case the Argies decided to come out of their warrens. Bergens, tents, ratpacks and shovels would be choppered up soonest. And, as an afterthought, a single platoon might as well continue to Chancho Point.

'I suppose that means 3 Platoon,' commented Rupert.

'Are you volunteering?'

'No, but we're closest.' Rupert squinted north. 'How far d'you reckon it is?'

'The map's a bit dodgy,' said Winter's Day. 'Contours aren't perfect, either. A couple of miles, say three, to the headland. You don't have to go that far. Not much of a gradient either way as far as the eye can tell. You'll be back in an hour, perhaps an hour and a half.'

'The Argentine Air Force permitting.'

'Yes. Still, you've got five hours of daylight. We'll keep in touch via radio.'

'Going to be a bit rough on my blokes,' said Rupert, 'if it takes longer. The other platoons will have trenches dug, sangars built. They'll be doing it in the dark.'

'So will you, Rupert,' said Peter, 'so the sooner you get going, the better. Do you want to go with them, Archie?' he added to Buchanan.

'No, I think I'll stick around here. I'll have to scrounge a ride back to the ships to file a report long before dark or my editor will have my head for allowing the BBC and ITN to scoop the cream. He's got some kind of idea there's a Falklands Hilton with telex facilities on tap.'

'We're bridesmaids, James,' said Rupert to Double-Eff. 'We're decorative and useful but no one wants to marry us.'

'Bugger off, Rupert,' said Peter.

Rupert pointed to Scarlett and placed a hand on the top of

his head in the universal military gesture which means 'fall in on me'.

'Same deployment up to Chancho Point,' he started to say when there came a sudden, urgent wail of ships' klaxons in San Carlos Water. Simultaneously 3 Platoon's wirelessman and the HQ signaller yelled: 'Air Red!'

On this occasion it was Pucaras from the south, with *Ardent* opening up with her 4.5 at long range, from Grantham Sound. The Pucaras sheered off momentarily before making a second pass with greater determination. A couple of Harriers bounced the Argentine planes from 15,000 feet, with the loss of one Pucara. Smoke could be seen rising from Wreck Point North.

Grantham, thought Double-Eff lugubriously, spitting out a mouthful of dirt. Town in Lincolnshire. Population 30,000 or so. Birthplace of Margaret Thatcher. Was somebody trying to tell them something?

3 Platoon were back in an hour and a half, having taken cover during two further Air Reds, and with nothing to show for their recce apart from sore feet. Wet feet, too. They had met just five people during the course of the recce, a quartet and a singleton. The foursome were desperately hard-looking individuals dressed in an assortment of gear and bristling with weapons. Not one of them appeared to have shaved for the best part of a week. On seeing them—and they seemed to come from nowhere in spite of visibility being excellent, out of the dead ground to the west and crossing the platoon on a diagonal, eleven o'clock to five o'clock—the platoon dropped to the earth on Scarlett's command, cocking rifles, machine guns and Sterling submachine guns. From two hundred yards away the leader of the quartet held up an arm and hailed them. 'Hold your fuckin' horses, mate,' he shouted in broad Cockney. 'SBS,' he added as the quartet passed. 'Been here since Christ was a carpenter.'

'Yes, you smell rather ripe,' said Rupert pleasantly.

'You oughta see the other guys.'

'I don't know what they do to the enemy,' Rupert remarked to Double-Eff, 'but by God they frighten me.'

'Now's your chance to tell them what you think of them,' Three-piece called over to Prawn Balls.

'I think I'll save it for another day,' said Cyril Ball.

The singleton sported a natty Clark Gable moustache and a rifle with telescopic sights. God only knew where he came from, either, for he was heading south-east from the direction of Chancho Point.

'Anything up front?' Rupert wanted to know.

'Find out for your fuckin' self,' growled the singleton. 'Who do you think I am, the RAC?'

'Sniper,' said Scarlett. 'They're a weird bunch of buggers, snipers. Half of them think they're Clint Eastwood and the other half Lee Van Cleef. They get pretty pissed off if they don't get a chance to shoot anyone. Still, not a job I'd fancy.'

Bergens, shovels and ratpacks had been choppered up by the time 3 Platoon returned to D Company's lines. Blowpipes too. The other platoons were already digging in. Scrunch showed Scarlett 3 Platoon's positions while Rupert sought out Winter's Day to report that the platoon had drawn a blank.

'Well, it had to be done,' nodded Winter's Day. 'Okay, carry on.'

On the slopes, the earth was soft and the trenches quickly filled with six inches of water. The deeper they dug, the greater the seepage. Some of the craftier troops tried putting stones at the bottom of their trenches, but the water always found a way through. Besides, on the hillsides there were not enough large stones to act as a base for the trenches and build walls for a sangar. For that matter, there were not enough stones period, and many of the three-foot sangars were constructed of peat bricks. In between digging, on all sides hexy stoves were fired and brews made, ratpacks opened. The culinary offerings were occasionally eccentric, with chicken frequently being boiled up with dried fruit in a manner that would not have been approved by any self-respecting Tandoori restaurant back home. But there were few complaints about food. Most of the men were too hungry. And too tired.

'Never thought I'd be glad to see the Catering Corps,' Groggy remarked to Legless Jones, shovelling down a disgusting mixture of apricots, chicken and what he presumed was an Oxo cube, 'but they can't get here soon enough for me.'

'I wonder if they'll bring any beer,' said Legless.

Archie was having terrible trouble with his own trench, which was anything but a rectangle and in which the sides kept falling in, until Scrunch showed him how. 'Not like that, you horrible little man, like this. Put some muscle into it.'

'No wonder I can never grow anything in my allotment,' said Archie, standing back and admiring Scrunch's handiwork until the CSM twigged that he was being used as cheap labour. He tossed the shovel to Archie.

'Here, catch. I don't give a bugger whether you've got the honorary rank of captain or not, I gave up navvying for officers when I was a lance-corporal.'

Archie wondered if he wouldn't be better off down at the beachhead, with Daddy and the remainder of Battalion HQ, who would undoubtedly have commandeered something better for themselves than a wet hole in the peat. He concluded he'd stay where he was for the time being.

'Going to be a long day,' said Prawn Balls to Non-Legless Jones, with whom he was sharing a trench and a brew.

'A bloody long day, boyo,' said Non-Legless, using the only adjectival intensive he ever permitted himself. 'But I'd rather be up here than down there.'

'Down there' was where the warships and the transports sat in San Carlos Water and Falkland Sound, and the *Ardent*, out of sight, in Grantham Sound, and where they were attacked again and again by the Argentine Air Force throughout the afternoon. A Pucara went for the *Ardent* without success, and a brace of Skyhawks were shot down by Harriers around 2.30. A few minutes later, while Daggers were distracting the Harriers over West Falkland, six Skyhawks came in from the north and pounced on HMS *Argonaut*, hitting her with two bombs. With both engines out of action and her steering gear damaged, the ship was heading for disaster until the officer of the watch had the presence of mind to race onto the exposed deck and release her anchor.

In the same sortie *Ardent* came under the hammer again. From their vantage point on Wreck Point North, D Company, without being able to pick out *Ardent*, could see her returning fire from her Oerlikon cannon and light machine guns. Tracer hurtled towards the low-flying Daggers, whose pilots pressed home their attacks with considerable courage, not knowing as they swooped that the *Ardent*'s skipper was unable to bring his 4.5 to bear.

Fifteen minutes later *Brilliant* was strafed by cannon and some of her crew injured. *Canberra*, huge and white and seemingly unmissable, came under repeated attacks until, later, she slipped away under the cover of darkness for South Georgia.

But the Argentine Air Force seemed to have it in for *Ardent* above all, possibly because she was by herself in Grantham

Sound. Skyhawks, Daggers, Skyhawks again, with the *Ardent* hitting back with everything that could be fired, which wasn't much. Whereas the *Argonaut* could still fight though barely float, the *Ardent* could float but scarcely defend herself.

The ground troops—out of it for now, safe in their trenches and behind their sangars, though shooting with small arms, without success, whenever an Argie plane came near—experienced overwhelming compassion for the ships' crews, many of whom they knew personally, and bitter hatred for the Argentine fliers, no matter how heroic their exploits. While far from having it all their own way in running the gun line, the planes were able to strike and get out, go home, while the ships were stuck there, massive targets. The Rapier batteries were not operational in sufficient numbers to give the enemy air force trouble and the Blowpipes were inadequate. For the present the grunts were little more than spectators, Colosseum crowds watching the Argentine lions versus the British Christians. But there'd come a time of reckoning. Oh yes. There'd come a day when the British ground troops would meet Argentine ground troops, and then there'd be hell to pay. Whatever sense of chivalry, however infinitesimal, had been felt for the enemy in the past, for the sailors in the *Belgrano*, for example, was now non-existent. There was no room for pity any longer.

It wasn't all one-way traffic, however. For the loss of a Lynx helicopter destroyed with the *Ardent*, the two Royal Marines Gazelles and a Harrier taken out by anti-aircraft fire over Port Howard on West Falkland, the task force—or, more accurately, the Harriers—were able to claim five Skyhawks and five Daggers, as well as miscellaneous helicopters and a Pucara.

A further task force success, the most important one insofar as the success of Operation Corporate was concerned, was that during May 21 over 3,000 troops and 1,100 tons of stores were landed for hardware losses, other than aircraft, of a frigate abandoned and three frigates and a destroyer damaged. By courageously drawing the fire of Brigadier Lami Dozo's pilots, the warships had rendered the transports and the assault troops an invaluable service, though over a score of men had been killed and many others wounded. Nevertheless, the land forces were ashore and, as yet, there was no sign of an Argentine counter-attack.

•   •   •

'You can't say that,' said an MoD minder, vetting Archie Buchanan's copy before he transmitted from one of the ships.

'Why the hell not?' snarled Archie. It had taken him two hours to hitch a lift in a chopper, from 3.30, when the Argentine planes seemed to have called it off for the day, to dusk. He'd been promised a ride back to the beach in a LCVP if he could make it before 6.30 and he had no time to bugger about with old women. And, although the wardroom beckoned temptingly with its promise of drinks and decent food, Archie wanted to return to the battalion rather than spend the night aboard. Other considerations apart, Archie judged it safer ashore. The Argies were reputed not to fly by night, but Archie had heard it said by a high-ranking American officer in Viet Nam that the Viet Cong would never occupy Saigon.

'Because I say so, that's why not,' said the minder, blue-pencilling the offending lines.

'For Christ's sake,' exploded Archie, 'what can it possibly matter that I tell my editor the Argies haven't counter-attacked? The fucking Argies know that!'

'You can say "resistance throughout the day from Argentine ground forces was light", if you wish.'

Archie was appalled. 'I've never written a sentence like that in my life. I don't work for *The Times,* you know.'

'It had come to my notice.'

'My paper's a tabloid. It wants blood, guts and adjectives, not syntax.'

'Take it or leave it. There's a rota for the satellite link, and you have ten minutes starting three minutes ago.'

'I can't see what the problem is,' complained Archie. 'The MoD will vet the whole story in London.'

'They'll also vet me out of my pension if I don't obey the rules. Make the most of it, Archie; it's going to be pooled dispatches from now on.'

Archie snatched at his copy.

'What if I say the Argentine ground forces attacked heavily in small numbers?' he asked sarcastically.

'You now have six minutes.'

Above Red Beach, on which Daddy Rankin and his HQ staff had established relatively comfortable quarters in the abandoned refrigeration plant, albeit with a little opposition from a team of naval surgeons who were setting up a field hospital there, D Company stood down for the night. It was becoming bloody cold, with a wind getting up. Although the chances of a counter-attack were considered to be remote during the hours of darkness, perimeter pickets had been posted with orders to shoot anyone who didn't have the password of the day.

The last 'O' group was over, both at BHQ and D Company HQ. Tomorrow was another day, and platoon officers were advised to tell their men to get some sleep.

'So far, so good,' said Winter's Day to Peter, with whom he was sharing a sangar. Peter would rather have bunked in with the CSM and picked his brains regarding what was likely to happen in the morning, but he knew that Scrunch would not have welcomed that, the class differentials between officers and other ranks in the British army being deep-rooted on both sides of the invisible barrier. Besides, the ORs needed an opportunity to grumble in private about their officers.

Working by shaded lamp with a clipboard on his lap, Peter was going over the platoon commanders' reports on stores and ammo. Current thinking was that a break-out from the beach-head would take place on May 27 or May 28. When it happened, each member of each platoon would be required to carry, as well as his personal kit, spare mortars and machine-gun ammunition. It was trying to calculate precisely how much weight a man was capable of humping while still remaining a viable fighting unit that was giving Peter a headache. Then Scrunch appeared.

'Sorry to bother you, sir,' he said to Winter's Day, 'but I've got the medic we asked for.'

The battalion had its own medical staff, but the numbers were geared to peacetime operations and Northern Ireland tours, where hospital facilities were never far away. Along with the other unit COs, on Ascension Daddy had asked for further RAMC personnel, hoping to be allocated at least two men per company. But that had proved a difficult request under the circumstances and up till now D Company had seen neither tail nor whisker of any medics.

'You deal with it, Peter,' said Winter's Day.

The RAMC private's name was Philip Beavis. He was twenty-one, shy and reserved, and came from Wolverhampton. Although he was slightly built and looked as if a zephyr would blow him halfway to Buenos Aires, he had lugged a fairly heavy medicine chest plus his rucksack up seven hundred feet in the dark. In civilian life, he had wanted to be a doctor but his education wasn't up to it. He had tried private nursing and found it not to his taste before joining the Royal Army Medical Corps.

Wrapped up as he was, Peter could hardly make out his face. But he put a stop to Beavis's half-hearted attempt at a salute.

'Not in the field,' said Peter. 'You salute me in daylight and some Argie sniper's going to be putting a notch on his rifle butt. Where's the other one?'

'Other one, sir?'

'We were expecting two medical orderlies.'

'There's just me, sir.'

'Well, let's hope you don't have much trade. Where are we going to bed him down, CSM?'

'How about with Mr Buchanan, sir? Sarn't O'Hara's in with him as of now, but I can find room for Scarlett with me.'

'If you say so.'

'We can talk about his wife,' grinned Scrunch. 'You know how he misses her.'

Scrunch's solution to the sleeping arrangements was interrupted by an almighty explosion in the south-west, which lit up the sky for several minutes. Men came tumbling out of tents and trenches, and the ominous sound of nervous pickets cocking weapons was heard although everyone had been warned to expect the *Ardent*'s magazine to detonate before morning. Thus rifles and submachine guns were lowered, as if in homage, while the men witnessed a vision of some distant hell. Even for landlubbers, there was something frightful about a ship dying, the more so because she had been abandoned. It seemed an ignoble, lonely fate.

'Ah well,' said Rupert, 'here today, gone Gomorrah.'

'Not funny,' said Double-Eff, uncharacteristically sharp.

'No, you're right,' intoned Rupert, instantly regretting his attempt at humour, 'not funny at all. I take it back.'

Scrunch blew his whistle and adopted his parade ground voice.

'All right, all right, there's nothing more to see! Get your heads down!'

'Put Private Beavis on the ration strength and show him where he's to kip,' said Peter.

'Right, sir.'

'And you might apologize to Sergeant O'Hara on behalf of

the company commander for disturbing him at this hour. I suppose we have to do that? I mean, I suppose Archie's coming back tonight?'

'Your guess is as good as mine, sir. If I were him, I'd stay put, get myself a toddy and a shower, maybe a change of clothes.'

'Me too. Even if he gets off the ship, I doubt he'll be able to make his way up here.'

'Most of them couldn't, sir,' said Scrunch. 'Most of the hacks, I mean. Most of them couldn't find their cocks with a six-inch refractor and a guide dog, but I'd be surprised if Mr Buchanan didn't make it back to company lines. There was a time when I thought he'd rather be with the Paras or the Royal Marines . . .'

'Bunch of brigands,' interrupted Peter, recalling that Scrunch had once served with 40 Commando.

'. . . Quite agree, sir. Anyway, I think Mr Buchanan's quite happy with us now.'

Which was not what Archie Buchanan was thinking as he scrambled back up the slope to D Company. Archie Buchanan was thinking that Mrs Buchanan's little boy was a frigging idiot. He could have stayed on the ship, being wined and dined. He could have stayed down at Ajax Bay with BHQ. Instead he was being stopped, with terrifying aggression on occasions, by sentries demanding verbal identification. Somewhere at the back of his mind he remembered that it was opening time in El Vino's right about now, GMT. The night editor and the subs would be downing a few drinks. Must be hell, he thought, being stuck in London, with nothing to look forward to except the World Cup, the Derby, a few Test Matches, Wimbledon, and lazy afternoons sipping Buck's Fizzes.

'Guy the fucking Gorilla,' he panted in answer to the latest challenge.

'Oh, it's you, Archie. Might have known it wasn't the Argies. You're making more noise than a squadron of tanks.'

'Can you keep your voice a little lower,' asked Archie, passing the perimeter picket and keeping a tight hold on the guide rope that stretched, supported by stakes, from the beachhead to the summit of Wreck Point North. 'Pronouncing it the way you do, there's not a lot of difference between ''Archie'' and ''Argie''. Why the hell don't they give all you guys radios, anyway? Then the guy at the bottom could tell the next guy up that there was someone coming through.'

'Don't ask me, I only work here. Will you send a message to my mum in your column?' the picket called after him. 'Tell her my feet are cold.'

'It'll be my first priority tomorrow. I won't even use the latrines until I've typed that.'

'And can she send me a ham and a crate of beer and a few Mars Bars.'

Hunting for his trench, and still attached to the guide rope, Archie stumbled across Rupert doing the rounds of 3 Platoon.

'Welcome back,' said Rupert. 'I'm sure you could use a large whisky and water.'

'Damned right,' said Archie eagerly.

'So could I. Will you settle for a brew?'

'I thought you were an aristocrat,' grumbled Archie. 'Whoever heard of an aristocrat travelling without booze?'

'Not exactly travelling without it, old chap, but rather saving it. Until Stanley.'

'You think you'll live that long?'

'One never knows. However, the beauty about being the younger scion is that the line continues, regardless of deaths.'

'Fuck me,' said Archie.

'I'd rather not, with due respect. People might talk.'

'You're unreal, you know that?'

'A little eccentricity is good for the soul. Is that an affirmative to the offer of a wet?'

'Didn't I hear something about no hexy stoves after dark?'

'You did. Fortunately I carry a thermos.'

'Well, if that's all there is.'

'That's all there is.'

'Then I'll settle for it. My mouth tastes like an Arab's jockstrap.'

'Ah, you journalist johnnies certainly get around. Over here. There's been a bit of a reshuffle regarding your accommodation, by the way. I was asked to explain it if I saw you.'

'I wish to Christ he'd shut the fuck up,' said Sammy to Twiggy, listening to Rupert. 'You'd think it was manoeuvres on Salisbury Plain the way he goes on.'

If Sammy sounded edgy it wasn't due to fear. He was just pissed off and tired. He had given up the unequal struggle with the seepage in the trench and was now perched on the edge, inside his sleeping-bag with his knees up and using his bergen as a back-rest. He was warm enough except for his feet, which were freezing, and he knew from experience that it was almost impossible to sleep with cold feet. He doubted he'd get more than a few hours, if that. How the hell could anyone expect them to fight if they didn't sleep?

Twiggy remained in the trench. He had constructed for himself a mattress of peat slabs, through which the water, in theory, permeated only slowly from bottom to top. It was no more than forty per cent effective, but there was no way Twiggy was going to sleep with his body exposed, just in case the Argies did the unexpected and launched an air or mortar attack in the dark.

'What's the shortest book in the world?' he asked Sammy.

'*The Biafran Cook Book,*' said Acne Hackney from an adjacent trench, overhearing the question.

'*Prominent Negroes in the Third Reich,*' said Jomo.

'Fockineytiebooko'fockinwarheroes,' said Branston Pickles, who was sharing with Acne Hackney.

'*How to Win Friends and Influence People* by General Galtieri,' suggested Sammy. 'Okay, what's the answer?'

'*British Foreign Office Successes Since Suez,*' said Twiggy.

'Pathetic,' said Sammy.

'Chip butties,' said Twiggy, changing the subject.

'What?' said Sammy.

'Chip butties. I was thinking about them a minute ago. Two thick slices of real bread, not that ready-sliced muck, lashings of butter, salt, and deep-fried chips the diameter of a gimpy barrel.'

'Jellied eels,' said Sammy, warming to the theme.

'Haggisanmash,' called Branston.

'Toad-in-the-hole,' said Acne Hackney.

'Lancashire hotpot,' drooled Twiggy.

'Salt beef sandwiches.'

'Pints of John Smiths.'

'Pints of Watneys.'

'Gnat's piss,' said Twiggy. 'They haven't got a clue how to make beer south of the Wash.'

'That's all you know. At least beer down south tastes like beer and not soup.'

Twiggy chuckled.

'What's so funny?' demanded Sammy.

'Us. Talking about beer and sandwiches and jellied eels and shit when we're eight thousand miles from any of it.'

'That's funny? You've got a weird sense of humour, Twiglet. Anyway,' he added seriously, 'it's what we're fighting for, ain't it?'

'Beer?'

'Not exactly. But doing things our way and not the friggin' Argie way. Yeah, beer, I suppose, when you get down to it.'

'That's not what Scrunch reckons.'

'What does Scrunch reckon?'

'I heard Archie ask him what he thought he was fighting for while they were digging Archie's trench. "For the Queen," says Scrunch. I thought Archie was going to have a fit. "For the Queen?" he says. "Yes," says Scrunch. "And for the ace, king, jack, and ten." '

'Like I said, Twiglet, you've got a weird sense of humour. I find that about as funny as gonorrhoea.'

'I didn't say it,' protested Twiggy. 'Scrunch did.'

'And Scrunch is going to bang a couple of heads together unless you shut up,' called the CSM from a distance.

' 'bout bloody time too,' muttered Two-Shit to Jomo. Two-Shit was zipped up in his sleeping-bag but standing in the trench, leaning on the butt of his gimpy. He'd managed to 'liberate' a couple of ammunition boxes from the beach. These he had hammered flat and was now standing on. They were keeping his feet and the bottom of his sleeping-bag relatively dry, but they did not cover a broad enough area to lie down on. 'Bloody Argie patrols can hear that a mile away.'

'They won't be out tonight,' said Jomo. He was crouched in the base of the trench, his own gimpy propped up beside him, catching a crafty smoke and shielding the glowing end of the cigarette between cupped hands. 'Stands to reason. If I were them I'd keep well clear and lob a few long-range shells in our general direction from somewhere like Goose Green.'

'Why don't you talk a little louder?' said Three-piece from close by. 'Maybe they didn't hear you.'

'Up yours,' said Jomo amiably.

'After you with Sweet's,' said Yank.

Slowly, with the passing of the hours, conversations grew fewer as men managed to doze off.

TWENTY-TWO

Winter's Day

SATURDAY MAY 22, dawned bright and clear, and by mid-morning there could be little doubt that the beaches and the high ground around were securely in British hands, although the Rapier batteries were giving some trouble and would continue to do so until the operators solved the teething troubles. With that in mind senior officers waited anxiously all day for the return of the Argentine Air Force, which did not put in an appearance until late afternoon and then only in the form of a brace of Skyhawks, whose pilots quickly fled after releasing their bombs without success.

May 23 was a different matter. Shortly after 2 p.m. a small force of Skyhawks evaded the Harrier CAP and attacked the shipping in San Carlos Water, singling out *Antelope* for special attention. The frigate was hit by two bombs which failed to explode immediately but which detonated later while a disposal team was trying to defuse them. The subsequent fire burned its way to the magazine and the ship disintegrated, finally sinking the next day.

May 24 saw three of the LSL 'Knights'—*Sir Galahad, Sir Lancelot* and *Sir Bedivere*—also hit by bombs which failed to explode on impact, that fact being given out over the BBC World Service from the Ministry of Defence and thus telling the Argentine pilots that they were setting their fuses wrongly.

Three Daggers and a Skyhawk were destroyed on May 24 for the loss of a Sea Harrier from *Hermes*.

Tuesday May 25 was Argentina's National Day, and the troops were warned to prepare for something spectacular. Towards midday small forces of Skyhawks were driven off by fierce ship and ground resistance, but during the afternoon a quartet of Skyhawks attacked *Broadsword* and *Coventry*. *Broadsword* was hit by a bomb which failed to explode, but *Coventry* wasn't so lucky. Three bombs penetrated her hull and detonated, smashing a yawning gap in her port side through which the sea immediately poured. Within minutes she was rolling over. Sea King and Wessex helicopters winched up survivors and attempted, by using their blades, to fan away the survival dinghies from the stricken ship.

In all nineteen men died in an attack lasting thirty seconds.

Later on in the afternoon the container ship *Atlantic Conveyor* was attacked by a Super Etendard-launched Exocet one hundred miles north-east of Port Stanley. The warships in the same group fired antimissile chaff. *Atlantic Conveyor* had no such defences; she was hit and abandoned. Lost with her were ten helicopters, among them three giant Chinooks, something that would cause a severe logistics headache in the days to come and result in the manpacking of munitions across East Falkland.

But the junta had shot most of its airborne bolt by the end of May 25. For five days it had tried to sink either the transports or the carriers; it had largely failed in its first objective and totally failed in its second. It had also lost thirty aircraft in the trying and the same number again to Harrier and SBS/SAS ground action before the arrival of the land forces. The Argentine navy had retreated to home waters; the army on the Malvinas seemed not to know what to do next.

Throughout the air/sea battles the British assault troops had watched more or less impotently while the RAF and the Royal Navy had fought their fights for them. Now they wanted to do something, get on with it, make a contribution. But the build up of essential supplies for a push forward was slow, and for the ground troops boring since on the Falklands at that time of year darkness was twice as long as daylight. Thus for fifteen or sixteen hours a day there was nothing to do but talk or sleep. Or eat, though the Arctic ratpacks, whose main constituent was chicken, were beginning to pall. 'I'll end up cockadoodling and chasing fucking hens,' Sammy grumbled to Twiggy.

The Catering Corps, when the Argentine Air Force allowed, performed small miracles, cooking in oil drums cut in half or anything else their ingenuity could conjure up when all else failed. Their efforts were not always appreciated. 'What's this?' 'Goat shit, what does it look like?' 'Okay, just thought it was something I shouldn't eat.'

When break-out became imminent and unit objectives were allocated, they raised a few eyebrows. Hitherto, Goose Green had been considered irrelevant. When Stanley fell, Goose Green would follow. It was only necessary to isolate the hamlet to preclude a flanking counter-attack, not go for it head on. Or so the senior officers thought. The politicians in London thought differently. They needed a victory, and quickly. Thus 2 Para would take the hamlet, pulling out of their emplacements on the Sussex Mountains on May 26. In tandem, 45 Commando, 3 Para and Daddy Rankin's battalion would break out of the beach-head and march, 'yomp' or 'tab' the length of East Falkland since there were no choppers to airlift them. With the battalion on its right flank, 45 Commando would take the northern route, via New House, Douglas and Teal Inlet, accompanied by a troop of the Blues and Royals in Scorpion and Scimitar light tanks. 3 Para would 'tab' a more southern route, skirting Bombilla Hill, making directly for Teal Inlet. Later, two companies of 42 Commando would head for the lower, western, slopes of Mount Kent, the vital first hill for the assault on Stanley, probably in all the available helicopters. 40 Commando would hold San Carlos.

Few of the unit commanders believed that a march across East Falkland could be accomplished now that the weather was changing for the worse, or, if it could be done, that the men would arrive on Mount Kent in any condition to fight. Several senior officers were openly rebellious at being hurried for political reasons. On East Falkland there was a lot more at stake than a ministerial portfolio. When he heard about Goose Green, Daddy Rankin said, 'They're all raving mad.' It was an unnecessary side show. Too much could go wrong. 'Thank God it's not us,' said Winter's Day, who would not, as it turned out, have been involved anyway. . . .

. . . And who should not have been in the brigade maintenance area at Ajax Bay in the late afternoon of May 25; who should have deputed Peter to see if there was any chance of obtaining more light machine guns for D Company. Better still, he should have gone through the Battalion Quarter Mas-

ter. He went in person because he overestimated his powers
of persuasion.

The three Skyhawks which bombed Red Beach should have
been picked up earlier, except there was a lull in the air
attacks and, in any case, the ships were still reeling from the
previous raids. Moreover, the pilots of the Skyhawks, whose
orders were to fly to the limit of their range and attack the
carrier group, would have done precisely that had it not been
erroneously confirmed by the Super Etendard pilot who sank
the *Atlantic Conveyor* that the ship his Exocet had hit was
Hermes. Thus informed, the Skyhawk fliers opted not to
press on but to bomb Ajax Bay as the strategic alternative.

Finally, in retrospect perhaps munitions dumps should not
have been placed so close together, except where else, a
Royal Marines QM lamented later, were they to put the
dumps, space being at a premium?

In any event, the Skyhawks made their bombing run and a
successful escape. The attack killed six men and wounded
twenty-eight others, among them Winter's Day, whose entire
right side was peppered by shrapnel from mortar rounds
exploding in the fierce fire that followed the bombing. Torso
wounds were minimal and the surgeons reckoned they could
save his right arm. They were not so sure about his right leg;
a sliver of metal had neatly removed part of the knee-cap. It
would probably be all right but he'd never walk properly
again. That notwithstanding, he was now out of the fight.

Although aware that the company commander was on the
beach, the first Peter knew about Winter's Day being wounded
was when he was summoned to Battalion HQ by the adjutant.
Daddy Rankin saw him personally and explained what had
happened.

'Good Christ,' said Peter, shocked. Winter's Day was the
company's first casualty, the battalion's, to the best of his
knowledge. 'How is he?'

'The last I heard he was semi-conscious, under sedation,
and receiving blood. He's got about half a pound of metal in
him by all accounts.'

'What are his chances?'

'Well, he's hors de combat, if that's what you mean. He
might lose a leg, but that's in the balance at present.'

'Are they operating?'

'Not yet. There are a good number of chaps worse off.
They'll get round to him, probably save his leg too if I'm any

judge of the calibre of surgeons we've got with the brigade. What the hell was he doing down here anyway?'

'On the scrounge for machine guns.'

'Silly bugger. Hasn't he ever heard of channels?'

'I wouldn't have thought it was the sort of day for doing things by the book,' said Peter wryly, thumbing to where the blaze started by the Skyhawks was still burning fiercely and where ammunition was detonating at intervals.

'Perhaps you're right.' Daddy put a match to his pipe. He had heard just half an hour ago about Goose Green and about the forced march across East Falkland, but he had yet to have an 'O' Group of his company commanders. He wondered if Peter Ballantine should now be one of them.

'The thing is,' he went on, 'it now looks as if you've probably inherited D Company.'

'Probably, sir?' What the hell was Daddy talking about? Companies had 2 i/cs in order that the chain of command would not be broken if something happened to the company commander.

'I had the adjutant dig out the seniority list the moment I heard about Major de Winton-Day. There are three captains senior to you in the battalion. One's the adjutant, who doesn't count. Another's Bill Peckham, whom I choose to leave where he is for reasons that don't concern you. The third's Toby Lomax.'

'I hope that doesn't mean what I think it means, sir,' said Peter, reddening beneath the camouflage cream. 'Neither the officers nor the men would accept Lomax. He doesn't know anything about D Company.'

'I don't run this battalion by committee,' said Daddy sharply. Then, as though regretting his tone, he added in a more friendly manner: 'Besides, you misunderstand me. If I put Toby Lomax in command of D Company it would be no reflection on your ability. I also looked up the seniority of D Company's subalterns. You'd need a 2 i/c to take some of the work load, and that means Lieutenant Parker-Smith. Parker-Smith is commander of 3 Platoon with young ffolliott under him. You see my predicament. If you get the company Parker-Smith becomes 2 i/c and ffolliott inherits 3 Platoon. Do you think he's up to it?'

'He's a good man, sir. A bit green, but Sergeant O'Hara can nurse him. Until he's used to it—ffolliott, that is—Rupert can double up as 2 i/c and 3 Platoon commander.'

'You think Rupert's that capable?'

'I do, sir.'

'Good. I'm happy to say Major de Winton-Day agrees with you. That's that then. As of now you're OC D Company.'

'Thank you, sir.'

'Don't thank me. You may live to regret Winter's Day buggering about looking for machine guns. You don't know it yet—there'll be a company commanders' ''O'' Group at first light tomorrow—but the battalion's in for quite a hike.'

'Break-out, sir?'

Daddy tapped his nose. 'You'll be told in good time.'

'Right, sir.'

'Oh, one other thing, Peter,' Daddy called after him.

'Sir?'

'There's a world of difference between being number two and being number one. I know I don't have to tell you that, but bear it in mind. I'm always available if you need any advice.'

Peter sought out Winter's Day in the field hospital. The former company commander was more than half conscious and receiving blood. Peter wasn't squeamish by nature, but Winter's Day was a mess. The right-hand side of his face was scarred and burnt, his right arm bloodied. But it was his right leg that had caught the worst of the exploding mortars. The medical orderlies had applied a tourniquet and one was attempting to extract the larger of the shell fragments. Evidently Winter's Day had been pumped full of local anaesthetic, for he didn't seem to be in any great pain. There wasn't much left of his right knee-cap, though it was difficult to tell the full extent of the wound, there being so much coagulating blood.

'Bloody stupid, what?' Winter's Day recognized Peter and managed a rueful smile. 'How does it look?'

'Could be worse.'

'Tell me the truth. I can't feel a thing down there, and every time I try to sit up this bugger pushes me down again.'

'Now, now,' said the medic, 'no slagging the nurses.'

'Like something from the Battle of the Somme,' said Peter.

'Going to fuck up my pheasant shoots, I suppose. I should have sent you.'

'Thanks a lot.'

'No offence. Army rules are there for a purpose, one of them being that you don't do anything yourself that can just as easily be done by a subordinate. I didn't get the damned machine guns, either. I was arguing with the QM when those bastard planes came over. Have you seen the CO?'

'Yes.'

'And you've got the company?'

'Yes.'

'Rupert as 2 i/c?'

'Yes.'

'That'll shake him. Fewer jokes now, I shouldn't wonder.'

'I doubt that. You know Rupert.'

'You next, my old china,' said a second medical orderly, a burly individual who unceremoniously elbowed Peter out of the way. 'The knife awaits.' He glanced down at Winter's Day's leg and shook his head. 'Jesus Christ, you look like the front window of Sainsbury's. You can send him some grapes,' the medic added to Peter.

'I'll try to keep in touch,' said Peter, knowing he was being absurd. Winter's Day would be casevacked to the hospital ship *Uganda* as soon as it was humanly possible.

'You'll do nothing of the sort,' said Winter's Day. 'Forget me, look after the company. I'll see you in the UK.'

'Dear Lord,' said Rupert later, when Peter informed him of the new chain of command. 'I suppose that means I've now got to take the war seriously. Any idea when we break out?'

'Soon,' said Peter. 'Tomorrow night, maybe. The 27th at the latest.'

TWENTY-THREE

Peter

PETER WAS RIGHT IN his second guess.

On May 27 45 Commando and the battalion rubbish-skipped across San Carlos Water to Port San Carlos, and from there, at 10 a.m. local time, 1400 hours Zulu, set off, accompanied by 3 Troop of the Blues and Royals and several BV Volvos, tracked snow vehicles belonging to the Royal Marines, on what would be known thereafter as the Long March: fifty miles of rivers and marshes and peat bogs and hills, in weather that was never warmer than bloody cold and where freezing rain was a constant companion, when it wasn't snowing. And all this for much of the way with 120 pounds of equipment per man.

The ultimate objective for this phase of the assault on Stanley was the lower slopes of Mount Kent, a dozen miles from the capital. Since there could be no guarantees that the Argentine Air Force would not change its tactics and attack the columns or that Argentine ground forces would not offer resistance in the form of a fighting retreat (though in the event the air force was conspicuous largely by its absence and the ground forces pulled back without engaging the British columns to form a defensive horseshoe around Stanley), much of the trek would have to be made at night under strict radio silence. Thus darkness as well as the weather and the Argentines were adversaries to be considered, and it was estimated by brigade that 45 and the battalion would not reach Mount Kent until June 3 or 4.

Also from Port San Carlos (with 4 Troop of the Blues and Royals), 3 Para had moved out on foot for Teal Inlet, midway between the coast and Mount Kent, a little ahead of 45 and the battalion, while 2 Para closed on Camilla Creek preparatory to launching the attack on Goose Green. 42 Commando was staying behind, partly to relieve 2 Para on the Sussex Mountains and eventually Goose Green, and partly to be helicoptered forward to Mount Kent when the time came. 40 Commando was just staying behind.

With the light tanks of the Blues and Royals skirmishing ahead and the BV Volvos carrying some of the heavier equipment, 45 Commando and Daddy Rankin's battalion, six hundred men in each, marched parallel to one another and a mile apart, with the battalion south of the marines. A distance of ten to fifteen yards separated each man. Thus each unit from first to last stretched across four or five miles of East Falkland, though by the time a halt was called on the first day, long after dark, with the information being passed down the line by word of mouth, what had begun as two echelons recognizable as being military in origin were now long columns of exhausted men. And some who were already falling by the wayside due to sprains and blisters and general debility occasioned by the weather. D Company had lost four individuals to the elements and accidents in the dark, the other companies in the battalion ten between them. 'We'll be down to about enough men to mount a guard of honour before Mount Kent at this rate,' commented Daddy acidly when he heard the casualty report.

Though now officially with Company HQ as 2 i/c, Rupert sought out 3 Platoon when D Company bivouacked for the night. He was relieved to hear from Double-Eff that the platoon had lost not a man. 'Though I'd hate to stake a lot of money on how many will be fit to go on tomorrow,' said the new platoon commander, who was also feeling the pace but whose marathon runs around the troopship to combat seasickness had left him fitter than most. 'What's it like at HQ where the rich people live?'

'Boring, quite frankly, my dear James. A great deal of basic arithmetic to ensure that everything is where it should be. I don't think anyone informed the commanding officer when these new arrangements were considered that Old Etonians are not good at adding up. We generally employ accountants and factors to take care of such mundane matters.'

Double-Eff smiled.

'Do you mind if I do the rounds with you?' asked Rupert courteously, not wanting to step on Double-Eff's toes or undermine his authority but genuinely concerned about the men in what he still considered partly his platoon.

'I'd appreciate it,' said Double-Eff, who was only just starting to realize the difference between having someone at your elbow ready to take the burden of even minor decisions and having to make them oneself.

The men had the hexy stoves going, preparing brews and hot food at Scarlett's insistence (when most of them would willingly have settled for a couple of slabs of nutty and sleep), there being no option but to cook in the dark. Not that any Argentines around would be able to see much now that it was snowing heavily. 'God's dandruff,' remarked Rupert, huddling deeper in his Arctic gear and wondering whether— and concluding not—this was the time to break out the two bottles of Glenmorangie he'd brought, and so far left untouched. There would be occasions, if he were any judge, when the whisky would be needed more than now, and he wasn't necessarily thinking of Port Stanley. 'You'd think He'd have the courtesy or wisdom to recognize which side has more right in this little conflict. Still, I expect there are Argentine officers berating the Almighty for the same reason. Odd, don't you think, that we're both asking the same God for the defeat of the other side? Something wrong there.'

Crouched over their hexy stoves, warming their hands by the same flame that made their brews and cooked their food, the men had little or no shelter from the snow. They would sleep, after eating, as best they could in their bags, within the lee of a convenient rock or against their bergens. Rupert found he was missing the platoon more than he would have thought possible in just forty-eight hours. They moaned a lot and they were bloody insubordinate at times, but they didn't know the meaning of the word 'quit'. They would go on until they dropped and then go on some more. Pray God the people in the UK and the Falkland Islanders understood that.

Idiotic sentimentality, he chided himself. They were a bunch of bolshevik no-goods who impregnated young girls and broke up bars, who would willingly see the estate burn to the ground and dance on the ashes under different circumstances. They ate because they were hungry and warmed themselves because they were cold. They would sleep because they were tired and march and fight because they were ordered to. Not a man jack of them possessed a soupçon of the nobler instincts. And yet . . .

And yet he would not have chosen different companions had he been offered the pick of Caesar's legions. Though they were no longer his, they were magnificent. And bloody foolish he'd be to tell them as much, of course.

'How's it going, Sarn't O'Hara?' asked Rupert, raising his voice to make himself heard and recognizing Scarlett not so much because of his bulky six feet but because of the crafty manner in which the NCO was arranging HQ section's bergens in a circle, like a wagon train's, to protect those within from the wind and the driving snow. 'Sorry you volunteered?'

'Not a bit of it, Boss.' Scarlett saw Double-Eff alongside Rupert and recalled that Rupert was no longer 'Boss' in 3 Platoon. No point in diminishing young ffolliett's authority. 'Not a bit of it, sir. What have I got at home that I haven't got here? Sergeants' Mess'll be more or less deserted, with no one to check what the rear party's drinking and them having to be taken on trust, as it were, to sign their own mess bills without too much fiction. Mid-evening television. It's Thursday at home and I can't remember whether that means *Dallas* or a film on the other channel. Sausage, egg and chips and a walk by the river just before the last pint. Young girls in mini-skirts and tight jeans. No, what the hell is there at home?'

'You're making me think, Sarn't.'

Rupert was surprised to see Archie still roughing it with 3 Platoon; he'd have thought the journalist would be up with Battalion HQ, especially now 2 Para were about to attack Goose Green. He was also surprised to see Archie fiddling with the magazine of a Sterling submachine gun.

'What on earth are you doing with that?' asked Rupert. 'If you intend carrying it, I'm not quite sure that's within the rules.'

'Fucking defending myself, aren't I?' answered Archie, wondering if his occasionally dubious command of the Queen's English, written and spoken, would ever be the same again after this operation. Something also told him that he was getting a bit long in the tooth to be gallivanting around strange islands where people were trying to kill him. 'Picked it up from one of the dropouts.'

'Really?' said Rupert. 'You'll forgive me for being importunate, but to the best of my recollection the British soldier doesn't exactly toss away his weapon because of a sprained ankle.'

Archie had the grace to look sheepish.

'Well, let's say I found it at Ajax Bay. It was lying there doing nothing, so I thought I'd save it from the sea air. You know how much these things cost.'

'A very wise and thoughtful precaution.'

The medical orderly, Philip Beavis, was attending to Acne Hackney's feet. Davey Binns had his boots and socks off—unwisely, in Rupert's opinion considering the temperature—but Beavis seemed to know his business. In the dim light from the masked torch, Rupert could see that Binns had several blisters the size of twenty-pence pieces. Beavis was pricking them with a needle he heated in the flame of the hexy stove, to sterilize it. Nothing unusual in a man having blisters; most of the company did. But the flesh at the base of Acne Hackney's toes, which Beavis was rubbing, was unpleasantly pale.

'And what did your last servant die of, Binns?' asked Rupert.

'I can't feel a friggin' thing, sir,' said Acne Hackney. 'I can see Phil rubbing the bejesus out of my feet, but I don't feel anything.'

Rupert nudged Double-Eff, who took his cue.

'Anything really the matter, Beavis?' asked Double-Eff.

'He'll be okay, Boss,' answered the medical orderly.

'I'd ask Scarlett to keep an eye on him if I were you,' Rupert advised Double-Eff sotto voce. 'You know how he managed to wangle his way out of a medical discharge to come along. He'll keep going whatever condition his feet are in.'

'Mind you, sir,' said Acne Hackey, realizing that the officers were talking about him, 'my feet might look like something off a fishmonger's slab, but this climate's worked a miracle on my spots.'

Which was more or less true. Beneath the camouflage cream Acne Hackney's skin condition was clearing. He'd lived rough for almost a week. He'd witnessed bombings and strafings and occasionally come under fire himself. He'd eaten reconstituted food almost exclusively and hadn't had a really decent wash or a shave since leaving the assault ship. Yet in spite of all that his skin was getting better. He didn't push his luck by asking himself why.

'Did you see the penguins earlier, sir?' asked Three-piece, when Rupert and Double-Eff came to where he and Yank were gulping hot drinks.

Rupert had, along with the remainder of the battalion. A small colony had followed the battalion's route, while keeping their distance, earlier in the day. Until the birds recognized that these strangely clad beings were not some unknown variety of fauna.

'That I did, Sweet,' said Rupert.

'Fucking good advertising campaign, that, don't you think,' asked Three-piece, 'naming a bird after a chocolate biscuit?'

Sammy Finch was flaked out, already in his sleeping-bag. Twiggy was making the brews and supper.

'Everything okay, Finch?' asked Rupert.

'Tired, Boss,' said Sammy. 'I could use about twenty-four hours' sleep.'

'Not this week,' said Rupert. 'Wait until Stanley. Then you can sleep all day for ever.'

'Huh?'

'I mean, you can sleep all day when we get there.'

'No, I don't think you meant that, Boss,' said Sammy wistfully. 'You meant what you first said.'

'I'm not with you.'

'Well, dying's a bit like sleeping for ever, isn't it?'

'You're not going to die, Finch,' said Rupert, concerned. A comment like that was most unlike Sammy Finch. 'In a month or two we'll be back in barracks and you'll be the same insubordinate little bastard you've always been. I'll make you a small wager, say a pound, that you'll be up before the company commander on a charge at least twice before Christmas.'

'You've got a bet, Boss,' said Sammy, feeling better already.

Back at Company HQ Rupert found Peter in the process of dismissing the other platoon officers at the end of a pow-wow. Scrunch had been taking notes from the light thrown by a hexy stove.

'Where the bloody hell have you been, Rupert?' demanded Peter sharply.

'Hunting up a hot bath.'

Peter counted slowly to ten before motioning Scrunch to move out of earshot.

'I asked you where you'd been,' Peter repeated. 'And no jokes, if you don't mind.'

'Looking up 3 Platoon, making sure everything was as it should be. You recall you wanted me to keep an eye on Double-Eff for the time being.'

'And I also recall mentioning something about no officer wandering off without letting this HQ know where he's going. I've just held a company "O" Group, which you missed. You also caused ffolliott to miss it. Where do you think 3 Platoon would be if I'd decided to push on before first light, if the CO had altered the companies' dispositions and moved us up to the van?'

Rupert felt the hairs on the nape of his neck bristle.

'I told you I was going. You nodded.'

'Don't accept anything other than the written or spoken word as consent in future. And try not to stray without making sure I don't want you here. I thought you'd disappeared to bring ffolliott back with you.'

Peter conceded that he was handling this badly, allowing a minor incident to blow up out of all proportion. Damn, he thought.

'Got it,' said Rupert tersely.

Peter's criticism was unjustified, Rupert knew. Equally, he realized that Peter had a lot on his plate since taking over the company from Winter's Day. That Peter could hack his new responsibilities Rupert had no doubt. But it had been a long day and everyone was tired. The men could make a brew and turn in, the junior officers and NCOs too. The company commander was allowed no such luxury until he'd dotted the i's and crossed the t's. It was inevitable that a tyro in the job would become irritable, worry that he'd forgotten something. It was a bit like playing chess: the pieces and pawns were in position, but there was always a danger that something had been overlooked.

Scrunch, who had not gone far, moved back into the hexy-light.

'With due respect, Boss,' he said to Peter, 'your voices are carrying.'

Peter nodded his appreciation of the CSM's attempt to defuse a potentially unpleasant confrontation.

'Right, Sarn't Major. Thanks.'

With a map shielded from the thickening snow by two bergens, Peter spent ten minutes with Rupert going over the company positions in relation to the remainder of the battalion. He also asked Rupert about the condition of the men in 3

Platoon. Rupert told him that they were okay as far as it went.

'Fine,' said Peter eventually, shutting the map case. 'I guess that's about as much as we can hope for. But damn this snow. I hope it doesn't hang around all the way to Mount Kent. Or all day tomorrow, for that matter. I don't think the battalion can take another night in the open in conditions like this.'

'We should be at Douglas settlement tomorrow. There'll be shelter there.'

'True. No Argies, either, according to information Daddy's had from an SAS patrol. I dunno, part of me's hoping they haven't buggered off. The sooner we get to grips with them, the better. If they're all pulling back to the mountains around Stanley, there's going to be a hell of a scrap there.'

'Agreed. On the whole I'd say I preferred Belfast.'

'I'll second that.'

'Well, if that's all,' said Rupert, getting up from his haunches suddenly and reaching for his shovel, 'I rather think that this afternoon's chicken supreme is getting to me.'

'Right.'

Rupert hesitated. 'Sorry about the misunderstanding earlier. And about making a joke of it.'

'Don't apologize about the jokes,' said Peter. 'God knows, if it were not for some of your idiotic cracks we'd all be about ready for the asylum.'

'No, you were right in the first place,' said Rupert, surprising Peter with his apparent sincerity. 'There's a time and a place for being a comedian.'

Clutching his shovel, Rupert disappeared behind a curtain of snow. Ten paces away from the dozen bergens that were Company HQ he was invisible. But after a moment he returned.

'By the way,' he said, 'I may be away some time. G'night, Cap'n Scott.'

Peter had to grin. Rupert was incorrigible, but his sense of the absurd was worth a machine gun platoon.

'Good night, Captain Oates.'

While D Company slept, 2 Para moved forward from Camilla Creek House for the attack on Darwin and Goose Green, the opening salvos of the assault being fired by HMS *Arrow* at 0230 on May 28. To start with the paratroopers made rapid headway, and by dawn they were within striking distance of the enemy defensive bunkers though being harassed mercilessly by enemy 105s. With virtually no support from British artillery, a company of paras fought a bitter and bloody battle to gain a foothold on Darwin Hill, during which engagement 2 Para's CO, Colonel 'H', was killed.

While a single company secured Darwin Hill, three others attacked the airfield and the hamlet of Goose Green, being forced to fight for every yard of ground throughout the afternoon of May 28, and coming under fire not only from artillery and heavy machine guns but from the deadly 35 mm anti-aircraft guns being used in a ground capacity. Skyhawks and Pucaras also bombarded the paras with rockets and napalm.

By evening, when the weather cleared sufficiently for a Harrier strike to be mounted, casualties were heavy on both sides, and Goose Green had not yet fallen. Furthermore, a patrol established that over a hundred East Falkland civilians were locked up in the community hall. It did not seem likely that these non-combatants would escape unscathed if the Argentines chose to make a fight of it, which they elected not to after a written ultimatum had been delivered to their commander, who was convinced he was capitulating to a far superior force.

Even the paras were shocked when file after file of Argentines came out to lay down their arms, for they had been outnumbered by more than three to one. They had lost sixteen killed (some while moving forward to accept a white flag in an earlier firefight) and thirty-six wounded. In return they had killed 250 and taken 1,400 prisoners plus weapons.

News of the victory at Goose Green was like a shot in the arm to the rest of the task force, though it was now recognized that there would be no easy victories, no 'walkovers'.

On May 30 45 Commando and the battalion arrived at Teal Inlet, a small settlement overlooking the estuary. 3 Para, taking the shorter route across the centre of East Falkland, had already been and gone, leaving for their next objective of Estancia House, a grand-sounding name for a few farm buildings, at the foot of Mount Estancia and within sight of Mount Kent.

The snow alternating with icy rain and hail had hardly relented since Port San Carlos, thirty marching miles west, though there would be the occasional break in the weather that made everyone think the sun was about to shine for a few hours and dry the sodden (and sodding) ground. Not a chance. Why anyone, Britain or Argentina or for that matter the sheep-shagging kelpers, could possibly wish to lay claim to this miserable few hectares of South Atlantic nothingness was beyond the comprehension of the troops. They had other things to consider, in any case, mostly the state of their feet and hands and whether the Argie Air Force would come out of its shell. Which it didn't except for a few marauding Pucaras rapidly driven off by the Harrier CAP when the weather permitted take-off from the carriers, and by Blowpipes, whose operators were becoming more skilful and daring with the passing of time. Occasionally in the distance, east, there was heard the rumble of artillery, but what the Argie gunners were aiming at was a mystery. And could remain so, thank you very much, until reinforcements arrived. 5 Brigade was due to land the Gurkhas, Scots and Welsh Guards at San Carlos on June 1 if the rumours were correct. Along with Major-General Moore, who would be taking over from Brigadier Thompson now that the ground forces comprised two brigades.

At Teal Inlet everyone had a chance, during a thirty-six hour restover, while K and L Companies of 42 Commando were being helicoptered forward to Mounts Kent and Challenger after a previous attempt had been whited out, to take stock.

For a few in Daddy's battalion the examination revealed frostbite and trenchfoot. Six more casualties were added to the previous fourteen incapacitated. Two of them came from D Company but none from 3 Platoon, though Phil Beavis, having taken another look at Acne Hackney's feet, told him that the raw blisters weren't healing as they should and if he were Davey Binns he'd put in a chit to see the battalion MO with view to being casevacked to Ajax Bay for proper treatment. Beavis had seen these things before. A raw wound exacerbated by constant marching in wet boots suddenly turned septic. The next thing a bloke knew he was being issued with a set of crutches and being called Hopalong. Acne Hackney informed Beavis, who was otherwise now an accepted member of the company, that the medic would find a Blowpipe up his jacksie if he allowed his diagnosis to go any further. Davey Binns hadn't come all this way to be hospitalized.

Others too were feeling the strain, not always because of foot problems. When, courtesy of a Teal Inlet resident and in a snowstorm, Twiggy stripped to the waist and threw hot water over his torso, Sammy remarked that Twiggy looked

like a sub-Arctic version of E.T. Which was accurate enough.
Twiggy had been sleeping badly when he slept at all. Lightly
built anyway, his cheeks were now sunken and his eyes those
of a congenital hyperthyroid. He wasn't sure he could go
much further. But he would, as long as everyone else was
pressing on.

Which they did on June 2, heading east at first and then
south-east, over the Malo Hills to Lower Malo House. Then
east again, towards Mount Kent.

Each man in the battalion, in D Company, in 3 Platoon,
kept going the way he'd been taught, or in ways he'd learned
for himself; the way they'd done it on exercises a hundred
times, the way they'd marched the sixteen miles up to the old
Marston range before Christmas. A man didn't think that
there would be another two miles before a ten-minute break.
Or that there were another two miles after that. A man
concentrated on the next step, then the next, cursing when
someone dropped to the ground exhausted, forcing the man
behind to change pace. It would all end sooner or later, that's
all that could be said. Everything ended sooner or later.

Two-Shit Tyler knew he could hack it. Carrying the gimpy,
belts of ammunition and a mortar round just for the hell of it,
he wasn't going to allow a few more lousy miles to break
him. No, sir. You didn't get promotion to sergeant because
you knew how to read a fucking map and take a drill squad.
They were looking for other things, those selection boards,
and Mike Tyler had what it took. He'd get to Stanley with the
machine gun if it killed him, which he was bright enough to
realize it might.

With the other gimpy, Jomo Mason wasn't feeling as confident, though they'd have to stretcher him out before he'd go.
No doubt about it, however, he chuckled to himself, wondering if he was losing his marbles, De Law'God hadn't meant
fo' black folks to be exposed to de cold and de snow. No, sir,
massa, dis wedder wus stric'ly fo' honkies. Right on.

Branston Pickles, much to his surprise, was helping Acne
Hackney along, his trench mate. Swearing at him too. Not
that Acne Hackney got more than a quarter of the drift.

'Ye'ssupposedtaebemarchin'infockincolumnsyedumbfocker.
I'mnaesupposedtaebesupportin'yelikeafockinbairn.'

'Thanks, Branston.'

'Dinnaefockinthankmeyefocker. Ye'safockindrugonthefock-
inmarket.'

'Thanks, Branston.'

Non-Legless Jones had decided he'd had enough long before Lower Malo House. He'd forgotten the honeyed words of the recruiting officer all those years ago. This was too much. He wasn't injured in any way; he was as fit as he'd ever been. But he was frightened—and envious of those he saw being casevacked to Ajax Bay because of injuries. He had some vague idea of deliberately twisting his ankle, wandering off the track as though exhausted, and stumbling. Until, remarkably, Prawn Balls read his mind.

'If you're thinking of dropping out, boyo, you'd better forget it pretty fucking quick. What you don't carry some other bugger will have to, and that might be me.'

'Who's thinking of dropping out?' demanded Non-Legless indignantly, wondering how the hell Prawn Balls knew.

'You are, you little Welsh bastard. But let me tell you something. You won't have to wait for the Argies to put a round in you. I'll shoot you myself if you contract something that as much as needs an Elastoplast.'

Maybe it wasn't such a bright idea after all, thought Non-Legless, seeing the expression on Prawn Ball's face.

Time became meaningless as they trudged on towards the western slopes of Mount Kent. They marched, they stopped, they ate, they slept, they marched again, platoon NCOs urging on the stragglers by a combination of threats and mockery and savage humour. *Come on, Groggy, you lazy bastard. The Argies are cutting the balls off anyone they capture. You too, Legless. There's beer in Stanley. Pints of the friggin' stuff. They've run out of your blood group, Hobart, so if you're shot out here in the sticks you're going to bleed to death. Move it, Finch. Pick your skinny fuckin' knees up, Twigg. Jesus Christ, I've got a six-year-old niece who could do better. Still got your condom, Sweet, the one with the feather, you dirty little man? You're gonna need that in Stanley. I hear they're setting up brothels for us from volunteers. So far they've got three women, one who's not quite sure what he is, and a hundred and three thousand ewes. Pretend that ground's my face. Grind the heels down. Right down. Grit bag, grit bag, dirty old shit bag.*

A buzz went down the columns that 5 Brigade was finally ashore, unopposed, at San Carlos. No one gave a toss. The Pope was supposed to be in England or on his way to England, after which he'd go to Argentina. No more than a handful gave a stuff about that either, though maybe *Il Papa* could get the whole war called off before the mountains. And maybe not too. Galtieri was reputed to be saying that he now sincerely wanted peace, to which Rupert remarked that Galtieri was to peace what Benny Hill was to culture.

Helicopters flew overhead in endless procession, ferrying forward troops and artillery pieces. Somewhere up front on one occasion came the noise of an artillery barrage, British, which was short-lived and was the Forward Observation Officer calling down a salvo on Moody Brook barracks, now overlooked by a party of marines for the first time since the Royals had been ejected in April. The SAS were on the high ground north of Stanley. 42 Commando held the upper reaches of Mounts Kent and Challenger. 3 Para were well dug in on Mounts Estancia and Vernet. Argentine resistance had been minimal, but these mountains were only the first line of defence. After them came Two Sisters, Longdon, Tumbledown, Harriet, William. A long, long way still to go.

45 Commando and the battalion reached Mount Kent on June 4, having marched every yard of the way from San Carlos, the trek that some senior officers had reckoned couldn't be done. Suddenly the order came down the line to halt. Another friggin' 'take ten' was the first grumble until the troops realized they were there.

After a brew and a meal, wearily they began to dig in. They would be there a week, the buzz had it; a week of consolidating and sending out fighting patrols to soften up the Argies before the assault on the last of their mountain-held positions, which on this occasion the enemy could be expected to defend since there was nowhere for him to go afterwards except Stanley and the sea.

Another effing week of friggin' misery, the moan went up. And then the mail arrived.

TWENTY-FOUR

Letters From Home

Dearest Rupert:
 . . . and the estate is looking wonderful. Daddy and
McGregor argue a lot—and isn't that an earth-shattering eye-
opener!—mostly about next season's shooting. I've come to
the conclusion that Daddy deliberately provokes McGregor in
order to raise the temperature a little. He loves a good battle,
our esteemed father, though perhaps I shouldn't write so
flippantly about battles knowing where you are. Or rather, not
knowing where you are!
 . . . Mummy wasn't looking too well when Oliver and I
went to see her last time. Poor dear, she tries to hold a
conversation, and frequently manages to for some minutes on
end. But then everything drifts away and she's in a world of
her own again—one that ended, I think, about 1950. She's
tremendously lucid about events that took place thirty years
ago, but quite hopeless about last week. She wanted to know
where you were. She cannot take in this hideous business
over the Falklands, although she has a television and should,
therefore, be fairly au fait with current events. The 'camp
commandant', as Oliver calls the principal, is quite liberal
with the 'inmates'—another Oliverism—allowing them to watch
whatever programmes they wish providing they do not appear to be disturbed . . .
 . . . you might also tell Peter when you see him that I had
lunch with his sister a couple of days ago. Sara's a lovely girl

and her mother's delightful, but because of her Argentine fiancé she's going through a very difficult time. But enough of that. Let's all pray that it's over soon without any further loss of life.

I'm writing to Peter separately and I only mention the business of lunching with Sara in case, knowing what the mail can be like, my letter to him is delayed or goes astray. Oliver is writing to you also and Daddy attempts one or two scribbles which he tears up without posting. I think he finds it hard to express himself on paper. If you get a letter it will probably be in the tenor of: Well, my boy, show'em cold steel, that's the way to deal with Johnny Dago.

Take good, good care of yourself.

Your loving sister. . . .

My darling Peter:

Your letter posted from what I assume was Ascension Island arrived only yesterday. What an age these things take! Mustn't grumble, though. Saw some television pictures of the Mill Hill Depot. They seem to be doing marvellous work there.

. . . am writing this in the tennis court having just scribbled a few lines to brother Rupert. I was thinking this morning about our weekend together and hoping that there would be something in the post from you—and lo, there was! How clever of you to arrange for its delivery just when I was feeling down. It seems ages—because of course it is ages—since I saw you, and I can't wait for the next time. We're both a bit careful about the word 'love', aren't we? I suppose that's only natural. But for what it's worth, if the misery I'm feeling at your absence isn't love, then I don't think I ever want to experience the real thing. It doesn't seem possible that on the last shoot before Christmas we were sparring with each other. All right then, *I* was. Aren't men and women foolish to waste so much time on the preliminaries? And no, I don't mean *that* sort of preliminary! That can never be a waste of time!

The weather here is quite splendid. (Good grief, and I vowed I wouldn't write to you or Rupert about the wretched weather. How dull can one get? Is it only the English who are so obsessed about whether or not the sun is shining?)

I had lunch with your sister on Tuesday. In London. I'll bet that surprises you. I was lucky and phoned your mother at home before she left to spend a few days with Sara, otherwise

I wouldn't have known her number. However, our lunch was à deux. Clever old stick, your mum, diplomatically declining to make it a threesome, though I wouldn't have minded in the least. She's a dear. I won't tell you what Sara and I ate, but it was frightfully fattening and odiously expensive. We went dutch.

You must tell me if these are the sort of letters you like to receive, by the way, or if you'd rather know the County Cricket scores and suchlike. There's such a lot I don't know about you.

. . . also Sara made me promise I wouldn't mention the following to you, but I'm afraid I have to break that promise. She's been terribly torn vis-à-vis Ricardo and the events of the last two months, and is extraordinarily depressed. I'm telling you this only because you might find her letters somewhat strange when you get them. One cannot wipe out the past, as Sara says, but her natural reaction is to feel deeply for both you and Ricardo. I don't know, perhaps I shouldn't have mentioned it. I've said it all wrong anyway, but I hope you can read between the lines.

I'll close now or this will never get posted. It's coming up to tea time and I need a shower. I also have to get some figures ready for Oliver.

Take care of yourself. With very much love, Lavinia.

My dear Peter:

I was going to make this only a few lines and pop it in with Sara's, but I saw her dash out to catch the evening post a minute or two ago so I suppose I'm left to provide my own envelope.

She came home on the afternoon train. I saw the condition (mental) she was in when I met up with her in London, and decided she needed a rest. No arguments, I told her sternly. She's very run down . . .

. . . and Barney's in fine form you'll be happy to hear. He certainly doesn't seem his age, though I get the impression he's puzzled by your non-appearance, albeit that you were an irregular visitor in the recent past. Still, he pricks up his ears at the sound of cars, wondering if it's you.

. . . Edward is studying fiendishly hard at school, though I know that events in the South Atlantic are distracting him, as

they are several of the other boys. I think he said there are ten
or eleven boys with close relations in the task force, and
naturally they are always on the alert for news flashes. Life in
England, sad to say, is very much geared to radio and television bulletins these days. So far, thank God, none of the boys
has had a relation injured.

. . . and spoke to Lavinia on the phone, later meeting her
at Sara's flat. I like her very much.

. . . should be more I should tell you, but I prefer to write
regularly rather than at length. If I'm lucky I should be able
to make the post, even at my rate of hobble.

With fondest love, Mother.

Dearest Peter:

. . . Well, it's six minutes past nine in jolly old London
town and I'm taking a day off from the factory, having
decided that the Foreign Office can get along quite nicely
without my help, thank you very much. However, the reason
I'm mostly slutting around in a robe that could definitely use
a trip to the washing machine is because I have a hangover
that is worthy of being filmed as a sequel to *Lost Weekend*.
For Ray Milland read Sara B. Bit of a shindig with Poppy D.
last p.m. during which yours truly disgraced herself nobly.
Poor poppy seems always to catch me in one of my let's-tie-
one-on moods these days. She's a friend, as far as it goes, but
I rather think my number will be struck from her diary from
now on. Details a bit boring, so I'll skip them.

Mummy was up to see me for a couple of days earlier in
the week. Or was it last week? Forget. However, she's gone
now, having made me promise to head for the old homestead
this weekend and there take some time off. I probably will. I
might even go today. Depends how I feel when I've shaken
up a couple of Bloody Marys. I have a new recipe for those,
my own invention. One no longer mixes the vodka, tomato
juice, fresh lime, celery salt and all that stuff into one glass.
One drinks (or licks or sucks) each ingredient separately, very
fast, and then exercises through pages one to seven of Jane
Fonda's book. Marvellous. One becomes one's own cocktail
shaker. If I do decide to go home today I'll probably finish
this there, in case there's anything Mummy wants to pop in.

And aren't you a slyboots! By which I mean that I met

your Lavinia the day before yesterday (or a time approximating to that). I remember her, of course, from battalion functions, but I didn't realize she was quite so grown up. My recollection was of someone about fifteen years old which, my dear, is not the case at all, as you well know. When she telephoned me and asked if we could meet, I rather expected to be taking her to Macdonald's for a hamburger and a Coke, or around the Natural History museum, with clever Auntie Sara showing dear little Lavinia the big dinosaurs. Or that she wanted me to help her mend her hockey stick. Quite a surprise, I can tell you, when this marvellously svelte creature walked into L'Escargot, turning heads as she perambulated to the table. I doubt I'd have recognized her if she hadn't recognized me first. This carroty mop of mine, I expect.

Well, she's a beauty, and evidently wildly in love with you. No, she didn't say as much, but the distaff side of the human race has a way of knowing about such matters. You are well in there, my lad, if that is your objective.

I seem to be babbling on without saying a hell of a lot. I'll close here pro tem and catch a train home. I think that's probably wise. The Bloody Marys first, of course.

Later!!!

Am now home and have rather run out of things to say. Mummy will doubtless give you all the home news so I'll skip that, wrap this up, and dash to the box. Coincidentally the last post leaves at the same time as the pub opens. I witnessed huge frowns emanating from Mummy when I took a casual swig of the brandy on arrival, so I shall make sure she sees me dancing gaily down the drive with an envelope in my hand. Barney can come too. I'll get myself a pint of something, I think, and sit in the pub garden, remembering times when life was kinder.

Take damned good care of yourself, and give the bastards hell.

Love, Sara.

Dear Chris:

Mum knows about the baby. There was no way of keeping it from her, but she took it very well. Dad knows now too, and *he* didn't take it well at all. I think he'd have throttled you if he could have laid his hands on you in spite of Mum and I trying to make him see that it takes two to tango, as they say.

The thing is, Mum's trying to talk me out of getting married—if I don't want to. She's going on at me about how difficult it's likely to be living on a private soldier's pay. Don't misunderstand me. She means well and is only trying to look after my interests. I didn't expect her to react like that and it's confusing me. Dad hardly talks. We only told him tonight. He's not rational.

I know you'll probably read this as if I'm having second thoughts, but that's not true. I just think we should all have a good talk when you come home. Don't get me wrong. It's not that I don't love you. I think I do. I'm *sure* I do. But this is for ever, as Mum says. If we get married for no other reason than the baby, well, maybe we'll regret it. We must talk it over, that's what I'm saying . . .

. . . and badminton's now out of course, on Doctor McCauley's advice. Apparently I've got some kind of anaemic condition and he wants me to take it easy for a month or two. And after another couple of months I'll be too heavy to play.

. . . and I'll keep writing obviously. (And then something scratched out.) With lots of love, Carol. XXX

Hi lover! (Sammy read):

I thought you might like the enclosed centrefolds snipped from some old *Mayfairs*. I saw them lying around the office and, knowing what you're like, lifted them, shall we say. I was going to cut out a picture of my head from an old snapshot and gum it over the 'lady's' face in the photograph I've marked with a red asterisk. The one with the outsize mammaries. Then I thought I'd better not get you too excited. All that fresh air and exercise—well, it can make a man frisky. . . .

(Bugger me, thought Sammy, she thinks I'm on holiday. 'Hey, Twiggy, forget the brew and fetch me a rum and Coke and a bowl of cashews.')

. . . and you really must be careful about some of the things you say in your letters. Not that *I* mind, but the last one I had wasn't sealed down. I'd die if anyone else got hold of it. . . .

. . . if I'm being faithful to you. The answer's yes. Mind you . . .

Sammy read on.

Three of 3 Platoon had not received any mail: Two-Shit; Acne Hackney and Prawn Balls. Two-Shit was enraged; there had to be a foul-up somewhere. He had lots of friends, male and female, in the UK.

Acne Hackney was a little disappointed. Although he didn't have many friends, he had written three letters to his local pub since leaving England, general chitchat, the envelope addressed to Tim the landlord, letting Tim know that he was fine and hoping that Tim would pass on Acne Hackney's good wishes to the blokes he drank with when he was on leave. He hadn't *really* expected a reply—he didn't know any of them *that* well—but perhaps one of them might have dropped him a postcard. Still, fuck it. That's how it went.

Prawn Balls had written no letters and didn't expect to receive any. He didn't care either way.

Three others in the platoon had received, among other items, letters they could well have done without. Groggy Butler's unwelcome epistle was forwarded from the off-licence he frequented near the barracks. It had been forwarded by the rear-party NCO i/c mail, and was for an unpaid account of £28.20. It was very much in the Dear-sir-or-else style, but Groggy felt he could safely leave the matter of payment until he got home. Legless Jones also received a demand, in his case for a boxed collection of records he'd ordered by mail and not paid for. The company's computer, the obvious author of the letter, had got as far as being hurt. 'We really cannot understand why our previous requests for payment have been ignored . . .' Legless knew very well why they'd been ignored. He'd ordered the records just after Christmas, when he was flat broke, for £29.95. He had also immediately pawned the collection, unused, for ten pounds. Five pounds had been spent on a bottle of supermarket whisky, the other five on what he had been assured was a certain winner in the 2.30 at Haydock. The horse had run fifth, the whisky had acted as consolation. The mail-order company could whistle for its money for now. Non-Legless Jones's unsolicited communication was from a bible-reading group he belonged to in

Wales, a single roneoed sheet that was headed: Matthew 26, verse 52. Non-Legless knew the quote by heart but he read the words anyway. *Then said Jesus unto him, Put up again thy sword into his place; for all they that take the sword shall perish with the sword.* Non-Legless didn't care for the implications of that at all.

Yank Hobart received six adventure comics from a company called War Picture Library, which had been forwarded by his mother in a plain brown envelope. The stories involved super-macho heroes who accomplished impossible deeds of derring-do, and had such titles as *Special Forces, Air Commando,* and *Fortress over Berlin.* Yank was an avid devourer of this adolescent fiction, but in private. He knew he'd be mocked unmercifully if he was caught reading them.

Three-piece hit the jackpot with seven letters, three of them in the same handwriting and all, bar one from his parents, from girls he knew and had been to bed with back home.

Two for Winter's Day were delivered to D Company in error. Scrunch took them for redirection. Scrunch himself had received a couple from his estranged wife and one from his twelve-year-old daughter, who lived with her mother. One of the letters from Mrs Watkins enclosed a newspaper advertisement placed by a television rental company offering preferential terms for video recorders. Could she go ahead and hire one? The letter from Scrunch's daughter was a single page in rather large handwriting, in which the young girl said she loved her Daddy very much and hoped he would come home safely. The words were poorly formed since the girl was trying to write with her left hand now, her right arm having been amputated above the elbow a year ago after an accident with a farm tractor while she was on a school field trip. Scrunch missed his daughter terribly and often wondered whether he and his wife should not try to make another go of their marriage, for the girl's sake. The answer always came out negative. In spite of them loving their daughter, the parents were incompatible. Good people apart, awful together.

Among Double-Eff's batch was one from an elderly, and batty, aunt, whom he had not seen for some years but who always sent him a pound note on his birthday and at Christmas and to whom he always wrote a thank-you letter, trying to convey without offending or hurting the old biddy that there was really no need to send him money nowadays. This letter also enclosed a pound. 'I know it's not your birthday and of course not Christmas, but I thought I'd send your regular gift now, in order that you may spend it before you get killed.'

Double-Eff read the sentence twice, unable to believe his eyes, before bursting into helpless laughter.

Branston's letter, just the one, was a beauty.

Dear Jim (wrote his father):

Well, son, I've been seeing a lot on the TV what it's like in the S. Atlantic. Now, can you see your way clear to sending me a couple of pounds as you won't be spending anything down there? Five would be good, ten better. I've been having a bit of bad luck lately and could use the cash. I've heard on the grapevine that slut of a wife you've got has moved in with Billy McNamara. Just thought you'd like to know. Good riddance say I. It's the kids I feel sorry for. No cheques, son. A postal order will do, cash better. Well, son, must close now. I know you're busy but the cash is needed. I'll keep an eye open for you on the TV. P.S. If you can't raise five, anything you've got to spare will be okay.

Branston set fire to the letter in the flame of the hexy stove.

Scarlett received three, all from Eileen O'Hara, all in the same vein. He read the first few lines of each.

Dear Harry:

I've spoken to Julia Lomax and she agrees that it would probably be better if you left HM Forces on your return . . .

(It took Scarlett a few moments to work our precisely who Julia Lomax was, and when he had the answer knew that Eileen was telling a lie with that statement.)

Dear Harry:

Gwen's husband Trevor says that there are some good openings in his firm. Of course you couldn't expect a car right away . . .

Dear Harry:

Kathleen has come down with a rash, which the doctor says is certainly due to stress passed on to her from me . . .

(Dear God, thought Scarlett, would there never be an end to it?)

Jomo's single letter was from his Kenyan mother, who wrote far better English than her husband and who, had the chips not been stacked against her because of her colour, would undoubtedly have been employed in a more responsible capacity than that of a hospital cleaner.

Dear Henry:

It goes without saying that your father and I are proud of their son and the part he is playing in this horrible fiasco. Your sisters too look up to you. I don't have to remind you that some of the other children have been unkind in the past, to Faith especially as she was born with pigmentation more resembling my side of the family than either you or Janet. However, Faith, at seven years old, came home the other day and said: 'Mum, one of the boys gave me this.' It was a drawing made by one of her classmates, also aged seven, of some soldiers with guns. Childish aeroplanes overhead too. You know the sort of thing. It wasn't a class project—I don't think the teachers would encourage that sort of artwork; it was a drawing the little boy had made at home. There were six soldiers in the picture and one of them, obviously the leader, is black. 'That's your brother,' the lad told Faith. It made us all feel—awed, is I suppose the word.

I would have sent you the drawing except Faith won't let me have it. She sleeps with it on her pillow.

We say a prayer for you each night, privately, of course. We ask the Lord to look after you, and your companions.

With love from us all. . . .

On other parts of East Falkland, in Stanley and the mountains, Argentines too waited for mail which rarely arrived in the huge Hercules transports that were still managing to land during the hours of darkness at Stanley airport. Letters were being written, of course, from the Argentine mainland, but delivery was low on the list of priorities. Ammunition came first, for in Stanley no one was in any doubt that the final push was imminent.

TWENTY-FIVE

Ricardo

THE SIX-MAN PATROL that Major Carlos Tomba, Ricardo's company commander, had sent out just before last light on June 4 had not returned by dawn. Nor had it been in wireless contact since midnight. That could either mean that it was trapped at daybreak or earlier so close to the British lines that breaking radio silence would have been hazardous, or that it had been wiped out. Tomba feared the latter. Company HQ had reported the sound of distant machine-gun fire in the small hours and the perimeter pickets had witnessed the night sky being streaked with red and green tracer far to the west. Not that that necessarily meant anything sinister. Few nights went by without some sort of activity up ahead. That the patrol might have surrendered at the first opportunity did not occur to him. Officers and regular NCOs had instilled into their men that the vanguard British troopers were largely SAS, who were taking no prisoners waving white flags. And as added insurance all patrols since June 1 (when there was some evidence to support the contention that a four-man unit had shot the NCO leading them and handed themselves over to the British) were conducted in the dark hours, in spite of the dangers from the Argentine's own minefields. White flags could not be seen at night, nor was it likely that the British, fearing a trap, would accept the spoken word. They would shoot at anything that moved.

The patrol's mission, one of several being undertaken in

concert with other companies in the battalion across three kilometres of front, had been to probe the enemy defences as far as the eastern slopes of Mount Kent, assess his strength, then return or radio back its findings. The weather was against air reconnaissance and, in any case, the British too were moving at night, rendering useless air photographs taken during the course of the previous day.

Colonel Jorge Filippi's battalion was well dug in on the upper reaches of Two Sisters, with Alpha Company, Tomba's company, on the right flank of a forward-facing slope. The fierce British artillery barrages from land and sea that were to be a nightmarish feature of the assault on Stanley were largely a thing of the future, and all the trench-bound troops had to contend with for the present were the cold, the snow, the wet, and inadequate food and sanitation. And fear, for Alpha Company had lost, apart from the missing patrol, six other men to Harrier attacks while it was positioned north of Stanley airfield; the battalion had a casualty list of dead, missing and wounded of over fifty, some of whom had been replaced by conscripts taken from other duties and transferred to front-line regiments. Among these was Beto Jordan-Arditti.

Ricardo had fought a minor battle with Tomba, and then a major one, in Tomba's presence, with Colonel Filippi to get Beto transferred from his anti-aircraft gun post once Goose Green had fallen to superior British forces. (The BBC World Service could lie as much as it liked; no Argentine in Stanley believed that Goose Green had been overrun by a single paratroop battalion outnumbered three to one.) After the success enjoyed by the 35 mm anti-aircraft gun in a ground capacity at Goose Green, Ricardo thought that the SAS would be targeting all such weapons for destruction, killing the crews and the army guards. He knew he wasn't doing Beto much of a favour, moving him up front, but at least his brother would be where Ricardo could keep some sort of an eye on him, prevent him being used as cannon fodder when the going got rough.

'Can't be done, Ricardo.' Tomba had turned him down flat.

'Then I'd like your permission to talk to the CO.'

'You think he hasn't got other things on his mind? The answer's no to that too.'

'I'm going to see him whether you like it or not,' said Ricardo. 'You'd better get used to the idea.'

'I could have you court-martialled for that remark.'

'Your privilege. I doubt there'll be anyone left to court-martial me in three weeks.'

Tomba shook his head. He liked Ricardo and knew him to be a thoroughly efficient officer with that something extra which sorted out potential generals from the rank and file.

'I'm owed this,' said Ricardo determinedly. 'I was here long before all but a handful, taking shit from these bloody islanders. Please,' he said, adopting a more conciliatory tone. 'If Colonel Filippi says no, that's it.'

Colonel Filippi did say no. He was low on sleep and the American cigarettes he chain-smoked, and in no mood to indulge mere captains.

'Do you think you're the only damned officer on the Malvinas with a kid brother or cousin or some damned relative or other in the services here? You're not.'

'I didn't think I was, sir.'

'I can't have my officers wet-nursing their kin.'

'That wasn't my intention, sir.'

'Of course it was. Why the hell do you want him in Alpha Company unless it's to look after him?'

'If you'll allow me to explain, sir . . .' Ricardo held what he hoped was a trump card, but did not want to play it with the CO in this mood. 'I meant, sir, that I had no intention of wet-nursing him. He'll get no preferential treatment from me, no light duties. If his platoon gets assigned a hazardous patrol, he'll go.'

'Rubbish! That would defeat the whole object of this little exercise of yours.'

'With respect, sir, you can take my word that I mean what I say.'

'You'll be mollycoddling him instead of attending to your other duties.'

'I take exception to that, sir.'

'Do you? Do you indeed!'

Colonel Filippi looked as if he was about to explode. Then he calmed down, with an effort. He too liked Ricardo and knew, naturally, of the part he'd played with the gas workers. He also had him earmarked for high rank. He did not want to goad young Jordan-Arditti into saying something he might live to regret, something that would go on his dossier. This damned war; it had changed everyone.

'What do you think, Carlos?' he asked Major Tomba.

'The same as you, sir.'

But Ricardo would not be denied. Until Colonel Filippi actually ordered him to dismiss, he would keep trying. And Filippi, if Ricardo was any judge of character, would be willing to grant Beto's transfer provided it could be justified, providing it wasn't bending the rules more than a fraction and creating a precedent.

'We're asking for replacements, are we not, sir?' he asked Filippi.

'Of course we are. Don't be a damned fool. We're not asking for conscripts, but that's doubtless what we'll get. I'd swop all fifty of them for half a dozen regulars. They're no bloody use to anyone, least of all a fighting company. Besides, you're forgetting something. Your brother is not a member of this battalion. It's not within my purview to transfer him.'

'A word with his commanding officer would do it, sir. You said it yourself, he's a conscript and no bloody use to anyone.'

'Granted,' agreed Filippi grudgingly. 'His battalion would doubtless be thankful to be rid of him. On the other hand, why should *this* battalion be compelled to feed another useless mouth?'

'We'll be feeding fifty of them anyway, in your view, sir. I don't see that it makes much difference if one of them's my brother.' Ricardo sensed that this was the moment to slap down his ace. 'Besides, my brother's a little less useless than most of them.'

'How so?'

'He speaks excellent English,' Ricardo exaggerated. Beto's English was fairly fluent but heavily accented. Still, Filippi, who spoke only a few words himself, was not to know that.

'How does that help us?' Filippi wanted to know. 'You speak excellent English, but I haven't noticed you winning the war for us single-handed.'

'The British had a Spanish-speaking officer at Goose Green, by all accounts. He wrote the ultimatum dictating the terms of surrender. I wonder if we're not missing out on something.'

'Explain.'

'An English-speaking private with a patrol might be able to get his comrades out of an awkward situation. Or, better, by talking English get the enemy to reveal a concealed position. Or . . .'

'Enough.' Filippi held up a flattened palm for silence.

'You don't have to tell me what any lance-corporal knows.'
Still, it was an intriguing notion, thought the colonel. And the
battalion would be getting fifty bloody conscripts anyway!

'You realize,' he said, 'that if I were to agree, you've more
or less condemned your brother to more patrols than he might
otherwise draw. It would be foolish, would it not, to have a
linguist on our strength and not maximize our use of him?'
Filippi permitted himself a tiny smile. That would teach
junior officers to try their little tricks on him. 'And if he
speaks English as well as you claim, I'm surprised you
haven't volunteered him for intelligence duties with brigade
wireless, down in the capital where. . . .'

Colonel Filippi saw the trap too late. Ricardo's expression
was all innocence when he said, 'Now you come to mention
it, sir, perhaps he would be more use here at Battalion HQ,
monitoring the enemy's radio frequencies alongside a trained
operator, than up front with a fighting patrol. God knows,
we're going to need all the help we can get. Of course, we
could let him go to brigade, but then . . .'

'Hold on, Captain!' said Filippi, recognizing that he had
been outmanoeuvred but perceiving the logic of Ricardo's
suggestion. 'You've made your point, don't beat it to death.
Let me have some paperwork and I'll see what I can do.'

'Thank you, sir.'

Ricardo turned to leave, a pace behind Tomba. Filippi
called him back.

'Tell me,' said the CO, 'just for my own enlightenment. If
it was your intention all along to see your brother installed
with HQ wireless section . . .'

'I only just thought of it, sir,' lied Ricardo, 'when you
mentioned brigade intelligence.'

'Balls. Still, what I don't understand is why you didn't
come right out with it and offer your brother's services as a
wireless monitor. You have a valid point. He'll be useful.'

'Would you have accepted my argument, sir,' asked Ricardo politely, 'eminently reasonable though it now seems?'

'Of course. I just have.'

'But the suggestion came from you, sir, in effect. If I'd
made it you would have said I was trying to find a safe job
for my brother.'

'In other words I'm intractable.'

'Oh, I wouldn't say that, sir.'

'But you would say that if you fired the one shot in your

locker and it missed because I wasn't receptive, you'd have nothing with which to follow up?' Ricardo held his peace. 'Get the hell out, Ricardo,' said Colonel Filippi, not at all unkindly. 'You make me uneasy. I have the feeling when you're around that you have one eye on my job and that you could smooth-talk your way into making me give it you.'

Surprisingly, Beto was less than grateful when the transfer came through and he and his kit were helicoptered forward from York Point to Two Sisters. He didn't want special treatment, he told Ricardo when the brothers met up. Nor was he happy about leaving the others who were to remain with the AA gun because they didn't have connections among the officers. That smacked of privilege.

Ricardo wasn't sure whether to put down Beto's sullenness to apathy or fear. The latter, probably, he conjectured privately. He'd seen such manifestations before. Beto had felt comfortably secure guarding the gun. Harriers had attacked York Point and positions right and left of the 35 mm had been bombarded by naval gunfire. Others had died, Beto had not. No matter how potentially dangerous the AA site was, Beto felt safe there. The trench he was in or the people he was with were lucky. Moving was asking for trouble. Like the nervous air traveller who sits rigidly in his seat for fear of, by fidgeting, offending the gods of destiny, Beto wanted to remain in his nice deep hole.

Before he left the battery on the morning of June 3, Beto composed a short poem which he left with the three other conscripts who were part of his watch, who had shared each other's miseries and deprivations for two months; who had studied him in hurt and envious silence when a junior NCO told him to pack his kit and be ready to move out in thirty minutes; who would have to remain with the gun because they were nobodies.

Usually, because of natural shyness mostly, Beto showed his poetry to no one outside a small circle of friends, and this trio, he was honest enough to admit to himself, would not have been included in that group in civilian life. But he wanted to leave them something. They had promised each other, as soldiers will, to meet up after the war, talk about their experiences over a glass of beer. Beto knew that would not happen. He would not be seeing them ever again, he was sure.

The poem read:—

Listen to the empty echoes
Evangelizing peace
Prosecuting war.
Look upon the dying embers
Personifying grief.

'What does it mean?' they asked him.

'It means what it says.'

After Beto had gone, the trio agreed among themselves that he had always been a little crazy, talking for hours during the night watches about literature and music, using words they couldn't understand. Oh, he was okay, considering he was probably stinking rich, but crackers definitely. Later, one of the youngsters used the sheet of paper on which the poem was written as a spill to light a cigarette from the fire they had going. At least it saved a match.

Ricardo hadn't seen Beto since May 25 and thought that, if anything, his brother looked worse than he had then. He seemed to have lost even more weight, though apathy regarding his personal hygiene (admittedly not unique to Beto among the conscripts) was a contributory factor to his air of general dereliction. Still, rations were better up front, even for conscripts. Not much, but better.

'Get a shave and smarten yourself up, for God's sake,' said Ricardo, speaking as a soldier rather than a sibling and impatiently waving aside Beto's objections at receiving special treatment. 'I know it's bloody cold, but try and buck your ideas up. Where you'll be working you can expect to see the CO at regular intervals. He'll have you shot if he sees you looking like that.'

'Then he'll only be anticipating events, won't he?' remarked Beto with studied coolness.

For the first time in a dozen years Ricardo felt like hitting his brother.

'You're going to survive this, do you understand that?' he demanded fiercely. 'Whatever happens, no matter how bloody it gets, *you're going to survive.*'

'If you say so.'

That was on June 3. Now it was June 5, and Major Tomba was debating the wisdom of sending out another patrol at dusk, to do the job the missing six-man party hadn't.

'I've spoken to the other companies,' said Tomba to Ricardo during the afternoon, both men ducking automatically and then racing for the nearest trench as British 105s opened up from the west. Two Sisters was not the target; the salvo landed three kilometres south of them, on Mount Harriet, sending up clouds of frozen earth. In the dug-out, Tomba had to shout to make himself heard. 'All bar one either lost men killed or have men missing, and we achieved nothing in the way of hard intelligence. The thing is, I'm not sure it's all worth while. We know they're coming.' He thumbed skywards. 'We can judge their strength by that lot. What have we got to gain, I ask myself, by sending out a fighting patrol? We'd be better off, surely, staying put in our prepared positions and picking them off as they advance. What's the point in risking men's lives simply to establish where their greatest strength is? They've got to take these mountains and they'll advance across a broad front. So we wait for them. But I wanted to hear your views before having a word with the CO.'

Ricardo shook his head in despair. Carlos Tomba was a good officer but subscribed to the same school of thought as General Menendez, C-in-C Malvinas. Menendez did not believe that the largely inducted Argentine ground troops stood a chance against the better-trained British. It was the general's strategy to fight a holding campaign, retreating where necessary to what he considered to be the unbreachable fortress of Stanley. There would then be a stalemate and a political settlement before the Argentine officer corps was disgraced.

'You know what I think,' said Ricardo, who took the opposite view, who had bitterly resented pulling back from the mountains that were the first line of defence—Vernet, Estancia, Kent and Challenger—without offering more than token resistance. The British had taken that ground largely unopposed, which was tactical lunacy. They should have been made to pay for every yard. Why should they even contemplate a political settlement when they were gaining a military victory gratis? In any case, Ricardo did not believe in the impregnability of Stanley. 'If we hadn't pulled back we wouldn't be sending out these damned patrols now. There'd be no need. We'd still hold those mountains instead of being boxed into this horseshoe.'

'Concentration of forces,' said Tomba mildly, unwilling to resurrect this ancient argument.

'Concentration of forces be damned. We retreated without

a fight, that's all there is to it. If we're going to have a fight, for God's sake let's choose the ground.'

'We have. This is it.'

'You'll forgive me if I suggest that that decision was a strategic error. The British have taken the initiative. They're always attacking, we're always defending. Now that may look highly attractive on a wargames board and earn staff points, but it's no damned use here. We're waiting for them, certainly, but they can afford to let us wait while they bring up more matériel.'

A second, third and fourth salvo of 105 shells crunched into Mount Harriet. The Argentine defence bunkers were deep and well enough constructed for the shells to be doing little damage to anyone not caught out in the open, but killing was hardly the purpose of artillery in this instance. The salvoes were designed to sap morale. Not difficult given the calibre of most of the troops. But the conscripts would have to learn how to fight sooner or later, in Ricardo's view, or God help them. And the sooner a few of the replacements in Alpha Company got that fact drilled into their stupid skulls, the better.

'Where on earth are they getting the shells?' said Tomba, mostly thinking aloud and knowing quite well that the shells were coming from San Carlos because the air force, bravely though it had fought, had not finished the job. 'And where's our artillery?'

'Keeping its head down so that it won't be spotted and picked off,' said Ricardo savagely. He had a thought. 'You asked my views regarding another patrol. I'm for it. They're not magicians, the British.' He indicated Mount Harriet. 'They've got a forward observation officer on the high ground correcting the range for that little lot. We should do something about him.'

Tomba laughed. 'Come on, Ricardo, you're not seriously suggesting that a patrol can locate and destroy their FOO. Or that they couldn't replace him if you did.'

'No, I didn't mean that exactly. What I meant was, we should at least let them know that we're not sitting here quivering with fear, waiting for their next ground attack. We should do something positive, if only to stiffen morale. If that also means that we get some idea of their dispositions on Mount Kent, so much the better.'

'Then you're for another patrol?'

'I am. For that matter, I'll lead it. A dozen men plus myself and Sergeant Gonzalez. I'd like four of the men to be conscript replacements. No, make that two. I'm not about to commit suicide.'

'I'm not sure I can sanction that.'

'You have to,' insisted Ricardo. 'As of now, eight per cent of the battalion's fighting strength is conscripted. I don't think any of us can afford to have that percentage unaccustomed to battle conditions when the time comes, or they'll be throwing down their arms at the first sign of trouble and it might be your flank they're supposed to be covering. For that matter, it's not a bad idea to suggest to Colonel Filippi. Every patrol from now on takes two replacements with it.'

Tomba mulled it over. What could he lose—apart from Ricardo, Gonzalez and a dozen men?

'Very well, I agree. How many replacements did Alpha Company get?'

'Ten. I'll ask Gonzalez to pick a couple at random.'

'Don't worry about me. I'll coordinate timings with you later, but I'll probably be asking for a diversion around midnight. About eight hundred metres south of where I expect to be by then. Flares, machine guns, tracer. About five minutes' worth of noise to see if it can't draw someone's fire.'

'Anything heavy?'

'I doubt you'll get the CO's permission for that, not for a small patrol. Besides, I don't want to wake them up too much.'

Sergeant Gonzalez, a hardened veteran five years Ricardo's senior, was delighted at the prospect of action.

'We leave at last light?'

'A few minutes before, yes. Not that it matters a lot. There's a moon tonight.'

'Weapons?'

'Small arms, two machine guns, two mortars with HE and smoke.'

'So we're not going to walk away from a fight.'

'No, we're not going to do that even though we're essentially reconnaissance.'

Ricardo's personal weapon was usually an FMK 3 9 mm submachine gun, similar to the British Sterling and deadly at close quarters but unlikely to be much use on a patrol such as this, for which he would draw a rifle.

Gonzalez nodded his approval. He picked his teeth with a wooden splinter, and frowned.

'You're sure about taking conscripts?'

Ricardo smiled. He had known Gonzalez for four years and had served as a section commander with him as the section's senior NCO on first joining the battalion. Gonzalez had no time for amateurs.

'I'm sure. Pick a couple who look as if they might know what they're doing.'

'You're asking the impossible. Not one of them has enough sense to come in out of the rain.'

'Well, do your best.'

One of the pair Gonzalez selected was Ernesto Martinez, who had been drafted forward from the airport perimeter guard on June 2. Martinez did not yet know the name of the company 2 i/c. Nor would he recognize it when told, for he had virtually forgotten his meeting with the tearful Lucita Jordan-Arditti in the Plaza de Mayo.

Half an hour before last light Ricardo heard an angry voice he thought he remembered and whose owner turned out to be, beneath several layers of all-weather combat clothing, Major Vila, the special forces officer who, with Major Corino, had escorted Ricardo up from Rio Gallegos. Ricardo had not seen him for six weeks. Indeed, had he been asked he would have answered that Vila was now probably back in Buenos Aires. Vila was carrying a rucksack and a sniper's rifle with telescopic sights. Slung across his shoulder was a bandolier of ammunition. He was over by the victualling bunker, helping himself to tinned supplies above the protests of the supply NCO.

'Tell this silly bastard to mind his own business, will you?' Vila asked Ricardo when the latter hailed him.

'It's okay,' Ricardo told the NCO, who turned his back muttering mutinously. 'What are you doing up here?' Ricardo asked.

'Stocking up. I'm no bloody use down there.' Vila thumbed east, towards Stanley. 'There's nothing for me to do.' He brandished his rifle. 'If Menendez thinks I'm surrendering to the British when the time comes, he's mistaken.'

'Surrendering?'

'You don't believe it will come to that?'

'It's not something I'd make a lot of noise about even if I did.'

'Well, each to his own, but you should hear some of the talk at headquarters. They're very big on honour, short on action. That's not for me. I'm taking this'—he waved the rifle—'a week's supplies, and heading north. I've had some experience of survival techniques. I'll make out, and there'll be a few British dead, I can tell you, before it's all over. And maybe after it's over.'

'Major Corino?'

'Is staying put.' Vila spat noisily. 'His explanation— excuse—is that maybe General Pastran will fly in one of these nights aboard a Hercules.' Vila laughed without humour. 'Imagine that. Pastran here. No, Corino's looking after himself. I don't necessarily blame him. As I said, each to his own.'

Ricardo had not particularly liked Vila from the moment of their first meeting, but he had to admire the major's fortitude. A few more like Vila and maybe it would have been the British forming the defensive horseshoe.

'North, you say?'

'Well, maybe. I'll see where it takes me. A lot will depend upon our minefields. I've got the plots of most of them firmly fixed in my head, but the engineers scattered others like shit from a goose. Why?'

'I'm taking a patrol out tonight. There should be some activity around midnight. On the forward slopes of Mount Kent. Maybe before if we run into someone coming the other way. I wouldn't want you to mistake us for them. That's quite a weapon you have there.'

'Yes, it's a beauty, isn't it.' Vila fondled the sniper's rifle lovingly. 'With the 'scope I reckon I can take the balls off a fly at five hundred metres. I've been getting some practice in, and a handful of us have been dining on mutton pretty regularly.'

'The SAS are in the mountains.'

'Half the British army's in the mountains. They won't get me.'

'I hope not. Good luck.'

Vila waved a hand as he left. 'Same to you.'

The patrol set off in single file, Ricardo in front, Gonzalez bringing up the rear—'Just in case one or the other of the replacements decides he doesn't like the idea of a stroll, sir.' Five yards between each man, no talking, and absolute radio silence unless there was some pressing need to break it.

Ricardo was not too worried about mines. Unless someone had done something completely idiotic in the last couple of days—and Tomba assured him they hadn't, that no fresh mines had been sown in a week—he knew where the fields were and that there were single strands of barbed-wire half a metre above the ground if he strayed from a true path. Not that that was likely. He was as familiar with his proposed route between Two Sisters and Mount Kent as he was with the back of his hand. He should be; he had studied the terrain daily through binoculars and had pulled back on foot from Mount Kent across the same route with the remainder of the battalion a week earlier.

From summit to summit it was around seven kilometres as the crow flew, a little further on the ground. From the battalion's trenches to the lower slopes of Kent was six kilometres, no more than a good, sharp walk achievable in forty minutes on a tarmacadamed road, but likely to take five or six times that long allowing for conditions underfoot and the need to be particularly wary, for the first kilometre, of nervous sentries and identify oneself in good time, and the fact that there were three thousand enemy troops up ahead ready to blow the patrol to kingdom come. That the moonlight made the surrounding, frozen landscape eerily bright was neither here nor there. In its combat gear the patrol was no more than a slowly moving serpentine shadow virtually indiscernible against the shadows cast by natural land features. In any case, many British units, like many Argentine units, had image intensifiers or passive night goggles, instruments capable of seeing in the dark. There was nowhere to hide if a set of those were focused on you.

So the moon was not a worry. Heavy machine gun fire to the northeast and the occasional whirring of helicopter blades were. So was the lack of enemy artillery. That particularly. It could mean that the British were still in the process of ferrying forward supplies and had none to spare for unsustainable barrages at night, or that they had their own patrols out and were taking no chances of maverick shells falling short and killing their own troops. Ricardo was glad he'd brought the machine guns. Two weren't going to be a hell of a lot of use if the patrol ran into stiff opposition, but they'd make some noise and might convince the British that the patrol numbered more than it did. He hoped Gonzalez hadn't been over-ambitious and included tracer in the ammunition belts, but it was too late to ask him that now.

Progress was slow once the patrol reached the open ground between the foothills of Two Sisters and Mount Kent, though neither range really deserved being dignified as mountains even at the summits, being only 326 and 458 metres respectively. Now the patrol was in bandit country, where every boulder or patch of gorse could conceal instant death. Still, there was no hurry. Tomba's fireworks display was not due to start until midnight unless the fire teams received a wireless message otherwise, and Ricardo did not wish to be too far forward with possible escape routes blocked before close on that hour. He could afford to take his time, play it cautiously, use the eyes before using the feet, and, if in doubt, sweep the countryside ahead with night glasses—which he did every few minutes and which made it all the more surprising that he saw no tell-tale movement before four machine guns (quickly joined by ten times that many rifles) opened up simultaneously from cover three hundred yards in front, two from either flank using tracer, arcing in on the patrol and making it, as it were, the apex of a triangle. In tandem half a dozen flares illuminated the night sky, momentarily freezing the patrol into petrified immobility, like a Lowry snowscape, before self-preservation took over and the Argentines dropped to the ground, with Ricardo shouting for the mortar teams to set up and zero in on the British gimpies with HE.

In a matter of seconds, while Gonzalez and the second machine gunner swung their weapons from their shoulders and started returning fire, and the riflemen crawled for the nearest cover and also began shooting, Ricardo assessed the patrol's predicament while waving frantically at the wireless operator, who was a regular soldier, a good man, and already doing it anyway, to contact Tomba and inform him that they needed help now, for the pyrotechnics to begin even though they would hardly do more than distract the British since the agreed arcs of fire were to be eight hundred metres to the south.

Ricardo's first thought as he fired on the enemy machine guns at ten o'clock from his position and, a moment afterwards, saw the first of his HE mortars overshoot considerably, was that the British troops were not SAS or SBS. They had opened up too soon; they should have allowed the patrol to get a hundred and fifty metres closer. The SAS or SBS would not have made that mistake. His second thought was that the safety of denser cover was two hundred metres behind them, and likely to be bloody difficult to reach under the circumstances. His third thought judged the opposition to be no stronger than a platoon, perhaps two platoons, otherwise there'd be a damned sight more machine guns hosing down in their direction. His fourth thought was that this fighting recce was a dead duck, as dead as its participants were likely to be unless they got out fast, outnumbered as they were and with the possibility that these were not the only British in the vicinity. The enemy machine gunners would finish off or come close to finishing off a belt of ammunition apiece, reload to give covering fire, and then the riflemen would advance across the open ground, their platoon/company commander now having obviously perceived that the Argentines facing him were only a handful. The infantry would come either full tilt, weaving, or carefully, using cover, depending upon the courage of their leader. And whether those fucking mortars could polish off the machine guns. They seemed to have the range, the mortars, but the machine guns kept firing. They'd be well dug in, of course, probably in abandoned Argentine trenches in what had once been the reverse slope of Mount Kent. And the patrol was carrying only twenty mortars, fourteen of them HE, the remainder smoke.

'How's that radio?' Ricardo shouted.

'In contact. They're opening up now.'

'Now', to Ricardo, seemed an eternity, though it was no more than twenty-five seconds before a barrage of flares illuminated the sky in the distance and heavy tracer made pretty, lethal patterns. Or patterns that would have been lethal had anyone been on the other end. Briefly the two machine gunners at ten o'clock swung right, still firing, to counter this new threat. Then they realized they were in no danger from that direction and concentrated again on the patrol. Tomba, or whoever was controlling the Alpha Company fire teams, could obviously see the British tracer and there was some attempt to correct the Argentine arcs. But they were way out of range and, had it been otherwise, could not have corrected too much for fear of hitting the patrol, since there could be little doubt from the upper slopes of Two Sisters precisely where the patrol was pinned down.

'HE,' called one of Ricardo's mortarmen, and the nearest patrol riflemen tossed him the spares they were carrying.

'Smoke?' the other mortarmen wanted to know.

'Not yet,' shouted Ricardo.

They would need the smoke to withdraw. They did not need it now, when it would be as much use to the British, concealing an advance, as it was to him.

So far the action had occupied thirty-five seconds. Ricardo yelled at Gonzalez and the other machine gunner to limit their rate of fire. They were having little effect and the last thing Ricardo needed was for Gonzalez and his opposite number to run out of ammunition and be forced to change belts if the British began moving forward.

Except they did not move forward. Their machine guns had stopped firing either on command or to change belts and there was continuing rifle fire from the boulders up ahead. But no sign of any advance. Maybe the moonlight was putting them off or they were waiting for their flares to expire. Maybe they'd misjudged the size of the Argentine force. Maybe—Christ—maybe *they* were organizing mortars or calling up tanks. One thing was for sure: this was the moment to get out.

Ricardo took stock, asking if anyone had been hit, asking, above the din, for each man to check with his nearest neighbour and report back. No one had received so much as a scratch. Amazing, thought Ricardo. Probably any one of the British machine gunners could have knocked hell out of a static target at twice the distance. But in all the excitement . . . And the British had made the mistake of opening fire *before* their flares went up. Green troops, maybe, seeing their first combat. Lack of coordination, also, for which someone would get it in the neck.

Ricardo asked if the wireless operator was still in contact with Alpha Company. He was. Could Tomba do anything, Ricardo wanted to know? Tomba could not, not immediately. He might be able to organize some 105s in ten minutes or so, but from what he could see of the firefight from up top the patrol and the enemy were too close to one another to risk artillery without precise coordinates.

'Tell him we'll be dead in ten minutes anyway,' said Ricardo, thinking: Jesus, we came out in part to look for the British FOO, and now we could use one of our own.

Orchestrated with rifle fire, the British machine guns had again opened up from ten o'clock and two o'clock. The

Argentines were replying with two- and three-shot bursts to conserve ammunition. Ricardo shouted for the patrol to toss all the spare mortars to the mortarmen, HE and smoke, but for the mortarmen to do nothing for the moment. There was still no sign of infantry movement up front. What the hell were they playing at?

He went over the terrain in his head. They were three kilometres from Two Sisters, roughly the same from the Kent foothills and scrub. Were there any gullies around he'd forgotten about, any ravines down which the British could advance unseen while the patrol was concentrating on the machine guns? He couldn't recall any.

A minute had now elapsed since the British first opened fire. Ricardo belly-crawled over to where Gonzalez was spread-eagled behind his machine gun.

'Tactical withdrawal,' he yelled in Gonzalez's ear.

The NCO nodded, disappointed but accepting the situation. The British wouldn't wait much longer before charging (or bringing up heavier weapons) and that would mean odds, if he was any judge, of about four to one against. He didn't feel like dying this night.

Ricardo crawled from man to man, telling each of them what the patrol was about to do. He instructed the wireless operator to inform Alpha Company. One of the conscripts— Martinez, was that his name? wondered Ricardo—seemed paralysed with fright. Nor had his rifle been fired. Ricardo hit him twice about the face.

'Move when we move!'

The mortarmen and the machine gunners, the most important elements of the withdrawal, knew what was expected of them.

First, each mortarman would fire two rounds of HE followed by one round of smoke. Through the smoke Gonzalez would fire half a belt of ammunition in the general direction of the British positions, to keep their heads down. To discourage the medal hunters. While that was happening the mortarmen, the second machine gunner and the rest of the patrol would retreat at the double for two or three hundred metres. Once there they would re-establish a defence base. The mortarmen would lower their weapons' angle of elevation to give greater range and fire a single round of HE. That would be the signal for Gonzalez to withdraw. He would leapfrog the patrol, retreat a further two hundred metres, and set up a second fire point. In the meantime, the mortarmen would discharge another round of smoke, through which the second machine gunner would empty half a belt while the rest of the patrol retreated beyond Gonzalez. Once they were two hundred metres behind the NCO, the mortarmen would again change elevation and fire the remaining HE, at which the second machine gunner would withdraw, beyond Gonzalez as far as the patrol, where the entire group would set up a third fire point. When the second machine gunner was in sight of the patrol, the last of the smoke would be fired to cover Gonzalez's final withdrawal. At this point they should be six to seven hundred metres back from where they were ambushed, and a whole kilometre away from the British lines. A kilometre closer, also, to Two Sisters and relative safety. Ricardo doubted whether the British would want to take the pursuit too far.

All went well during stage one, the first of the smoke. Then the British commander obviously realized what was happening and called up his own mortars—51 mm with HE rounds and a range of 800 metres. Nor did the machine guns or the rifles cease firing.

Neither British nor Argentine high-explosive rounds were very effective in the soft ground of a Falklands winter, and Gonzalez had luck—and perhaps God, he was to reflect later—on his side. The patrol saw him charging through the smoke, instinctively weaving as he ran carrying the heavy machine gun, though weaving would not have done him much good with the killing range of a 51 mm had one exploded close enough. It didn't. Gonzalez leap-frogged the patrol, pausing only to snatch up an extra belt of ammunition.

The British increased the range of their mortars. So did the patrol. An artillery battle in miniature, and one that could have but a single outcome, considering the availability of ammunition, had Ricardo elected to stand and fight. He did not. The patrol was fucked. He stuck to his original plan of withdrawal and suffered only one casualty, a fatality: the death of Ernesto Martinez, who was sprinting within thirty metres of Ricardo during the second stage when he was hit in the back by a fluke burst—through the smoke no one could have been aiming accurately—from the British machine guns.

Ricardo sensed Martinez was wounded at least from the moment it happened, but he was too busy zig-zagging himself to take much more than peripheral notice. Carried forward by his own momentum and the impact of the heavy 7.62 mm rounds, Martinez ran, or stumbled, for a further dozen steps before he collapsed, his heart and lungs ruptured.

Waving the others on, Ricardo went back to him. He was obviously dead, though, curiously, there was no blood to be seen. Damned conscripts, thought Ricardo, recognizing the still features of the man—boy—he had slapped. Then he heard the sound of distant shouting. Realizing that the Argentines were on the run, the British were advancing at speed.

Gonzalez kept his head. Through the smoke from the last of the mortars he could see eight, perhaps ten, figures running towards him, from his own right, the British left. He had half a belt of ammunition remaining, a few seconds of sustained fire. He aimed at the British vanguard, keeping the machine gun steady, allowing the natural spray of the rounds to take its toll. He was delighted to see two or three, maybe four or five, figures fall before the machine gun jammed. He then slung the weapon over his shoulder and ran towards Ricardo and the patrol.

'A fuck-up,' Ricardo said to Tomba later. 'A complete fuck-up.'

'You were unlucky,' said Tomba sympathetically.

'I was a jerk-off. That sort of operation needs a company.'

'Which I'm not going to give you. Which I'm not going to allow you to try again.'

'Which I understand. Gonzalez was magnificent,' Ricardo added.

'I'll see it's noted in my report to the CO.'

Later still, Ricardo went through Martinez's kit, prior to writing to his family—his responsibility, he thought, as opposed to Major Tomba's. He found little more than books, school books, some of them dealing with elementary architecture. He vaguely recognized the name Ernesto Martinez, but it was a fairly common name and, for the life of him, he could not remember where he'd last heard it.

Also later, Peter Ballantine held an 'O' Group of his platoon commanders, particularly those of 3 and 4 Platoons, demanding to know what the fuck had gone wrong when they'd had the Argie patrol in their sights.

'A complete fuck-up,' he snarled at Rupert, Double-Eff and the sergeant i/c 4 Platoon, who would not be earning his commission if he did it again. The flares were too late, there was no coordinated fire pattern. There was also a distinct lack of aggression and imagination.

'If you'll forgive me . . .' began Rupert.

'Shut the fuck up,' snapped Peter. 'Speak when you're spoken to. You,' he said to Double-Eff, 'what went wrong?'

'My mistake,' answered James ffolliott. 'No one else's. The flares were my fault.'

'The result being,' said Peter, 'two men dead and three wounded. Think yourself lucky that that was the total.'

3 Platoon did not consider themselves lucky. Of the casualties, only one, a fatality, had belonged to them. And, even though they'd all, most of them, thought him a pain in the arse, Non-Legless Jones had been one of them.

TWENTY-SIX

Girl friends and Wives (iii)

THE TELEPHONE IN THE HALL rang and rang. She counted about fifteen double tones, by which time anyone who knew her, and who knew her flat, would conclude she was either out or not in the mood to answer, and ring off. This caller didn't.

Another ten rings. Okay, so maybe it was urgent.

She sat up with a start. It couldn't be, surely . . . No, if anything terrible had happened, it wouldn't be announced this way. There would be a personal visit.

She got out of bed still wearing her black slip, the only item she had on and in which she had slept. Through force of habit she checked her appearance in the full-length mirror, patting her hair into place. She had often thought it would be a good idea to have an extension in the bedroom, but always argued herself out of the notion because she did, after all, live somewhere where all the rooms were on the same level. From the bedroom to the telephone was only a few paces.

'Hello,' she said sleepily.

Heather Rankin's voice, full of house-matron joviality, boomed down the receiver. Oh Christ, thought Julia, not today.

'Good morning, my dear,' said Daddy Rankin's wife. 'Sorry to disturb you so early on a Sunday, but I wanted to catch you before you went out.'

Julia peered at the hall clock, squinting. 8.30. *Eight-thirty*!

Who on earth went out shortly after 8.30 on a Sunday? Good God, this had better be important.

'Good morning,' she responded, trying to inject a little enthusiasm into her tone. 'You didn't disturb me. I was awake anyway.'

'Oh, that's a relief. I'd hate to think I'd ruined your beauty sleep. Not that you need any aids to beauty the way some of us do.'

Yes, yes, thought Julia. Get to the damned point.

'The thing is,' went on Heather, and then rattled on for five minutes about some pre-lunch function she was holding for senior NCOs' wives at her house that morning and how she'd been let down by Major Thomas's wife who'd called late last night to announce that she had incipient 'flu and couldn't make it. Would Julia be kind enough to deputize for Anne Thomas at 11.30 sharp?

'I realize it's short notice, my dear, and I apologize for that. But if you're not doing anything . . . ? I tried ringing you last evening but there was no reply. Presumably you were out. And it is, of course, D-Day.'

'I'm sorry?' said Julia.

'D-Day. The anniversary thereof, I mean. June six. Today. You understand?'

'Oh yes, of course,' answered Julia, not understanding at all but accepting that she'd been nabbed and for some reason that would doubtless be explained to her later she was to deputize for that insipid weakling Anne Thomas at a pre-lunch thrash for a handful of NCOs' wives.

'Then you'll do it?'

'Naturally.' Never fall out with the CO's memsahib.

'Splendid. I'll expect you at 11.30, then. Nothing too chic, may I add.'

'Fine.'

'And you'll be happy to hear that Sergeant O'Hara's wife is *not* on the guest list.'

'Thank God for small mercies.'

Damn the woman. Still, it was her own stupid fault for answering the bloody phone. Anyone that persistent just had to be Heather Rankin or some other do-gooder with a lame-duck cause.

In the bathroom she brushed her teeth, straightened her slip, dabbed scent behind her ears and on her bosom. Then she returned to the bedroom, where John Maxwell blinked up at her from beneath the sheets.

On the other hand, she thought taking off her slip, persistence had its advantages, for John Maxwell had phoned her every other day since their first gin and tonics back in May, and she had always refused his invitations to dinner until yesterday. And happy she was, now, she'd finally accepted and allowed him into her flat and her bed. For someone who worked for the Department of Health and Social Security (she'd always thought of such people hitherto as men with little beards, degrees from Warwick, SDP voters and just-a-half-a-lager drinkers), who was only twenty-four, and who, while pleasant enough to look at, was scarcely the stuff of which young girls dream, he had proved a remarkable lover, full of vigour and imagination.

'Leave the slip on,' he said.

Ah yes, that was it. He'd wanted her like that.

'As you wish,' she said demurely, climbing between the sheets and thinking that she had two hours before she need bother about getting up and having a bath. Then Mr Maxwell would be shown the door and would not be seen again. When all was said and done he was, after all, quite a common individual.

Sunday breakfast in the Bannister household on the morning of June 6 was the same grim, cheerless affair it had been the previous Sunday and the one before that. Carol's father did not work on Sundays and, in happier times, would have been out on the golf course before nine, having breakfasted alone. These days, however, he insisted on eating with his wife and daughter and every so often glared sullenly at Carol from behind his newspaper; looking at her, she thought, as if she were a refugee from a leper colony. Now that he knew of the baby his moods alternated between deep hurt ('How could you possibly do this to your parents?') and accusation ('You little slut').

Mrs Bannister had a theory about her husband's attitude, one that was too shocking to repeat aloud: deep down, Mr Bannister held incestuous feelings towards his only daughter, feelings that he could hardly know he owned. And she had betrayed him like an unfaithful wife.

Carol wasn't sure how much more of it all she could take, and occasionally she was horrified to find herself despising the thought of the baby and even despising herself for being so stupid as to get herself into this condition. Despising Chris, too, at times. If he were here, of course, it would be different. They could all talk it over, resolve it one way or the other, get married or stay single.

And there was going to be another six months plus of this. She would grow perceptibly larger, her father would become more crusty. Her mother said he'd get over it sooner or later, but she was beginning to doubt the accuracy of that prediction.

The sound of church bells floated through the open breakfast-room window. Carol's father looked up from his paper.

'That's where you should be.'

For Carol it was the last straw. They were not a church-going family. He was having another go at her, and she'd had enough.

'Oh, sod off,' she said irritably.

He was round the table in a flash, knocking over a chair and pushing his wife out of the way as he came. Then he had his daughter in a headlock and was punching her in the stomach. My God, she thought, panic-stricken, unable to scream, he's trying to kill the baby.

Her mother scratched at her husband's eyes, pulled his hair, shrieked for help. It was all over in seconds. Mr Bannister standing white-faced by the window, aghast at his actions, Mrs Bannister hugging her near-hysterical daughter.

Then the breakfast-room was full of neighbours, including Libby Rees from a few doors down. The police came, summoned by a passerby after the first screams. An ambulance arrived, called for by a cool-headed Libby who, with a uniformed constable, accompanied Carol to the hospital, holding her hand, the other policeman in the squad car insisting that Mrs Bannister remain in the house to give him her version of the fracas. At the hospital, after an hour, Libby was told by a doctor that Carol had lost the child she was expecting, the doctor assuming incorrectly that the two girls were related. Carol was in no danger but needed to rest for a while before seeing anyone.

The constable got a nurse to organize two cups of tea.

'She wasn't married the way I understand it,' he said to Libby. He didn't have his notebook out, wasn't taking evidence; just being friendly.

'No.'

How could something like that happen, wondered Libby?

Mr Bannister was such a quiet individual, pleasant, cheerful. And in a matter of seconds he'd wiped out a life.

'Steady boy friend?'

'He's in the Falklands.'

'Poor bugger.'

Mr Bannister would regret it tomorrow, later today, was probably regretting it even now. But it was too late. Nothing would bring Carol's child back.

'What will happen to him, her father?' Libby wanted to know.

'That's not for me to say. We'll take the evidence and it'll go upstairs. Someone else will decide if he's to be prosecuted. A lot will depend on whether he's ever done anything like this before . . .'

'He hasn't.'

'. . . and the attitudes of his wife and daughter. It can get complicated. I mean, even if he's not prosecuted, or prosecuted and receives no more than a fine and a warning, how is he going to be able to face them again? How will they be able to live with him?'

'It's stupid, isn't it,' said Libby, fumbling for the answer to a question she'd never considered before, 'that no one has any control over how and when they're born—or if they're born at all—not much over how and when they die, and very little over the bit in the middle? Go here, do this, do that, don't do the other. Rules.'

'Stupid maybe,' said the constable, 'but that's life.'

'Then it's a bloody awful arrangement. Do you need me here?'

'No. I'll need a statement from you, but that can wait. Are you going somewhere? I'd have thought you'd want to stay until—Carol?—was well enough to see you.'

'Oh, I'll be back,' said Libby, 'but I'd like to go home for an hour or so and talk to my parents. You see, the bit in the middle, the bit we can do something about, they've been controlling for the last few weeks. It's got to stop.'

In Eileen O'Hara's married quarters she was serving lunch for her sister Gwen and her brother-in-law Trevor. Tinned salmon and salad; a beer for Trevor, a glass of white wine for Gwen. Trevor had bought the wine and the beer, knowing full well that his sister-in-law would have no alcohol on the premises. Knowing also that eating Sunday lunch with Eileen was going to be bad enough without eating it dry. Nor had he understood, when Eileen telephoned the invitation, why they had to go. Sunday was meant to be a day of rest. 'Because Harry's in the Falklands, that's why, and she's my sister.'

While nowhere near as hen-pecked as Scarlett (and not hen-pecked at all in his own estimation), Trevor had been brought up in the sort of environment where women had the last word and where, if they didn't get it, they kept going until they did. Anything for a quiet life was now his yardstick, but Eileen was beginning to get on his nerves, banging on and on about the same old subject of Harry's underhandedness in 'sneaking off' to the Falklands. And receiving murmurs of sympathy from Gwen who was, Trevor suspected, secretly afraid of her sister's waspish tongue.

'Change the record, will you,' he said.

There was a moment's shocked hush while the two women, and Eileen O'Hara in particular, attempted to fathom the meaning of this extraordinary statement. Gwen got there first.

'Trevor,' she said sharply.

'Well for God's sake, she never talks about anything else. Harry did this, Harry did that. Harry didn't do this, Harry didn't do that. It's getting on my nerves.'

Eileen found her voice.

'You'll not address me in that tone in my house, Trevor.'

'That's the whole damned point.' Trevor pushed his plate away. Christ, if there was anything he hated it was tinned salmon. 'This isn't your house. It's the army's house first and Harry's second. You should get that into your head. You wouldn't have a house if Harry wasn't in the army.'

'I'd have a house of my own, like Gwen, if Harry wasn't in the army.'

'And that's another damned thing. The house you've just called Gwen's isn't Gwen's at all. It's mine. I pay for it. I sell frozen food five days a week and sometimes six to afford the mortgage and the rates and all the other bloody things that make up the house.' Trevor was beginning to enjoy himself. Or rather, his tongue was on a rollercoaster and he didn't want the ride to stop. 'I do a job that drives me crackers to pay for the bloody house. If I wanted to chuck it all in tomorrow and go away to Tahiti to paint, do you think I could? I couldn't. Because the building society wouldn't let me. Neither would the bank or the hire purchase company. Or the local council who want the rates. Harry does a job he actually enjoys, and that's worth more than owning any stupid bloody house.'

'But *I* don't enjoy him doing it,' said Eileen.

'I didn't know you wanted to paint,' said Gwen.

'Oh for Christ's sake!' said Trevor.

'He has to think of me and his daughter,' persisted Eileen. 'He has a family and he has to look after that family. That's his job for the rest of his life. He's had his youth, he's had his fun. He should now look to his responsibilities.'

'He's twenty-six, for the love of God.' Trevor was twenty-eight. 'You make him sound fifty. Living around you, I'll bet he *feels* fifty.'

Another shocked silence.

'You should take that back, Trevor,' said Gwen eventually.

'The hell with taking it back. She's a whining crone and she knows it. Nothing's ever good enough for her. She doesn't give a bugger about anything as long as she gets her own way.'

The sound of Kathleen crying came from the bedroom.

'There, now you've woken the baby,' said Eileen, with evident self-satisfaction, as if the whole masculine gender was conspiring to prevent women and children taking their rightful place in the world, preferably on the sunny side of the street.

Trevor finished his beer and got to his feet.

'Well, you've got your daughter complaining at an early age also. I hope you're satisfied. I'll be in the usual pub for half an hour,' he said to Gwen. 'If you haven't joined me by then you can get the train home or stay here, I don't care. And the next time your sister invites us over for lunch or a drink or to provide the audience for her moaning, tell her we're busy.'

The door slammed behind him.

'I never heard anything like it in my life,' said Eileen, also getting to her feet to attend to Kathleen. 'You'll have to give him a good talking to when you get him home. He's starting to develop some very funny ideas.'

Gwen stared at Eileen's departing back. 'I never even knew he *could* paint,' she said to an empty room.

Shortly before tea-time on the Parker-Smith estate, in the library, Lavinia and Sara Ballantine, who had driven over for lunch and stayed on, were composing a letter to Peter, taking a paragraph apiece, while Oliver practised potting on the billiards table and the Viscount snored in his favourite armchair.

Sara, Lavinia had been happy to see, had driven over sober and had remained sober, succumbing only to a pre-luncheon sherry and two small glasses of wine with the meal, which she had helped prepare with Lavinia and Helen, Oliver's wife. She, Sara, had been charming throughout, enchanting the Viscount in particular and entertaining everyone with her stories of the FO and the largely self-serving worried little men who ran the place and who had succeeded in turning mediocrity into an art form.

Lavinia wouldn't let Sara see everything she had written, which Sara pronounced to be unfair.

'How do I know I'm not repeating precisely what you've just said and boring Peter rigid?'

'If you're writing what I'm writing you're going to need the sympathetic ear of a good psychiatrist.'

The telephone rang in another part of the house.

'I'll get it,' said Oliver. 'I'd hate to break up the act.'

'Act?' spluttered Lavinia indignantly. 'You think this is acting?'

Oliver was back in a moment.

'It's your mother,' he said to Sara. 'The phone's in the hall to your left.'

'Something the matter?' mimed Lavinia to Oliver, who shrugged I-don't-know.

'It's my brother Edward,' said Sara when she returned. 'He's just arrived home unexpectedly from school, having been sacked forcibly or done a bunk deliberately. I couldn't quite make Mummy out. He's been in a fight or something.'

TWENTY-SEVEN

Mothers and Daughters (ii)

'. . . so I thumped him once or twice, heaved him around the common-room, which didn't please Quidgely, my housemaster, at all. I got the Class A lecture. "This is not a zoo, Ballantine. Nor is it a bear garden." He's very big on animals, Quidgely, "If you have a grudge or an argument that cannot be resolved by civilized debate, there is always the gym for three two-minute rounds." Anyway, I told him to bugger off and start living in the 1980s . . .'

'Very bright.'

'. . . and he went a peculiar colour and ordered me from his room, telling me to come back before evening prayers, which would have meant a whacking before everyone trooped in to sing a few verses of "Holy, Holy" and listen to the chaplain pi-jaw about just causes. Well, that did it. They can still beat the Lower Sixth for certain offences and I gathered I qualified for that category. If I'd reported back and he'd touched me with his cane I'd have wrapped it round his neck, and that would have meant the sack for sure. So I suppose I took the easy way out and hopped the first train home.'

'Easy way out is right,' said Sara.

They were walking in the copse that was part of the grounds, with Barney barking excitedly at everything that moved. Elizabeth Ballantine had remained in the house, and not only because a lengthy walk was beyond her capabilities. She suspected that Sara would be able to talk more sense into Edward than she could.

'It seemed the thing to do at the time.'

'They always do. And all because some idiotic oaf starts slanging the Argentines.'

'It was offensive. This guy knows about Ricardo . . .' Edward threw a glance at his sister. 'Do you mind talking about this, incidentally?'

'Not at all. That's why I'm here.'

'Then it wasn't just slanging. He was being obscene about what the paras and the marines were going to do when they got stuck in. Rip the Argies from belly to throat with serrated bayonets, cook them with napalm. All dagoes should be put in ovens like Jews. You know the kind of thing. Then he started having a go at Peter, who would doubtless have wangled himself a job in the cookhouse, at the rear, to avoid having to hurt his precious wog—that was the word he used—friend. He made several uncomplimentary remarks about you too.'

'Such as?'

'I wouldn't care to repeat them.'

'Then I'll do it for you. Any Englishwoman who'd get engaged to a dago can't be much of a woman. She's only after one thing, believing the Latins to be better at it than anyone else. Little more than a tart.'

'Don't,' said Edward. 'You've got the drift. Anyway, at that point I hit him. Actually, what I did was dive at him and catch him in the midriff, which rather knocked the stuffing out of him. Then I picked both of us up and bounced him off several walls.' Edward grinned in spite of himself. 'It was a bit like squash, if you want to know the truth. He'd go "ping" one way then come rebounding back. Then I'd "ping" him the other way.'

'And the rest of the common-room were doing what throughout this?'

'Egging us on, mostly egging him on. They have a peculiar public school mentality, which I suppose is not unique to them at this time. We're right, the Argentines are wrong. I can accept that. I can believe it, as a matter of fact. But the thing is I happen to like Ricardo . . .'

'So do I.'

'And Beto, if he's there.'

'So do I.'

'And I'm finding it very hard, impossible, to equate the Jordan-Ardittis we sang with at Christmas with what's going on down there.'

'So am I.'

'And Peter's there too, don't forget . . .'

'I haven't . . .'

'. . . and I guess there can't be many people in this country who have a brother fighting for our side and great friends—no, more than that—fighting for the other. It's very confusing.'

'For me too.'

'Yes, it must be even worse for you.'

'No, not worse. But just as confusing.'

They walked on.

'I had some absurdly romantic notion of taking a train in the opposite direction when I was at the station,' said Edward after a moment, 'going to London, to a recruiting office and joining up.'

'For Christ's sake, Edward!'

'I know, I know. It wasn't a serious notion. I'm afraid I'm a bit too practical for the noble and the futile.'

'And they wouldn't have taken you anyway. You're not seventeen yet.'

'It's also Sunday. They're closed.'

'And by the time you'd done your basic training and all that crap, this war would have been over and probably the next one as well.'

'I said it wasn't serious.'

'And if things were different you might be in Peter's position, having to fight Ricardo and Beto. Not the action of a friend.'

'I also said I was confused. I dunno, it all seems so puerile, sitting in a lecture room listening to abstract mathematical theory while that lot's going on. I feel I should be doing something constructive, but there's nothing constructive to be done.'

'You should be with my mob, not that I'm noted for regular attendance these days, then you'd really understand deconstruction.'

'Deconstruction? Is that a word?'

'It is now. It should be in the FO manual. To deconstruct: verb transitive: How to Fuck Up by Fence Sitting.'

'No chance of a settlement before the bloodbath?'

'My dear, I'm not exactly privy to the inner councils. Not that I'd understand a damned word they were saying if I was. But as far as I can understand it's all about punishing naked aggression and not losing face. The Foreign office, the MoD, and for that matter the whole of Whitehall are very good about not losing face. They are the original plastic surgeons in the face-saving department, the Max Factors of international buffoonery.'

Barney brought a stick. Edward took it from him and threw it. It hit a tree and shattered into a few small pieces. Barney hunted for the biggest, wailing with rage at this arboreal perfidy.

'Ricardo was probably in this from the beginning,' said Sara. 'From way before the original invasion, I mean.'

'So I've heard you say. You can't be sure.'

'I am. That's a betrayal—if it is a betrayal—I've had to come to terms with. There's he and his merry band of pilgrims planning a hostile act against this country and telling me lies while he's doing it. There's me lapping it up and expecting summer wedding bells. Then the crunch. It was hard to understand.'

'Have you come to terms with it?'

'No, I haven't come to terms with it,' said Sara. 'Obviously nothing can ever be the same again, but we'll have to see. I've tried liquor and that doesn't work, brings out too much bitterness. But it does anaesthetize the senses for a while. The bugger of it is, I'm prone to the most appalling hangovers. The cure is considerably worse than the disease. And I also concluded a couple of days ago after a severe dressing down from one Elizabeth Ballantine, that I was feeling more than a little sorry for myself. As you are now.'

'Me?'

'You. People say wretched things and you can't handle them. You're confused. You want to be doing something and you can't. Yes, that's feeling sorry for yourself. Have you seen the television pictures from the Falklands?'

'Yes.'

'Then you've seen the conditions they're fighting under. You've seen people burnt and killed, and there are a few women not a million miles from where we're standing who've lost husbands and brothers in recent weeks.

'We're being a bit selfish, aren't we, you and I? *We're* confused. *We're* hurt. *We* feel betrayed. There's a certain Colonel Jones's wife and a few others I could mention who'd be more than happy to accept a little betrayal today as opposed to the alternative. Then there's Mummy, Lucita, Mrs Jordan-Arditti, Peter, Ricardo, Beto. A great many others.

Yes, I think selfish and self-pitying just about covers it. Come on, let's walk back. It's going to be a long drive.'

'Drive.'

'Back to school. Trains are going to be awful at this time on a Sunday.'

'Oh, now look here . . .'

Sara planted herself squarely in front of her brother.

'No, you look here. Work it out. Are you planning to stay at home for ever? Or a week? Or just a few days? And what's that going to do to Mummy? What would Peter think if he'd heard you'd done a bunk? Okay, someone became objectionable and you thumped him. Good for you. If he says it again I hope you'll do it again. But telling Squidgely or whatever his name is to bugger off and come out of the nineteenth century won't solve anything. Nor will turning his cane into a necktie. I suggest you see him and apologize—for bad manners if nothing else. I also suggest you tell him, firmly but without raising your voice, why you got into the fight *and* that you'll get into others if people insult your friends, your brother and your sister. I'm sorry if all this sounds like the Queen's Speech to the Commonwealth, but that should take the wind out of his sails.'

'And if it doesn't?'

'You're on your own. I only read the first chapter of Teach Yourself Homespun Psychology. You really have no choice when you think about it.'

'Go back, face the music, take what comes. I guess you're right. I reacted like a bit of an idiot, didn't I?'

'You're a mere beginner in that department. I've graduated.'

After depositing Edward, Sara did not get back home until almost midnight. Her mother was still awake.

'You must be exhausted. A drink, a sandwich, tea?'

'Drink, I think. I've earned this one.'

'I'll join you.'

They took their brandies into the sitting-room.

'How did it go?' asked Elizabeth Ballantine.

'I didn't wait to see, but he marched off as if someone had just offered him a blindfold and a last cigarette. You know, I think I sometimes forget he's only sixteen.'

'Yes. Did he tell you the bit about wanting to head for the nearest recruiting office?'

'Oh God, he didn't say that to you, did he?'

'Yes. I didn't take him too seriously, but I must confess I

swallowed heavily several times. I thought . . .' Elizabeth Ballantine hesitated.

'Go on.'

'I thought I wouldn't have been able to stand it if he'd been in the army and old enough to be in the Falklands. Having one son down there is frightful enough. But two . . . Do you know what I'm trying to say?'

'I think so. In all probability, Maria Jordan-Arditti has both of hers on the islands.'

Midnight in England, British Summer Time, was 8 p.m. in Buenos Aires, where the nine million *porteños,* as the inhabitants of the capital's metropolitan area choose to describe themselves, no longer knew what to believe regarding the war in the Malvinas. There were rumours and counter-rumours, tales of great victories, hints of massive defeats. Some said the British were on the run, having lost their aircraft carriers and other warships, dozens of planes, thousands of men. Others queried those statements. Where were the pictures? And, if Argentina was winning, why were there so few letters being received from the troops? Those with experience of war remembered that mail was generally only given a low priority by the side that was losing, for reasons of cargo space aboard aircraft, and censorship. Why, too, were the citizens being exhorted to tighten their belts, conserve fuel and food? Certainly the heady days of April and May were things of the past, and only the junta's most fanatical supporters accepted as indisputable fact the contents of the official communiques and the nightly bombast delivered by television and radio. Most people preferred to trust their own instincts—that, at best, the war was at stalemate—and hope for Papal intervention, the Holy Father being due in five days' time. The anti-clerics didn't have much faith in the Pope arriving as a deus ex machina, pointing out that the Church in Argentina had shifted its attitude considerably in the last two months, from the belligerent 'joy at this reclamation of our sovereign territory' to 'our legitimate rights cannot be gained at the expense of others or against others'.

In the Jordan-Arditti household, at seven minutes past eight on Sunday evening, June 6, these arguments became academic when Maria Jordan-Arditti, who a few seconds earlier had been talking quite happily to Lucita, suddenly seemed to have great difficulty with her breathing, made a curious rattle in her throat, and collapsed on her pillows.

Lucita's screams brought the nurse running from the guest-room across the passage and, a few moments later, Alfredo Jordan-Arditti up the stairs.

The nurse was a no-nonsense middle-aged widow who knew her job. She ushered father and daughter from the room without ceremony, ordering the former to telephone for an ambulance on the emergency number the doctor had left, and then pulled to the bedside the portable oxygen equipment.

An hour later, at the private nursing home where a bed had been reserved in Maria's name for several months, the family's personal physician accompanied by the nursing home senior resident informed Lucita and her father that Mrs Jordan-Arditti was in an oxygen tent and doing as well as could be expected.

'Will you operate?' asked Alfredo.

'Impossible. She's too weak. Her body wouldn't survive the shock.'

'Then what?'

'We'll have to see how she responds. The next forty-eight hours will be critical. I'm sorry to be so blunt, but that's how it is.'

'And after that,' asked Lucita, 'after forty-eight hours?'

'She needs to build up her strength. Nourishment, peace and quiet. Then, I'm afraid, it has to be surgery.'

'What are my mother's chances?'

'I'm not in the clairvoyant business.' The doctor corrected himself. He had known Lucita since she was born and Alfredo for years before that; they were his friends. 'I'm sorry, I didn't mean that to sound so harsh. I can't calculate her chances. Much depends on her own will to live. The body is a peculiar mechanism . . .' He broke off. This was no time for a lecture on elementary pathology.

'Is there anything you need, anything we can do?' asked Alfredo.

'Yes. You can get her two sons safely home where she can see them.'

TWENTY-EIGHT

D Company

WALKING THROUGH THE BATTALION LINES towards last light on June 11, Daddy Rankin looked upon the anxious, grimy, tired young faces around him with affection and pride. Briefly he remembered how they were in full dress kit on the parade square back home, six hundred of them ramrod straight and proud as Punch in their light-blue berets. He supposed the COs of the other battalions were at that moment thinking something similar, remembering their commandos in their green berets, their paras in their red, their Guards. What a sight to see the cream of the British army lined up in the prime colours of the rainbow, though with rainbows, as everyone knew, there was nothing at the other end except disillusion. No, that was wrong, he corrected himself. At the end of any *particular* rainbow there was disappointment at not finding the pot of gold, but there would be other rainbows, fresh hopes. And one day . . .

Daddy marvelled at their youth and at what he had asked them, through their company and platoon commanders, to do. What they had already done.

Each night since arriving on Mount Kent his battalion and the other battalions had sent forward fighting patrols in their designated areas to probe the Argentine defences around Two Sisters and Mount Harriet and accompany the engineers, whose job it was to find a way through the Argentine minefields. Many of the patrols had encountered the enemy, in several instances at close quarters where bayonets had spilt blood. The young men who had marched from San Carlos were no longer green; some had dealt out death, some had been killed or wounded. All of them had tasted fear unlike anything they had known before, experienced 'dry mouth' and legs that refused to obey the mind's commands. Battalion casualties had increased by an extra dozen: three fatalities, six wounded, and three back to Ajax Bay with trench foot. It could have been worse. For some regiments it had been worse.

No one was yet quite sure, or was not admitting, why the Guards had not disembarked a bit more smartish from the LSLs, *Sir Galahad* and *Sir Tristram,* at Bluff Cove and Fitzroy on June 8. But the fact remained they hadn't, had been spotted by a high-flying Canberra reconnaissance aircraft, and were sitting targets for the Argentine Air Force Skyhawks and Daggers which pounced early afternoon. In all, fifty-three men died and forty-six were wounded, many seriously from appalling burns. Most of the dead were Welsh Guardsmen, youngsters; and worse, if anything could be worse, the survivors' kit was largely destroyed, which effectively rendered the Welsh Guards hors de combat for several days.

A few minutes earlier, in what was later reckoned to be a diversionary attack in Falkland Sound, five Daggers of 6 Group from Rio Gallegos had swooped on the frigate *Plymouth,* hitting her with four bombs which failed to explode but which detonated an armed depth-charge. *Plymouth* survived with wounded but without fatalities.

But that was June 8. Today was June 11, and at 2330 local time, 0330 Zulu and, even more confusingly, 0430 BST, the battalion would cross the 'start line' and take the open and occasionally highish ground north of Two Sisters, while 45 Commando took Two Sisters itself.

The basic strategy was simple and classic and virtually failsafe (and so, a Royal Marines captain was heard to remark, in theory is oral contraception). With the battalion on its left, 45 would make a two-pronged attack on the twin peaks of Two Sisters, while 42 Commando would attempt to skirt Mount Harriet, south of Two Sisters, and take the Argentine defenders unawares. 3 Para, in concert, would assault Mount Longdon, north-east of Two Sisters. When these objectives were gained and the high ground secure, the Guards, the

Gurkhas and 2 Para would move through, 2 Para heading for Wireless Ridge and Moody Brook, the Scots Guards for Mount Tumbledown, due east of Two Sisters, the Welsh Guards and 177 Gurkhas for Sapper Hill, east again of Tumbledown. The entire operation was to take place, as far as it was possible, over a forty-eight hour/seventy-two hour time span, and naval gunfire support could be expected from *Avenger, Yarmouth* and *Glamorgan*, coordinated by FOOs. Land-based artillery fire would be stepped up from the intermittent bombardments of the last two days, and was being stepped up to a frightening crescendo even as Daddy walked the lines—fierce and distant instruments of death that made men shiver.

There would be no stopping for anyone. The impetus had to be kept up, to frighten the Argies out of their socks. If an oppo fell, he had to be left for the medical teams, 'no matter if he's your brother or owes you fifty quid'. There was to be no, as Daddy inelegantly put it, fucking about. The battle was the thing. That was why they were paid 'the huge honoraria (he pondered the alternative plurals) a grateful country sees fit to bestow'.

Daddy had also given his company and platoon commanders, his senior NCOs, a pep talk earlier in the day. Although it went against the grain, he kept it short and sweet and mostly monosyllabic. It was his job to convince the officers and NCOs that it could be done; it was theirs to convince the men. The time for maps was over—they all knew the ground and their assigned objectives now—and as Daddy began speaking he 'cammed' up, a deliberate piece of theatre to put his audience at its ease.

'Ready for the close-up, Mr de Mille,' called Rupert.

'Lousy butler part,' riposted Daddy, surprising Rupert with his knowledge of *Sunset Boulevard*. 'And that will be an end of the repartee, if you don't mind.'

Rupert got the message. Between 2330 and sun-up men would die. Some badly, some well; some British, some Argentines. But all men. Daddy was right. Wrong time for levity.

'Now I don't know what the marines are going to do and I don't know what the paras are going to do,' said Daddy. 'I don't know what the Guards are going to do and I hope to high heaven I'm nowhere near the Gurkhas when they put on their killing face.' This brought a chuckle, as intended. The

Gurkhas had a reputation for not much caring whose blood they drew as long as blood was drawn. 'Nor am I going to reveal the tenor of the conversation unit commanding officers had with the Commander Land Forces except to repeat the caution that anyone found with a serrated bayonet will not see the light of day this side of the next century. I'm simply going to tell you what this battalion will do. Which is as it's told. As I tell it. We shall go in hard. Very hard. We shall take our objective regardless of the cost.'

If to an outsider it all sounded unbelievably gung-ho—and hardened journalists who heard this and similar briefings could scarcely believe their ears at some of the exhortations—Daddy didn't notice it and neither did his listeners. Nor would they have cared if outsiders thought they'd wandered on to a film set. Civilians knew shit. Civilians weren't important. A battalion, any battalion, was its own self-contained unit with its own shibboleths, a family based largely on paternalism but nonetheless fiercely protective of its own. Civvies would never understand that, never understand that a bloke would do more for his mates than he would for his own flesh and blood. Many wives didn't understand it; many were envious of a world from which they must for ever be excluded.

As darkness fell Daddy came across Archie, who tried to hide the Sterling submachine gun he had liberated under a poncho. Daddy saw the action but made no comment. In any case, Archie wouldn't be shooting anyone. By common agreement between Daddy and the journalist, Archie would remain with Battalion HQ. Unless the attack went terribly wrong, Archie wouldn't be anywhere near the sharp end.

'Hello, Archie,' said Daddy pleasantly. 'Writing nice things about us?'

'How about this,' said Archie, tilting his notebook and squinting at the words. 'In the early gloom of a Falklands winter's evening, with the snow mercifully for once an absentee though, like an unwelcome gatecrasher, it can return at any moment, I watched six hundred young and not so young. . . .'

'I suppose that's me.'

' ''. . . men daub their faces with cam cream and check their weapons.'' '

Archie paused, slightly embarrassed. He hadn't meant to read so far. It all sounded absurdly stilted when spoken aloud and had very little to do with what was going on around him.

'Continue,' said Daddy.

' "With the frightening rumble of artillery blasting Argentine positions, and helicopters, even at this late hour, ferrying forward supplies and ammunition, the young men huddle over their hexy stoves and prepare a final brew . . ." Look, that's enough.'

'Agreed. I must say your prose style's improved since Day One.'

'Thanks very bloody much.'

'My pleasure. However, you can scrap that lot, Archie. You should simply write that they're bloody brave, these blokes. That they're tired and cold and more than a little scared, but that they'll do the job they set out to do. That if anyone back in England ever talks disparagingly about "the youth of today" they should come and take a gander at this cross-section. That if they don't get some recognition when they get home, that if all this is forgotten within a year, then England should be bloody well ashamed of herself.'

'Can I quote you?' asked Archie. It was the longest unprepared speech Archie had ever heard the CO make. He would not have thought Daddy to be capable of such emotions.

'I haven't finished. You should also write that the next time one of these little buggers gets himself or a girl into trouble, people should remember that a great many of them are only eighteen or nineteen, and that most blokes that age in the UK haven't got enough sense to cross the road unaided.'

'Yes, but can I quote you?' Archie was scribbling furiously, cursing the fact that his tape recorder wasn't handy.

'Well, perhaps not, not attributably, anyway.'

Archie threw down his pen in disgust. 'Because you want to be a brigadier.'

'Not at all.' Daddy didn't take offence at the remark. 'I shall be more than happy if my lords and masters see fit to add another pip to this crown and a half. No, because they wouldn't thank me for saying it, the blokes.'

Archie nodded, accepting the argument. Although he would not have thought it conceivable ten weeks ago, he was starting to like the British army.

In D Company lines Rupert had broken out the two bottles of Glenmorangie and entrusted its distribution to Scrunch, with the caveat—not that Scrunch needed telling anyway—that each man got something of a tot. It wouldn't be much, a thimbleful. With ninety men in the company and sixty-four pub-optic measures in two bottles, they'd be lucky to taste the whisky. But there was no point in saving it any longer. Port Stanley might be only forty-eight to seventy-two hours away on the battle plan; it was a hell of a sight further in reality. Rupert did not expect to survive those hours and was not entirely surprised to find that he was unafraid to die. Except for one reason: a big, roaring fire and a couple of his favourite dogs around him.

Ah well.

Also in D Company Phil Beavis was making sure that each man had a syrette of morphine. Just the one, to be carried in the same pocket as his field dressing. And making sure each man knew how to use it. Slam it in, press the tit. Wait for peace. He continued to worry about, among others, Acne Hackney's feet. Davey Binns was less worried than Phil Beavis, though in some pain. A few more hours and it would all be over. Then he'd chuck it. In the meantime, he wasn't going to let Zebedee down. Or himself down. Fuck it, there wasn't anything back home anyway. Bloody pub hadn't even written a postcard. Though it would be ironic, he thought, if he lost not only his spots but a few toes to go with them. Yeah.

In 3 Platoon they no longer thought of Non-Legless Jones. They'd all seen him dead, though the suddenness of it had not made sense at the time. His lack of life, that is. From a living, breathing, boring bible-punching human being to so much dog food. One or two of them had also seen him fall, or rather be blasted, into an untidy, jerky heap that became the earthly, bloody remains of Non-Legless. A couple of them thought irreverently (because treating it as a cosmic joke was the only defence they had against going mad or breaking down) that they hoped to Christ Non-Legless had something to look forward to on the Other Side, because he'd sure fucked up this one. They'd seen Phil Beavis scuttle over to him when the Argie patrol was on the run through all that fucking smoke and shit, and, despite Phil's apparent frailty, pull Jonesey into cover because the Argie machine gunner was still firing. Then Phil had opened his satchel and got down real close to see if anything could be done for Non-Legless. Which nothing could. Phil had also moved forward, unarmed, with the rest of 3 and 4 Platoons to examine the dead Argie, to see if he could help. Which he couldn't. Then Non-Legless and the Argie disappeared. A couple of other medical teams and Burke and Hares moved up, and then they were gone. Fucking gone. Just like that. Like a comic conjurer doing one of his crazy tricks, except this time there was no funny ending, no stuffed chickens. Fucking gone.

They didn't think too much about either corpse thereafter apart from considering their own mortality at the wrong end of an ounce and a half of lead. And speculating with gallows humour on what Captain Ballantine might be writing to the next of kin.

Dear Mr and Mrs Jones: Well, your son fuckin' copped it, already. Whooosh. Right through the chest and neck. What a fucking mess. Like M.A.S.H. when Hawkeye hits the wrong artery. Bang. One minute he's yelling in some strange foreign tongue (Welsh, I think it's called), running forward with the rest of the gang. The next he's strawberry jam. Bingo. Eyes down for a full body-bag.

And. Dear NOK: So much for religion.

And. Dear Sir or Madam: Bits of your son's back and chest are currently distributed over areas of Mount Kent and points east. Will you kindly move him. He's making the snow look untidy.

Then they forgot about Jonesey. That was best.

And they'd been lucky, 3 Platoon, in their subsequent patrols, meeting up with the enemy only twice, and only once at close quarters, when Three-piece and Yank became the first members of the platoon to kill someone with a bayonet, two scared machine gunners in a trench. They didn't fire, the Argies, and there was some speculation afterwards that they'd wanted to surrender, join the 'ostriches'. But they didn't put up their hands and, in any case, Yank and Three-piece were on a high, drugged on momentum and noise. They were also taking no chances. There was a lot of shooting prior to taking the trench and the Argies might have been dead from rifle bullets before the bayonets went in. Neither Yank nor Three-piece knew or cared, and they didn't hang around to find out. Into the trench. Shoot. Stick. Yell. Out of the trench. Run on. Until there were no more Argies in sight. None alive and dangerous, that is. A few prisoners, a few wounded. Some crying.

Wisely, Double-Eff sent Three-piece and Yank to the rear while the rest of the patrol rounded up the ostriches, and, later, Three-piece and Yank seemed disinclined to talk about it all. However, on several occasions during the following day they were both seen, individually and collectively, polishing their bayonets with more elbow grease than was strictly necessary, and examining the blades for traces of blood. Then polishing again.

Double-Eff asked them if they were all right, any problems. Both denied there was anything wrong, seemed surprised at the question.

And indeed they seemed to be fine, except for the regular polishing and the fact that both of them, never great gag tellers in the past, now seemed to have a vast reserve of idiotic jokes. Peter Ballantine figured it out, not that there was much to figure.

'I've never actually stuck a bayonet in anyone myself but I can imagine what it's like. They won't crack because we've taught them otherwise. They don't want to talk generally because the patrol might crop up. But they have to say something. So they tell jokes.'

Three-piece was telling one when Scrunch reached Scarlett with 3 Platoon's share of Rupert's scotch.

'There's this old tramp, see, who walks into this pub with a pig on his shoulder and a notice round the pig's neck that says: Before anyone asks, this pig is intelligent and can talk. The bloke walks up to the counter and says: "Two pints of bitter, please. One for me, one for the pig." The barman takes one look and says: "Hang on, get that dirty fucker out of here." The tramp says: "Wait a minute, you can't talk to us like that. This pig's a friend." The barman says: "I was talking to the pig." '

Nobody laughed.

'Aw, bollocks,' said Three-piece.

'You've got the sense of humour of a sheet of Andrex,' said Two-Shit.

'Piss off.'

'Piss off, Corporal,' said Two-Shit, not biting.

'All right, piss off, Corporal.'

Three-piece stabbed his bayonet into the snow and the peat beneath the snow, dug it out, and wiped it against his thigh. Then he started polishing it again.

'Tell you what,' said Sammy Finch, 'let's have a real laugh. Get Branston to tell that gag.' Sammy gave a passable impression of Branston's rusty-nail accent. 'Therewuzthisfockingpiginthisfockingbarsee . . .'

'YefockinwatchyerfockingmouthFinch,' said Branston, which brought the house down.

Yank tried one. They'd be going again soon, but he wasn't scared. Well, he was, but he wasn't going to let these bastards see it.

'There's this guy who's being shown round a biscuit factory by the foreman and they come across one of the workers with his flies open and his cock in a box of Jacob's.'

'I think I got one of those biscuits in the last ratpack,' said Prawn Balls.

'Anyway,' said Yank, glowering at Cyril Ball, 'the foreman says, "Don't worry about him, he's fucking crackers." '

'I don't know why you don't go on the stage, Yank, I really don't,' said Legless Jones. 'Christ, with material like that . . .'

'Naafi break,' said Scarlett, distributing the platoon's ration of the scotch from a water canteen, using a mug with a mark on the side as a measure and leaving it to the individual to decide whether he wanted it in his brew or preferred to gulp it straight. Most preferred it straight. Groggy held his own half mouthful for thirty seconds before his taste buds got the better of him and he was forced to swallow. Christ, he was going to drink it by the bucketful the first opportunity. We shall fight them in the hills, we shall fight them in the streets, we shall most especially fight them in the saloon bars . . .

'Who's this down to, Sarge?' he asked Scarlett.

'The old boss.'

'Crafty old friggin' Zebedee. Is he sure he can spare it?'

'Shut it, Groggy, before I shut it for you. This is it, all he had. He could have kept it for himself and Captain Ballantine.'

'Well, maybe, but if you want my opinion . . .'

'I'll wait for the paperback.'

'He's trying to get us pissed, is what he's doing, the old boss,' said Sammy. 'They used to do that in World War One, didn't they, Sarge . . .'

'How the fuck old do you think I am?'

'Ninety-six. They used to give guys a tot before they went over the top. I remember the movie with Kirk Douglas . . .'

'Just drink up and shut up, Finch. Christ, you're mouthy.'

'It's being a Londoner that does it . . .'

Time passed slowly. Then the time passed quickly. The land artillery was still firing. So too were the naval guns bombarding the reverse slopes of Two Sisters and Harriet. The ground troops did the 'jumps', moved around violently to see if anything rattled. Anything that did was removed and left behind with the bergens. Grenades were attached, magazines checked. Bayonets fixed. Clunk-click every trip. Three-piece shivered. It was fucking cold and there was snow in the air, but he didn't think that was why he was shivering. Like stabbing a side of beef, sticking a bayonet in was. A side of beef covered with an old coat. Pffffsssh. Squelch. Nothing like the practice dummies. Not that bloody easy to get the bayonet out, either, not until you'd fired a round. That made a bigger hole. Easy then. Piece of piss. Friggin' hard to get the bayonet clean afterwards, though. There was always a spot of something or other there. Get hell for that on parade, spots on your bayonet. Wham. Into the slammer.

Your feet won't touch the ground, Sweet, you 'orrible little man.

All the perfumes of Arabia will not sweeten this little hand.

Not that Sweet knew those lines spoken by Lady Macbeth. He would have appreciated them had he known, for his circumstances and those of Lady M were broadly similar. He might also have appreciated the pun on his own surname and the transitive verb.

He wondered if he could fall behind, drop out. It was possible. D Company was going in with the second wave, leapfrogging with B Company A and C Companies. It wouldn't be hard to go missing, though he concluded he'd be a fool to consider anything of the sort. Scarlett would see him. Or Scrunch. If they didn't then they'd find out later. Then he'd be in trouble. 'In the rattle,' as Scrunch called it. Easier to motor in with the others, trust to luck.

Rupert had a word with Phil Beavis.

'Okay?'

'Thanks, Boss.'

'Keep well out of it, you know that?'

'I'll watch it.'

'Because we might need you. You get hit, one or two of us might get stuffed.'

'I'll watch it.'

There was excitement in the air as well as fear. As well as artillery shells, which Double-Eff hoped to God someone had reminded the gunners to ease up on before D Company got anywhere near its objective. Not that the FOOs had made many mistakes, if any, up to now. From all accounts they'd been performing exceptionally, taking great risks and calling down barrages with pinpoint accuracy within a few dozen yards of their forward positions. Still.

The sustained-fire machine-gun platoons checked their tracer for the tenth time. Gonna be a fuckin' party, this bastard.

Peter squinted at his watch, waited for the word from his HQ wirelessman, saw A and C Companies move off into the night. Right.

All went well for an hour, with what was, in effect, a massive advance going undetected. Then 3 Para was discovered on Mount Longdon—someone stepping on a mine, it was immediately hazarded—and the Argies knew a full-scale attack was underway.

On Two Sisters, 45 Commando came under heavy machine-gun fire. This was followed, now the Argies were awake, by mortar and recoilless-rifle fire, with the marines replying in kind with small arms, Milan bunker-busters, and 66s, an American-built throwaway rocket launcher carried by infantrymen. South of 45 on Mount Harriet, 42 Commando had got close to the summit without being detected, whereupon they attacked the Argentine trenches with 66s and machine guns, small arms and grenades.

On 45's left flank the battalion's positions were being illuminated by Argentine flares and then assailed with devastating power from fixed-position machine guns and mortars. Tracer from attacker and defender alike hosed through the night sky like party streamers flung by bad-tempered children. Conscript army or not—and many in the Argentine trenches were not, were crack troops and continued to fight well until their officers and HQ forces began to desert them, to pull back—the Argies were putting up a hell of a scrap.

All notions of stealth were now out of the window. With Daddy directing the battalion's battle via wireless and, when that didn't work, via runners, A and C Companies stormed the middle ground, the first of the trenches, using 66s, Milans and heavy machine guns to take out the first line of opposition. Mortars too, though the mortars were being used on the second line of defence, the rear trenches, to put the fear of Christ up the Argentines in the hope they would make a run for it, back across the open country towards Tumbledown, into the air-burst artillery barrages that were even now being coordinated.

Then B and D Companies began moving through, howling like banshees, urged on by their officers and NCOs. Peter caught a brief glimpse of Toby Lomax, his huge frame unmistakable, diving forward ahead of the remainder of B Company. Then Peter had other things on his mind, for temporarily he lost his wirelessman and thought, Oh fuck it, now I'm in trouble. But a moment later the signaller appeared out of the gloom, hunting his company commander, having fallen, though being unhurt, in the last fifty-yard rush.

Around Peter, other men were falling, British troops. In the mêlée it was impossible to see if they were taking cover or if they'd been hit, or even to identify platoons. There was a hell of a clatter coming from Peter's right, where 3 and 4 Platoons seemed to be pinned down. And in being pinned down were slowing the momentum. Unable to raise either platoon commander via radio, Peter sent Rupert to investigate. He thought briefly of sending Scrunch, then calculated, quite coldly if logically, that he could afford to lose Rupert more than he could the CSM. In any case, Scrunch was fifty yards to Peter's left, reorganizing 2 Platoon, whose platoon sergeant was down.

The D Company 2 i/c ducked and weaved across to 3 Platoon, where Double-Eff and Scarlett were redeploying Two-Shit and Jomo into some kind of sustained-fire pattern prior to malleting the two enemy trenches that were slowing the advance.

Rupert took over. This was no time to fuck around. He'd sort it out with Double-Eff later.

'Get the machine gunners close together,' he shouted at Scarlett, who scuttled away to do just that. 'Milans and 66s?' he asked Double-Eff.

'Gone.'

'Jesus, you're profligate, James. Okay, then we'll open fire with the machine guns. A substantial burst for ten seconds. Then we advance. Corporal Tyler!'

Rupert's cry was lost in the explosion of a mortar landing close by, throwing someone up into the air. But Two-Shit had got the message before Scarlett reached him and had opened up in concert with Jomo. He might be a pain in the neck, Two-Shit, but, as he'd correctly deduced, promotion boards didn't hand out three stripes for no reason.

'Go!' shouted Rupert, knowing that the platoon machine gunners would cease firing long before the men were in

danger of being killed by their own oppos. Knowing too that
the sustained-fire machine-gun platoon had its broad trajectory way over to the right.

Rupert hesitated before going with them. Peter Ballantine
might need him. No he wouldn't. Peter had Scrunch.

Rupert led the assault on the two trenches, a pace ahead of
Scarlett and Double-Eff, who were both carrying, Rupert
noticed, SLRs with bayonets compared with his own Sterling.
Fuck it. Next time, if there was a next time, he'd grab a rifle.

On Rupert's left Branston Pickles was uttering some weird
kind of Scottish war cry. Or maybe he was just shouting
normally. Whichever, he was sure as hell scaring the bejesus
out of the Argentines, who swung their machine guns in
Branston's direction, allowing the right flank of the 3 and 4
Platoon attack to develop.

A moment later Acne Hackney was hit, on the right of
Branston, who momentarily slowed his charge.

'Keep going!' yelled Rupert.

'Getupyedumfocker!' Branston bellowed at Acne Hackney,
who, his stomach now being spaghetti, could not comply.

While 3 Platoon took the left-hand trench, with Three-piece
(earlier worries gone), Sammy Finch and Twiggy lobbing in
grenades before diving after them with fixed bayonets and
destroying the trench's occupants, 4 Platoon hammered the
right-hand trench, losing two men in the process, which only
made their assault more frenzied. Grenades. Wait. In. Stab.
Out. Move on. There were other trenches and resistance was
nowhere near what anyone could yet reliably term weak.

Behind the main arm of the attack, behind 3 and 4 Platoon,
that is, came Phil Beavis. He was crying, trying not to but
failing, as he helped, or attempted to help, Acne Hackney
shovel back his spilling guts inside his gear. Acne Hackney
was screaming unbelievably, though his cries could scarcely
be heard above the surrounding tumult.

'Teams, teams!' yelled Phil Beavis, asking for extra medical assistance. But there was none near. In any case, Davey
Binns would certainly not survive. Phil's limited medical
knowledge told him that much. He was ripped from crotch to
armpit. He was dying and it could only be a matter of minutes
before he expired. He was also in the most enormous pain,
which no single syrette of morphine could do anything about.

'Bravest thing I ever saw,' said an A Company officer
later, talking to his platoon sergeant. They resolved after-

wards, the pair of them, never to mention to anyone what they had witnessed.

Phil Beavis picked up Acne Hackney's rifle and shot the East Londoner in the head, killing him instantly from close range, with Davey Binns' half-seeing eyes on him throughout. Beavis would have nightmares about what he had done for the rest of his life, but for the moment he could not afford to think about the consequences of his action. He was needed elsewhere.

The man Rupert had seen blown up by the mortar was Yank Hobart, and in the curious manner of mortar blasts the shell had wounded only Yank, no one else. But Yank had lost a leg. He couldn't believe it was happening, seeing the spurts of blood long before he felt any pain and went into shock. Or rather, seeing a gusher of oozy, sticky liquid, warm liquid, cascading away from him as he lay on his back, wondering why the hell he couldn't get up. And his own leg, or what was left of his leg, lying beside him like a dead pike that had been badly gaffed. Hey, he thought, hang on a fucking tick. This isn't right. I did my bit. Hey.

'It's okay, Yank, it's okay,' Phil Beavis was saying somewhere near his head, just before Yank gave a low moan of pain and passed out, with Beavis trying to find Yank's morphine before realizing that it had gone with Yank's leg. Then trying to find his own spares and cursing his stupid, fumbling hands for being so slow and inefficient.

He slammed in a syrette and managed to find the artery and staunch the flow of blood, getting covered in Yank's blood in the process. Then two stretcher-bearers were beside him, telling him they'd look after the injured man. That Phil should go and look for others he could help.

There was plenty of trade, some of the wounds minor, some major. One man had been hit in the head by machine-gun rounds or mortar fragments but was still walking around, his arms out in front of him, for he was blinded. Prior to sailing with the task force he had been the battalion's middle-weight boxing champion and had got as far as the inter-service finals. No more of that for him, and not much more of anything.

After dealing with him, the rest of the night for Phil Beavis became a blur.

Up front the attack was going well, with the battalion overrunning more trenches and bunkers, killing more Argentines, and taking many prisoners, though Argentines only became ostriches if they made it perfectly clear they wanted to surrender, by throwing away their arms, leaving their funkholes, and putting up their hands so that there could be no mistakes about intentions. Everyone had learned from 2 Para's tragedy at Goose Green, and no one wanted to become a casualty of a 'misunderstanding'. If there was any doubt, and sometimes when there wasn't, the occupants of the trenches were killed unceremoniously. Three-piece, Twiggy and Sammy, who never seemed to be far apart from one another, were quite foolishly noble about taking and disarming prisoners. Groggy, Legless Jones and Branston, who also seemed to operate as a trio, never buggered about. Any Argentine in the way was an enemy, and there was only one way to deal with enemies.

Somewhere in the small hours, when many Argentines were on the run, getting out, fighting a tactical withdrawal before they were swamped, Dippy Hendricks of C Company died in a hail of small-arms fire when he unwisely got too far ahead of the platoon he was leading and was shot from a trench he had not seen. He died without his teeth.

Shortly afterwards HMS *Glamorgan*, until then providing naval gunfire support for 45 Commando, was hit fifteen miles offshore by a land-based Exocet. The explosion was seen on the high ground of East Falkland as a distant, and at that time inexplicable, fireball.

Not all the Argentines elected to surrender or run. Some of them were hard men, particularly those of the 5th Marines, and small groups of that unit chose to take the fight to the British, get out of their trenches, which they now recognized to be death-traps, and advance. 3 and 4 Platoons D Company— with Rupert now back with HQ Platoon but having a roving brief from Peter, because it seemed to work, to go where he liked—came across an octet of 5th Marines and at first mistook them for British troops because it didn't seem likely that the Argies would do anything so foolish as counter-attack in section strength. Not that a handful of them weren't brave, but fighting from fixed positions against a mobile and determined attacker did not lend itself to flexibility.

Double-Eff, Scarlet and the sergeant i/c 4 Platoon, with Double-Eff having rough command of both platoons since he was the senior rank, quickly realized their error when the 'friendlies' went to ground and opened fire with machine guns and submachine guns, wounding two members of 4 Platoon severely and Prawn Balls less so, Cyril Ball taking a single bullet in the fleshy part of his thigh—the jackpot wound, as the battalion termed it, for it put a man out of the fight, back to Ajax Bay and then the *Uganda,* without doing serious damage. Then Double-Eff earned his salary for that day by getting 3 Platoon deployed behind cover and waving 4 Platoon forward in a flanking movement. The Argentines were stuffed from that moment. They were most especially stuffed when Double-Eff called down a mortar barrage and, once that was over, led the assault which finished off the surviving Argentines with bayonets and small arms. No prisoners on this occasion. Total elapsed time from first contact to all-clear: eight minutes. Double-Eff was feeling quite proud of his performance until Scarlett nudged him and gestured forward. The Argies weren't finished yet.

But almost, at least in these positions.

The night wore on, and dawn was imminent before fire from the Argentine trenches became sporadic. 42 Commando had held Mount Harriet for several hours, but were still moving forward into the cold morning with fixed bayonets to clear up pockets of resistance. 45 Commando controlled the high ground of Two Sisters, and the FOO with the marines was busily calling down a fierce artillery bombardment on the fleeing enemy. 3 Para would finally occupy Mount Longdon before first light, having suffered the worst of the casualties but, in the process, adding another battle honour to the Parachute Regiment's standard. And Daddy's battalion on 45's left flank had largely reached its objectives and was now mopping up.

Throughout the battle Peter Ballantine had felt curiously out of it. No Argentine position in D Company's area had required what he would have called an all-out company attack to finish it off, and he had been left, he thought, with the shitty end of the stick, that of administrator, of coordinating his platoons without getting into the thick of it himself. Going everywhere with his wirelessman, who looked about on his last legs, he had made sure that each platoon was where it should be, or if it wasn't, get it there. He had signalled battalion for more Milans, more mortars, more 66s as required. He had fired only one magazine from his Sterling. Although he had done a good, competent job, he hadn't done an exceptional job. He was pretty pissed off. He was beginning to think that being Company OC was not all it was cracked up to be, and wishing Winter's Day hadn't been such a damned fool. He was also wondering if he'd be allowed to keep D Company, with a promotion to major, when the battalion got back to the UK.

He rather doubted it. It didn't work like that.

Rupert had had most of the excitement, scuttling around like a terrier to where he was most needed. Tireless.

In the final stages of the advance, with night now retreating and snow falling, Peter found himself dog-trotting alongside a helmetless officer he recognized as a Pay Corps lieutenant. The lieutenant was carrying an SLR, bayonet fixed, and looked as if he meant business. Peter wondered aloud where the hell he'd come from.

'We don't all toss off into the balance sheets, you know,' said the subaltern, not taking offence in the least. 'I tried shooting at them with my calculator but the batteries must be low or something. Fuck it, I'm a trained soldier.'

'What happened to the helmet?'

'Curious thing. It got hit by a piece of shrapnel or a ricochet or some such about an hour ago, and went bounding away like a tennis ball. I decided not to go after it. I figured I'd had my share of luck from that one.'

'Bit bloody dangerous to go around without a tin hat,' said Peter. 'You should pick up another one.'

'No, I'll wait. You see, if I find one lying around I also figure that the previous owner has had *his* share of luck.'

'Ah,' said Peter.

Scrunch appeared at dawn clutching a sheaf of papers. Intermediate casreps. The CSM too had missed the bulk of the fighting because his place was with the company commander, and for an ex-Royal Marine, especially when other bootnecks had taken Two Sisters and Mount Harriet, this was intolerable.

'Four dead, six wounded,' Scrunch reported, 'as of now. And two missing we're not sure about.'

Peter looked at the names. Up ahead D Company and the other companies were still sorting out Argie stragglers, while in the air choppers were flying to ferry back the wounded. The prisoners would be dealt with later, sent to the rear when time permitted. Away from Peter's eyeline the open ground between Two Sisters and Mount Tumbledown was being bombarded unmercifully with air-burst and phosphorus shells. The Argentine 105s and 155s around Stanley were not yet replying, presumably because there were still hundreds of Argentine troops in the captured ground.

Private Davey Binns—dead. Private Billy Hotchkiss—wounded, blind maybe. Private Colin Gordon—dead. Private Cyril Ball—wounded. Private Hobart—wounded, an amputee. 2nd Lieutenant Mike Riley—wounded. Corporal Ronald Smith—missing. Private . . .

It was a distressing list, but no company commander could afford to consider the casualties as people while there was still fighting to be done.

Peter handed the casreps back to Scrunch.

'Get it all into the proper form and up to BHQ. Liaise with the RSM regarding burial details. I'll round up the company. We ought to think about digging in before anyone settles down for a brew. Their artillery will be having something to say about it all in an hour or two. We'll use the Argie bunkers as far as they're habitable.'

The HQ wireless gave out with a broken-biscuits squawk. Peter's signaller said that Sunray—Daddy—had called an immediate 'O' Group of company commanders. Acknowledge.

'Right,' said Peter. 'Call up the platoons and establish Mr Parker-Smith's whereabouts. Tell him to get back here soonest and see the CSM. Those bloody prisoners are going to give us problems,' he said to Scrunch. 'Christ, where did they all come from?'

In twos and threes and sometimes double figures, the Argie ostriches were being herded to the rear. Many of them were very young, some were evidently frightened, but the majority seemed relieved that, for them, it was all over. In that respect they were more fortunate than the British troops, for whom there was more to come.

'We should leave them out there and tell the Argies in Stanley what we're doing,' said Scrunch. 'That would put paid to their evil little notions with 105s.'

'Ever heard of the Geneva Convention?' asked Peter.

'Bunch of Swiss beefers.' Scrunch waved the casreps. The CSM was a boxing fan. He'd known all the blokes who had been killed and wounded, had more often than not given most of them hell back in barracks, but Billy Hotchkiss being possibly blind for the rest of his life upset him. 'Somebody should remember who started this.'

'Yes, well,' said Peter, 'I think we'd better go along with the rules while we still have rules. The MPs can look after that lot.'

'Sunray says now, Boss,' said Peter's signaller.

'I'll take these with me,' said Peter, holding out his hands for the casreps. Scrunch seemed pleased to be rid of them.

Daddy had only one piece of unexpected news after absorbing the casreps and discovering that his battalion was thirty-two men fewer than the night before. The Scots Guards, Welsh Guards and the Gurkhas would not be going for their objectives of Mount Tumbledown, Mount William and Sapper Hill at last light today, June 12. Due to a shortage of helicopters to ferry his troops forward to the start line, the 5 Brigade Commander had asked for, and been granted, an extra day. The attack would now begin after dark on the morrow, June 13. 2 Para, whose job would be to move through 3 Para's positions and take Wireless Ridge and Moody Brook, were known to be unhappy about the delay. Even more than the men now digging in on Two Sisters and Mount Harriet, 2 Para would be exposed to the enemy's 105s and the even more vicious 155s for longer than they thought necessary. But there it was.

There were groans of exasperation among the assembled company officers, which were quickly silenced by Daddy with a raised hand.

'They're not as acclimatized as we are,' said Daddy. 'Nor as prepared. We had a week to probe the defences and plan last night's attack.'

'They didn't march from San Carlos either,' muttered someone.

At the conclusion of the 'O' Group, Daddy motioned Peter, Major 'Dick' Barton, OC B Company, and Toby Lomax, Barton's 2 i/c, to stay behind.

'There's also another slight hiccup,' said Daddy. 'The best laid schemes of mice and men syndrome. Brigade wants two companies from this battalion to look after the low-ground left flank of the Scots Guards when they go for Tumbledown. We're closest. 45 is on Two Sisters, 42 even further away on Harriet. I've selected B and D Companies for the job, and I'll be coming with you with a small Tac HQ. Any questions, apart from the obvious ones of how, when, where, bloody minefields and so on, which we'll get around to later?'

'My blokes are pretty near exhausted,' said Dick Barton.

'If they're going in again tomorrow, they'll need all the rest they can get today. I mean, prisoners, digging in, and so forth.'

'I've taken that into consideration,' said Daddy. 'As soon as the immediate round-up is over, I'm pulling B and D back. A and C and HQ can do whatever's necessary. Peter?'

'Nothing to add for the moment, sir.'

'Good. Then get back to your companies. I'll talk to you later.'

Scrunch was dismayed when he heard. So too was Rupert.

'Fuck me, Boss,' said Rupert, 'they're asking a lot. I mean—well, take a look around you.'

Peter already had. At Chris Twigg and Sammy Finch, Jim Pickles; Jomo Mason and Corporal Tyler. At Phil Beavis, whose gear was covered in blood, none of it his own. At the others. Well, they'd have to go again, and that's all there was to it.

'Look on the bright side,' said Peter. 'It could be worse.' He gestured towards the heavens where British artillery was still shelling the hell out of the retreating Argentines. 'They could be under that lot.'

TWENTY-NINE

Beto

BETO JORDAN-ARDITTI was. And terrified.

On direct orders from Port Stanley, Colonel Filippi's battalion had been told to start pulling back in the small hours, when it became apparent that 45 Commando on Two Sisters was winning this battle. At least, *half* the battalion was ordered to withdraw; with other units, two companies would remain in their trenches to cover the retreat and prevent it from becoming a rout. Two companies would therefore be sacrificed, to become POWs at best.

Ricardo was enraged. So too, for once, was Major Tomba, who immediately volunteered Alpha Company for the rearguard. Colonel Filippi turned him down. The commanding officer had had very little sleep for forty-eight hours due to the incessant British artillery barrage. Neither had anyone else in the battalion, naturally, but Filippi had decisions to make, or so it seemed, every few minutes. Important decisions that could effect whether men lived or died. He was also down to his last pack of cigarettes.

'Why not Alpha?' demanded Tomba boldly. 'Are you implying my company isn't good enough? Sir.'

Filippi hesitated. Oh well, Tomba would have to know sooner or later—as would the other officers—that it didn't matter a damn whether Alpha Company stayed or not. Because Tomba would not be staying with them.

'I said two companies were to remain. What I actually meant was that two units of company strength would stay.'

'Sir?' Tomba did not understand.

'This is unofficial, you must realize, because nothing has been put in the form of a written order. But all officers above the rank of lieutenant will retreat. The rearguard companies will be commanded by junior officers and NCOs.'

Tomba could not believe his ears.

'You cannot possibly be serious, sir.'

'I'm afraid I am. I've been given some discretion, of course, but I can read between the lines as well as the next man. There's a certain logic to it, when you think about it. This isn't the final battle, not here. That will come outside Stanley. We're going to need our senior ranks there, to help hold the line in case there can still be a political settlement.'

'And what use will we be, sir,' Tomba wanted to know, 'if we have no men to command, no seasoned troops, that is?'

'Ah, that's another thing,' said Filippi. He seemed embarrassed. 'The larger proportion of the companies left behind will consist of conscripts. Not exclusively, but largely. And that doesn't only apply to this battalion.'

'They'll be murdered.'

'Some of them will, doubtless,' said Filippi realistically. 'The majority of them will surrender sooner or later. They're there to buy us time, Carlos, and that must be the end of this discussion. Just do as you're told, please. This headquarters is packing up as of now. We'll take only what we can carry.'

'Jesus, not that again,' swore Ricardo, when he heard the dreaded words 'political settlement'. There was a brisk firefight going on over to his left, several hundred feet below the summit of Two Sisters, with the British commandos assaulting a trench with rockets. Having dispensed with his wirelessman to save time conveying instructions, Ricardo muttered a rapid order into the radio he carried, whereupon trenches to the right and left of the one being attacked swung their machine guns on to the commandos' position. That was where he should be, Ricardo thought, with the forward echelons, not stuck in this funkhole with Carlos Tomba. Except one extra rifle or submachine gun wasn't going to do much good down there. At least from above he could see what was happening with his night-glasses and direct fire to where it was most required. 'Hasn't Menendez got it through his thick skull yet that the British are not going to listen to any peace formula short of unconditional surrender while they're winning the land battle?'

'Filippi didn't say the order came directly from Menendez.'

'Then who the hell has it come from? His cook?'

'Maybe the Casa Rosada.'

Ricardo ducked involuntarily as a rocket exploded fifty metres below, down slope. He heard men scream as they died. Whoever would have thought in April that it would come to this? He supposed there were British officers thinking the same.

In his estimation the Alpha Company frontline bunkers would hold out for forty-five minutes, perhaps sixty, no more. Then the Royal Marines—the attacking regiment had been identified early on in the battle, once radio silence was broken—would overrun them. Two hours after that the marines would have the hill, cleaning up with bayonets and those bastard 66s. Fuck it, he'd stay, take his chances. What was the point of being a soldier if you quit because the going got rough.

Tomba read his mind.

'Think of your brother, Ricardo. You got him up here, if you remember, to keep an eye on him. There are three kilometres of open ground between here and Tumbledown. Part of it's mined, and Christ knows where the engineers sprinkled the bloody things. Snow or no snow, getting out is going to be tough enough in daylight, when their artillery really gets going. It's going to be almost impossible for an inexperienced man in the dark. We still have to get down the reverse slope of Two Sisters.'

'Damned mines. We should have kept those bloody sheep, driven them ahead of us.'

'We had to eat.' Tomba paused. 'Face it, Ricardo. I have, or did when I listened to Colonel Filippi just now. It's over. We might be able to damage them a bit on Tumbledown, but mostly it's over. Look after Beto.'

Ricardo thought about it. It was good advice. Or rather, it was lousy advice—abandoning one's men to their fate wasn't in the manual—but it was practical and sensible. He'd just be another candidate for an icy grave come dawn, and he had a duty to Beto and their sick mother the equal of that he owed the battalion. It might have been different had the C-in-C adopted a policy of greater aggression, made the damned British pay for every inch of ground. But he hadn't.

Ricardo shook his head in the darkness. No, he couldn't swallow that argument, not even privately. He would attempt to get Beto to the relative safety of the rear because that was the clever thing to do, because his mother would not survive Beto's death. What he would have elected to do had Beto not been on the islands he didn't choose to consider.

'What's Battalion HQ doing?'

'Pulling out immediately.'

'Does everyone in Alpha Company know what's expected of them?'

'I've got runners to each trench. I couldn't risk the radio.'

'They can't have many people who speak Spanish.'

'That's not what I meant. How do you think those who are being left behind are going to feel when they know the rest of us are leaving?'

'We won't be able to save our forward positions, let them know what's going on?'

'No.'

'Christ,' said Ricardo.

Then he felt a surge of sympathy for Carlos Tomba. Alpha Company was Tomba's in a way that it could never be anyone else's. He was the company commander. He was also having to leave some of his men to be killed or taken prisoner.

A combat-ready figure appeared over the rim of the dugout. Ricardo jumped. Sergeant Gonzalez said, 'Hold it!'

He seemed surprised to see Ricardo.

'Ready when you are, sir,' he said to Tomba.

'Right. See you at Battalion HQ, Ricardo,' said Tomba.

'You're not coming?'

'In a minute or two. There are still some things to be done here.'

Ricardo scrambled up the slope, keeping low and calling out the day's password every few seconds. Then a flare went up, an Argentine flare, followed by another, to give the defenders some light on the advancing British. Ricardo leapt into a shell crater. Flares worked both ways. While waiting for the illuminants to expire, he looked back to the dugout he had just quit. Impossible to tell from the distance, of course, but the two figures who had just left it must be Tomba and Gonzalez. And they were going downhill, into the fight.

They were too slow seeking cover. The flares had been unexpected. Ropes of tracer from British machine guns zeroed in on them like lightning to a conductor.

God only knew how much a British general purpose machine gun cost, plus ammunition. Say a thousand pounds, and there were two of them hosing in on Tomba and Gonzalez. Add in the local support weapons and the cost of training, say six men at around ten thousand pounds apiece, and another few thousand each for transporting just that half dozen from the UK to the Malvinas, and there was something like one hundred thousand pounds attempting to reduce two men, whose body chemicals taken as a whole on the open market would be valued at approximately twenty pounds, to so much fertilizer.

Ricardo saw both of them fall. Then one staggered to his feet and moved forward a few metres before falling again to the same gunner. After that neither figure moved, and gradually the flares died.

Ricardo remained rigid in the crater for several minutes. Or it could have been ten. Unable to move. Psychologists call the phenomenon negative panic; others call it shock. There was no sign of Gonzalez or Tomba following him. Damn it, he thought finally. Damn it.

Kit had been left behind, sleeping-bags, radios, even belts of machine gun ammunition. Battalion HQ, what was left of it, was a shambles. So was the retreat, with vague shapes stumbling after one another, and occasionally into one another, down the reverse slope of Two Sisters. Ricardo grabbed the nearest man. Boy. Eighteen at the most. He was shaking with fear.

'Where's Battalion HQ?'

'I don't know. Gone.' The boy tried to loosen Ricardo's grip, but Ricardo held him.

'Are you HQ?'

'Yes. They left me. I didn't know they were going.' The lad was crying. 'They just left me.'

'Do you know Beto Jordan-Arditti?'

'No.'

'About your age, a bit older. With HQ wireless section. An interpreter.'

'No.'

Where's your rifle? Ricardo wanted to ask the lad, for he

was weaponless. But the question was stillborn. How could he condemn the kid for tossing away his weapon when he'd seen his officers turn tail.

'Go on,' said Ricardo. The boy ran.

Ricardo spent a further forty minutes on the reverse slope, stopping fleeing men as and when he could, asking them if they knew Beto or his whereabouts, examining the dead—and there were quite a number, even on this side of Two Sisters— fearing what he would find. But he didn't find Beto before the time arrived to either get out himself or to perish. The sounds of battle behind him were diminishing and dawn wasn't far off. A few flakes of snow were starting to fall, which might aid the retreat. No, the rout. Beto must have made it, must have got out, would have left when Colonel Filippi left, might even now be on Tumbledown.

Which Beto wasn't. Thirty minutes after first light—though the snow and the early-morning mist made it difficult to tell what time dawn had arrived, and his watch was broken—he was lying in a shell-hole with a youngster named Ruben Sanchez and another called Arturo Mendoza, both conscript riflemen with Colonel Filippi's battalion who had decided to run and worry about the consequences later when, on ammunition replenishment detail, they saw HQ Company leaving. They were replacements, like Beto. The trouble was, Sanchez was nursing an ankle broken when he fell on the way down Two Sisters in the dark. His companion Mendoza had called out for help, and Beto had paid heed. He was not alone in this humanitarian gesture; other men were helping other wounded comrades. But it was then that Beto lost HQ, and subsequently he and Mendoza had half dragged, half carried Sanchez to the foot of Two Sisters. It was useless asking other refugees from insanity for assistance; aiding Sanchez was no more than a two-man job. Ricardo had passed within a hundred metres of the trio twenty-five minutes earlier, without seeing them. And then the shelling started, forcing them to take cover.

But they couldn't stay where they were for ever. While a shallow crater was reasonable enough protection against conventional shells, it was less effective against the air-burst variety and phosphorus. And soon the British would come with bayonets. They were taking few prisoners; that much had been drummed into every conscript's head. The choices were between staying put and certainly being killed, or moving on and taking that chance.

Sanchez was in too much pain to do more than groan, but Beto could see Mendoza looking at him, at Beto, waiting for a decision.

The majority of his fellow Argentines, Beto saw, were in the middle ground (some running, some walking, some loping), which was where most of the enemy artillery fire was being directed. Over to his right, which would mean approaching Tumbledown from the south, there was no one. And no shells.

'We'll go that way.'

He and Mendoza helped Sanchez to his feet, or rather, on to his remaining good foot. Then they heaved him out of the crater and, bent double, with one of Sanchez's arms around the shoulders of the man on either side of him, hobbled and scrambled a few dozen metres at a time before taking a rest. Curiously the three of them were the only ones following Beto's chosen route. He wanted to shout to some of the others to come this way, away from the terrifying shells. Then self-preservation took hold. The more who came this way, the more the British artillery observers would redirect their guns.

Run a few metres. Stop. Crouch. Keep low. Pause for breath. Look round for danger. Look up for the fearsome shells. That was the pattern for sixty minutes, during which they covered less than a kilometre.

But they were going to make it, thought Beto. He could see men on the forward slopes of Tumbledown, Argentines, presumably with field-glasses on the trio to be certain they were friendly and not British. Some of the men were waving—encouraging them, thought Beto, though it would be a damned sight more useful if a few came out to help them with Sanchez.

Beto waved back with his free arm. So did Mendoza, and it is always possible that this pair, at least, recognized the hand signals as gestures of alarm and understood why no one else was taking this route fractions of a second before the Argentine anti-personnel mine beneath them exploded as one of them stepped on it and it blasted the three to smithereens, hurling Beto, as metal entered his groin and abdomen, sideways, where he landed on a second mine that finished the job.

What remained of the three youngsters was eventually found by a British patrol and, in the course of time, buried in a communal grave. Identification tags had also been destroyed in the detonation and there was nothing on the cross to indicate who lay underneath. Beto, Sanchez and Mendoza were simply posted as missing, believed killed, but as their fate was far from unique no one, even afterwards, ever found out precisely how they died.

THIRTY

Peter

'THERE'S THIS BLOKE trying to work his ticket, see,' Three-piece was saying to Archie Buchanan late afternoon on June 13, beginning another of his jokes to a background of Argentine and British artillery exchanging rounds. 'Get a medical discharge,' he translated, when the journalist looked at him blankly. 'But the CO won't have any and sends him to see a psychiatrist. The bloke walks into the shrink's office and instead of sitting down and answering the questions, he saunters around the room fiddling with bits of paper, ink-stands, pictures, the telephone. Each time he picks up an item he examines it carefully from every angle before putting it back, saying, "That's not it, that's not it." The shrink watches him. Calendars, blotting pads, the whole issue. All the time saying, "That's not it, that's not it." Finally the shrink decides that this bloke is most definitely nutty, writes out his discharge and hands it to him. The bloke looks at it and says, "That's it," '

Archie laughed politely, pleasing Three-piece. Everybody else was getting a bit cheesed off with his gags.

Archie pondered the significance of the joke's subject matter: crazy soldiers. He remembered Three-piece coming ashore at San Carlos with that ridiculous feathered condom covering his rifle muzzle. And although Archie hadn't witnessed the incident himself, it was apparently Three-piece who had been one of the prime movers in The Great Erection Race. Brian

Sweet might be a little eccentric but was obviously a young man who enjoyed himself. Or used to. Now his eyes were glazed, distant. Part fatigue, part something else.

It was a wonder, thought Archie, that a few more hadn't gone the way of the guy in Sweet's story, considering what they'd all been through. There was a piece to be written on it somewhere, though it could wait until he got back to the UK and had a chance to research it properly. *Would* have to wait, for that matter, as there was no way that articles on instability would be sanctioned by the MoD. But instability was there, right enough. And understandably. He made a mental wager with himself that a good percentage of the men who had fought the Falklands war would apply to buy themselves out once home. Or would crack when it was all over, probably weeks or months later. They'd bury their experiences deep within themselves, then one day they'd snap, thump an NCO or officer—or a wife or girl friend like as not. Archie hoped to God the army would understand, had considered the price of victory. What was it Wellington had said? Something about the only thing more melancholy than a battle lost was a battle won. Soldiers were not supposed to have any imagination according to the rule books, except they did. Probably on both sides.

It was a damned crazy world that resolved its differences by asking young men of one nation to stab, shoot, bomb or otherwise dispose of the young men of another nation. The human race had crawled out of the slime sightless a million years ago and was still blind.

B and D Companies and the Tac HQ plus, as an afterthought of Daddy's, a sustained-fire machine gun platoon were due to begin their move forward half an hour before midnight. They would ford Moody Brook and keep it on their left while they advanced east to support the Scots Guards, the object being to pin down or otherwise engage any Argentine units in the open ground between Moody Brook and the northern features of Tumbledown and prevent them withdrawing and attacking the Guards' left flank. It was known that Argentine troops were in the designated area. A fighting patrol from A Company, escorting a mine-clearing detachment in the small hours of June 13, had run into a dozen or more, who had fled after a short firefight, leaving behind three casualties without inflicting any damage on A Company. The route was clear of mines as far as it was possible to tell and, in Daddy's view, the battalion didn't have a hard job to do. Nowhere near as hard as the Guards, anyway, who had advanced and dug in the open ground between Two Sisters and Tumbledown during the hours of darkness and who were now being shelled. Nor as hard as the paratroopers charged with taking Wireless Ridge.

Daddy's opinion of the difficulties wasn't wholly shared by some of the men in his battalion. 'Why us?' Sammy Finch was heard to lament to anyone who would listen. 'Why D Company?'

The battle for Two Sisters thirty-six hours previously was the first full-scale offensive any of them had ever participated in. Prior to that it had been only fighting patrols and keeping your head out of range of the bastard Argie artillery. They thus hadn't been petrifyingly scared because they hadn't known what to expect—and they hadn't been scared during the fight because the adrenalin was flowing and everything was happening so fast. But now they knew what it was like to lose mates. Instead of Acne Hackney, Prawn Balls, Dippie Hendricks and Yank Hobart, it could have been any one of them. During June 12 the QM had brought their big bergens forward and the Catering Corps had set up field kitchens to provide hot food that wasn't chicken fuckin' supreme. ('It's arse-licking good.') Comparatively speaking, they'd tasted some luxury and they didn't want to give it up. They especially resented the ostriches being looked after as well as they were treated themselves. They didn't hate the ostriches as people; there was none of that. But there was already talk of repatriation for the Argentine POWs—just a few hundred miles across the water. They wouldn't have to fight again.

Why us?

A and C Companies were no bloody help either. 'You shouldn't have joined,' they jeered whenever they saw members of B and D Companies.

They were afraid, in a word, and they were ashamed of being afraid. Scrunch, of course, was not going to allow them to be afraid. Or rather, he was not going to allow fear to paralyse D Company.

'You shaved today, Twigg?' he asked, doing the rounds while the company officers received their final briefing from Daddy.

Twiggy was surprised. Nobody had shaved for forty-eight hours.

'No, Sarn't Major.'

'Just thought I'd ask, Twigg. The way you look, you look like the Black Death.'

'Cam cream, Sarn't Major,' said Twiggy cockily.

'That's the new sort, is it? Grows hairs. Where will it all end, I ask myself.'

'Dunno, Sarn't Major.'

'Well, shave tomorrow.' Scrunch had the knack of making everything seem normal. He virtually guaranteed that there'd be a tomorrow. 'For tonight, in there, up there, and stick it to 'em. Right?'

'Right, Sarn't Major.'

'After that, Bob's your mother's brother.'

'Bet he's not like this back in the UK,' muttered Sammy. Scrunch turned.

'Did I recognize your dulcet tones, Finch?'

'Me, Sarn't Major?'

'You, Finch. You said something.'

'Not me, Sarn't Major.'

'Must have been the fairies, then, eh, Finch? The little people. The wee ones who live under toadstools.'

'Must have been, Sarn't Major. Little buggers, they are, for getting a bloke in the rattle.'

'Must have been, Sarn't Major,' repeated Scrunch. 'You and me are going to fall out, aren't we, Finch, you start making snide comments behind Scrunch's back? We're going to be in trouble, aren't we, Finch, when we get back to the UK?'

'Dunno, Sarn't Major.'

'Yes, you do, Finch. I say we're going to be in trouble, and Scrunch is always right, isn't he?'

'If you say so, Sarn't Major.'

'I do say so, Finch. I do say we're going to be in trouble if we have any more cracks from little men like you. What's the bayonet for, Finch?'

'Sarn't Major?'

'What's the flaming bayonet for, Finch? Is it for cleaning your nails, picking your teeth, removing piles?'

'Killing people, Sarn't Major.'

'*People*, Finch?'

'Killing Argies, Sarn't Major.'

'Which you're going to do, aren't you, Finch? You're not going to let old Scrunch down, are you?'

'No, Sarn't Major.'

'Good, good. It'll work up a nice sweat, malleting a few Argies. And you need to get warm, don't you? Because you're all cold, aren't you?' Scrunch put a cupped hand to his ear. 'Let's hear it. ARE you cold? ARE you wet? ARE you miserable?'

'YES, SARN'T MAJOR.'

'Then the sooner we get the fuck out of here, the better. RIGHT?'

'RIGHT, SARN'T MAJOR.'

Scrunch kept on hyping them up, kept their minds occupied. He had them in the palm of his hand, and one of the ways to stop them being frightened was to get them to admit openly that they were.

'Are we afraid?'

'You're fucking A-right we're afraid!'

'What are we afraid of?'

'We're afraid of dying and disembowelment and all sorts of other shit!'

'So what are we gonna do about it?'

'We're gonna run in the opposite direction.'

'No we're bleedin' not. We're gonna go in like John Wayne and Rock Hudson and Tab Hunter . . .'

'Tab who?'

'Forget it. We're going in singing our battle hymn.' This was familiar stuff to D Company. 'And what is our battle hymn?'

'We are the Ovaltinies . . .'

'Louder.'

'WE ARE THE OVALTINIES HAPPY GIRLS AND BOYS . . .'

'Right! And who's looking after you?'

'Jesus!'

'Who wants you for what?'

'A sunbeam!!!'

'A what?'

'A sunbeam!!!'

'So let's hear it. Follow the bouncing ball. All together now. Jesus wants me for a sunbeam—a sunbeam—a sunbeam . . .'

'Jesus wants me for a sunbeam . . .'

'AND?'

'AND A FUCKIN' GREAT SUNBEAM AM I!'

'They're in good voice anyway,' said Peter to Scrunch a couple of minutes later, returning to D Company's lines with Rupert and accompanied by Daddy. 'They must have heard that in Stanley. You almost had me singing.'

'You mean you didn't?'

'Don't know the words.'

'Ah yes, I forgot. Wrong religion. You're a Pancake Tuesday Adventist or something like that.'

'Something like that.'

Rupert spotted a couple of sheep grazing quietly between artillery bursts.

'In any case,' he said, 'it was too high a key for the sort of voices we have. We're more the crooning type. Embrace me, my sweet embraceable ewe . . .' he sang.

Daddy chuckled and glanced at the sky, now darkening. The weather didn't seem to be able to make up its mind what to do: snow, rain or stay dry. He suspected it would rain and then turn to snow before morning, which would make the half-battalion attack rough going. The main road to Stanley was just a couple of hundred yards north of his proposed line of advance, but he'd rejected the notion of sending a company along it. The Argies would certainly have it covered one way or another, to stop light tanks—one of which he'd been promised if the Guards could spare it—using it.

'If there's ever another battle like his on terrain such as this, I'm going to suggest to the MoD that we bring along a few dozen dolphins and use them as rigid raiders.'

'The Americans had a scheme like that once,' said Peter, 'if my memory serves me correctly. Attaching warheads to dolphins and training them to attack Russian subs.'

'What a frightful idea,' said Daddy.

'Though what else can you expect from Americans, I ask you,' put in Rupert. 'I have several American second cousins who, when they're talking about "old money", mean about 1860. And even the New England ancien régime's claim is based upon their ancestors going over on the *Mayflower*. Good grief, my great-great whatever to the power of five owned half of Somerset two hundred years before those pilgrims set out. Mind you, he did acquire it in rather an unpleasant manner. In English terms, their country is scarcely out of the Stone Age.'

'With a great deal of advanced technology, however,' said

Daddy. 'Though I wish to God they'd offered it a little earlier instead of playing politics.'

'I say, sir,' said Rupert, adopting his most foppish mannerism, 'that's a bit unfair. I mean, dash it all, some of their UN people have yet to reach emotional puberty. This is hardly their war.'

'You can sit on the fence for so long,' remarked Daddy, 'and then your bloomers get torn climbing off.'

'Do you want to say anything to the men, sir?' asked Peter.

'I don't think so. I don't have Scrunch's way with words and anything I say can only diminish what he's already achieved.'

Daddy finished speaking just as two Skyhawks came hurtling in unannounced from the east, causing everyone to dive for the nearest trench.

'Good God,' said Daddy, when they'd gone, 'don't tell me *they're* still with us.'

They weren't. With the exception of a high-flying Canberra shot down by a Sea Dart launched from the destroyer *Exeter* late that night, that was the last anyone saw of the Argentine Air Force, though many men in Daddy's battalion would willingly have gone back to San Carlos Water and relived their first days on East Falkland a hundred times over rather than take part in the carnage that was to come, which lasted until dawn with only the occasional lull and which proved more terrifying then their worst nightmares until they each more or less decided that there was no way to survive and that they might as well do as best they could before Phil Beavis's services were required or the Burke and Hares came up with their dustbin liners.

'A' Company's reconnaissance patrol had seriously underestimated the strength of the Argentines in the open ground on the Guards' left flank, guessing at no more than a couple of well dug-in platoons which could be pinned down or destroyed before they could turn their fire-power on the Guards. 'A' Company was well out. Daddy calculated during the course of the fight that he was up against two companies, which made it a one-on-one battle until he signalled C Company forward, leaving A in reserve. Nor did he get his promised Scorpion tank. The Blues and Royals lost one early on when it struck a mine, and the remainder were having their work cut out half a mile to Daddy's right, supporting the Guards, who appeared to have come up against, for their first encounter with the enemy, highly disciplined soldiers, many of them with night-sight sniperscopes on their rifles. 2 Para, for its attack on Wireless Ridge, had claimed the other troop of light tanks, and was throwing everything it had at the objective: as well as the tanks the paras employed two batteries of guns, naval gunfire support from a frigate, and a sustained-fire machine gun platoon. To make matters a little harder for everyone concerned, it began to snow from the moment the attackers crossed the start line. Some malevolent deity in an ethereal grandstand seat was determined to create as much mischief as it could before the fun was over.

B Company, on D's left, made a first contact soon after both companies crossed Moody Brook at midnight, drawing withering machine gun fire from four bunkers which killed two men and wounded B Company's CSM. Daddy dispatched D Company to outflank the Argentine trenches and positioned the sustained-fire MG platoon in the centre of both companies to give the Argentines something to think about. But far from outmanoeuvring the enemy, D Company itself came under attack from three more Argentine bunkers before it had covered fifty yards. The advance shuddered to a halt as men sought cover. Then Milans, 66s and 51 mm mortars using HE came into play, with some effect but not as much as Peter had hoped for. From the three trenches facing D Company—and three machine guns per trench, he calculated, counting the tracer arcs—eight machine guns were still firing. Soon afterwards the ninth came back on the scene. So far D Company had achieved precisely nothing.

Via radio Daddy urged D Company forward, desperately anxious that it should not become bogged down, lose its momentum entirely, when the men would begin to think about their own survival instead of the job at hand.

For Peter, two hundred and fifty yards, at a guess, separated the nearest Argentine trenches from D Company's point, which he led. Behind those trenches there were doubtless more waiting their turn. But those three were causing all the trouble for the present. B Company could look after its own four. Bayonets were already fixed to every rifleman's weapon, and every officer in D Company was carrying a rifle. Peter wirelessed Daddy for some heavy machine gun support from the sustained-fire platoon beginning in one minute. Then he told the platoon commanders over the radio that they would be moving forward on the Argentine positions in sixty-five seconds. Rupert would have overall command of 3 and 4 Platoons; Peter would take care of 1 and 2. Scrunch was mobile, cursing, swearing, encouraging, concerned to get on with it. Aggression was the greatest weapon. The Argentines had to be convinced that there was no way they could survive this assault, that it was in their own best interests to chuck it in here and now, before they found themselves ripped from arse to navel. There would be no damned mercy once the company was close.

Scrunch used his parade-ground voice to scare the living daylights out of those who might be reluctant to move when the company commander said move. Get in, get on with it, get those bastard machine gunners. Kill them before they kill you.

On flat ground a fit athlete can cover 250 yards in approximately thirty seconds. Most of D Company would not have taken much longer given the same conditions. But here they were encumbered by bulky fighting gear and carrying rifles and spare ammunition. They were also, because they weaved, covering closer to four hundred yards, perhaps five hundred. And in snow that was thickening and with the ground underfoot resembling undercooked pizza prepared for someone the size of Gulliver. It thus took them three minutes to reach the first of the Argentine trenches, by which time D Company had lost two men killed and three wounded including Legless Jones with a bullet in the groin. Legless would survive thanks to sterling work by the surgeons at Ajax Bay and the skills of the medical teams before he reached there.

Then it was every man for himself and his nearest mate, and a score of individual hand-to-hand fights were taking place in and around the Argentine trenches, with the defending machine gunners startled and scared by the rapidity of the assault and unable to bring their weapons to bear at close quarters.

Groggy had seen Legless fall but knew there was nothing he could do to help. His drinking partner might be dead or alive. All Groggy could do was to make sure that some of the bean-eating bastards who'd shot him paid the penalty. Roaring like a madman, he rammed his bayonet into the face of the Argentine he first confronted. Then he vaulted the trench and ran on.

Double-Eff had outstripped the rest of 3 Platoon in racing for the platoon's objective. Tracer hurtled by him, but it was far too high. Now that 3 Platoon was close, the enemy machine gunners had to shift their trajectory, and inevitably they made mistakes. But it wasn't easy to kill his first man. He lunged with his bayonet and missed as the Argie ducked and swung his machine gun barrel. Double-Eff fell into the trench. There were six men in it; four alive, two dead or cowering in a corner, Double-Eff didn't know which. He thrust again at the nearest man, and felt the satisfying (at the time) contact of metal and flesh, fired a round, then turned on a second man, who was fumbling with a rifle, trying to bring it to bear. Scarlett appeared over the rim of the trench, a primed grenade in his hand. He recognized Double-Eff in time—or rather recognized the figure of a British soldier, and hurled the grenade forward, into the distance, where it exploded harmlessly, injuring no one. After that he disposed of the Argentine trying to kill Double-Eff with a fierce stab in the back.

One man tried to escape the trench 3 Platoon were attacking. And almost succeeded. When he saw the way the fight was going he hopped out of the dugout like a rabbit and started to run towards the rear. At that moment a barrage of illuminants exploded overhead, brightening the fighting area. The Argentine kept on running. Except he didn't run in a straight line or weave like a trained soldier. He ran like a child in a game of tag, or a football hooligan trying to escape the police. Panic-stricken. In figures of eight. Round and round. Three of 3 Platoon were chasing him trying to catch him and bayonet him. Fifty yards away Jomo was screaming at them to stop, give up the pursuit so that he could get a shot in. But Three-piece, Sammy and Twiggy, the pursuers, were all on a high, could not have given up the chase for the world.

Anyone who thinks death is noble or dignified had better think again. It's a nasty, dirty, stupid, fucking business that is without honour. There isn't any glory or fine adjectives in dying. On the receiving end a man's like a bullock in an abbattoir. You're alive, you try to escape, then you're dead. There isn't even any time to say your prayers, no more than a few half-formed sentences beseeching God to intervene, anyway. All you know is that you want to live, that your underwear is being soiled, that the people behind you are determined to murder you, that there's no place you can run to and cry 'safety', grin, and make your pursuers try to catch someone else. Everyone dies fearful. The knife goes in. Or the bullet. Or the mortar shell fragment. Or the bits of rocket. Blood isn't dignified. Nor is a ruptured kidney or spleen. It isn't the films; it's a fucking mess.

Which is how the Argentine Three-piece, Twiggy and Sammy Finch were chasing died, when he tripped and fell in the rice-pudding ground and was bayoneted to offal by all three of them, though later not one of them could recall doing it.

Then the three trenches facing D Company were cleared. When they saw that they were not only outnumbered but being outfought by these maniacal British, those Argentines who had survived up to now attempted to surrender. No way. D Company hadn't the time or the inclination for prisoners. They killed even those who wanted to quit. The Argentines had been trying to kill them. The Argentines couldn't just say, 'Okay, lads, it's a fair cop,' just because they were losing. That wasn't how wars were fought. Besides, the battle wasn't over yet. The Argentines had pals in other trenches up ahead, pals on Tumbledown, on Wireless Ridge. When they packed it in—and made it perfectly fucking clear that they were packing it in, without any bloody nonsense—D Company would pack it in. Until then, those friggin' Argies had better watch their balls.

Peter Ballantine had also killed his first man with a bayonet, in the trench adjacent to the one Double-Eff had stumbled into. He'd hardly noticed the Argentine's death. The man was there, a hooded face, a figure. A voice screamed something unintelligible. He was in the way. And then he was gone.

After that, now the flanking movement was complete, it was time to take some pressure off Dick Barton's company. Which D Company did without much style but clinically. Pivot on an axis. Bring forward Two-Shit's machine gun and Jomo's machine gun, plus the rest from the other platoons. Bring up the Milans and the 66s. Set up arcs of fire. Distract the Argentines facing B Company. Blast the buggers. Allow B Company to finish off its own opponents.

Then regroup, count the casualties, re-establish radio links with the platoons and Tac HQ. Replenish ammunition stocks. Go firm in present positions while C Company moved through and set up forward fields of fire before the next attack.

The entire action had taken under thirty minutes from first contact, and Daddy, while surveying the next line of defence as far as it was possible, was highly delighted with the way it had gone. Though there were more trenches to be taken, and over to the right the Scots Guards seemed to be taking a fearful pasting, the battalion was a few hundred yards closer to Tumbledown. It was going to be a long night, however. And a tough one. The time was not yet 1 a.m. and the battalion's objectives had to be taken before first light in case the Guards and 2 Para hadn't won their own battles by then. If the Argies still controlled the high ground at dawn, the battalion would be slaughtered.

It wasn't all fear, though, while the troops waited for the order to go again. Peering over the edge of an occupied trench, with two dead Argentines at his feet, Three-piece tried to quieten his thumping heart with his own version of 'The Ball of Kirriemuir', his opening line being: Four and twenty Argies came down from Wireless Ridge. In the same trench Branston told him to shut up, that this wasn't an audition or a seaside concert party. At least, that's what the others who overheard the Scot assumed Branston had said. It could well have been that he'd recited the opening scenes of *Macbeth*, playing all the witches. Sammy doubted if Branston himself knew what the fuck he was talking about half the time. How the hell could anyone understand an accent that sounded like a couple of rabid dogs with bad teeth squabbling over the ownership of a bone?

Scrunch went around from position to position, keeping their spirits up. Groggy was worried about Legless until Phil Beavis, checking for casualties, told him that Legless was okay as far as he knew. Got one close to the balls though. 'Bloody near circumcised him.' Stretcher-bearers had whipped him away, back towards Two Sisters from where he'd be flown to Ajax Bay in due course. He'd be sipping a nip of medicinal brandy before long.

'Jammy bastard,' grunted Groggy. 'Do anything for a tot.'

Then it was time to go again, with C Company flushing out the next Argentine bunkers by sending up illuminants and drawing their fire. The next attack was over a wider front, and time gradually lost all meaning for the troops.

Flares, mortars, Milans, 66s. Sustained fire from the machine gunners. Run like fucking hell. No time to be scared when you're mobile. They say you never hear the one with your name on it, so as long as your eardrums are bursting with all this fucking racket going on, you must be alive, right? Right.

Cries of 'Magazine!'—the signal that a man was temporarily out of ammunition and would be unable to give covering fire until he'd reloaded—were lost in the surrounding tumult, the endless kaleidoscope of changing events and fortunes. A soldier was supposed to count his rounds too, never hear the 'dead man's click', his firing-pin striking nothing that was about to go bang. On exercise, there were severe penalties if the 'click' was witnessed by an NCO, for it meant that a man wasn't paying attention. And a man who didn't pay attention rapidly became a candidate for a dustbin liner. But here it was impossible to keep count of the rounds fired.

There were individual acts of bravery that no one considered especially heroic at the time. When 3 Platoon were attempting to outflank an Argentine dugout, with the Argies thinking it was Guy Fawkes Night, the amount of shit they were flinging, Jomo Mason was knocked flat, hit by fragments of HE mortar. At least he thought he was hit, for the blast threw him off his feet and he lost control of his gimpy. Two-Shit Tyler was thirty yards away from Jomo when he saw the lad from Birmingham go down. Two-Shit would later claim—to the astonishment of everyone who considered he deserved his nickname—that he was less interested in pulling Jomo to safety and checking him for damage than in making sure that the platoon's flanking movements didn't falter. Nevertheless, Scarlett and Double-Eff and several others witnessed Two-Shit race towards Jomo and half-drag, half-push him into the nearest shell crater, while somehow hanging on to his own gimpy and collecting Jomo's. Tyler didn't stop firing for more than a few seconds, either. Then he discovered that Jomo's only damage was to his gear, that the mortar fragments had dissipated their lethal energy before reaching him, that the QM was likely to be a little angry with him—'That's Her Majesty's property you've managed to fuck up, Private Mason'—but that he was otherwise unhurt apart from being winded and shaken. 'You silly bugger!' shouted Two-Shit. 'Why can't you keep your stupid thick head down!' While Jomo was catching his breath, Two-Shit laid down an arc of fire that gave 3 Platoon the opportunity to knock out the trench and kill its occupants.

Phil Beavis was his usual no-fuss, no-bother self. When Twiggy was hit and went down under a hail of machine-gun fire that detonated a spare SLR magazine he was carrying and removed his left arm below the elbow as cleanly as any scalpel, Phil yelled at Sammy and Three-piece, part of the same charge but unharmed, to keep going, that he would see to Twiggy. Then Phil apologized to Double-Eff, who didn't hear him anyway, for trying to take command of the platoon.

Twiggy was unconscious and bleeding profusely when Phil reached him. He slammed in a syrette of morphine while shouting for stretcher-bearers. When none appeared—they were rather busy elsewhere—Phil picked up Twiggy in a fireman's lift and carried him out of danger.

Twiggy survived, and would eventually use his five 'O' levels to get himself a job with a builder's merchant. His only regret, apart from his infirmity, was that the explosion destroyed the very first letter Carol Bannister had written to him earlier in the year. He'd carried it with him as a talisman, but it became part of the detritus at the foot of Tumbledown.

Elsewhere as the battalion advanced, Scarlett O'Hara and Double-Eff, always within a few feet of one another, performed minor miracles with acts that were not so much individual bravery as encouragement. There wasn't an awful lot left of 3 Platoon as 4 a.m. became 5 a.m. with no sign of the Argentines taking the hint and quitting, but what there was Scarlett and Double-Eff kept urging forward, and were always, the pair of them, in the thick of the fighting, leading charmed lives but doing their jobs.

By common consent the bravest deed, in the purest sense of the expression, that night was enacted by Rupert, Toby Lomax, Scrunch and Branston Pickles.

The time was shortly after 5.30 a.m. and first light wasn't far off. From Daddy's Tac HQ it was difficult to see how the battles for the Tumbledown heights and Wireless Ridge were going, but if Daddy was any guesser the Guards and the paras were winning. It had to be a guess. Information coming over the brigade wireless net was confused and confusing, and Daddy didn't have time to take more than a passing interest in other people's fights, for his own battalion's offensive was being held up by fierce resistance from what he would later learn was the Argentine's last line of defence in the battalion's area: half a company of men cleverly dug in among the rocks on the lower northern slopes of Tumbledown. The battalion had to wipe out that pocket of Argies and press on for the reverse slope of the mountain, where it could then support the Guards coming over the top and also cover the paras heading for Moody Brook barracks, a mile or so north-east of Tumbledown. The Argies would then be caught in a bottleneck, and God help them, for no one else would.

The Argentine bunkers were being so tenaciously defended by machine guns, rifles, mortars and rockets that to take them out called for, by the book, a full battalion attack. But A company, being held in reserve, could not get forward in time, and Daddy was left with B, C and D Companies and his sustained-fire MG platoon. C Company took the left, B the centre, and D the right, but the advance managed only fifty yards in thirty minutes. The Argies appeared to have endless ammunition and machine guns with barrels that never seemed to get hot and need changing, giving the attackers a chance. Or their tactics were being cleverly coordinated by someone who knew his job.

D Company was travelling fastest, even if fast could only be measured in a few yards at a time. The Argies were weakest on their left flank, the battalion's right, and some-where along the line right-hand elements of B Company got mixed up with left-hand elements of D, to such an extent that Rupert found himself within a few yards of Toby Lomax, while Peter Ballantine's Company HQ was asking with ever-increasing irritation for more 66s to be brought up. More Milans. And Daddy was demanding to know via the wireless, his voice testy, what the fuck the delay was.

'And where the hell do you think I'm going to find Milans at this hour of the morning? I hope you realize you can buy a half-share in a rather fine racehorse for every one of those bastards you let rip.'

Leading 1 and 2 Platoons, B Company, Toby Lomax had wandered too far to his right, which was how he found himself close to Rupert and Scrunch Watkins, who were ready to move out with 3 and 4 Platoons, D Company, whether the bastard 66s came up or not, once Rupert got Peter's okay.

'Your AA guide's out of date,' said Rupert to Lomax, when he recognized the burly form of B Company's 2 i/c. Insanely, he wondered if Lomax had deliberately sought him out to put an 'accidental' round between his shoulder blades because of his relationship with Julia. It was that kind of night. 'You should be on the A3 to Portsmouth, not the A10 to Cambridge. I mean, how come you're here?'

'Lousy navigation,' said Lomax. 'You may also have noticed that the road's up in one or two places. I missed a turning.' Lomax studied the pretty picture the Argie tracer was making. 'Are we going to sit here all night?'

'I rather thought we might. Then breakfast at the Ritz. What do you have in mind?'

Lomax pointed. There was very definitely a weak link in the Argentine left flank. The machine-gun fire coming from a cluster of rocks, doubtless concealing well-protected bunkers, was less dense there than in other Argentine positions. Hammer them there and occupy the bunkers, and the Argies would be caught in the crossfire, to tumble like wheat before a scythe.

'I'm game if you're game,' said Rupert, when Lomax explained. 'What have you got with you?'

'A couple of platoons.'

'66s?'

'Three.' The high-explosive anti-tank man-portable missiles had not proved so effective in this latest attack as they had hitherto, but they were better than nothing. Especially as Daddy was being stingy with the Milans. 'Do you want to tell Ballantine?'

'It might be an idea. Don't you want to inform Major Barton?'

'Lost my wirelessman a couple of minutes ago. Silly sod not only got himself shot but buggered up the radio to boot.'

'I'll do it for you.'

Peter wanted to clear it with Dick Barton and Daddy before giving his sanction, but that took only a few minutes. Daddy needed the Argentine position cracked. He'd just heard from brigade that elements of the Guards were virtually at the top of Tumbledown and that 2 Para's attack was developing well. ('Which is probably where all the bloody Milans have gone to,' Daddy grumbled to the RSM.) He was determined his own battalion wouldn't foul up.

'Go,' said Peter. 'Keep Scrunch if you want him.'

'Do we want you, Scrunch?' Rupert asked the CSM.

'I'm going to feel pretty pissed off if you don't.'

The battalion's sustained-fire MG platoon hosed in tracer on the Argie trenches before the attack started. For a few seconds. To keep their bastard heads down. Then the three 66s were launched, thumping home and silencing at least one machine gun. After that Daddy called up smoke on the left, to try and kid the Argies that the assault was coming from that direction. And it fooled them for a while. For another few seconds. Until some bright spark saw Rupert and Scrunch and Toby Lomax galloping ahead of the four platoons they collectively commanded the one hundred and fifty yards that separated the British from the Argentines.

Lomax might have stood six feet four and weigh in the super-heavyweight division, but he could run a bit. In his hands an SLR looked like a toy.

He was half a dozen strides ahead of Rupert for the first hundred yards, at which point the Argentines got the message that the attack was coming from a different direction to the smoke and switched their fields of fire, tracer stitching its way through the ranks of the advancing British. Toby Lomax got hit when he was within thirty yards of the nearest machine gunner, but his momentum and will were such that he kept going, bellowing like a lunatic, part rage, part pain. He blundered into the first of the bunkers, where he lashed out with bayonet and rifle butt before he fell. A trooper from the 5th Marines shot him dead with a submachine gun from close range.

Rupert and Scrunch and Branston were close behind Lomax, making for the same bunker. Following this trio came the remainder of 3 and 4 Platoons, D Company, and 1 and 2 Platoons, B. By now the Argentines were panicking at the ferocity of the attack, trying desperately to beat it back. Seizing his advantage, Daddy launched the rest of the battalion at the central Argentine emplacements, taking some pressure off the right flank. But only some. A couple of machine gunners seemed to have it in for Rupert, Scrunch and Branston, directing their fire-power at the closest and most aggressive of the enemy.

Branston was shot in the neck and upper torso, and spun away like a top. Somehow he struggled to his knees, hunting for cover. Then he was hit again, and on this occasion he did not get up.

Scrunch and Rupert hurled phosphorus grenades into the bunker, trying to dislodge its occupants, get them out into the open. Each Argentine who appeared was dispatched by small-arms fire and bayonets, and before that fight was over Rupert, leaving Scrunch behind, was racing for the next breastwork. And being hit by machine-gun rounds. Four, five, a dozen. At Tac HQ, although they could not identify the casualty, they could see the tracer striking, punching home. No one could survive that, and no one did. When the medics found Rupert later, they discovered that the magazine on his SLR was empty, though at what point he ran out of ammunition no one could guess. People who knew Rupert well concluded that he'd not had time to change magazines, that he'd opted to tackle the next bunker armed only with a bayonet.

Unharmed, Scrunch rallied 1 and 2 Platoons, B Company, while Double-Eff and Scarlett led 3 and 4 in the rout of the trenches, getting in amongst and behind the Argentines. Nor was this attack on their weakened left flank the only problem the defenders had, because the bulk of the battalion was now moving forward at a brisk clip.

The battalion's war diary later recorded that this engagement lasted forty-five minutes. No one who took part believed that, though even among themselves they argued about duration. Some said they'd fought for no more than half an hour; others said two hours. Whatever the time-scale, it was a foot-by-grimly-gained-foot battle wherein the leitmotif was doggedness, a quality displayed not only by the attackers. Using phosphorus, small arms, bayonets. Mostly bayonets. Until dawn crept in through the snow. Until resistance began to crumble. Until those defenders who were left elected to take to their heels—or surrender and mean it, making it obvious by tossing away their weapons. Until the firing became sporadic and then virtually nonexistent in the battalion's area.

Daylight came, the sky the colour of a slag-heap. The battalion took stock, herded the prisoners into sullen groups, looked after the wounded of both sides. Peter Ballantine surveyed the remnants of D Company, at whom Scrunch was vocalizing. 'A bloody shambles, you lot, a bloody shambles.' They'd proved their mettle, this crew, some now tending to injured and exhausted comrades, some further afield mopping up bunkers whose occupants did not seem willing to call it a day. Peter made a private promise that, if he kept D Company, any man appearing before him on a charge when the battalion was back in the UK would be exonerated as of right for the first offence.

Peter had seen a preliminary casrep and found it difficult to believe that Rupert hadn't made it. He didn't get the opportunity to see Lavinia's brother before the body was whipped away by the Burke and Hares. Nor did he have time to consider such self-indulgent thoughts. The Argentines in Stanley were still shelling. He had to get D Company together for the next assault.

Which never happened.

Daddy flagged it in first, to all company commanders, during midmorning of June 14. One of his wirelessmen was on the brigade net and word was coming through from the paras and the Guards that the Argentines between Mount Tumbledown and Stanley were 'on their bikes' in huge numbers; that they had thrown down their weapons and were getting out, making for the capital. Hundreds of them.

'Christ, they've broken,' Daddy said to the RSM, and gave the order for all companies to be ready to move out in ten minutes.

It was an unnecessary instruction. Although one half-hearted counter-attack was mounted, it quickly dissipated. With the exception of a few minor skirmishes which did not affect the battalion, the Falklands campaign was over.

A 2 Para patrol reported seeing an armoured vehicle flying a white flag. Remembering Goose Green, the paras double-checked. It was genuine. Then other white flags appeared in the distance, in Stanley, and there was jubilation among the survivors when they realized that the enemy had surrendered.

An order came over the wireless net to remove helmets and don berets, a tradition at the cessation of hostilities. The red, the green, the blue. Afterwards came the long slog into Stanley in the snow. 'Just what we need, a fucking Christmas-card,' said Two-Shit to Jomo, whose kit resembled a string vest.

Peter Ballantine marched along the road above Moody Brook next to Archie Buchanan, checking every now and then that the men were okay. They were, those who were left, and already moaning in the time-honoured manner of the British soldier. The bloody paras were way ahead and would grab the best billets and whatever booze was going.

For Double-Eff and Scarlett, there wasn't much of 3 Platoon to lead. Acne Hackney was dead, Non-Legless Jones was dead, Branston was dead. Twiggy was wounded and Yank an amputee. Legless Jones had had his balls shaved and according to Scarlett, Cyril Ball had had his prawns shaved. It was a weak joke that made everyone laugh.

Sammy Finch had survived. So too had Two-Shit, Jomo, Groggy, Three-piece, a few others. A few less than the 3

Platoon that had tackled the climb up to the old Marston range before Christmas the previous year.

'How does it feel?' Archie started to ask Peter, when Peter suddenly stumbled and Archie noticed the red stain spreading across Peter's back as he fell. And a fraction of a second later Archie heard the distant crack of a rifle.

Major Vila, who had been determined not to quit, join the surrender, the rout, had notched up his last victim. Operating alone, he had outwitted the SBS four-man stick that had been hunting him for two days and nights. Then he had seen the white flags and decided to get one more shot in. Peter Ballantine was his target, and Peter Ballantine was the penultimate fatality of the war. The very last was Vila, when the SBS, observing where the round had come from and not about to allow the marksman another, moved in and destroyed him.

THIRTY-ONE

Ricardo

. . . WHO HAD TAKEN PART in the abortive defence of Tumble-down and who, along with the remnants of Colonel Filippi's battalion, had retreated at dawn to Port Stanley for fear of being cut off by the Welsh Guards and the Gurkhas advancing against Mount William and Sapper-Hill. Who still did not know that his brother was dead.

Long before the official surrender was signed at 2100 hours on June 14, columns of British troops were marching into Stanley. Ricardo searched their ranks for the light-blue berets of Daddy Rankin's battalion, and when he saw the first of them detached himself from a tiny group of forlorn Argentine officers. An NCO tried to bar his way and send him back with a triumphant obscenity, reinforcing his argument by a gesture with his submachine gun. Ricardo was prepared for this.

'I'm enquiring about Captain Peter Ballantine,' he said politely, in perfect English.

Major Dick Barton, whose B Company it was that Ricardo approached, overheard the request. Motioning the NCO with the Sterling to stay with him, he waved the rest of the company on and questioned Ricardo, who kept his answers brief. He'd known Peter at school in England; he was a friend. Not any more, said Barton. Captain Ballantine was killed by a sniper two hours ago.

'Ah,' said Ricardo sadly, and turned away.

Major Barton called him back, thinking he might be of some use in the negotiations to come. Ricardo paid no heed. The NCO cocked the Sterling, but Ricardo seemed neither to hear nor care.

'Leave him,' said Major Barton. 'He's going nowhere he can't be found.'

THIRTY-TWO

The Viscount

FROM AN UPSTAIRS window Oliver watched his father clamber into the Range Rover, a bottle of whisky in each hand. McGregor was behind the wheel. The two elderly men held a brief conversation before the gamekeeper put the Range Rover into gear, driving towards his cottage. Then Oliver went to comfort his sister.

THIRTY-THREE

Barney

THEY FOUND BARNEY in the red barn where once, many years earlier, Peter had nursed him back to health. Old age, said the vet. Labradors go quite suddenly when they're his age. Sara knew differently.

THIRTY-FOUR

The Rt. Hon. Margaret Thatcher, MP

'Rejoice, rejoice.'

Epilogue

THIS SORT OF BOOK should have an epilogue, which should tell how Maria Jordan-Arditti died because she had lost the will to live and how those who survived the Falklands spent the remainder of their days. It should show whether Twiggy married Carol, or did not, and whether Sammy and Libby ever got together again.

Equally, epilogues should relate how Lavinia coped with losing the man she loved and her brother, and what actually happened between the Viscount and McGregor.

And what about Mr Bannister? Was he prosecuted; did he continue to live with his wife and daughter? Did Lucita Jordan-Arditti grow up to sing? Did Legless Jones recover from his wound and stay in the army? Did Archie Buchanan ever write a think-piece on what he had witnessed?

Epilogues should be like that. Epilogues should tie everything up with a nice bow. Life is not like an epilogue. Epilogues are full stops; life goes on.

But I suppose Julia Lomax will get married again (and continue to sleep around). And Eileen O'Hara will moan on and boringly on until either Scarlett capitulates and quits the army, or more hopefully, socks her on the jaw one day and tells her to button up. And Daddy gets promoted to full colonel and Winter's Day is invalided out, maybe to get together with his estranged wife.

Life should be like epilogues, like the end of a book. File

it, put it on the shelf, take it down once in a while and re-read the bits one liked.

And what about Sara Ballantine and Ricardo? Well, they met again in 1984, looked at one another a couple of times, had several drinks, then decided to fold their tents and softly steal away. It should have been different, forgive and forget. But life isn't like that.

Men lived, men died. Both sides. As Hemingway might have written: You know how it is on the morning streets when the bums are out and the fish are jumping and you don't know whether this will be a good day or a bad day but what ever the hell kind of day it is, it's all you've got. Make the most of it.

Epilogues should be neat and tidy. Wrap it up, tie it off. Dinky parcels. Big deal.

There is a tide in the affairs of men . . . Shakespeare's useful too for epilogues. But the best's a bit of Captain Scott, he of the Antarctic.

Had we lived, I would have had a tale to tell of the endurance, hardihood, and courage of my companions which would have stirred the hearts . . . These rough notes and our dead bodies must tell the tale.

And Laurence Binyon.

They shall not grow old, as we that are left grow old. Age shall not wither them, nor the years condemn. At the going down of the sun and in the morning, we will remember them.

Right.